LADYBIRD FLY

LADYBIRD FLY

Tessa Lorant Warburg

The Thorn Press

First published by **The Thorn Press** in 2011

This book is a work of fiction. The characters and incidents are largely fictional and the product of the author's imagination. However, the story is based on some of the actual events which happened to a real family originally living in The Villa Gehben, Altenbruch, Cuxhaven, Germany between 1907 and 1938. Some of the older inhabitants of Altenbruch may recognize several character traits of the main protagonists, but this book is *not* a biography of the Gehben family, it is a work of fiction loosely based on that family.

Ladybird Fly is the final volume in **THE DOHLEN INHERITANCE** trilogy, spanning the years 1948 — 1992.

ISBN: 978-0-906374-09-2

The Thorn Press Ltd
Lansdowne House, Castle Lane
Southampton SO14 2BU, UK
www.thethornpress.com

Printed and bound in the UK

DEDICATION

This book is dedicated to the memories of **Ralph R Lorant, Medora Gehben Cox** and **Franz Xaver Bosch**.

ACKNOWLEDGMENTS

I would like thank Madeleine Warburg for her continued support and help with **THE DOHLEN INHERITANCE** trilogy. I would also like to express my unbounded gratitude to Gillian Geering for not only copyediting the final manuscript of *Ladybird Fly*, but also for her perceptive insights and research into historical material, her understanding of the German parts of the text, and her continued and invaluable support.

The Blue Room writing group of 2010-2011: Deanna Dewey, Claire Violet Hanley, Evelyn Harris, Mike Hayward, Jenni Jacombs, Donna McGie, Mike Plumbley and Ann Roberts all offered, as ever, invaluable constructive criticism. It is a joy to be able to read some of the work to them and gain from their perceptive insights.

I am, once again, indebted to the publishers, Männer vom Morgenstern, for permission to translate and incorporate a number of fascinating North German myths and legends from the book *Hake Betken siene Duven*, Das grosse Sagenbuch aus dem Land an Elb-und Wesermündung, zusammengestellt von Eberhard Michael Iba.

This comprehensive collection of stories from the North German fens bordering the estuaries of the Elbe and Weser rivers was first published in 1993, ISBN 3-927-854-41-6.

BY THE SAME AUTHOR

Fiction, written as Tessa Lorant Warburg
The first book in *THE DOHLEN INHERITANCE* trilogy:
The Dohlen Inheritance
The second book in *THE DOHLEN INHERITANCE* trilogy:
Hobgoblin Gold

Science Fiction, written as Emma Lorant:
(Tessa Lorant Warburg with Madeleine Warburg)
Cradle of Secrets
Lullaby of Fear
Baby Roulette

Non Fiction, written as Tessa Lorant Warburg:
A Voice at Twilight, Diary of a Dying Man
Winner of the ODDFELLOWS Social Concern Book Award 1989

Non Fiction, written as Tessa Lorant
The Batsford Book of Hand and Machine Knitting
The Batsford Book of Hand and Machine Knitted Laces
Yarns for Textile Crafts

THE HERITAGE OF KNITTING SERIES
Tessa Lorant's Collection of Knitted Lace Edgings
Knitted Quilts & Flounces
Knitted Lace Collars
Knitted Shawls & Wraps
The Secrets of Successful Irish Crochet Lace
Knitted Lace Doilies

THE PROFITABLE KNITTING SERIES
Earning and Saving with a Knitting Machine
Choosing and Buying a Knitting Machine
Yarns for the Knitter
The Good Yarn Guide

Jeremy Warburg and Tessa Lorant
The Grockles' Guide

Richard Warburg and Tessa Lorant
Snack Yourself Slim

ILLUSTRATIONS

I would like to thank **Claus Brusen** for his very kind permission to use his painting *Ladybird Flying to the Land of Makebelieve, Opus 134*, for the cover illustration. The image exists as a Glicee print, signed and numbered to an edition of 275, for sale at €100 plus postage.

This artist is profoundly original. His paintings appear deceptively innocent, but they have an undercurrent of strong emotion as well as providing tongue-in-cheek entertainment. His world consists of his own distinctive outlook, and so features a unique perception of the human state. It makes his 'Ladybird' very apposite for illustrating this last book in THE DOHLEN INHERITANCE trilogy.

Claus's two 2011 exhibitions are being held in: Phantasten Museum Wien, Österreichisches Kulturzentrum im Palais Palffy, Austria and Be my Valentine, group show at the NovaBelgica Art Gallery, Belgium.

Claus sells some of his work to HRH Prince Henri of Denmark..

You may also be interested in his book: *The Fantastic World of Claus Brusen*, Ole Lindboe, First Edition 2006, ISBN 87-990636-1-1, available from Amazon.

www.clausbrusen.com

I have also been very fortunate to have found an illustrator for some of the German legends translated in this book to amplify some of the stories told. It is remarkable how several of these myths and legends are reflected in the characters of the two main protagonists.

Andrew P Jones has a method of working which is particularly suited to these stories, and I would like to thank him for his contributions. He has a distinctive style which, though reminiscent of MC Escher, is entirely his own.

INKTASTIC, The Thorn Press, 2011 is a collection of fifty of his black and white drawings, available from Amazon and good bookshops.

Some of the original images are for sale. Write to:

enquiries@thethornpress.com

OLD SCHWANENBRUCH

PART 1

HARROWING

HOME

1948 – 1951

THE VIENNESE VILLA

CHAPTER 1

St Gilgen, Austria, Summer 1948

Gabriele Dohlen Bosch — nicknamed Gabby because she talks so much — arrives home with mixed feelings. Her all-too-short holiday, the first for many years, has made her long to stay in Schwanenbruch. She adores walking across the flat marshes, loves watching the ebb and flow of the North Sea breakers against the pebble beach, is entranced by boats plying the Elbe. Striding along the top of the dyke, with the clean wind blowing the cobwebs of unhappy thoughts away, she wonders: will she ever have the chance to live here again, or is she destined to stay in Austria?

World War II changed so many things in Schwanenbruch: the beautiful villa her father built belongs to Cuxhaven Council now, many of the young men she went to school with are dead, there's virtually no food except for basic swede and potato mash. And coffee made from dandelion roots or, as a treat, from acorns.

But it's still Schwanenbruch, still the village she grew up in, still the

beloved place where her parents cast anchor when they returned from
the United States. It's where her father built the Villa Dohlen across
the street from the twin-spired St Nicolaikirche, the house on which
he proudly engraved the year it was built, as well as her parents' view
of German traditions:

1908
DEUTSCHE ART TREU BEWAHRT
GERMAN WAYS UPHELD WITH PRAISE

'I'd like you to remember those words, Gabby,' she hears her mother
say. 'They're there to remind us how proud we are to keep our German
traditions alive, to keep faith with them.' Mutti's hands pressed hard on
Gabby's shoulders, long ago in 1913, the very morning of the day she
died. 'Honour, loyalty and duty are the most important ones.'

Gabby remembers complaining that her mother was hurting her,
digging into her shoulders.

But Mutti didn't even hear her, just went on to recite more German
virtues: 'Together with honesty, diligence, sobriety, responsibility,
discipline, courage.'

Gabby tries to hold back tears, feels them trickle down whitening
cheeks. What on earth is she doing, living on the shores of the
Wolfgangsee, in the Franzosenschanze, the Emperor Franz Joseph's
one-time hunting lodge? Set in the heart of picture-postcard Austria,
where the natives wear Dirndl and Lederhosen and have sinewy legs
from climbing up and down mountains. They yodel reverberating
sounds to make themselves heard from one mountain peak to another.
And the weather, alternating between summer thunder storms and
winter snows, isn't to her taste. The climate's worse than the maligned
English one she lived through, first as a refugee from Hitler, then
because central Europe was in no state to return to until 1947.

Her recent visit to her sister Dorinda in the Sussex countryside has
made her nostalgic for the nine years she, her girls and her second
husband Franz Bosch spent surrounded by the gentle downs of the
Home Counties of England.

True, it's hard to believe she's actually making a home in a hunting
lodge the Habsburg emperor Franz Joseph adored. Pretty enough, in its
chocolate-box way, but it lacks even the basic amenities: no electricity,

2

no running hot water, uncomfortable antiquated wooden furniture. Why is she spending time in this Alpine region, right beside a glacier lake and, worst of all, on the shadow side of the mountain?

She hates mountains. They squat, fat and stolid, casting dense shadows, ruining the distant view. You either go round them, or you climb, far too steeply, up or down. Either way is hard on the calf muscles, and when you reach the summit you see more bloody mountains, ranges of them.

The Franzosenschanze perches uneasily on the shady side of its particular craggy precipice: no sun, no far horizons, just the enviable view of what sun there is shining on the white roofs of St Wolfgang on the opposite shore. She could, given enough schnapps to warm her up, learn to cope with that. But she misses Vienna, the life she and Bosch — she never uses her husband's Christian name — lived before the war. Their lively political chat, their belief that they could stop Hitler because they imagined Chamberlain read their far-sighted editorials, and the meeting of like minds in Viennese cafés, particularly the *Café Herrenhof*.

She thinks back to the Heurigen — the inns where they drank the new wine — they used to enjoy, frequenting the leafy Viennese suburb of Grinzing with its many agreeable places to savour the new season's offerings. She pictures her splendid villa on the edge of the Vienna Woods now occupied by conquering Americans. Will she really be able to make a tolerable life for herself and her family beside the glacial Wolfgangsee while they wait for Bosch to be offered a suitable position in Vienna? Who is there in this backwater, among the yodelling mountaineers and sailing enthusiasts, with whom they can discuss politics?

Or is it worse than that? Does she actually loathe the place, however charming, however picturesque, however many interesting local people they might find? Hate it with a passionate detestation of all things relating to rural Austria? She can begin to understand how sixteen-year-old Nina feels, realises that the teenager is desperate about living here rather than in the idyllic Surrey cottage they rented during the war. She had a horse there, and friends, and a school she enjoyed. Now, in Bosch's beloved homeland, the child has nothing. Maybe she has more sense than Bosch.

***

3

Gabby's return isn't greeted with great enthusiasm. Because she hasn't brought any money. Tante Martha's life savings have gone to her sister Dorinda — nicknamed Doly — while the Cuxhaven Council pointed out, politely and accurately, that they paid Gabby for the villa: the day before the Anschluss with Austria in 1938. They can't be held responsible for the Nazi party taking over all foreign-owned bank accounts.

'They voted Hitler in, didn't they?' Bosch, in threadbare clothes he hasn't had the money to replace since the thirties, is sitting with one leg over the other, jiggling it. The sign he's spoiling for a fight.

'In 1932, Bosch. Long before Moppel and I sold the villa. I should have known better, I should have put the money into an American bank. I just had no idea, it didn't occur to me that governments, even the Hitler régime, could simply take over a foreigner's private account.'

'You're thinking about Emil.' He doesn't refer to her brother by the childish nickname Moppel she and Doly still use. The jiggling stops. 'You couldn't very well let him handle it.'

'Exactly.' Eyes still bright and birdlike, but faded to a lighter shade of blue than in her younger years, shine determination. 'He'd have collared the lot, just like the Nazis. And I'd have lost a brother as well as the money.'

Bosch stands, staring across the lake, lighting a new Austria Tabak cigarette from the old one. They have managed to find one or two agreeable acquaintances. Not kindred souls they can have political discussions with, but people who do have other qualities: an amiable American Colonel who supplies them with cigarettes and alcohol, and a GI who manages to rustle up tins of spam. This curious American comestible is a spiced ham particularly popular in the United States and, being one of the few meat products available, is considered a delicacy in post-war Europe. Though most American food is, by European consensus, disgusting.

'So how is Holy Doly?' Bosch asks, his cigarette end flaming red, using the name he dubbed her in one of his more astute moments. He's never been able to stand Dorinda, normally can hardly bring himself to speak of her. But even he can sympathise with a woman whose husband mortgaged the house she bought, then took off with another woman just when Doly returned from the States with their first, long-awaited child. After thirteen years of marriage.

'She's staying on at Dramlings. Getting a lodger to make up the shortfall from the derisive amount Erskine contributes.'

'She's staying on? Miles from anywhere, no car, pumping her water, shovelling coke for the back-boiler?'

'She adores the primitive life-style. Not sure the baby will, but then he hasn't got a choice!'

The cigarette flourishes a circle of red. 'I think your sister's crazy.' A cough now often interrupts his words. 'But I do admire her spunk.' He breathes heavily, sits down. 'She's really holding on to that cottage in spite of Erskine mortgaging it and leaving her to pay off the debt?' He steadies the cigarette in his mouth, pulls down the paraffin ceiling lamp, removes the strawberry glass shade, then the chimney, trims the wick, lights it. Diligently puts everything back.

Gabby is amazed at Bosch's skill at menial tasks. Brought up in a houseful of servants obedient to his every whim, he's managed not only to learn the menial chores of basic living but to be good at them. 'So she maintains.'

'Good luck to her!' Bosch expertly raises the lamp above their heads. The gentle swings cast shadow movements, as though an army is about to charge.

'She's living in cloud-cuckoo land. Plucky enough, but it can't last.' Gabby shrugs indifference. She's never been able to understand her sister's priorities.

'Very droll. From your description of the woodland setting there must be flocks of them about.'

Gabby's nose lifts like a hunting dog's. 'You know what, Bosch? Doly has given me an idea. We don't use our top floor here. Why not sublet it?'

The hunting lodge may be a fairytale gem but few modern people would undertake the hard back-breaking physical work needed to live there. It's as gingerbread as Dramlings is Tudor, in a Grimm fairytale sort of way.

Bosch leans over the functional etched globe of a table lamp. Lights another cigarette by holding it over the searing chimney. Blows clouds. 'You think the Countess would stand for that?'

'Assuming the right tenant, absolutely. I ran into her in Bad Ischl. Otto Habsburg — one of Karl's sons and the putative heir — is longing to come to Austria for a holiday. Terribly homesick, apparently. He can't possibly stay with the von Langens. They couldn't keep that from the authorities. Frau von Langen mentioned how much he used to love being taken to the Franzosenschanze as a boy, how he'd give anything to be in our shoes. I wondered why she rambled on about how they'd manage if they were here. She must have thought me pretty thick. I've only just grasped what she was trying to get across!'

A cumulus of smoke above their heads. 'You're talking about the Habsburg heirs living in our attic? While we're in the main rooms?'

'Even royal beggars can't be choosers.'

'What makes you think they'll pay?'

'Because money isn't the problem. We're a brilliant cover, they get the chance to relive their youth. All we have to do is keep our mouths shut.'

'How much?'

'I haven't a clue. Nothing as indelicate as an actual sum was mentioned, but it was labelled generous. Enough to keep you in cigarettes for several years I'd guess. The Countess explained they always travel with their own maid. She sees to personal needs.'

Bosch sits, jiggling again. 'There's no bathroom up there.'

'Exactly. A delicate reference to chamber pots and washing bowls. Their Swiss castle doesn't go in for mod cons either. Perhaps they prefer old-fashioned ways. They can have water taken up to them in jugs. Royalty never share utilities with commoners.'

Bosch's cackle rebounds from the huge expanse of window glass overlooking the Wolfgangsee. 'We can live with that. Neither of us ever goes upstairs. Gemma can share with Nina and Kamilla.'

'And they eat separately. An Archduchess's mastication is not for our eyes.'

'That so? Splendid.'

'There's one crucial requirement. You'll never believe it.'

'We have to give them our bed?'

Gabby laughs. 'Nothing as practical as that. A bloody game — to pay for the privilege of having them here. Not chess this time. Tarock.' Weird how they got their English cottage by playing chess with the owner in lieu of rent. The tables turned but still playing a game. This time it earns the rent for them.

Bosch's eyes slant heavenward. 'I knew exactly what you were going to say.' Several rapid puffs on his cigarette. 'Tapp Tarock, you mean, don't you? A stupid card game.'

'The Countess mentioned it was an Austrian version of Tarot, whatever that is. Otto is crazy about it.'

'The others were always playing it at my school.'

Surprise gapes Gabby's mouth. 'I've never seen you play cards.'

'Not me. My schoolmates. I find card games unbelievably tedious.' Rapid-fire puffs. 'I'm not sitting around playing some idiotic game just to amuse past royalty.'

'I'm told Tarock is a game for three. The deal — if you'll forgive the pun — is to find two players to join Otto. His wife doesn't play.'

'That's ridiculous!' Snowy-white hair pushed back, deep-holed cheeks sunk deeper in despair. 'Damn it all, how are we supposed to do that?'

'We need the money, Bosch. Why not rope in Gemma and Nina? It isn't only that I can't stand playing cards, I'm a complete duffer at it.'

'You're saying two of us should take it in turns to play with Otto? What about after the summer, when Gemma goes back to England?'

'There'll be other victims. I heard that that writer — Lernet-Holenia — lives just across the lake in St Wolfgang. Probably bored to tears in this backwater. He can row over in his boat. And there's Fassbinder, in Salzburg. Maybe the Count will come over from Bad Ischl...'

'But every day?'

'We're allowed Sundays off. They're strict Catholics. No card games on Sundays.'

'That's Calvinist. No matter. Thank God for religious fanatics.' Bosch stares across the lake. 'You really think we can handle it?'

'They're only planning a couple of months. Mostly while the girls are still on holiday.' Gabby's eyes light up. 'You know, I've had a brilliant idea. Remember that American, Colonel Tippets, who's always helping us out with Care parcels? Maybe we could teach him to play.'

'Don't talk such rubbish. It's illegal for the Habsburgs to come to Austria. They've got to smuggle themselves over the border. We can't let an American Army colonel in on it. He'll think they're breaking the Treaty of Yalta, not Versailles!'

Gabby's grin is as wide as she can make it. 'No need to worry about that. His girlfriend's Austrian, remember. She'll sort it out because he loves playing cards.'

'You know Otto Habsburg and his wife are staying on the top floor for two months.' Gabby feels unusually nervous. Can she really cope with royalty — even past royalty — in her house? Will she make all kinds of faux pas? Will the girls behave?

'So what? Just tenants like any others, aren't they?' Gemma's first year at university has turned her into a socialist. But she's underage, barely nineteen, and under Gabby's and Bosch's care whether she likes it or not. She'll have to tow the bloody line.

'No, they aren't. They're paying an excellent rent, on the understanding that we treat them in the way they're accustomed to.'

'Pandering to their grandiose pretensions is disgusting coming from a woman like you. You're a political revolutionary, not a royalist!'

'You know nothing about politics, Gemma. You live in an ivory tower of high-flown ideas. I have to pay the bills.'

'Which means Nina and I are supposed to perform like circus clowns. You might as well spell it out. What do we have to do? Play silly games?'

Gabby has always found Gemma's direct challenges a nuisance. The girl has no finesse, no understanding of social nuances. She sees everything in red and white. 'Tarock, yes. And the Archduchess likes to bathe in the lake.'

'To make up for the fact there's no bathroom upstairs, I suppose!'

Gemma's summing up is not unreasonable. Gabby has found the Habsburgs oddly lacking in cleanliness. Though godliness is there in good measure: a local priest is smuggled in for Sunday Mass, and any others he can manage.

Not having a bathroom doesn't, of course, preclude washing. The maid has been offered hot water galore.

'Perhaps. The point is that it isn't suitable for anyone else to bathe at the same time.'

'You're saying the whole of the lake is reserved for her gracious non-majesty?'

'Not the whole lake. Our private bathing strip.'

'I get it now. Nina and I are out of bounds there.'

'You can bathe when she doesn't.'

'Big deal. The sun's only there for two hours at the crack of dawn. When there is any sun, that is. I've no idea why people call the English climate wet. This place is much worse.'

Gabby has also been dismayed by the way the mountains catch

the clouds and precipitate rain at regular intervals. 'You can always walk along to Strobl, Gemma. It's only half an hour away. And much nicer.'

'Right; no bathing except in the shady part of the day. What else?'

This is going to be the really hard bit. 'Well, there's the way you behave when you come across either of them.'

'Behave? I'm not going to attack them or anything.' Gemma grins. 'Or even sing political slogans.'

'You're supposed to curtsey. And walk out of the room backwards.'

Gemma laughs. 'You can forget that. Ridiculous even for you, Gabby.' The girls decided some time ago that the childish Mutti was no longer a suitable address for their mother. Gabriele is too formal, and Gabby so appropriate they've settled for that. 'Count me out of curtsies. I'll make sure I don't come across them at all. That way we can all coexist.'

The Otto Habsburgs stay for two months. Their intrusion into the Bosches' lives is minimal, their contribution adequate, if not substantial. Bosch orders a new suit in readiness for the job he assumes he'll be offered any time now in Vienna. Gabby makes do with a new wig from the impressive hairdresser on the Kärntnerstrasse. It is one essential she cannot do without.

Gemma and Nina cooperate reasonably. They play Tarock, they refrain from bathing while her Royal Highness takes the waters of the Wolfgangsee, and they disappear into their room as soon as they hear royal footsteps on the stairs, so obviating the need to walk backwards.

Bosch's mood becomes sunnier. He smokes as much as ever, and now adds a few glasses of local wine every day. Gabby joins him and begins to relax. It's possible that the Franzosenschanze interlude could turn into a reasonably pleasant one. Nevertheless, she's sure she can only stand it for at most a year. She spends hours working out how to get them back to Vienna. So far she hasn't had one of her usual brainwaves.

CHAPTER 2

Sussex, Summer 1948

The knock on the door is soft but Doly recognises it. Bland, unassuming, genteel. Erskine. What does he want? How dare he trespass on her territory?

'Yes?' She's usually so hospitable, so welcoming. Even now she finds it hard not to jump up, fling the door open, and welcome back the prodigal husband. He wouldn't be here if this wasn't some sort of peace offering.

'It's Erskine, Doly.'

Her front door is always unlocked, always open to all and sundry. She's been told that's dangerous but waved all fears away. What is there to steal? A few second-hand pieces of furniture, fruit and vegetables from the garden, the odd bottle of home made wine? Hardly what thieves are looking for.

'I know. I recognised the rat-a-tat.' Thirteen years of marriage aren't that easy to forget.

She can hear he's already inside the little front porch, sees the door to the living room opening. Slowly, gently.

Doly's heart flips as she sees remembered tousled hair flicking into blinking eyes, the tall figure stooping under the lintel. He stands, eyes flittering, hands in a gesture of supplication mixed with that very English attribute, helpless self-effacement.

She has to sound businesslike. 'You've forgotten something? You've come to pick it up?'

He nods. 'I have indeed. Something important.'

'I haven't come across anything…'

'We have a son. He matters more than anything else.'

So that's the way of it. He can't resist both fatherhood and the fact that Ross is a boy, an offshoot, a sprig off the old tree. The only sure immortality known to man. He may prefer Sheelagh Dickson in many different ways but they haven't, at any rate as yet, got a son.

'It's taken you nine months to work that out?'

He sighs, tousles his hair in the gesture she used to crave. 'I know. I must have been mad.' That smile, that very Erskine look of helplessness. The boyish grin, the blinking eyes. He holds out a bottle.

'Any chance of giving it another go? For the little one's sake?'

She hunches over the baby on her lap. 'You expect me to just forget the way you've behaved and take you back? Just like that?'

'I don't expect anything. I just hope.'

There's a whole litany of crimes. She can't bring herself to mention the fact that he mortgaged her beloved Dramlings behind her back, when she was in the States and too ill to return until after Ross's birth. Can't snarl that he mortgaged the cottage she not only found but bought with *her* money. He didn't contribute a single penny. Then took the cash and spent it on a drinking spree with that awful woman. How could he? How does he have the gall to come here…

All right, so maybe the Sheelagh episode is over, maybe that's why he's crawling back. But he's responsible for their being hard up instead of, at last, free to spend his salary on a reasonable standard of living. Contributed, finally, by him. Now that he's head of the Maths Department at Midhurst Grammar.

'What can I say? I'll make it up to you — honestly. And Ross needs a father.'

'It wasn't me who deprived him of one.'

He's come right into the room, advanced towards her. She's just finished feeding Ross, is burping him.

'May I do that?' He takes the baby, his eyes soft, his hands flirting the bib around the child's mouth. He pats a muslin nappy onto his shoulder, lifts his son and holds him upright against himself, pats his back. Gently, very gently.

Doly watches, eyes slit. If it's a charade, it's a very good one. 'Where did you learn to do that?'

'Some of the boys' mothers bring infants to the cricket matches.' Erskine's eyes have changed from the bored disdainful sweep she had to endure the last time he was here, more than a year ago, to one of amiable friendliness.

Should she really just forgive and forget? *Can* she?

'He's a great little chap.'

'Not exactly news to me.' Has he tired of Sheelagh? Is he offering himself as resurrected faithful husband? More like a devoted father, but still… It would be wrong not even to mull it over, to deprive Ross before she's even thought through the implications.

'So, what d'you think? Can you consider forgiving me? Think about taking me back on a trial basis?'

It would solve so many problems. She could stay on at Dramlings without counting every penny, Tante Martha's money could be used to buy decent togs for the baby, nursery furniture. She could relax, give her body the chance to recover properly at last, allow Ross his father, and bring friendship to what was once such a loving and affectionate relationship between her and Erskine. Never passionate. That was, perhaps, the problem. She hadn't realised Erskine was capable of that.

Perhaps that has its advantages now. Passion belongs to pre-parenthood. And they've waited so long for that. Who knows, they might return to the loving feelings she and Erskine had for each other all those years ago, during the war, when he came to visit her at Barrow Farm while she was doing her war effort stint as a Land Girl.

That was the apex of their love: a genial tender devotion which warmed her even when he wasn't there. She lets the time he helped her through those terrible months flitter through her mind, remembers the way he trekked to visit, overcoming snow and ice, to support her, cherish her. She's longing to return to that.

'I don't know, Erskine. I really have to think it through…'

'I wouldn't dream of rushing you.' A large burp as Ross brings up wind.

'It could only be on a trial basis. I'm not sure that I'd be able to get back to…'

'Of course not. I wouldn't want to hurry you. I'll sleep down here, in the study.'

'I've got a lodger at the moment. Brings in much-needed cash.'

He swallows, his eyebrows rise, he hides his head behind his son. 'Presumably you could give her notice.'

'Him. Chap from the riding stables. Too far out for a girl.' She's standing by the window, lighting a cigarette. 'He uses the outside facilities.'

'Right you are.' Ross gurgles delightedly, quite clearly enjoying his father's company. 'After a due time, then.'

She sees the question in his eyes. Does he really think she'd have a lover in the house with the baby? Surely he can't be that stupid.

Whatever he thinks, would it be proper to deprive her son of his father? 'Wilf and I agreed two weeks' notice either way.' She settles on the sofa, lights another cigarette from the old one, watches as Erskine and Ross get to know each other, apparently adore each other's company.

The past drifts by in a series of flashes. This is the man she nursed through septicaemia for many long years, the man whose hospital bills she paid, who nearly died and sat, weak and pallid, drinking tea while she dug their garden, organised repairs for the cottage, kept accounts. But he's also the man who admired her efforts, let her choose everything for the cottage, supported her when the farmer she worked for as a Land Girl nearly murdered her. Erskine made sure his father, a retired Army general, interceded for her, got her release from the Land Army when she was exhausted, vulnerable, unable to cope.

'Is this about Sheelagh? Has she gone off you? Found someone else?'

'She's moved back in with husband Dick.'

'Thought you said she couldn't stand him?'

Erskine's head lowers towards the baby, hiding his expression. 'He's very fond of her.'

'Still at the Egmont?'

'They've got a different place now, making a new start. In Bepton. Smaller, easier to run. A couple of rooms to let out gives them a bit of extra cash.'

He'd said it was a passionate affair, that he couldn't help himself, that there would never be anyone else. Surprising from a man who never showed real passion when with her. Not even in the early days. 'You're sure it's over?'

'Sure as one can be of anything.'

And that's precisely what he said when he told her that Sheelagh was the only one for him. So his opinion counts for nothing. She stands, stubs out her cigarette, holds her arms out for her son. 'I'll think about it, Erskine. Come back in a week.'

And turns her back.

THE DEFEATED

NIGHTMARE

If seven sons or seven daughters are born in succession, then the seventh child will become that curious, secretive being which rides horses at night while plaiting the horse's mane – a nightmare. Anyone foolish enough to disturb this dressage is likely to get a visit from the phantom.

Nightmares creep into a bedroom through the keyhole. Then they sit on the sleeper's chest in various guises. Very often they take the form of a black cat which mews until the victim is bathed in sweat. The only safeguard against such an unwelcome visit is to put one's shoes with their toes pointing away from the bed.

One day a young man forgot this precaution. The nightmare arrived the very next night. But he woke up before the creature could leave, rushed to the keyhole and stopped it up so that the nightmare couldn't escape. Suddenly he saw that she wasn't a demon, but a beautiful young girl.

The young man had to unplug the keyhole in order for her to leave the next morning. The nightmare immediately escaped, calling out:

> The bells of England ring,
> They're dancing for their king.

With that she disappeared and was never seen again.

CHAPTER 3

St Gilgen, Austria, Winter 1948/1949

Winter comes early to the mountains. The friendly lapping of the Wolfgangsee is a distant memory as icy winds turn the lake into a cauldron of swirling mists and buffeting waves. Large solid snowflakes settle with amazing speed. Passing jeeps driven by impatient conquerors spray a mixture of mud and snow into high banks along the road, narrowing it. Gabby's shoes are not fit for the long walk to St Gilgen, the nearest place for buying food. The prospect of carrying groceries back along icy roads is terrifying.

'We need a sleigh,' Bosch announces. 'And some boots.' Both objects the locals are willing to supply, second hand, in exchange for coffee or chocolate. The Bosches get a minimal supply from Rolf Ferent, Nina's father, now living in New York. He likes to send her parcels.

A stout pair of leather boots is purchased for the maid. As part of her salary, of course. She's the one who's going to do the shopping. Not only because of the hazardous journey. She speaks the local dialect, knows the best sources of supply. Young Trautl is worth her weight in cigarettes and chocolate.

The fifteen-year-old is brilliant. One of a large family cow-herding on the Alm, she's used to making do, has no problems using the kitchen stove fired by wood, sleeping on a cot in the nether regions where the cooking, the laundry and the cleaning are masterminded. Gabby had problems using the very adequate gas cooker in their English cottage. Trautl thinks having a cooker, even a wood burning one, is paradise. The girl also runs up and down two flights of stairs with hot water for the royals, makes beds, lugs laundry to a woman who lives nearby, cooks all the meals as well as baking brilliant pastries and special Austrian Mehlspeisen, those highly satisfying dishes which do duty for a whole meal. Her Buchteln — sweet dumplings made of yeast dough, filled with anything to hand: jam, poppy-seed paste, curd cheese, then baked in a pan so they stick together — are to die for. She has a remarkably light touch for such a stumpy girl. Gabby is so delighted with her cooking and general domestic skills she plans to take her to Vienna. Trautl is ecstatic at the thought.

The winter is long, dark, intensified at the hunting lodge by the tall mountain at their backs, and cooled by the glacier lake in front of them. Bosch passes time in lengthy correspondence. Letters to Vienna, to Linz, to Salzburg. Exhausting all his contacts, however peripheral. He receives short, friendly, non-committal replies. The Bosches feel frozen into a Christmas-tree life without the baubles.

Slowly, imperceptibly, the thaw begins. Pointed snowdrop buds spear bare earth, there's more blue in the sky between the mountains. A ray of sunshine glints over the roofs in St Wolfgang, is reflected off the lake.

'Listen to this, Bosch!' Gabby waves a piece of paper she's drawn out of an official-looking envelope. 'The American Army is leaving Neuwaldegg. They're returning the house to Rolf Ferent and me by autumn. Maybe earlier!'

Bosch, after a brief spell of energy lit when the Habsburgs were in residence, has become more silent each day. He deals with the oil lamps, plays with toddler Kamilla, shovels snow, wears a muffler to keep warm and stop his coughing. But the ready tongue and glinting eyes have gone.

'Back to Vienna at last?' Paraffin spills out of the lamp feeder. 'Wonderful!' His voice takes on a fuller tone, his eyes light up.

'You're thinking we can stay in the villa?' Gabby's peaky face tenses into a mask. 'We'd have to pay Rolf Ferent rent.'

'You're not married to him any more.'

'You know that's beside the point. He did pay for half the house. We'd do much better to sell the place for a decent sum.'

'And go on living here?' Smoke drifts ceiling ward. 'Nonsense. If the villa is free we live there.'

'I can't work miracles, Bosch. I'm not sure…'

'You always imagine difficulties. They'll offer me a job as soon as I return. Arrange for the move right away.' He wipes up the paraffin without his usual care.

So hopelessly impractical. 'I'll discuss it with Czezina.'

'This touching faith in a humdrum lawyer. What's he supposed to contribute?'

'He can explain Austrian property laws to me.' The lawyer is another one of the old boy network from the prestigious school Bosch attended. János Czezina has made it clear that Byzantine is the only word to describe Viennese property laws.

'The villa is exactly what we need to entertain my friends in the government. See Czezina by all means. We're moving in as soon as the Americans leave.'

Always that autocratic tone. He has no rights to the villa, no rights to anything. All his property was destroyed during the war. There's no restitution for political refugees, only for Jews. But Bosch, used to his pre-war standing and his coterie, acts as though Vienna belonged to him, was under his control. Fortunately the Neuwaldegg villa is owned by Gabby and ex-husband Rolf Ferent, both US citizens. Bosch has no legal control over the house or its contents, should those still be around. Gabby makes a mental note that she has to remember that.

Czezina welcomes Gabby into his office with an oily smile and a sweaty palm. Moist lips brush her hand: 'Küss die Hand, gnä' Frau.'

She's staying with Bosch's cousins, the Weisses. Hans, another old boy from Bosch's prestigious school, the Schottengymnasium, was the one who recommended Czezina, the one who arranged this meeting.

'The house is in a terrible state, gnä' Frau. Even if either you or Herr Ferent has the funds to bring it round there's no market for such a large house. No Austrian can afford it in the present climate.'

'What about renting it out, Herr Doktor?'

'Austrians are out of the question. Our rental laws stipulate tenants have right of tenure. For themselves *and* their heirs.' A little shorter than Bosch, the same age but looking years younger. Hair a glistening black, olive skin still smooth on cheeks and forehead. 'There's only one sensible solution.'

'Yes?'

'Rent to one of the occupying powers. Preferably Americans.' He flicks his head sideways, a robin pecking the early worm. 'The only certain thing in an uncertain Europe is that the Americans will leave. Sooner than the others.'

'But not before the Russians one trusts.' She frowns. Vienna, occupied by all Four Powers — Americans, British, French and Russian — is a long way from being a free city. The constant Four-Power jeep patrols keeping strictly to their own zones makes everyone aware of that.

'We must certainly hope so.'

'You'll look for someone?'

'Leave it to me, gnä' Frau.' He ushers her out of his office, invites her for coffee at the *Hotel Sacher*. Where the coffee is made from dandelion roots and still an outrageous price, and the famous Sachertorte is in abeyance.

Czezina is a vivacious, bubbling man who makes Gabby feel alive again. 'Go back to the Wolfgangsee until September, gnä' Frau. I'll have everything sorted out by then.'

Gabby rushes round a Vienna which bears only skeletal resemblance to the city she loved so much, the city she felt at home in, before the war. She was reluctant to move from Berlin, was dragged to Austria's capital by Rolf Ferent, who'd been promoted to heading the Eastern European division of IBM. At the time Gabby was convinced that Germany's vibrant capital was the only place to be. It was the glamorous city of Europe for theatre, for art, for cabaret.

For the first year or so, in 1929, she was bored in Vienna. Until she discovered the *Café Herrenhof*, the coffee house frequented by politicians, radicals, intellectuals. It had all the newspapers she could wish for, and even a four-sheet weekly she'd never heard of before, had never come across. *Sturm Über Österreich* sat, small and unobtrusive, among the giant bamboo poles bearing the other newspapers. She read it avidly, attracted by its anti-Nazi thundering. And met the owner and editor: Franz Bosch.

Not exactly love at first sight, more admiration, followed by the adulation accorded Bosch by his small coterie of friends. He certainly knew the politicians of the day, but they were not intimates. That is the point: his friends were a select band of like-minded people who included Jews and working-class men. No women, apart from Gabby.

Now that the Bosches are finally back in Austria those people cannot help him, they have no power. The Jews who managed to escape can claim restitution, but they can't help Bosch become a member of the present Austrian Government.

Gabby hurries along the Kärntnerstrasse — Vienna's Oxford Street and Bond Street combined. The main buildings at the two ends of the street, the Staatsoper — the opera house — and the Stephansdom are still standing. The city's proud cathedral, and the emblem of all Austria, has lost its roof to fire. Not to a bomb, rather less heroically. The German officer ordered to shell the cathedral until nothing remained disobeyed the order, but when the Russians arrived nearby looters caused fires which the wind spread to the cathedral roof. It fell in, and repairs are costly for a defeated nation.

Still, Vienna knows how to regenerate herself. She survived two occupations by the Turks, and she has also survived the Nazis. Gabby is confident the city will survive the Four-Power occupation. It may take a few years, but it will happen.

Somehow, miraculously, the money is being put together for a new Stephansdom roof and other repairs, not just by Vienna, but by the whole of Austria. The colourful glazed tiles for the roof are predominantly black and yellow. The Viennese jeeringly dub it the 'wasp roof', but recognise its significance.

Gabby is longing for Vienna to be her home again. Her heart aches for her native Schwanenbruch but her active mind, her calculating brain, knows Vienna is the place she has to live. And not in some tiny flat in the suburbs, that simply will not do. How is she going to achieve this miracle with a husband who cannot find a job, a young child to look after, and the money Ralph Ferent sends for his two daughters' maintenance soon to dry up? Gemma is nineteen, Nina fifteen. She has barely two years before she loses the contribution for Gemma.

THE DANCING BONES

THE DANCING BONES

A long time ago, well before the three small locks leading to the River Medem were accessible by anything larger than a rowing boat, a schooner with a full cargo of animal bones sailed down the Elbe. The captain was making for Otterndorf but it was such a harsh winter that ice floes prevented the boat from sailing on. That's when the captain decided to rid himself of his load, and to arrange for it to be ground down into fertiliser.

The seaman's search for adequate storage space was unsuccessful. The only suitable place he could find near the river mouth belonged to the lock keeper who also ran an inn with a large upstairs hall used for dancing. The innkeeper was reluctant to rent this out to the captain. However, all men have their price, and the captain finally persuaded the innkeeper to rent him his hall.

The cargo was duly unloaded and all seemed well for several days. Until the night of the full moon, when the reflection of moonlight in sheets of ice gave the impression of broad daylight. The innkeeper had retired to well-deserved rest in his bedroom below the hall when a curious shuffling noise woke him from a deep sleep.

He turned over, tried to go back to sleep. The noise went on and on. Only rats who'd found the cartilage, he thought. He'd set traps the next day. But he was wrong. The noise grew louder and stronger, until the poor man could have sworn that a crowd of people were dancing and skipping across the floor above him.

Fearful now, the innkeeper pulled his bedclothes over his head and tried to shut out the din. Impossible. A raging whirling roaring noise filled the air, followed by howling as though the winds of hell were blowing through his hall. The innkeeper cowered under his Federbett and blocked his ears. In vain. The howling turned into a shovelling sound, as though someone had come to scoop the bones away.

Worse was to come. The shovelling ceased, and he could hear

footsteps pounding down the stairs. His doorknob turned, the door opened, and a spooky figure walked into the room and up to his bed.

The innkeeper felt an icy fear crawl down his spine as he watched the ghost come nearer and nearer. Then it started to drag the bedclothes off the bottom of the bed. Terrified, the innkeeper jumped up, grabbed at the prayer book lying on his bedside table, and began to pray. At this the ghost disappeared.

The same theatricals were repeated the next night. And continued, night after night, until the innkeeper's pale face and black-holed eyes told their own story. The two customs' officials living in his house asked him what his problem was.

The innkeeper was reluctant to tell anyone of his experiences. He knew very well he wouldn't be believed. But his tenants, suspecting him of smuggling, finally persuaded him. And laughed at the explanation. At which the innkeeper invited them to spend the night in his room and see for themselves.

They smiled their disbelief and retired to the innkeeper's bedroom to prove him wrong. The midnight hour struck, and the ghost appeared on cue, starting towards the bed on which the officers lay. They bellowed for light and frightened the spook away. But they no longer made fun of the innkeeper. Instead, they suggested he have the bones examined by an expert.

The local butcher came and spent time rummaging among the bones. And was appalled. For, mixed in among animal cartilage, were obvious human remains.

Convinced that there was more to it than just an inadvertent mixture of animal and human bones, the innkeeper enquired further. He discovered that the bones had been scooped up by greedy looters picking over the carcases left on a battlefield. Human bones had been mixed with those of animals.

Now that the innkeeper knew why the bones whirled their dance of death he had the human relics separated out and given a Christian burial. From that day onward there was peace in the house.

But it was not the end of the story. When the sailors returned to load the remaining cargo into their boats, there must have been a few human ones left. For they swore their dogs never stopped howling until the last of the bones had been washed out of their holds.

CHAPTER 4

Sussex, Autumn/Winter 1948

Doly feels a chill creep over her shoulders, has doubts, begins to wonder. Has she made a terrible mistake? Was it wishful thinking that prompted her to take Erskine back? It seemed so good, so natural at first. The lazy days of the summer holidays, sitting in their fertile little garden surrounded by beautiful nature, their harvest in full swing. Wasps browsing the plums, apples coming into full bearing, marrows sprawling their languid bodies like reptiles, good crops of peas and beans. She even decided to let him share her bed again.

And Ross, of course. She never fooled herself, even at the start. He's the reason Erskine is here, why he came back. They both adore their son, but Erskine is obviously entranced. Already a year old, the child is a sturdy little boy, a determined little chap, crawling over the lawn, trying to catch butterflies. It all seemed so idyllic during the warm days of July and August, a dream come true.

Now term has begun and tranquil summer days have turned chilly at

24

night. Mists cover the garden, the fruit harvest is in store, frosts killed the last of the tomato plants a week ago, even the wasps have gone.

And Doly begins to sense a change. At first she put it down to her own shortcomings. Her legs are still giving her trouble, and she allows — encourages — Erskine to make breakfast, heat Ross's bottle, bring it all up to her in bed. But where he'd sat on the bed while she fed Ross and stayed to drink a companionable cup of coffee during the holidays, he now dashes downstairs, grabs a piece of toast and is gone without even kissing Doly and Ross goodbye.

She hears the news from Mrs Farley. The Dicksons are back in town after a spell abroad. Taking over the Bepton pub from the couple they'd left in charge.

Doesn't take genius to work it out. Always the same tell-tale signs. Shining eyes, suppressed excitement. Now, even when she brings Ross downstairs long before Erskine needs to leave, breakfast is rushed, his cup of coffee left half drunk.

When he comes home — a little later each day — his whole being looks altered, muted playfulness with Ross during the summer months now changed to enthusiasm, shining eyes. Not realising that Doly guesses what's driving his new-found fervour he shows uncharacteristic exuberance which occasionally even spills over on to his family.

She decides to skirt the subject of his day. Foolishly. 'Did you have lunch at the canteen?'

Slight pause as he heaves Ross up and down. Blinking eyes. 'No. Mince on Mondays.'

'So you skipped it altogether?'

He sets Ross on his knees, avoids looking at her. 'Yes. Is it important?'

'I just wondered. When you do that, d'you stay at school?'

He's clasped the child to himself, kisses his head. 'Generally, yes. Why the inquisition?' Tone tighter, gruffer than before.

If she doesn't indicate she knows he'll just go trotting back to Sheelagh and think he can have it both ways. 'Well, you didn't today, did you?'

Eyes open, nostrils whiten with anger. 'If you must know, I went out and had a beer.' He swallows, his Adam's apple moving rapidly. 'And I thought I'd take the opportunity to go to Knight's. See about the mattress.'

Another sop, of course. Pretending to get a new mattress to replace their upstairs sagging one. At least no indignant outburst.

Instead: 'How are your legs today?'

For the first time since he's been back, more than twelve weeks ago, he actually asks about her health. A dead give-away. The husband proclaiming consideration, a gift of conscience to his wife. The old, old story. But it's easier to make a solicitous enquiry than face the coming storm.

He's forgotten they live in the country, and Midhurst is a small country town. It was Mrs Farley who brought the news of Erskine in the Bepton pub.

'Why go all the way out to Bepton to get a beer when there are pubs aplenty in Midhurst?'

He hides behind Ross. 'Can't say I appreciate being spied on.'

'We live in the country. The grape-vine works overtime.'

'So I gather.'

Doly doesn't trust herself in his company any longer. It's safer to be out of the way. She takes Ross upstairs to ready him for bed.

When she comes down after her rest, well before their evening meal, he reminds her it's not yet time for the ten o'clock bottle.

'I came down to make supper.'

Suddenly the real Erskine erupts, the fury at being found out. 'I won't stand for this prying.'

He must have thought her securely tied, fettered, trussed up, imagined himself safe to do as he pleased. Though he must be wondering how she worked it out.

'Just thought you might like to take a packed lunch tomorrow. Mrs Farley saw you wandering round Midhurst like a lost soul.'

'Here this afternoon, was she?'

'You know she's here every Monday afternoon. Today was no exception.'

She's so exhausted she goes to bed right after supper. He comes up to say good night and asks should he warm the bottle. She thanks him for his kind offer, then hears him come upstairs again. Knows what he's forgotten and come up to fetch. His jacket with his wallet, his car keys. To go out for a drink.

And that's how it is with them. Doly has taken a stand before, but she's the loser in this game. It works for a day, and then he can afford another sally and a better one, and even more of their relationship breaks down. She dries her tears, resolves to get on with it on her own, to build up a new life for herself and Ross in this season of separation.

But how? The scandal of a divorce will endanger Erskine's job, leave them without income of any kind. Naturally she knows he despises her weakness and self-abasement — doesn't she? — but he can't cope with cold indifference either. And she's a useful background for the time being. She settles for keeping mum.

What really matters, their marriage, is no longer of any consequence to him. The only thing he cares about, the only thing he's here for, is Ross. He wouldn't give Doly a second thought. So if he can somehow get by with wife and mistress, he's fine with that. While making sure he's not found out, of course. Because that isn't useful, possibly more for Sheelagh's sake than his, possibly because of his real love for Ross. Which means this uneasy chain of duplicity and underhandedness will go on for as long as Doly allows it, and can stand it.

Even bad news is better than none. And so it is with Doly. Perhaps there'll come a time when she'll get to be as indifferent as Erskine. The only thing that provokes him into all loss of control is any reference to Sheelagh.

She's laughing aloud at this angle of it. Erskine is perpetually burying bones and Doly is perpetually digging them up again. He peers to left and right to make sure no one is looking and takes care to cover his tracks. And then he's found out again.

> Rub-a-dub-dub
> Three men in a tub,
> And who do you think they be?
>
> The butcher, the baker,
> The candlestick maker,
> They all jumped out of a rotten potato!
> Turn 'em out knaves all three.

He seems to have forgotten that Doly is on good terms with all three. Poor boy must think he's jinxed.

As everything is brushed aside as supposition, or poppycock, she's now letting him have his frequently repeated joke that she's a reincarnation of the Gestapo. The fact is that the moment he thinks she's worked out what he's been up to he comes across with the goods.

So mad the last time he called her a first-class bitch. And she merely smiled, and just said yes to it.

When she mentions that his drinking with friends is using up money he explodes: 'Anything which makes me forget this bloody place is money well spent.' He picks Ross up. 'And I never thought I'd say that to you.'

She twirls a postcard from Tante Martha. It has a picture of the Villa Dohlen on it. She shows it to him. 'Those were the halcyon days.' But in those days, of course, there was money attached. To it, to her.

'You seem to be able to think of nothing but money these days.' He stares at Ross, at his blond hair. Plentiful, clearly Nordic, not affected by Doly's dominant gene for early hair loss. 'Almost as if you had Jewish blood in you.'

Has he turned into a Nazi? 'If I had I wouldn't be ashamed of it.' Pure Aryan, but still despised by the stalwart supporters of the Blackshirts because of the errant gene. 'It's not money which counts, it's the attitude towards it.' She stares at his new pullover. 'That's new, isn't it? And very nice. Must have set you back a bit.' A new mattress, on the other hand, was considered too dear. Lordly munificence abroad and skinflint at home.

He dabs at some of Ross's dribble. 'Always that constant nag. You might like to think about this: who, in their right mind, would want to support *you*?'

They're in a cleft stick. Separation is out of the question, Erskine would lose his job. And if they divorce the ramifications are even worse. They'll have to stick it out for Ross's sake. And something to eat.

Sussex, Spring 1949

Dear Diary,

Back to silence. So I write it down here to make it tangible. What did Rilke say? 'Life is so often a matter of the longest patience.' And even more apposite: 'A person isn't who they are during the last conversation you had with them — they're who they've been throughout your whole relationship.'

Now that I'm so much stronger I realise, as I did not last winter, how much lack of resistance was bound up with utter physical exhaustion. So I must hoard my strength, gather it to me like my child — and look after both.

For a time it went better with us. Sheelagh disappeared from the Bepton pub, her husband stayed. Devon, the rumours had it. The atmosphere relaxed, I even remember quite agreeable evenings.

Until our statements from the bank arrived. I'd written for them because Erskine insisted he'd not been sent anything since last October.

I waited for him to come home to open them. When he did I asked him if he'd put anything by for the hospital expenses in the States. Reluctantly funded, after all, by cheapskate brother Emil. We still owe him. He hasn't badgered me. Better than I expected.

'We're about even on that,' Erskine said, nostrils wide.

I blinked, stared. What was that supposed to mean? And when I looked at the statements I saw that he'd had an overdraft of £165 for several months that it now stood at over £200.

'I'd no idea!' he spluttered. Shocked — or so he pretended.

I showed him the black and white, or rather the black and red. 'You took it out.'

'Oh well,' he brushed it off. 'We'll be in the workhouse soon.' That irritating laugh.

'And are we?' I said, my voice suddenly choking. 'What I can't work out is on what security you got that money.'

He flared up at once. 'Damn well keep your nose out of my affairs. And don't get so bloody hysterical. If you must know, the bank relies on my integrity.'

Even a public school education and an Army background won't stand up to debts in the long term.

I contacted the faithful Roger Quinnel, asked him to forward the deed of transfer of Dramlings to the bank. I have no choice so use compulsion and the law because there's no longer anything to give — except what is extracted by threat.

I feel wretched, utterly defeated, long to be shot of it all. It's as if circumstances have turned me into a potential blackmailer, holding fear of exposure over Erskine's head. As if behaviour out of fear of punishment is worth having.

What is there left for me to do? There are no decencies left. All is quicksand. Nothing to rely on, so I have to put what strength I can muster into getting my freedom.

The weirdest thing is that even now he tries it on, pulling me up short with solicitous suggestions: 'Would you like to go and visit your sister?' hiding the unspoken question: 'What exactly do you want?'

Once upon a time this elephant fell into an elephant trap which nearly did for him. Now he spots camouflage a mile off. It has to end, whatever the cost.

Sussex, Summer 1949

Doly sits down at the little desk under the window in her living room. The house is all hers. So is the full responsibility, and the bills. But she is not unhappy. Instead, she's energised, starts writing letters to everyone she knows.

Dear Gabby,

The inevitable has happened at last. Erskine and I are getting a divorce. We were trying to keep up appearances so that he could keep his job, but it's gone too far for that. He's been seeing Sheelagh on a regular basis. Then she suddenly disappeared and I thought we were home and dry. Not a bit of it. She went home to Devon, to her parents. She and Erskine now have a daughter.

I know you will ask how will I cope, what will I do. But we've already been there, and it will be better to have some sort of legal protection than to rely on Erskine's decency. It doesn't exist. I have to fight for everything. The only thing that kept him here for so long is Ross. He adores that child, can never get enough of him. And vice versa. I'm nothing to Ross in comparison to Erskine.

What can I do? I've spent a year trying to cope with lies, evasions, money spent on drink and petrol to see his precious Sheelagh, and virtually nothing for us here at Dramlings. The lies, the evasions, the pretence… I can't do it any more. Not even for Ross.

Erskine has tried to change my mind. It's the end of his career as a schoolmaster. Well, whose fault is that? He still tries to cajole me, to pretend I'm imagining everything. And when I showed him in black and white that he has an overdraft of over £200 and no means of paying it off he turned surly. Even raised his hand against me. I rushed upstairs and locked the door, threatened him with the police. He desisted.

The prospect of having Dramlings to myself fills me with happy anticipation, with peace. To be no longer involved with him, to have the days pass without stress. So strange: before Ross was born I couldn't bear to lose Erskine. It was all heartbreak. Now his presence oppresses me. His things and clothes scattered about make me sick. Even the great physical need I felt for his homecoming last summer is now almost revulsion. No longer shot through with painful desire for his approval, his answer, his pleasure. Better so. Also sadder so. It was dreadful to have a relationship so one-sided, so heartbreaking.

When I asked what his attitude to all this is, he said he hadn't got one. One cannot love in a vacuum, I said. He simply shrugged his shoulders. 'Perhaps the atom bomb will solve it for us.' Even that said grudgingly, with his back turned to me.

As for the divorce proceedings, his only question was: 'Would you mind if I were to notify it elsewhere?'

Because of getting a job, of course.

I've forgotten what else was said, but it was all laced with his usual 'baloney' and 'poppycock' about things I knew had happened. I fetched all the presents he had ever given me from upstairs — a pathetic little collection of trinkets: a pencil sharpener, a compact, earrings and a lipstick. I gave them to him. 'Here,' I said, 'is what I have amassed during the years of selfishness.'

I saw that that struck home for once.

This morning I asked him to sign what he recently agreed to: twelve yearly contributions of £200 for myself and child in the court of separation. Until the divorce comes through.

He still tried it on. 'I may have said a bit more than I meant to in the heat of the moment. I didn't really mean it.'

'You said you wished to come and go as and when you pleased. Not on. I'd like this agreement in writing. And there really isn't much beyond this which concerns us any longer. That's what you'll get from here on in. You won't be annoyed by me any more and I shall not be called 'bloody bitch' again. Which will be nice.'

He was quite taken aback by it all. A little later he offered to fry some eggs and was very polite. But this is it, I'm not going to change my mind. He hasn't left before because of Ross. Well, Ross comes at a price he isn't willing to pay.

The divorce will take time. Meanwhile Erskine sleeps in the study downstairs. We pass like ships in the night, though the seas are a little crowded. But he'll do anything to be with Ross, can't get enough of him.

He's looking for a new job. In Devon. That seems a good long way away. Now I understand why Sheelagh left months ago: to be with her family, have her child, and wait for him to join her.

CHAPTER 5

St Gilgen, Austria, Summer 1949

A late spring turns to summer, spirits lift. Gabby thinks longingly of Schwanenbruch but can't afford to escape. Doly writes she feels the same but hasn't a hope of going.

Gabby has a brain wave. 'Why don't we invite your cousin Hans to stay, Bosch? And ask Doly at the same time?'

'You're matchmaking?'

'Why not? He's a good-looking man who's never going to find himself a wife unless he's helped. Doly's still reasonably presentable.'

'You're out of your mind. She's an ageing slut whose looks have gone down the drain. And she has a small child. What's in it for Hans?'

'Ross is one of Doly's attractions, I would have thought. Hans is always asking after Kamilla. A frustrated father if ever I saw one.'

Bosch shrugs indifferent shoulders. 'Kamilla is a girl, and the last of the family line. Not sure he's interested in a stepson.'

'Why on earth not?'

'Too much like competition.'

'You're being absurd, Bosch. Anyway, a last chance. After this summer we'll be back in Vienna. In the villa.'

'Really? How?' The lighter flicks flame into faded eyes. 'You've spent months preaching that it can't be done.'

'I've worked out a solution.'

'*You*? What on earth are you talking about? I thought that was Czezina's job. If he can't find a buyer...'

'I know all that. But I've been thinking. Doly is making it work for tiny Dramlings. Vienna has an acute housing shortage. That huge villa must be able to house us as well as get us a decent return.'

'And how are we going to work this miracle? Especially as you insist on paying Rolf Ferent rent.'

She holds back from screaming at him. 'His share of the rent. You know very well that half the villa is his. If we divide the place up so that we live on the top floor, we can live rent free and offer to handle his percentage of the rest of the place.'

'And the rent laws?'

Gabby's hands flick problems away. 'I'll find suitable foreigners as tenants, preferably Americans. We end up living free in the penthouse, plus a little pocket-money. As well as back in the land of the living. I know it's a risk but I have no intention of spending another winter yodelling in Alpine isolation.'

His fingers, redeemed from cleaning chores, are as thin as the cigarettes placed into the holder. 'I do believe you've come up trumps again. I'll write and invite Hans. Someone to talk to while you and your sister gossip.'

'Must we invite Greti? I can't cope with that damned dog.'

'She's got some woman friend she goes doggy hiking with. Anyway, my invitation. No one can blame you if I don't ask her.'

Hans Weiss accepts Bosch's invitation by return of post.

'I can't think of a better way to spend three weeks than under the same roof as you and your lovely wife,' he writes. 'And it will give me a chance to get to know Kamilla better.'

'You're obviously an enormous hit with him.' Bosch's long-toothed grin is reflected in his eyes.

'Whatever do you mean? He's always been a hanger-on of yours.

Handsome, clever, appallingly well-read, educated up to his eye-balls
— and doesn't have a clue what to do with himself. You turn his dull
life into excitement.'

Bosch flashes the letter at Gabby. 'What about this, then? I hardly
think this refers to me:

> Hail to thee, blithe spirit!
> Bird thou never wert,
> That from Heaven, or near it,
> Pourest thy full heart
> In profuse strains of unpremeditated art.

'*To a Skylark*, Bosch! Shelley. I thought you went to the same school
as Hans. Obviously not to the same classes! He's droning on about
the wonders of nature in the beautiful Austrian mountains. Like all
your compatriots — crazy about the wretched things. Can't think why.
Damned mountains stop one from taking a decent walk and keep
the sun away.' In fact she did notice Hans's furtive eyes stray towards
her when they first met. Frequently. At the time she thought he was
assessing her hair. She grins as she thinks: what a lark!

'Whatever you say. You've got it all worked out, as usual.'

'You have no objection to inviting my sister?'

Bosch cackles. 'She's going to have her work cut out competing
against you.'

'She hasn't answered yet.'

'Such a surprise.'

'She does have to find someone to look after Ross for her. Says she isn't
bringing him, she needs a proper holiday. Apparently Erskine and that
barmaid he's gone to Devon with offered to have the boy to stay.'

'She's agreeing to that?'

'Why on earth not? He *is* Ross's father, has to be allowed access.'

'He might keep him.'

'Not very likely. Even if he wanted to, unlikely that Sheelagh would.
They say Ross and their new daughter are brother and sister, and will
enjoy playing together.' Gabby shrugs. 'Could even be true. That child
must crave his father at times.'

Bosch laughs. 'Familial bliss.'

'Exactly. And they've already got another on the way.'

'He certainly didn't waste any time once he got going, did he?'

Gabby remembers the many years of illness and infertility Doly had to handle, the large sums of money she spent on doctors, how she used the last of her capital to pay them. Then, virtually overnight, the newly-discovered penicillin worked its miracles. Erskine's septicaemia cleared up, and he begat a son on Doly. Then, obviously with just as little trouble, a daughter on Sheelagh.

'All that bloody stuff about the high-and-mighty Army types. How we weren't good enough to meet them. I always did think he was just after her money.'

Bosch's knee jiggles. 'Got what there was left to get, at that.'

'A bounder, my English friends call him. Doly fell for a fortune-hunting bounder.'

'Bound to come a cropper, then.' Long teeth flash.

'He hasn't yet. It's Doly who's taking all the flack. Poor thing is being run ragged.' To her surprise, Gabby finds herself feeling for her sister. Maybe she can find a nice solid dependable Austrian husband for her. Incredibly, after years of being the beautiful younger sister, Doly now looks older than Gabby, shabbier. In earth coloured clothes from her Land Girl days.

Gabby lost her hair in childhood, Doly still has hers. But it's a dingy brown and thinning. Gabby wins with bought locks.

Doly's date of arrival in Salzburg, the nearest mainline railway station to the hunting lodge, has not been divulged, is clouded in quotations from Wordsworth written in hard-to-decipher script. As ever.

'Don't worry about me,' her last letter scrawled. 'I'll turn up like the proverbial bad penny; ha'penny more like!'

'How exactly will she know where to come? We're not on the phone. There's no way for her to get in touch.'

'She's got the address, Bosch. Someone or other will put her right.'

Hans Weiss, already installed in one of their attic bedrooms, wears a shy smile. 'I would be happy to go to Salzburg every day and meet the Arlberg Express. If your sister is on it I will be happy to escort her here. If not, I will try again the next day.'

'For God's sake, Hans. She's twisting you round her little finger.'

'Nonsense. I am on holiday, Bosch. Salzburg has thirty-eight churches for me to explore. Of course I already know them, but I'll happily reacquaint myself. I do assure you I will be contentedly employed.'

It's a mystery to Gabby how a man as erudite and intelligent as Hans Weiss can spend his free time poring over ancient manuscripts and exploring decrepit buildings. He seems more dead than alive, a tall animated corpse whose hunched back bows courtesies from a bygone age. Instead of engaging in political discussions he infuriates her with his long-winded speeches of praise and thanks. Punctuated by abstruse quotations she doesn't recognise. Making her feel inferior.

'Up to you. But how d'you think you're going to recognise her? She doesn't know you'll be there, after all. And it's far too late to write.'

'Your wife has kindly shown me some family photographs. And your sister-in-law is remarkably like your lady wife in looks. I'll manage.'

Gabby stares at Hans. Quaint how impossible Bosch's relatives find it to use her Christian name. Apparently that embargo extends to her relatives as well. Impossibly formal. He even puts the Habsburgs in the shade. Hans, if absolutely forced into using some form of direct speech, addresses her as gnädige Frau, gnä' Frau at his most informal. He sticks resolutely to the formal 'Sie', though of course he is on 'du' terms with Bosch. And kisses Gabby's hand at every opportunity. Which, when she's longing to get at her drink, can be inconvenient.

The photographs she showed Hans are ten years out of date. She and Doly no longer look all that alike. Doly's delicate features have coarsened with ill fortune and the hard physical work in the Land Army. As well as around her cottage and garden. Whereas Gabby finds others to do the rough work for her: maids if she can afford them, charladies. Bosch and Gemma are pressed into service if need be. Which means Gabby's hands remain white, smooth and dainty. Her features show creases of worry, but the skin is unblemished. Her hope for the future shows.

Bosch nods. 'She's older than the photos show. But her English clothes will be unmistakable. There'll be crowds of locals dressed in the local Tracht, or military personnel. She'll stand out very clearly.'

Salzburg, Summer 1949

'Küss die Hand, gnä' Frau!'

Doly walks along the platform, carrying a small case, when a tall handsome man dressed in Austrian Tracht — Lederhosen which come to below the knee, a stylish Lodenjanker jacket in that soft grey green the Austrians love — raises his Alpine hat to her. 'You are Mrs Courtling, yes? I am Hans Weiss. Cousin to Franz Bosch. I am come to meet you.'

'My goodness! How very kind.' Presumably Bosch's age, around fifty. 'How on earth did you know which train I'd be on?'

'I have been coming to Salzburg each day for five days. It is an honour to meet you.'

'How charmingly gallant of you.' She allows him to take her case. Wonders at the height, the determined Austrian garb, the jaunty Alpine hat with an Edelweiss set at an unjaunty angle, as well as the benign and somehow unworldly expression. Certainly not a wolf in sheep's clothing. A white docile puppy dog. She shouldn't have come. This is going to be more boring than all of Erskine's misdemeanours.

'I hope you had a pleasant trip. You slept on the train?'

'I didn't have a sleeper, no. But I did sleep in my seat, and it's a lovely morning. I feel fine.'

'Perhaps I may invite you to a coffee house? Unfortunately we do not offer real coffee as yet. The concoction is made of roasted chicory roots and acorns, or you can choose dandelion roots. However, both are served hot and may, perhaps, be refreshing after a long journey.'

'How delightful. I always make elderflower champagne when I can't get hold of the real McCoy.'

The suitcase wavers in his hand. 'You are able to make champagne in England? I always understood the climate is not good for grapes.'

Doly's giggle is loud and high. 'We make do with all kinds of substitutes — Ersatz — just like you do. Elderflowers — Holunderblumen — can be fermented with sugar and wild yeast to make a pleasant alcoholic drink with fizz. We call it champagne. During the war I used young marrows dusted with a bit of sugar to simulate melons. So using dandelion roots for coffee is something I understand.'

'The coffee may be Ersatz, but Salzburg itself is still remarkable, the most baroque of towns. I will escort you to the Café Tomaselli, founded in 1705 but moved to the Alter Markt Square in 1730. Afterwards I think we have time also to visit the Domplatz, where they play *Jedermann* during the Festspiele. It is very nearby.'

Doly takes in an amazingly pretty town. 'It's very picturesque.' But does she really want to go to boring festival theatricals in German?

'Then in two hours we take a small train. It is a single-gauge local train, the Salzkammergut Lokalbahn, a very scenic route between Salzburg and Bad Ischl. Also the train stops very near the hunting lodge your sister is living in.'

'How convenient.'

'Assuredly so.' He takes a cigarette packet out of his breast pocket. 'You permit I smoke?'

'Delighted to join you.' Doly's hand is already stretched out.

Heavy eyelids open wide. 'Excuse me I did not think to offer one to you.' There's a questioning expression in appraising eyes. 'It is the time of the Festspiele now; always for five weeks from late July. Perhaps you are familiar with our music festival? As I mentioned, there are performances of *Jedermann* — the story of Everyman — playing in the square in front of the Cathedral. A most interesting outdoor theatre. I have already taken the liberty of buying tickets. Also, one of my favourite operas is being performed. *Orfeo ed Euridice.* I hope you will do me the honour to accompany me.'

'I'm afraid I don't think I know it.'

'Christoph Willibald Gluck was born in Italy, but he spent much of his musical life in Vienna. And all the better for that. *Orfeo ed Euridice* is one of his Neapolitan style operas.

'He wrote about thirty-five completed works altogether, plus ballets and instrumental works. This will be a wonderful performance. The conductor is Herbert von Karajan, himself born in Salzburg.' A hang-dog look which Doly finds hard to understand. 'I regret to tell you he joined the Nazi party. He was "denazified" in 1946, and has taken great interest in the Salzburg festivals since then. We are fortunate to be able to hear him.'

'It's really most kind of you, but…'

'It will be my greatest pleasure.'

It would be churlish to refuse to go. Even though opera is by no means one of Doly's passions. Far from it. 'Gluck, Gluck,' she murmurs to herself. Not her idea of Glück — good luck.

'I am so sorry. What is it you said?'

'So good of you to ask me.'

CHAPTER 6

St Gilgen, Austria, Summer 1949

'So you've actually found her. Pretty good going, Hans.' Bosch has wandered down to the Strobl stop to meet the late afternoon train, as he has every day. He blows smoke in Doly's direction, bows. 'Welcome to the Wolfgangsee, Dorinda. I am happy to escort you to the Franzosenschanze, just a few hundred metres from here. I hope you will have an excellent holiday.'

'Franz.' Doly is horrified by how much Bosch has aged. His hair isn't just grey, it's white. And he's thin, almost gaunt, with a sallow complexion. 'Very good to see you again. You're looking a bit peaky. Are you all right?'

'Never felt better in my life. The mountain air, the walks into St Gilgen, even swimming in the lake when the weather is good. That will make a new woman of you as well.'

Doly isn't sure she wants to be a new woman. She wanders along the road between the mountain on one side and the lake on the other, flanked by the two Austrians. Bosch doesn't wear the local Tracht. He's still in the corduroys he bought in England. They're wearing thin.

The place is undeniably picture-postcard beautiful. The lake is surrounded by craggy spectacular mountains, the waters are the clearest blue Doly has ever come across and reflect white clouds skipping with wind. Sailboats are dotted over the surface of the lake.

'And you live just around here?'

'Another few minutes and we'll be there. Strobl is on the line between Bad Ischl and Salzburg, should you want to play the tourist.'

'Gabby! How very healthy you look!'

'Hello, Doly!' Calling her fat first thing? Gabby knows she's put on weight. The diet of bread and Austrian dumplings, with very little protein. But not excessively. By Austrian standards she's still sylphlike. 'Kamilla, say hello to your Aunt Doly.'

The bouncy three-year-old is dressed in a Dirndl complete with lace blouse, petticoat and apron. 'Hallo, Arnt Doly.' She takes Doly's hand and pulls her down the small path towards the lake. 'We go rowing today. We go rowing now!'

'Kamilla!'

'She's absolutely right, Gabby. Why not? Such a hot day.' Doly shrugs off the jacket draped round her shoulders.

Gabby is horrified to see it revealing a sleeveless dress whose deep neckline shows a cleavage devoid of restraining underwear.

Doly grins at her sister. 'Have you really got a boat?'

'A rather ancient rowboat, yes.' Bosch lights another cigarette.

'Let's hop in then.'

They troop Indian file down the steep slope to the lakeside. Hans Weiss takes off his jacket, revealing ornate braces, folds the Lodenjanker carefully, sets it on a rock. The two men take their places on the bench flanked by oars while the two women sit opposite with Kamilla between them.

'It's rather shady here. Why not make for the sun?' Doly points towards St Wolfgang on the other side of the lake. Bathed in late afternoon brilliance.

'I don't think we should go too far, Dorinda. The weather in these mountain lakes is very treacherous. A storm can blow up within minutes.'

'Come on now, Franz. It's an absolutely beautiful day. Just because your wife calls you Bogey you don't have to imagine them all over the place.'

Doly grips the bench on either side of her, leans back. To Gabby's fury she's pulled her dress up over her knees and spread her legs.

'It's really hot! What I'd love to do is skinny dip in the lake.' She sees the horror on the faces around her. 'After we get back, naturally.'

'Please bear in mind the train passes right above you. People will be able to see you!'

'Don't suppose there are that many trains a day, are there? Just let me know what times to avoid.'

Hans Weiss's eyes are magnetically glued between Doly's legs. The colour rises in his face as his eyes pop into saucers. Bosch follows his gaze, and his pupils enlarge as well. He looks away.

'Clouds coming up already.' Gabby, sitting alongside Doly, is puzzled by the men's discomfort. Presumably Doly is wearing *some* underwear. Then sees a welcome diversion. She points to rapidly advancing banks of grey over the mountain behind the hunting lodge. A sudden wind begins to churn the lake.

Bosch cranes his neck to look. 'We'll have to turn back.' He signals Hans and they make a complete turn. The wind, now blowing hard, is causing havoc among the sailing boats.

'Let's get our backs into it.' Hans wipes his hands on his handkerchief and rows with vigour. 'These glacier lakes are notorious for sudden storms.'

'You two really are a pair of pathetic landlubbers…' Doly stops short. The skies, so clear just minutes ago, are dipping clouds into the lake. It's hard to make out the shoreline they left a bare ten minutes ago.

'One of the boats is down, Bosch. The idiots are too far out to swim back.' Hans Weiss holds up his oar. 'We'll have to go and help.'

Bosch takes his oar out of the water, flattens his eyes against spray leaping over the boat side. 'I suppose we have to. If we can…Look! The *Austria*'s making for them. Thank God for that.'

The small steamer which plies between St Gilgen and St Wolfgang is already nearing the capsized sailing boat. Even though steam-driven it's taking her a fair amount of time to get there.

'These squalls are really dangerous.' Bosch is putting his back into the rowing. 'They come up without warning, then go just as quickly. Bear that in mind, Dorinda. Don't go out rowing on your own. Or even swim out too far.'

***

'Let's walk down to St Gilgen, Gemma.' Doly is bored. She can't maintain that the Franzosenschanze isn't rural enough — though she can and does maintain that she prefers plains to mountains — but she can't stand the long philosophical discussions Gabby, Bosch and Hans Weiss indulge in. Never seem to tire of. She decides to look for better company and recruits her niece. A young girl as much in search of bright lights and entertainment as she is.

'Good idea. What are we going to do when we get there?'

'They have a lot of cafés overlooking the lake, don't they? And a lakeside band?'

'You mean pick up some men?'

'I don't know about picking them up. Have a few dances, a few drinks, a few laughs. The atmosphere at the lodge is too high on the intellectual side for me.'

Gemma laughs. 'Too intensely political, at any rate. And woe betide you if you raise the pink flag. Just one small problem. What do we buy the drinks with?'

'American soldiers have lots of money. We'll get them to stand us a few.'

'Better than the average night at the Franzosenschanze.' Doly giggles as she sways back along the road winding from St Gilgen between the mountain and the lake. 'My conquest was enormous. At least twice as tall as me. My nose was sort of squashed against his manly belly when we danced.'

'Mine was a normal size. Bit pressing, which was the trouble. I think he was so thrilled to come across an English-speaking girl he thought he'd hit the jackpot.'

'Must have been hard to get rid of him.'

'I threatened him with my fierce step-father. Said he knew the chief of staff, or whatever they're called. Anyway, I drummed up the name Colonel Tippets and turned the poor chap stone-cold sober.'

'Poor booby. You might have given him a bit of a break.'

'You're kidding. It may be boring at the house, but it's not half as boring as trying to escape the embracing clutches of a GI.' She grabs hold of Doly's arm. 'I can hear jeeps. Let's get behind this bush to avoid trouble.'

It takes forty minutes to walk from the St Gilgen lakeside back to the Franzosenschanze. When they return the house is quiet, there's no one in the living room.

'All gone to bed already? It's only half past ten.'

'Gabby needs her beauty sleep. Look at this! We're in luck. An ancient gramophone. I've got one just like this at home, so I know how it works.' Doly cranks the handle, rummages among the records. 'Polkas and Austrian waltzes. Better than nothing, I suppose. Here's something lively. Let's have a go at the *Tritsch Tratsch Polka*.'

Aunt and niece limber over the floor covered in furniture and rugs.

'This is impossible. Let's climb onto the table.' Doly grabs a chair, stands on the seat and mounts the large table in the centre of the room. 'Come on, Gemma! Just because you're Gabby's daughter and swotting for your degree doesn't mean you have to be completely dull!'

The music becomes faster, they gyrate, clicking their shoes on the table, laughing aloud. The room resounds with the notes of merriment. They do not hear, or see, that they have an audience.

The crashing of a door. 'What is going on here?' A furious male voice.

Gemma and Doly freeze as their whirling skirts settle around their knees. They see Gabby, Bosch and cousin Hans standing, mouths agape, eyes popping wide. The record reaches its last groove just as Bosch screeches the needle across.

'What on earth d'you think you're doing?'

'Enjoying ourselves.' Doly's voice has lost its gaiety. But not its vigour. 'Why don't you join in? We'll teach you the steps if you don't know them. Won't we, Gemma?'

'Get down from there at once, Gemma.' Bosch's voice isn't cold. Polar. 'You're making an exhibition of yourself.' He turns to Doly. 'As for you, I've had enough of sluttish behaviour in my house.'

'Sluttish?' Doly's voice a little less firm, a little less sure. 'You can't be serious. Gemma and I are simply practising our dancing.'

'You know precisely what I'm referring to, Dorinda. Gemma can have no idea. She's an innocent young girl. I simply won't stand by and have you seduce her — '

'Really, Bosch, you go too far. You're talking utter gibberish.' Gabby puts herself between Doly and Bosch.

He grabs Gabby's shoulders, whirls her away. 'Your sister is a sex-starved woman who couldn't care less what decencies she flouts.'

'She is a guest in this house, Bosch.' Hans Weiss walks up to him, towers above him.

'And no longer welcome. She flaunts her body to all and sundry, spreads her legs with holes in the underwear, persuades Gemma to join her in God knows what adventures in St Gilgen, and now this. It's going too far, and I won't allow it for another second.'

'Compose yourself, Bosch.' Hans moves his body in front of the shorter man.

Bosch takes a deep breath, thrusts him aside. 'Gemma, go to your room.'

'But, Herr Bosch, we were only…'

'I'm disappointed in you, Gemma. I expected more from you. You're not to leave the Franzosenschanze on your own for the rest of the holiday.'

Gemma looks from her mother to her aunt and back again. 'I'm not a child any more…'

'You're under twenty-one.' The voice is somber now. 'As long as you're under my protection you do as I say. I owe it to your father.' Bosch lights a virtuously victorious cigarette, the lighter flame held high. 'If you choose to ignore my instructions I shall write to your University, and to the Warden of your Hall of Residence. To explain you can no longer attend.'

'Go, Gemma,' Doly rasps, pushing her niece out of the door. 'There's nothing for you to do. I'll see you in England.' She pats her back and shuts the door on her.

'I really don't think…' Gabby squeaks.

Hans places a restraining hand on Bosch's shoulder. 'Calm yourself, Bosch. There's no need for any of this.' His hand shakes as he picks up a bottle. 'Why don't we all have a drink?'

Doly glares at Bosch, widens her nostrils at Gabby, at Hans. Seduce her niece? Is that really what Bosch thinks? She's a lesbian about to ruin her niece's life? What on earth gives him that idea?

Bosch shakes his cousin off. 'I regret you are no longer welcome as a guest, Dorinda. You leave tomorrow.'

Doly picks up her handbag and scarf. 'Wrong as usual, Herr Bosch. I leave tonight.' She walks out of the room, crashes the door behind her, and clatters up to her attic room. She packs her small bag and sets out on the road to St Gilgen. Reckons that even Austrian hotels must rent out rooms after eleven o'clock at night. And if they don't she'll find a grassy patch to sleep on. She's used to roughing it.

'You telling me Doly's left?' Gabby's brother Emil — Moppel — has brought his wife Rachel to the romantic Wolfgangsee. 'Already?'

Lake Wolfgang is said to be the most beautiful lake in all Austria. Brought his bride to be introduced to the family. What he thought would be the whole family.

'How very nice to meet you at last, Rachel. What a shame Doly had to get back.'

'We thought she was staying here for a coupla weeks?'

Gabby prefers not to explain the real circumstances. 'You know how unpredictable she is, Moppel. Never mind. We'll make sure you and Rachel have a really splendid time.'

She's young, she's beautiful. She has long blonde hair. What can she see in Moppel? Gabby sniffs a story. 'Where do your people come from, Rachel?'

A faint smile. 'My parents are divorced. My mother was born in Frankfurt, in Germany. My father is coming from Amsterdam.'

Not a native American, obviously. 'Will you be visiting one or other of them?'

'I hope to visit my father. He is now back in Holland. My mother, I am sad to relate, died in an air-raid.' The young woman blushes crimson.

Bosch is looking at her in the way Gabby has come to recognise only too well. He likes pretty women. But he goes no further than paying exaggerated court. 'So where did you spend the war?'

'After my mother disap — died — my father managed to get me to join him in Switzerland. He has business connections there.'

'That was very fortunate. So how did you and Emil meet? Needless to say, he never wrote and told us anything!'

'Real romantic, Gabby. You know I got me a boat to sail on Long Island Sound. That's the real reason I moved to Seaford. Kinda reminds me of Schwanenbruch. I was doin' up the boat and saw Rachel walking by along the bank. Asked her if she'd like a ride.'

'And the rest is history, as they say.'

'It sure is.'

He doesn't amplify the history, though Gabby and Bosch are sure there has to be something more. Why would a beautiful young woman of twenty-three bother with vapid boring forty-something Emil who, though he owns a business, hardly qualifies for sugar daddy status?

Gabby looks at Rachel again. It's a Jewish name, and Moppel hasn't enlightened them about her maiden name. Did her mother die in the

Holocaust by any chance? Was Rachel visiting her father, and was he a Dutch Jew clever enough to move himself and his daughter to Switzerland before Germany invaded Holland?

Gabby decides not to ask any more questions, but speculates that Moppel may have bargained beauty for American citizenship.

THE LORD'S REVENGE

In the days when the banks of the River Elbe were still close enough for people on either side to shout meaningfully across, a prosperous village nestled on its banks, well outside the present foreshore. The land around the settlement was so fertile that no villager had ever experienced the horror of a failed crop. The whole community thrived and became prosperous.

The people of the village could have lived in peace and harmony until the end of time except for one small problem. Instead of feelings of gratitude and modesty for the blessings the good Lord had bestowed on them, the village men and women became arrogant and overbearing. They assumed the Almighty's gifts could be used in any way they pleased.

They did not even try to help their less fortunate neighbours. Instead they abused their good fortune. When the time came to cart their golden harvest to their barns they were too lazy to drive along roads and across bridges. They simply filled the drainage ditches with one wagon load of corn and used that as a bridge for their other wagons. Nor did they bother to attend God's house to listen to His word. Instead, they mocked their pastor, even played tricks on him.

The good Lord watched these antics of profligacy and pride with concern. Ever merciful, He sent many signs to warn the villagers to change their godless ways. Their women became barren, and their cows gave birth to calves with two heads or more than four legs. The worst sinners saw live frogs jump out of their bread ovens, a portent no one could possibly mistake.

None of these warnings was heeded. Instead, the people's intemperance increased. And finally, in their worst extravagance so far, the villagers built a new sluice made of the purest copper.

At this the Heavens lost patience. One dark winter night God sent a particularly high tide. The flood came so suddenly, so quickly and so silently that the villagers didn't even wake from their sleep. The water crept over the dykes and flooded the whole land. And it destroyed the sinful village with all its inhabitants. Even the copper sluice was submerged in the stormy waters.

When the flood finally subsided the River Elbe was much wider. Its waters now covered the former village and the fertile lands around. And, in the very place where a wicked people once set themselves against the power of the Almighty, there is the glittering dazzling flow of the waters of a mighty river.

There's nothing to mark the submerged village. No church spire, not even a trace of the copper sluice. But occasionally, if you stand high up on the new dyke built many miles inland, you may hear a drumming knocking noise. That is the sound of the waters of the Elbe hammering against the copper sluice.

CHAPTER 7

Vienna, Autumn 1949

The Neuwaldegg villa, set on the edge of the Vienna Woods, sags peeling green window shutters on an indifferent world. Chrome yellow walls are streaked with city grime deposited by rain. The garden is overgrown with nettles, the rose beds are all thistles, the once beautiful lawn a tangle of weeds. Only the spreading chestnut tree, overlooking the lower garden, stands clothed in glorious autumn colours. It guards the roof of a dilapidated shed Gabby no longer even recognises as the Hansel and Gretel house she had built for Gemma's fifth birthday, in 1934. The child played there during the day. At night Gabby used it as a cover for Bosch's anti-Nazi political meetings. Later she even hid fleeing communists from the authorities as well as her former husband Rolf Ferent.

After their divorce Gabby stayed on at the villa. She and Bosch still thought they could hold the Nazis back from Austria's frontiers. They were wrong: Hitler annexed Austria on March 12th 1938 and Gabby's whole world was catapulted into a shipboard marriage to Bosch as they fled the Nazis. They arrived in a disapproving England, penniless refugees frowned on because they spoke German.

She can hardly picture herself before that fatal day: young, rich, even beautiful she now realises. The villa was a showplace where she played hostess: first to Rolf's business associates, later to Bosch's political friends. Now the house is a wreck, a shell of a place she's scared of entering. She lets Bosch go ahead, feels her heart thump as the stench of neglect and decay overwhelms her. Should she even be bothering?

Exhaustion thickens her legs, distends her abdomen. The walls are crumbling, the parquet flooring pockmarked by bayonet daggers. Can she make the place habitable again? Comfortable and gracious are long-term ambitions.

'God, what a mess.' Bosch roams lacklustre eyes around the entrance hall, up the splendid staircase. Filthy, but whole. The niches in the walls are still there, but accumulated debris takes the place of woodland nymphs.

Gabby, exhausted, grabs the rail as she climbs the stairs up to the drawing room. There's no question of turning on the central heating. Even if it were still in working order. Or they could find fuel. The heating bills would be completely beyond their means. They'll have to make do with the Kachelofen — the ceramic woodstove she had the foresight to install on the top floor.

A slant of sunlight across the drawing room parquet highlights the white marble fireplace whose cost shocked Rolf enough to protest. Her former pride and joy is streaked sooty, and chipped. But it is there. Three gaunt, tall windows face towards the street. Three french windows across the room whistle draughts from garden winds, show puddles on the balcony outside. One sofa and two armchairs stand forlorn, brooding under one miraculously preserved chandelier. Sagging, soiled, there's a spring like a corkscrew in the middle of one chair.

Kamilla squirms out of Bosch's arms, patters across once perfect flooring, catches at dust floating on the sunbeams. She stumbles on dull wood gouged by bayonets, wails distress.

A pang as Gabby comforts her, thinks back to the time before the Anschluss eleven years ago. Her shimmering salon. Daring white leather sofas and easy-chairs, rosewood vitrines, Meissen displays, sparkling chandeliers. Elegant women in silk and diamonds, men in tails. 'What are we going to do, Bosch?'

'Let's see if there's a bed.' He lugs a suitcase through to the master bedroom. 'Thank God there is. At least we can get some sleep.'

A dipping mattress greets Gabby as she follows with the smaller case. Her former boudoir. No sign of the Louis Quinze dressing table and chairs, a cracked mirror on the wall, the bathroom beyond the bedroom has a green-stained bath and chipped tiles. But both basin and lavatory are intact. Running water. Cold, naturally.

'Things may not be as bad as we thought, Bosch.' They explore the whole house. The top floor, the former nursery, now has a kitchenette in the nursemaid's one-time room. There are two large bedrooms, and the old day nursery can be used as a living room. The bathroom, complete with the ancient geyser which once helped a desperate nursemaid to commit suicide, is functional. This floor is now a viable flat for the three of them. Nina, still at boarding school in the Gmunden convent, can share with Kamilla during the holidays. And Gemma can join them if and when she comes during her university holidays.

'You've seen the long letter from Czezina,' Gabby says, voice flat. 'I've contacted Herr Ferent and explained it's impossible to sell the place at present.' Her former husband, now working for the IBM in Manhattan, relies on her to do what she can about the villa they own jointly.

'You've explained it's the Korean crisis which is the real threat to European peace?' Bosch stares around the bare, dreary rooms.

'I'm sure he knows that.'

'You always said he was a political illiterate. Make sure he understands that North and South Korea represent Russia and America respectively. The uneasy truce is just like the one in Europe. Anything could upset the balance.'

'Yes, yes Bosch. If we get a decent income from the two lower floors we can arrange a deal. Maybe we can even chase up some of our things. Catch those thieves.'

A loud, hollow clanging. Of a repetitious kind. 'The telephone!' Gabby sprints out to the top landing, down the two long staircases curving down to the ground-floor hall. She's taken back to the trauma of the nursemaid's suicide, spelling the end of her first marriage. Shrill rings continue from the wall-mounted telephone just outside the kitchen door. She grabs the earpiece off the hook.

'Frau Bosch?'

Unmistakable Czech intonations. 'Herr Doktor Czezina! How did you know we've arrived?'

'I've been ringing every hour on the hour. Better sit down. Your luck has changed. I've found you the tenants you've been looking for.'

'You have?'

'A film director and his family.'

'Oh. An Austrian, you mean?'

'I know what I preached at you about the rental laws. But the thing is, he's seen the outside of the house and it's just the kind of prestigious property he needs. He's willing to take on all repairs, and pay one thousand Schillings a month. That still leaves you the flat on the top floor.'

'I'm not sure...'

'Three months' rental in advance.'

'But once he's moved in, you said yourself — '

'Naturally I have your interests at heart. What I have suggested is the following: The tenant takes over everything except the top floor flat. He refurbishes the whole of the house, including the flat, the garden and the outbuildings, and pays all utilities including central heating. Plus a rent of one thousand Schillings per month over and above all that. In return you grant him a lease for two years.'

'You said yourself that means for ever!'

'Officially you rent him the living room, the library and the bedroom plus the en suite bathroom on the first floor. Naturally he has the use of everything else, including the dining room and the veranda on that floor, as well as the kitchen floor below. However, if you ever wish to get rid of them, you simply take up residence in the kitchen, the dining room and the veranda. They won't stay long after that.'

'You think you can persuade them to sign such a contract? That sounds too good to be true.'

'He's a film mogul, so he needs to look good. He likes the locality, the prestige.'

'I'll have to cable Rolf Ferent in New York.'

'Understood. Just don't mention a second owner when you meet Herr Zachen. Meanwhile I'll stall them. Get them to give you a ring in the morning.'

It isn't Rolf Ferent who turns out to be the problem. It's Bosch. He's appalled at the idea of living in what he terms the servants' quarters upstairs while some upstart film director takes over the gracious part of the house.

Gabby blots out volleys of words re-echoing round empty dilapidated rooms. The work! Filthy kitchen quarters complete with a squalid cooker. Thank God their girl from the mountains, young Trautl, came to Vienna with them. She'll have to deal with all that.

Even Czezina's golden tongue cannot reconcile Bosch and the film director. He refuses to let Gabby go ahead. Leaving the Bosches in glorious possession of a ruined villa. Without an income. And owing Rolf Ferent rent.

'Our luck really has turned.' Bosch returns from calling on the Austrian Chancellor at the Ballhausplatz the following day. An official-looking letter flutters in his hand. 'They're offering me a position. Apparently they've been waiting for me to check in.'

Gabby's been nagging Bosch to put in an appearance. Her intuition told her something was brewing. She hardly dared to think of concrete developments rather than vague promises. 'A position?'

'It's not that out of the question!' The chrysalis has metamorphosed into the moth. His shoulders square, his eyes challenge and smile. Even his hair has a glint of former brown.

'I wasn't implying that. So what is it?' Part of the government at long last? 'Foreign Minister?'

'You really are a stupid woman. How could I possibly be in the cabinet without standing for election?' His hands are placed as though in prayer, a typed sheet between. 'The diplomatic service. As you can see.'

Ambassador to London? Or Washington, perhaps! Because his long years in England have perfected his English. And because he has an American wife? 'Ambassador?'

'For God's sake, woman! Can't you read?'

'You're holding it too far away and I haven't got my glasses on...'

'Cultural attaché in Paris.' The voice of enthusiasm has become a sibilating whisper.

'How very nice.' Damn those stab-in-the-back politicians. Minor job, minor official. In a country whose language they both have to brush up on. Still, Paris. Two or three up on the shady side of Lake Wolfgang. One up on post-war Vienna, at that. And money coming in. 'Congratulations, Bosch.'

His shoulders have sagged back. 'So you think I should accept? Just like that?'

A pat on the back is better than a yodel in the mountains. 'But of course you should! It's very exciting news. The first rung on the ladder. After all, you have no experience in diplomatic circles. I'm sure they'll offer you the ambassadorship to somewhere interesting within six months. Maybe even Paris. They need Stein here, don't they?'

'Meaning they can do without me.'

'It's not that…'

'No doubt you're right. As usual.'

'When do they want you to leave?'

'In two weeks.'

'That soon?' She has no presentable clothes, she hasn't settled the business with the villa, there will be nowhere for them to stay. 'You'll have to go without me to start with.'

The eyebrows, in sharp contrast to the hair, are still dark brown. They turn to triangles of astonishment. 'Go on my own? How am I supposed to cope without you?'

'Naturally my going is out of the question. We'll have to get you kitted out first. Find a decent tailor to alter an old suit, buy a couple of shirts. You know there's no material to be had in this country!' A rueful smile. 'I'd love to go with you. But I simply can't be seen on Paris streets in the rags I'm wearing now, let alone appear in diplomatic circles. You'll have to send me some decent fabric.'

The nod is eager. 'I'll go back into town right away to discuss things with my colleagues. And I'll go and see my old tailor. He'll sort something out.'

Gabby is shocked to discover that, though the reasons she gave for not going to Paris immediately were accurate, she's actually looking forward to some time without Bosch. He has just ruined a reasonable business deal and produced nothing himself. A cultural attaché hardly earns the money they need to keep up the appearances that are vital to a job like that. She's hoping to recharge batteries, come up with deals Bosch cannot get in the way of, start on building up some capital. She hears her father's voice, sees his eyes sparkle at his latest deal. She has to be free to do that.

The tailor is willing to alter two suits for Bosch — at a price. Gabby pays it out of Rolf Ferent's contribution for his daughters' upkeep. How would they have survived without that?

'I think it would be reasonable to ask the Austrian Government to pay your fare. First Class,' Gabby suggests.

Bosch is startled, but agrees. He needs new ties, a briefcase, shoes. She persuades her brother to send spare neckties from the United States, hoping Emil's taste is not too outrageous. Miraculously one of Rolf's old briefcases is found in his one-time study. Clearly neither the invading Russians nor the billeted troops considered it of value.

Shoes pose a problem only to be solved with money. Gabby reluctantly advances enough for a decent pair.

How can she go to Paris? What would she wear? And what about her hair? Her wigs are old, falling to pieces. She has to find the money to get at least one new one. And one isn't really enough; she needs two. One to wear, one to clean and set ready to wear. A very expensive business. What can she do, where can she turn? She hasn't much jewellery left to pawn.

She spends the fortnight making sure Bosch is in a fit position to be sent off. Then she takes him to the station, waves her goodbyes, rushes home, puts Kamilla to bed far too early and sleeps through till nine the next morning.

There is a sense in which she's worse off than Dorinda. As long as her sister can stay in Dramlings she can gather food and fuel from the woods around her. No need for fancy clothes or keeping up appearances. The countryside round the cottage provides wonderful walks, berries to eat, mushrooms for protein, the odd shot pheasant missed by the retrievers.

Gabby can only think of one way to get the cash she needs to feed herself and Kamilla until Rolf's next cheque is due: a visit to Bosch's cousin, Hans Weiss.

He is courteous, amiable, and immediately draws out twice the amount she asks for from the bank. He doesn't ask what it's for, treats her with the utmost courtesy. What would she do without him?

CHAPTER 8

Sussex, Spring 1950

Doly smiles at the postman. He parks his bike at the top of her lawn and walks the three hundred metres to her back door. She's always ready to exchange a word or two, even to offer a cup of tea. It can get lonely living so far out of the village.

''Ere be hanother o' they letters from Hamerica.' He hands her the airmail envelope, crooked teeth smiling understanding. 'Be quite 'eavy this time. I allus thinks as yer 'as yer own Alistair Cooke writin' to yer!'

'Sometimes the ones I get do read like that,' Doly agrees, her eyes scanning the typed address on the envelope. Moppel sending a card for her birthday? Unlikely. And, anyway, Elite not Pica. And postmarked Oklahoma. From Faith Bowler, then. 'Though I'm afraid they're nothing like as humorous.' She's torn between looking forward to reading the letter — anything out of baby routine is a treat — and afraid how her friend will sound. She's never been that stable, and she's had another episode in hospital. Not that they can do anything for her.

She stays until she's fit again — a few weeks, a few months — then goes back to her solitary apartment. She's lucky that her employers allow her this leeway. Obviously brilliant at her job. Anyway, this is the first letter since last autumn.

'Young 'un a'right?'

'Thriving, thank you, Tom. Cup of tea?'

'Too much on terday, ta all the same.'

She watches the postman striding back towards his bike before slowly, deliberately opening the envelope. The last time she wrote to Faith she told her about the disastrous incident with Bosch, when he threw her out of the house by the Wolfgangsee. Doly detailed her retreat without naming names, so Faith can have no idea that Gabby's husband, and so Gabby, were involved.

Doly has thought for some time that there has to be something wrong with Bosch. She can sense it, can't define it. A kind of change, subtle but pervasive, which the people living with him wouldn't necessarily notice. Physical or mental? Hard to tell. He's always been arrogant, discourteous to her — clearly he never could stand her — but she sensed a difference that last time she saw him. He was less snide, a great deal more direct. Will Faith have understood that it wasn't Doly's fault, that the man she described has become despotic?

A massive birthday card with a letter inside.

Dear Doly,

This is the first time I've managed to put pen to paper. I spent my last difficult interlude in Wisconsin, taken under the wing of some pretty understanding quacks. But I did gather your news and felt your desolation at your host's unsavory deportment.

Same old Faith, which is good, except for the writing style. Still competing about who's the better writer, the tone too smart, too high.

Some feuds are like The Wandering Jew — *without redemption. I wonder, my dearest Doly: are the feuds irredeemable or are the emotions which give rise to them over hot-housed?*

Odd way of referring to Doly's letter. Bosch may be a lot of things, but he's not a wandering Jew. He's back in his beloved Austria. Quite likely the Austrian Government turned him down for good and he took it out on Doly. Where else would he — could he — look for a job? Enough to make even a less volatile man aggressive.

Now I don't know the feud to which you were referring in your last letter. I gather, however, that it troubles you. Do you want to redeem it or would you rather weep to have that which you fear to lose?

Is she weeping, or fearing to lose? Not really. Her relationship with Gabby has always been strained. It was hardly wonderful when she was married to Rolf Ferent. It was better for a while, during the war. After Bosch's appalling behaviour Gabby wrote — to apologise, to stay in touch. Doly eventually replied. She knows Gabby always checks the Bosches' mail before handing it on. Doly disguises her clandestine letters by typing the address on the envelope. On the ancient machine she brought back from the States.

Uninformed as I am, and consequently entirely dependent upon my own resources, I must be content with registering tolerant scepticism of your decision. But it would seem that what won't bear the light of day has no business shutting out the sun.

I wasn't born a Jew so I can't very well say how I should behave if I were one. However, I was born a female with a very basic desire to live the life of a male. Naturally, I imitated the male. That brought me from earliest childhood into conflict, sometimes serious, with all manner of accepted orders. Being a person of strong tastes, I persisted in following them. I found that only so was I at peace with myself or the world. Of course I gravitated into what was ordinarily considered man's work. Aided, undeniably, by the war. And of course, too, I met women inclined as I was. Many of them, and good ones at that, bemoaned the difficulties of their position, upbraided the 'intolerance and injustice' of men when they returned to claim their jobs after the war, went about always with the chips of feminism on their shoulders.

Doly doesn't particularly feel that men are unjust, merely that they have the authorities on their side and are, consequently, convinced of their superior powers. Well, the sort of men she's used to socialising with: professionals of one sort or another. She has no problems with the butcher, the baker, the candlestick maker — and the builder. She thinks back to Piers, to the physical embraces, to his short, often ungrammatical, sentences so redolent with feeling. More of a gentleman by far than Erskine and his ilk. But Piers is abroad, in the Merchant Navy, on the high seas. Does he ever think of her?

Maybe because I was born after the bloodiest battles or perhaps for some other reason I found the 'intolerance and injustice' so rare and so minor as to produce for me no problems of importance. I have yet to see the man who will work peaceably with men who will not work peaceably with a woman who tries only to do her job. And I have yet to see the ardent feminist with whom I have much sympathy.

Some people, my family, my friends, are displeased with my life, some boast of it, some are shocked, some glory therein, some are amazed, some bored. To me it is just my life, very valuable because it is the only thing I own. So what has the Jew to redeem?

Have a terrific birthday, write and tell me about it. And what about a trip to the good old US of A? Great to go roam the prairies again, go riding with Ross.

My deepest love to you both,
Faith

Do these sentiments have anything to say to her and Ross, or are they just the ramblings of a lonely woman? Faith has been a good friend, a true friend. Without her help Ross might never have been born healthy, or even born alive. But it is hard to see how to extend her own hand of friendship all the way to Oklahoma. Maybe Faith would like to visit Dramlings. She can afford the trip across the Atlantic which Doly cannot even consider.

April 3rd, 1950
Dear Faith,

Your lovely birthday card arrived in good time. I need not tell you that occasionally cider and ciggies go flat for want of adult company. That all the colour is drained from strangely-patterned thoughts for lack of another being in tune with me to bring them to life.

> Intimately do I know
> Rivers white with mountain snow
> I have slept with stars and stone
> But my lover sleeps alone

It almost makes me self-conscious to use writing as a form of dressage, a kind of self-expression which is now ornamental rather than purposeful. Both used to be a habit.

My little musings about myself flit into past and future. Like children tossing toys aside because they haven't been taught how to play. I've been lying fallow for five years, and I'm ready for new crops. I think back to the many times when my yields were forced with artificial stimulants, when both soil and seedlings were cultivated beyond their capacities. Yet they still produced both wheat and chaff rotating in quick succession. In those days I was frightened of vegetating, worried I might be choked by weeds. When all the time any harvest is better than none.

Come and visit Ross and me, Faith. You haven't seen your godson since he was born. It will do your name justice, shower your soul with manna, restore vigour to your body. We are still in the same cow pasture under the same tree. Like Buddha. Which, I like to think, is a consolation.

And the gods give generously. Last week we harvested the electrocuted bodies of a couple of careless flying geese crashing into the electric cables crossing the fields in front of the cottage. I sent Buffy to fetch, and he did. A bountiful feast.

Ross is no slouch either. He's been able to walk several miles from the age of two so we can forage in the woods.. Our many generous neighbours donate home-made jam and offer rides to Midhurst. You'll love meeting them, living the life we live here.

Come soon. I'll deck the house with wildflowers and ivy, even if it isn't Christmas. We'll roast potatoes in my Elizabethan fireplace, large enough to roast a sheep, and we'll walk through the purple rhododendron woods with Ross. There we'll throw sticks for Buffy, and our thoughts will be bountiful with sweetmeats and sugar candy.

Hurry to book your passage over. We both look forward to welcoming you to Dramlings. Our little world within the world.

Love from Doly and Ross

Sussex, Summer 1950

Faith Bowler doesn't live up to her name. Though she tries. She blunders through mud and rain, slush and drizzle, the faint sun of an English summer, bewailing the strong rays of Oklahoma.

'Why don't we go for a slap-up meal somewhere, Doly?' Breakfast porridge is left untouched, the dinner of pigeon pie which Doly was so proud of pushed around until it resembled breadcrumbs, the beautiful vegetables freshly harvested from the garden viewed with disdain.

'You don't mind walking? I've only got one bicycle.'

Faith's deep laugh. 'No problem. We'll get a cab…'

'No phone, Faith. We'll just have to foot it. Or make do with the riches we already have.'

Faith looks dejected. What happened to the girl who rode wild broncos, played the guitar, let her hair down? She's become like spiralling tumbleweeds. Dry, dead, rolling in the wind like empty drums.

They sit in front of blazing logs. Natter over, under and between old times. Which are a kind of consolation, but perhaps not one to be indulged in too much.

Faith grows sentimental, mulling that past. Which plays a much larger part in her life than it should. 'Being there for you when Ross was born was one of the highlights of my life.'

How sad that it should have been. 'It was wonderful to have you standing by, Faith. Such a stalwart friend.'

'Anyone would have done it.'

'I'll always be grateful to you. We both will.' The cigarette smoulders, is smoked to the very end. The tiny butt is thrown into the fire, leaving tarred fingers.

Faith lunges the poker into blazing logs, showering sparks which land on the sheepskin rug in front of it, smouldering. She stamps on them while Doly watches, lights another cigarette.

'You sure you're OK here, my dear? Don't you get lonesome?'

Doly glances at the lumbering, old-before-her-time figure, lights another cigarette, takes a puff to hide what she's thinking. Surely Faith is the lonely one. Doly has Ross, and the occasional au pair from Germany sent by steadfast Tante Martha. Faith only has her job. Plus the money it brings in. How can that be compared to living in Dramlings, surrounded by some of the loveliest countryside in the world, with friendly neighbours and her Buffy terrier boy as well as Ross?

'I'm fine, Faith. I know I'm always short of money, and I'm really grateful that you help out so often but, as my Onkel Wilfred used to say, "He who has sufficient, has enough".'

'I guess you mentioned that before, Doly. My point is that you never do have quite enough. Being dependent on handouts can't be all that pleasant.' Her eyes gather Doly in embrace. 'I could look after you.' She blinks. 'Both of you. In the States, of course. That's where my work is.'

'And we're both very grateful to you, Faith. It's really sweet of you. But Dramlings is our home, and this is where we stay.' The smoke rings float serenely up as Doly pours out another glass of elderberry wine. 'Let me refill your glass.'

Faith winces.

CHAPTER 9

Vienna, Summer 1950

Dear Bosch,

It's only days since you left, and the problems are already piling up sky-high. Perhaps I should have gone with you after all. I'm not sure I can handle everything entirely on my own.

First, the pressing question of money. Herr Ferent's cheque was due. I waited for the post, having promised the Weisses their money back. No sign of it. Anyway, no one wants to exchange dollars because of the Korean crisis. Did the North Koreans have to attack South Korea just at this moment? The point is that people think the next war is just around the corner and that Austria will be overrun by the Russians before hostilities even start.

I can't even think about politics, I have nothing but debtors around my neck. I've paid off the loan shark because he physically threatened me. Apart from the Weisses we still owe your good friend Egi, the Archduke, the dressmaker and the hairdresser. I have to send Nina some pocket-money and the train fare to Vienna. Her summer holidays start soon.

You promised me four thousand Schillings to be getting on with. Egi and I went into town to meet the courier from Paris. Nothing. You must send me money by the next courier. In Schillings, not in francs. Even Egi's contacts at the Mint can't promise to get me a decent exchange rate. And it takes weeks.

There is a little good news. Czezina came across some Americans called Middleton. He's the Finance Director of the European Recovery Project in Austria, part of the Marshall Plan team, and looking for a suitable house. Just he and his wife, and no children. They have their own furniture and will buy anything else they need. They don't care what state the house is in, they just want gracious rooms for entertaining. Mrs Middleton loved the villa when I took her round it and begged me to cut off all negotiations with anybody else.

You won't believe the terms Czezina negotiated. Everything the film mogul offered plus six months' rent — six thousand Schillings — in advance. And three months' notice either side instead of a two-year lease. There's even competition. Quite a few ERP people are being posted to Vienna, all desperate for decent housing. And there aren't any rent laws to worry about because everything is based on American law.

The Middletons are so keen they'd have paid far more rent if I'd had the nous to ask them. But you can't go back on deals with Americans. Anyway, they're paying all the utilities and we can keep those pathetic bits of furniture. So I can live very cheaply until I'm ready to join you.

I wish you were here to discuss it all. I'm exhausted by the agreements for the lease and terrified at having to shoulder the whole responsibility. What I need is a month in Schwanenbruch. Moppel is coming over. He wants to negotiate sales of the land we still own jointly, as well as some of the outbuildings and the smallholding Onkel Hinrich ran for our father. I should definitely go. If only to make sure he doesn't make a mess of it or try to take all of it for himself.

However, I don't see how I can with Gemma and Nina to be catered for during the summer holidays. I could send Kamilla to Dorinda for a few weeks and leave Gemma and Nina to supervise the Middleton repairs. Let me know your thoughts.

Yours

GDB

Paris, July 1950

My dear,

This is an amalgam of several letters, and the answer to several of yours. I'm waiting to catch the courier. There's only one each fortnight. We can't risk the wretched censor.

I've found a nice little apartment near the Boulevard Haussmann, within walking distance of the Embassy. There's enough room for you and Kamilla. Until you can find us a villa out in Versailles. That's the place to be.

It has been easy to get back into French. The difficulty is the attitude of the Austrian legation. There's to be an exhibition of Austrian paintings from the Albertina, and I wasn't even sent an invitation! Neither was anyone else at the Embassy. Most embarrassing. I don't know what's wrong with Austrians these days. They seem to have lost their way. So my energies are taken up with petty quarrels among ourselves rather than spreading the word.

Paris is an amiable city to live in. I enjoy it and look forward to sharing its advantages with you. As well as the inevitable burdens of course. Your letter sounded so muddled and hysterical. I realise you have to cope entirely on your own, so I have taken the trouble to work out a detailed plan:

Do not rent out the main part of the villa under any circumstances. I have found a tenant for the top floor who is willing to pay five hundred Schillings a month. This will take care of all the outgoings, and leave the rest of the house for us when we return to Vienna. As, I am sure, we will shortly. As for your idea of sending Kamilla to Dorinda – I WILL NOT TOLERATE THAT UNDER ANY CIRCUMSTANCES.

I enclose a detailed list of how you should pay the debts, the moneys needed for dressmaker and hairdresser, and the preparations for coming to Paris. Please be sure to stick to them.

Your deals with the American Forces in Austria, asking for reparation for the stolen goods from the villa, seem to be going according to plan. It was a big mistake not to have sent me a copy of your complaints procedure. Of course you are entitled to go to the furniture depot and look for your belongings, or at least choose some like the ones stolen from you. Just do it.

As for my family jewels, I've no idea what the Dorotheum auctioneer is talking about. Naturally my sister has my mother's personal jewellery. Everything else is family heritage. There's no question of the Bosches owning fake paintings, paste diamonds or silver plating.

Be sure to put in your rightful demands to be reimbursed for your losses in the Miller Verlag immediately. As you know, Miller has done very well out of it and there is no reason why you should not. Naturally you are entitled to full compensation.

Yes, go up to Schwanenbruch and make sure your brother doesn't blunder about in his usual way. Use the opportunity to sell off the remaining land and outbuildings at a decent price. We need the money. You also have the right to demand your German villa money from the German government. All you have to do is put in a claim.

Gabby scrunches the letter into a ball. Throws it hard at an innocent bee buzzing against the window pane. The bee drops to the floor, recovers and zooms erratically around the room. Gabby opens the window to let it out.

She throws the letter into the waste-paper basket. The man's completely unrealistic and idiotically inflexible. He's sent a bottle of Armagnac — but no money — with the courier. She opens it, drinks eagerly. The money from Rolf Ferent arrived, and she has the six months' rent in hand. She allocates money for bills she has to pay.

Dorinda's last letter announced her intention to visit Schwanenbruch, so there's no chance of sending Kamilla to Dramlings. And it's become even more essential for Gabby to join her brother and sister. With any luck they'll be able to release some capital from the remaining German properties. She can try to recover at least part of the money the Council paid for the villa. Though she's pretty sure that's a lost cause. Of course, if she had Jewish blood it would be a different matter. Being Aryan isn't quite the advantage it used to be in the Third Reich. Anyway, she lost out even under the crazy Nazi rules. It was never useful for her.

Gabby scans the papers while taking calls from Czezina. Is history repeating itself? The war in Korea is in full swing. This time the Russians are actually in Vienna. Will they take over? If she leaves her three daughters here, will she ever see them again?

She comforts herself with the thought that Gemma is now twenty-one, and an American citizen. Rolf Ferent successfully claimed nationality for her when he was naturalised. The girl is very competent. Gabby decides to send Trautl back to her family until the autumn — so saving her wages — and to leave Gemma in charge of Nina and Kamilla. With strict instructions to take both her sisters to the American Embassy as soon as there is any sign of trouble. After all, the Middletons will be in the same house, and Gemma is supervising the Middleton refurbishment.

Gabby has to leave enough cash for Gemma to feed the three girls. Seasonal fruits and vegetables are reasonably priced, corn on the cob a filling food, Knackwurst provides cheap and adequate protein. She'll have to get some of her jewellery out of pawn and leave it with Gemma for emergencies.

SILVER TREASURE

According to legend, the hilly district known as the Wingst got its name from the giant Wingis. He originally hailed from the Harz mountains, where he became a rich man because he found silver, and mined it well.

After Wingis had made his money he decided to travel. He took his wife Grete and his son Bolik and wandered North, right up to the coastline of the North Sea. But once he had arrived the huge expanse of foaming water made him afraid. He decided not to travel further, but to look for a good place to build a pleasant home, quite near the coast. And to settle there.

Wingis travelled all over the lowlands of the North German plain, until he came across a range of small hills in an attractive, wooded setting. That's where he decided to build his home. He chose one of the highest peaks, built a house he called Giantwife Gretenberg, and settled down. And the whole upland area was called Wingst after the giant himself.

One day Wingis's son Bolik decided it was time to become independent. And, having heard the story of his father's silver find, he wanted to be just like him. He discussed his plans with his mother. She suggested that he might like to go back to the Harz mountains, to look for his treasure there.

Bolik hurried back to his childhood home. No sooner had he arrived then he found a glut of silvery stones. Thrilled, the young giant filled a large sack with them and hurried back to Wingst.

As soon as he arrived home Bolik opened his sack and poured out a hillful of stones. But to his horror the silver had disappeared, and only ordinary stones toppled out. It appeared that, in his haste, Bolik had mistaken winter-frosted stones for silver ones. Nevertheless the mound of stones, now the highest mount in the Wingst, is called the Silberberg.

CHAPTER 10

Vienna, Summer 1950

Dear Bosch,

Czezina came out to the villa and made me extremely nervous about the political situation. He maintained that it was entirely possible that American civilians would be evacuated out of Vienna because of the situation in Korea, and the effect this has on the Russo-American situation. He said the next step would be up to the Russians, and God knows what they have in mind. It terrified me, so I rushed off to the Consulate, saw to it that my papers were in order and registered myself and the girls – just in case. Of course, Kamilla is British, not American, so I had to make a special journey over the Semmering to get her 'gray card' for her. Yes, she needs one even at her age.

I can well imagine the problems you face settling into the job and Paris. But is it really necessary for you to take out colleagues' wives to expensive meals when your family is almost starving? Please don't think this is some sort of petty jealousy. You must send me more funds. I simply cannot go on like this. And I can hardly bear to talk to your cousin Hans, since each time I see him I seem to be begging him to lend me more cash.

I won't go into the terrible problems I have with money. Suffice it to say that we hardly get anything to eat, let alone anything decent. We live on cheap wine, potatoes and, thankfully, cheap corn on the cob. I've told you before to change the francs into Schillings in Paris. Everyone in Vienna is so terrified of devaluation they won't touch anything but dollars and Schillings. I had no choice but to pawn my fur coat.

Another thing: I was desperate about my hairdo. I was left in no doubt that I simply had to have a new one when one of your tactful Viennese burgers pointed my shortcomings out to me. I realised I simply could no longer go out in company like this and begged my hairdresser to fix me up and I would pay him when I could. He finally agreed, provided I left my pearls with him.

In between all these problems I went to USFA to instigate the case against Blenkindorff. I accused him of stealing furniture, fittings and personal effects, and gave the authorities a full list. The people in charge were very interested and wanted to make mine a show case. I gave them all the details I could muster. Then they discovered I'm not Jewish, so the case was of no interest.

Outrageous, of course, but I'm in such a state, rushing here and there, trying to get the girls settled before I leave for Schwanenbruch, seeing to the Middletons in so far as I can, that I wasn't able to do much about it. I'm being torn limb from limb by all these demands, and I haven't had a decent meal for weeks. So I'm leaving the Blenkindorff case for Otto Venn to sort out while I'm in Schwanenbruch. He was my lawyer before the war so he knows all the ins and out and has the inventory. Czezina saw the state I was in, took pity on me and invited me out to dinner.

There's a direct train from Vienna to Hamburg now. I can't face that cheap thirty-hour third class trip to Bremen in hopes of getting an Allied train to Cuxhaven. I don't have the strength for it, and so will have to spend the extra money on a ticket. Hard though that is to do.

Thank God Gemma is so competent. She will take her sisters to the American Consulate at the very first hint of trouble, and get them out to Switzerland. She will ring you first, so you can meet them and take them back to Paris with you. In the meantime she has been a marvel with the workmen. She arranged the best price for repairing the parquet, supervised the man who did it, got hold of a woman to polish it, saw to all the details. The Middletons are overcome with delight.

So far I've been able to keep the true state of our financial affairs from her, but she isn't stupid. She must have worked out that her father's money is not being used entirely for her and Nina. Anyway, all that stops in September. She's twenty-one, so when she goes back to university her father will send money directly to her.

Schwanenbruch won't be any sort of holiday. The best I can hope for is that I'll be able to agree a reasonable sale of our remaining properties with Emil and Dorinda. I have to warn you I see trouble ahead.

   Let's hope I can bring Kamilla to Paris by October.
   As ever
   GDB

Schwanenbruch, North Germany, Summer 1950

The man from the Schwanenbruch council is all smiles. A shadow of his former rotund self, like all the other natives Doly's come across. He pulls back frayed shirt-sleeves and flourishes the Dohlen siblings through the front door of their father's one-time magnificence.

'The stained glass windows are still whole.' Doly stops in the entrance porch to lovingly trace the figures of swans.

'We managed to avoid actual fighting in the village, Frau Courtling. All damage is superficial, caused by careless occupants rather than destructive vandals. As you know, one of the highest ranking SS officers and his family lived in the villa during the war years. An SS-Oberstgruppenführer no less, equivalent to the rank of General in the US or British Army. Then the British requisitioned it for one of their Generals. After he left, there was a certain amount of looting. Some of the locals helped themselves to furniture and fittings.'

'Really? People we know?'

The official looks nervous. 'Best not to look too closely. The real damage occurred after that. Refugees streaming over from the East had nowhere else to go. They squatted here, crowded together in the house.'

The building is shabby but structurally undamaged. The floors are filthy but intact, the walls smooth, the ceilings not shot full of holes. Paint is peeling off doors and windows, wallpaper is hanging in sheets, windowpanes are cracked. All that can be refurbished.

Herr Fosse's smile is obsequious. 'What we would like, if you can possibly bring yourselves to help us, is to reconstruct the way some of the finer rooms were furnished and decorated in your father's time. This house is a wonderful archetype of early twentieth century architecture. We'd like to encourage visitors.'

'You think it a good example of Jugendstil?' Gabby can still hear her father's dismayed roar at the builders' perceived idiocies: the substituting of metres for yards leading to too-large rooms, stained-glass windows too small for the openings left for them, high-tread stairs. 'Holy Moses! How in hell did this come about?' she can almost hear him roar.

'Absolutely magnificent. Your father left a very precious legacy for the village. The nation, come to that.'

Doly's puckish grin infects her brother and sister. Their parents' white elephant has become the golden calf. Which won't net them a single Pfennig.

'You'll love what I have to show you here.' The little man waltzes ahead, up the stairs and into their father's old study.

The black leather chair stands where it always was. And, above it, the oil portrait of their father. The three Dohlens stand, mesmerised, as if he were still alive. The old man's look has lost none of its aura of determination and success.

Herr Fosse pats the frame with a proprietorial air. 'No one dared take it!'

Doly feels a sense of belonging, of revival, as though their father were still looking after them. 'Marvellous that it's survived. And the painting of our mother? That's in another room?'

A sideways smile. 'I'm afraid that one has disappeared. Softer and prettier, of course. We haven't been able to trace it. We did try.'

Emma Dohlen no longer lives even in a portrait. All they have is a photograph. A mother surrounded by her three children. Taken when Doly was eighteen months, about six months before Emma's death in childbirth in 1913.

The tour continues to the Blue Salon. Doly hears echoes of the band which played when she and Lieselotte danced to the tune of *Petronella* — *Peel 'em off, Petronella, peel 'em off* — and shocked the worthy burgers by discarding all but their dresses. At the ball she and Gabby organised in 1925. Already knowing it would be the last time that the Blaue Salon would be used for such an occasion by the family.

'I do hope this is not too sad an experience for you. We're keeping the study, den blauen Salon — the blue living room — and the kitchen as showpieces. I'd just like to take you down there. Simply marvellous. The old range is still intact, and your father's farseeing installation of indoor plumbing, central heating and electric lighting are gems of historical significance. What a man!'

Emil Julius Dohlen Junior shuffles along the corridor which must hold memories he'd rather forget. Their fearsome Tante Hannah, still in her teens when left in charge of them after their father's death, wielding the wooden spoon, ready to be applied to his backside. The table where cook Rula whirled protection when Tante Hannah put his small palm on the hot cooker. Doly can see it, feels a tremor of sisterly love for the man who accepted too small a sum from her for her share of their father's house, who treated her so shabbily. He's suffering from scars he can't erase. They all are.

'Did you see I have a street named after me?' Emil Dohlen Junior sits at an *Elbfluss Haus* table by the window. 'More than can be said for either of you!'

'Don't be such a dope, Moppel. It was named after our father.' Gabby compares Moppel's rounded plenty with her father's lean abundance.

'That has crossed my mind some, Gabby. But it's still my name.' Their uncle Wilfred Bender's Doppelgänger. Smoked-eel complexion. Semaphore ears topped by a highly-polished nubbin. An obvious addiction to beer. Stubborn eyes.

Gabby pours more schnapps from the bottle on the table. 'Onkel Wilfred has put in a bid for the meadow. The highest one.'

'So why don't we let him have it? He did look after us when we were children.' Doly is puffing across the table. Sleeveless blouse, slacks. Schwanenbruch tuts judgment. Married women do not wear trousers. And even if she hasn't got a husband any more she's still a mother, still a woman of a certain age.

'Looked after us? He robbed us blind.' Gabby's notepad is criss-crossed with figures. She remembers multiplication tables with the best of them. The Cuxhaven grammar school built good foundations. 'My point is that he's had the use of it since Onkel Hinrich was killed in action. In 1916, remember? Wilfred owes us back rent, and it amounts to a tidy sum. What d'you think, Moppel? Shall we put the squeeze on him?' Cornflower blue blazes confidence.

Smoked eel turns to lobster. 'Why don't we just call it a day? He's offering over the odds.'

'Are you out of your mind? The rent amounts to twice the capital. You may not need the cash, Moppel. Doly and I do.'

Smoke rings surround Gabby. 'Onkel Wilfred is a wise old bird. "He who has sufficient, has enough," he always says. Dramlings is sufficient for me.' Doly, serene.

Gabby subdues her fury. Sufficient because others make it so. Tante Martha's savings, old boyfriend Bobby Hudwalker's generosity, Faith Bowler's godmother gifts of cash, neighbours putting transport and telephones at Doly's disposal, gifts of jam the vicar sends over. 'Bully for you. Bosch and I have nothing. The man who stole my Viennese furniture and household effects will go to prison but he doesn't have to hand them back. Courtesy of Austria's unique laws.'

Several more smoke rings. 'You have Kamilla.'

Gabby grabs the edge of the table, knuckles white. 'Well, Moppel? You settling for sufficient?'

'Don't think we need to make an issue of it.' His mumble is as clear as an admission. What's he been up to with Wilfred? Present or past deals behind hers and Doly's backs? Or does Wilfred actually have something on her brother?

'I am making an issue of it. Whether you two like it or not.' Gabby's hand encircles her glass, threatening breakage.

'You throw your weight around as though no one else counts, Gabby.' Moppel's three hairs stand to attention. 'I do remember one little incident you don't want referred to none.'

Still blackmailing her about the baby swap. If Nina is ever to find out that Doly is her biological mother she has to be told properly, not by some garbled version Emil might give her. And, from a more practical point of view, it would put an end to Rolf's financial contributions. Which, even though they've ceased for Gemma, still cover Nina. Money Gabby can ill afford to, simply cannot, lose.

Gabby's fist crashes on the table. Spilling beer. 'Maybe you think there's no dirty linen in your cupboard. I know better.'

Chaos among the drinks. The proprietor walks over and asks the Dohlen siblings to keep the noise down. Threesome apologies.

'Let's get on to the stables. Kurt Meyer is interested. He — '

'Kurt Meyer's father treated our mother shabbily. I thought let Wilfred have those, too.' Moppel chases his schnapps with beer in a litre tankard.

'You've discussed it with him already?'

'You two aren't noted for your business acumen.'

'And you are?'

'Guess I'm the best we've got.'

Gabby fights a losing battle. Outvoted by frivolity, abstruseness, blackmail. Her rage against her brother is unsupported by her sister. Wilfred Bender will bag the lot. Living proof that virtue has to be its own reward. Because vice scoops the goods.

CHAPTER 11

Schwanenbruch, Summer 1950

Doly and Ross are staying with Rula's daughter Anna. Doly remembers Rula: the wonderful meals she prepared during the First World War. Everything was in short supply and even her father's wealth couldn't get them all they wanted. She marvels that there was less to eat then than they had during World War II in England.

Anna lives in her mother's house, the one next to the house Emil Dohlen senior was born in, right behind the dyke and some way out of the village. She's thrilled to be looking after Ross. Who's already a veteran walker at a tender age because, living at Dramlings, three miles from the nearest village, he has to be. The Schwanenbruchers, no slouches themselves, are impressed by that.

Doly and Gabby are sitting in the little garden sheltered by the dyke. 'I've had a brilliant idea for earning more money, Gabby.'

'You mean the lodger isn't working out?'

'John's been a model. Out from early morning till nightfall, modest, on time with his rent. But he does crowd my space.'

'You've had a good offer for Dramlings? You're going to live nearer Midhurst?'

'No. I'm going to rent out the whole place for the duration of the summer.'

'You rent out the cottage, which is where you want to live, and live where?' Emil, successful enough to afford a room at the *Elbfluss Haus*, has bumbled over to join his sisters.

'Tante Martha is keen for me to bring Ross over every year. He can learn German, how to use a boat, even ride if a horse is made available. It's cheaper to live here than in England.'

'The whole summer?' Gabby's eyes moisten, showing that's how she'd love to spend her summers.

'Not all of it, no. I had a wooden structure built. With the money Tante Martha sent. Rather like a summer house, divided into two compartments. With bunk beds. That's where Ross and I will camp while I rent out Dramlings.'

'Ross and you live in a shed? That's gibberish, even you must see that.' Gabby's harsh piercing tones are redolent of her father.

'It'll be summer. We can bathe in the millpond, cook on a camping stove. Great fun. Our private log cabin holiday.'

'You can't be serious?' Moppel's eyes round like cherries in a tart.

'I've looked at the personal ads in *The Times* and *The Lady*. I can get twenty to twenty-five quid a week in summer. And sell them fresh vegetables. That'll bring in three hundred quid basic. Let's say fifty for the extra living expenses, a hundred and fifty for the mortgage, a hundred for clothes and the au pair. We'll be in clover.'

'You're not sheep.' Gabby downs the rest of her schnapps.

'Sheep don't eat clover. It distends their bellies and threatens their lives. My business plan is all agreed with Roger Quinnel and the bank.'

'You're going to expose Ross to living like a gypsy?' Moppel opens a bottle he's brought.

'He's a proper outdoor chap. Loves the country, knows all the places where the moorhens lay their eggs, can help me find mushrooms and blackberries. We'll have a wonderful time.'

'Still pie-in-the-sky, Doly. *If* you manage to rent the place out every week, *if* the English summer isn't as cold as winter, *if...*'

'Do stop blathering, Gabby. I am my father's daughter. If he could start out by sweeping the sawdust on the floor of the New York Exchange and became a millionaire, why shouldn't I start modestly?'

'Rent for a single cottage with no amenities is hardly going to make your fortune.'

'You don't have any vision, Moppel. The city slickers will swarm around the place like bears after a honey pot. They know it's the genuine article *because* there aren't any amenities.'

'Let's assume that. So you're going to camp out in a garden shed for several months?'

'I'll be here some of the time. So about twelve weeks. It'll be summer. Kind of fun.'

'And the au pairs? They'll think it fun?'

'I won't need them in the summer. The PGs will be around…'

'PGs?'

'Paying guests, no doubt with posh cars. Any emergency and they'll be there.'

'Just think what you're doing, Doly. Think about your child. Think about unforeseens! Leaking roof, broken window…'

'God, you two are such old fogies. Why think of what can go wrong? I'll work something out if it happens. Meanwhile, what could be more beautiful than the Sussex woods? Clean air, fresh food, all the time in the world to devote to Ross. Idyllic.'

'Liesl! At last. I was beginning to think you were avoiding me.' Doly holds her arms out wide. For too long. The girl she's known since she was six and went to school with, the girl who mingled her blood with Doly's so making them blood-sisters for life, the bosom friend she took with her on her European and Moroccan tours in the months before their studies began, doesn't seem glad to see her.

Lieselotte stays looking over her shoulder. Standing apart. 'I'm in Hamburg during the week, Doly.'

Where she's highly valued as an eye specialist. The tall body has become solid Hausfrau. She tends to their weekend home while husband Joseph works in his general practice in Cuxhaven. Their three daughters spend their weekdays at her father Karl Waldeck's farm. The same man who refused to fund his daughter's fees for medical school, who called Doly and all her family a shiftless lot of vagabonds who shouldn't be allowed to breed. Because of the pesky gene which, though upsetting enough — especially for girls — is hardly cause for total condemnation.

Disappointed that he only has granddaughters Waldeck has trained them into Rhine maidens. Blonde, blue-eyed, lusty.

'Your little Ross may be a boy, but he's a fragile English bloom beside my three valkyries!'

Will their children form friendships like their own? Can the bond be repeated into the next generation? The gap in ages and gender isn't the only hindrance. Ross asks with a smile. The valkyries demand with sneers.

'I can't stay long, Doly. Joseph likes me to prepare his evening meal.'

To which Doly has not been invited. Though Gabby has been honoured several times in the past. Even with the tiresome Bosch. 'You mean he can't stand me any more than he ever could.'

'He's tired out when he gets in. I'm so very sorry about Erskine and all that.'

'These things happen. Funny, I always thought it would be Joseph who'd leave you. Never occurred to me that Erskine would turn into a ladies' man, abandon me without a backward glance.'

'Joseph is steady enough. Hardworking, does his best for what he sees to be his country's interests.'

'And was a practising Nazi, needless to say.' Doly can't help remembering her last encounter with him. In the Berlin hospital after her fiancé Jake was clobbered to death trying to help three hapless Jews attacked by a band of Nazi hooligans. 'He didn't have to be forced to take their stand, I'll bet my bottom dollar.'

Joseph not only forcibly stopped her helping Jake, he as good as told her that if she stayed in Germany she'd be sterilised, or worse. Not only because of her mother's errant gene. He considered her behaviour outrageous, dubbed her a moral degenerate. Who, according to Nazi doctrine, would be sent to a mental hospital and, well, disposed of.

Lieselotte's eyes are no longer clear. Murky, deep pools of submerged thought. 'You know all doctors were forced to join the Party. I only escaped because I worked part-time while having my girls. There was no choice, Doly!' Her hands twist round and round.

'Except that Joseph agreed with them. Would just as soon have seen me and my family exterminated.'

'Must we spend time on recriminations? We get enough of that already, Doly.'

Hitler is dead. Long live Joseph. Congratulations to his parents for choosing another dictator's Christian name. 'Right. D'you like being a doctor?' She sees Liesi's neat hands touching swollen eyelids with her healing touch. Adoring patients, grateful parents.

Eyes slide away to examine perfect nails. 'What I really wanted to talk to you about was money. What I can do is to let you have a little every month...'

The withered branch of friendship is twisted into a crutch. 'I'm not looking for charity, Liesi.'

'I so much want to help. As you once helped me. After all, I wouldn't be a doctor if you hadn't paid my tuition fees.'

Love cannot be asked for, cannot be forced, and certainly cannot be bought. 'A gift so that you could use your talents. Not a storing up of treasure to be repaid.'

'It's illegal to send money out of Germany.' Her eyes are dull. 'Draconian laws, you see...'

'And Joseph. I understand. My aunt has been more than generous, and I've found a way to cope.' Doly embraces a stiff Lieselotte. 'I'd rather have your friendship than your money. Any day. Got time for a walk on the Watt with the children?'

''Fraid mine would find that a crashing bore. They like to join the other young people in the village. Fishing, sailing, riding. Flirting. My father has been wonderful to them.'

They walk where they once rode together. On a silver horse which stumbled in the fog, leaving them stranded. This time their steps form straight footprints in the sand. Washed away by the incoming tide.

'You need a telephone, Doly. You can't be out in the wilds without that. I have some money saved. Take it back with you.'

Doly nods. It isn't enough to install a phone. Because she'd have to bring the line close enough, and that costs hundreds. No matter. Giving and taking. She doesn't see the difference. Or the need for dissonant words.

THE DEVIL'S DEFEAT

THE DEVIL'S DEFEAT

The captain was in despair. He paced up and down Cuxhaven pier, hoping for a boat. No luck. Until he met a fine gentleman who promised him a seaworthy ship. On one condition.

'When you get back from your trip you have to find me a job. Something I'll never be able to finish. Because if ever I can, I'll come after you. And you'll forfeit your soul.'

For the well-turned out gentleman was no other than the devil himself.

The captain-without-a-boat was desperate and agreed to the bargain. And was presented with a splendid boat in excellent seagoing condition.

The captain lost no time in finding cargo to take to the other side of the world. The trip kept him so busy that he forgot all about his bargain with the Prince of Darkness. Until he was sailing home and saw the Elbe estuary right in front of him. Now he had no idea what to do.

The helmsman was his brother. He asked him what the problem was. While explaining the situation the captain realised just what a fool he'd been.

'Don't worry, brother. I'll sort it out for you. Go down to your cabin, get drunk. I'll fetch you when it's all over.'

The brother took the wheel. He felt the wind sharpening and set all the sails. The boat flew like lightning into the Elbe. She was about to pass Cuxhaven when the devil stepped on board and demanded that his promise be fulfilled. 'Or I'll take the whole boat and crew to hell with me,' he bellowed over the wind.

The helmsman ordered the sailors to drop the main anchor, with the thick hawser unwinding from the pin. If the devil wanted to take the boat he'd have his work cut out. He'd have to grab at the hawser to keep the boat going.

They were going so fast, and the devil held the hawser so tight, that he was dragged through the hawsehole and thrown out into the waves.

That's when he was told exactly what his job was to be.

He was to ferry travellers from one side of the Elbe to the other, whatever the weather, even on the stormiest days. And he was to do it here, right by Cuxhaven, where the river is a mile wide. And he was not to take a single pfennig for the privilege. Which meant he'd always have passengers, even on the sunniest days.

Since then the devil has been on constant duty. There's always someone who wants to cross, however harsh the conditions. That is, after all, the very time when no one else will take on the job. So the devil is always at work, at the beck and call of any would-be passenger. And the turbulent North Sea makes sure he has no time off. So the devil has enough work for all eternity.

CHAPTER 12

Paris, Easter 1951

Bosch has found an excellent apartment in central Paris. Gabby and Kamilla have joined him there. The tall living-room windows overlook a private square which is at the tenants' disposal. It's planted with trees and shrubs, and is somewhere for the maid to take Kamilla to play.

Gabby is bustling Easter spirit. Gemma has joined them from England. 'Trautl's busy with lunch, Gemma. Keep Kamilla busy while I go down and hide the eggs. And don't let her look out of the window!'

'Just where do you propose to hide Easter eggs?' Volumes of smoke from Bosch's Gauloises veil the room grey.

Gabby starts opening a window, thinks better of it. The fourteen-foot ceilings will swallow clouds of smoke out of harm's way.

'Down in the square. It's absolutely perfect — '

'In full view of other people?' A sudden burst of choleric coughing he makes no effort to control. 'Are you insane?'

Bosch has been impossible from the moment she arrived in Paris. Cantankerous, quarrelsome, tight-fisted, sarcastic. Even, on two occasions, physically abusive. Another woman? He's been wining and dining far too many. But surely nothing personal?

'There isn't a soul about, Bosch. The whole of Paris has migrated from the city. But even if there were…'

'I forbid you to make a spectacle of yourself. If you must go in for pagan customs hide the damned eggs in this room. It's large enough even for your inflated notions.'

Cavernous, actually. A huge gaping fireplace they can't afford to use dominates one wall. Sparse shabby furnishings. And so damned cold they have to wear nightcaps and socks in bed. If Gabby had hopes that Paris might be more comfortable than Vienna they've been shattered. The city may be less devastated by street fighting, but it's also less friendly. She and Bosch are newcomers among people who detest anyone from a German-speaking background.

'But Bosch! I promised Kamilla.'

The Gauloise shoots out of his holder as he whirls round and starts towards her. He stops as Gemma stands between him and her mother. The empty holder points at Gabby, an accusation of intending crime. 'You had no right to. I won't have you making yourself ridiculous.'

He walks towards the mantelpiece and lunges for another cigarette.

'Come on, Kammy. Let's go and see how Trautl's getting on with that special cake.' Gemma grabs the five-year-old's hand and leads her out.

Nina is spending the Easter holidays with a friend from school, delighted to get away from having to spend time in the same house as Bosch. The antagonism between the two of them is getting worse. Gabby is glad not to be a witness to it during this holiday.

'Are you unwell, Bosch?' Gabby keeps the large divan between herself and the man now trying to fit a cigarette into the holder. Less raucous coughing misdirects his aim.

'Your constant assumption that there's something wrong with me is really getting me down. Actually it's you who causes all the problems. Two dresses! Such ridiculous extravagance. I'm not made of money, you know.'

How could she fail to? A cultural attaché's remuneration is minimal.

Even augmented by the handsome rent Gabby has secured for the Neuwaldegg villa. Not just the Middletons. She's found another couple for the top flat.

Bosch's absurd suggestion that they rent a villa in Versailles was vetoed the day she arrived. The apartment's three rooms, kitchen, bathroom and a maid's room on another floor are very adequate. And barely affordable even without heating. Their money is spent on sartorial standards undreamed of in Vienna.

'Mr Ferent's allowance is due tomorrow. Then I can pay off the tailor.'

Never handsome, Bosch did at one time have a knack of projecting a masterful ennui, an arrogant lordliness which attracted the wives of important men. Because it signalled a high political intelligence and an active mind. Now he's shrunk to the dingy, wrinkled aspect of a Rumpelstiltskin. With that gnome's cackling malice.

Gabby feels her heart ache. The Anschluss not only signalled Austria's doom — it signalled Bosch's. Deprived of all his possessions, exiled, interned, he came back to a hostile Vienna which only compensated Jews, not those stalwarts who had fought to fend off the Nazis.

The job is a disaster. Instead of giving Bosch back his pride, setting him up for a closer connection to Austrian affairs, it's made him bitter. He quarrels with his immediate boss and woos wives of dignitaries rather than the men themselves. Not for sexual reasons. His excursions into that area were always minimal. Now they're non-existent as far as Gabby is concerned. She sees him pay court to other women in a knightly way. Though not to her.

'I need more housekeeping money, Bosch. I've mentioned before that now she's of age Gemma's father has arranged to pay her allowance straight to her.'

'How much longer am I expected to put up with this constant odious comparison with that boring Hungarian Jew you were married to? If you're so keen on him, go back to him!'

What on earth has got into him? This isn't the Bosch she used to know. Overbearing, certainly not suffering fools gladly, he still used his one-time wealth to encourage the young, protect the politically naïve, help starving writers. Now he seems to be losing all reason. Surely he knows his family would have been sunk without Rolf Ferent's contributions. He's been decent and generous. Considering his own reduced circumstances and his need to support a second family.

She tries one more ploy. 'Look, Bosch. I've got six Easter eggs for the whole family. Why don't you hide them? Kamilla will be so disappointed if you don't.'

'If you must go in for sentimental claptrap, do it yourself.' Cigarettes spill over the floor as he grabs the open box. He stuffs some into his trouser pockets, kicks the rest aside and storms out.

Desolation stalks Gabby like the fabled Schimmelreiter — the ghost rider — riding the crest of the North Sea dyke. Bosch's despair is spreading its pall on Kamilla. She prefers Trautl's company, no longer asks when her Bogey is going to read to her. Because he never does.

Gabby stares at the face in the mirror. The sags of middle age are accented by the relentless drag of worry. Her lively eyes puff black shadows into her cheeks, her hairdo straggles lanky ends which don't quite fit. They stand aside in a curiously lifeless way, showing they aren't a part of her.

'Does he actually hit you, or just threaten to?' Gemma offers her mother one of the blouses she can now afford to buy. 'This one could work with your black skirt.'

'Once or twice. I'd be better off in Neuwaldegg than playing Cinderella to Bosch's grandiose ideas.'

'Why not just leave him?'

'I have a small child to bring up. She needs a father.'

'Not one who slaps you about. That may escalate to her as well.'

'He's never behaved like this before.'

'Not remotely. Even when Nina drove him to distraction he never came near to using violence.' Gemma, always a Bosch admirer, frowns puzzlement.

'Exactly. I suppose it's his way of coping with *the slings and arrows of outrageous fortune.*'

'You know I like him, Gabby. He's been a good father to me, helped educate me where my own father would have thought it a waste of time for a girl. And he's never been bothered by the Dohlen gene, always boosted my ego by saying I look like a Botticelli Madonna. I owe him a lot.

'But I can see something's wrong. I've no idea what it is, but get out while you can before it's too late. Take Kamilla to Schwanenbruch, give yourself time. You can always go back to Vienna, live in the top flat of the villa with Kamilla and Nina, get half the Middletons' rent.'

The unaccustomed sympathy makes Gabby's eyes water. 'Certainly better than being here!'

'You're gifted in languages, you know. Bilingual in English and German. And your French isn't bad. Why not try for a job as an interpreter?'

'You think someone would actually offer me a job? I have no qualifications.'

'Not formal ones. You're brilliant with people. A natural. And you're making a good job of sorting out tenants, as well! You don't need a husband, you know. You can stand on your own two feet. You'll be better off.'

What can a young girl like Gemma know? Gabby realises she herself contributes substantially to the family income, to the family welfare, that she's the one who keeps it all together. But cut loose on her own? Be responsible for bringing up Kamilla in a cold bleak world without a father? 'You really think I should leave him?'

'At least get away to think about it. You can't go on like this.'

'The hand life deals you is a given. What counts is how you play the game,' Gabby hears her father's thunderous voice. Is Gemma a granddaughter with her father's spirit? Is she right, and telling her mother what she should be doing?

Gemma belongs to a new generation of women who are convinced they're men's equals. Gabby realises she's forty-five, forty-six in September. Not that much time left to start out on her own. Should she take the plunge now, while she still has the energy to make something of her life?

CHAPTER 13

Schwanenbruch, Summer 1951

When the summer is kind, and the Elbe is as still as a mill pond, the will-o'-the-wisp lights flicker and flake in the dusky air. They dance and gambol, shimmering green like tiny dragons which guard the entrance to the North Sea.

Gabby sits on the bench outside the *Schleuse Inn* set on top of the dyke. She never tires of staring at the water, the boats which steam up and down, listening to the wheeling shrieking gulls. Nothing can replace the feeling of belonging, the sense that the wind-whipped grasses are a part of her. She is at one with sea and sky, earth and wind.

'Back for a little holiday?'

"Abend, Herr Fosse. I've brought my youngest daughter up for the summer. So good for her to get several weeks of fresh air after living in Paris and Vienna.'

'How fortunate you are, Frau Bosch. Always in the thick of what's going on. We lead such dull lives here.'

She's on her own: no Moppel, no Doly, no Bosch. Gabby relaxes down to her toenails for the first time since leaving the Lingfield haven. The war was a lull of humdrum life in spite of rationing, bombs and doodlebugs. And she was innocent enough to consider it dull to live on England's green and pleasant land, the unexpected refuge which soothed her heart and caressed her spirit.

Maybe Doly chose the better straw after all. As she did long ago, when they were dividing up their father's East Side properties after Doly came of age. Her letters now, full of chirping chaffinches and ripening corn, insist on heavenly ups amongst the downs of English country life.

Bosch, left alone, writes diligently, evidently missing her. Temperate letters which seem to shorten with each three day interval. A state of affairs he attributes to a bout of 'flu he hasn't been able to shake.

Paris, July 22nd, 1951
My dear,
I am still under the weather. I have actually been to see the quack. He couldn't find anything wrong, but said I really must take a few days in bed to get over whatever isn't there! The office reluctantly agreed to a week's leave. You'll forgive me if I'm not in touch for a while. Look after Kamilla for me. I miss you both.

The flimsy paper bends back and forth in Gabby's hand. Bosch went to see a doctor? Without being nagged to do so? Taking an interest in bodily health isn't one of Gabby's talents. But she has noticed Bosch age more than she would have expected. And lose substantial weight with each passing week. While gobbets of phlegm require the constant boiling of far too many handkerchiefs.

An intemperate man whose quick wit spiced dull days, pricked pomposity and chivvied boredom away was stimulating. Bad temper married to physical abuse is unacceptable. Illness may be a mitigating factor, but it will not persuade her to return.

'Another letter for you, Gabby.' Their one-time nursery maid, now a war widow, Ursula bustles into the charming room she's put at Gabby's disposal. Chintz curtains, an easy chair, a steaming cup of coffee in the morning, fresh bread. Ursula has a way of making the best out of nothing. 'You have more letters in a week than the rest of Schwanenbruch has in a year!'

Gabby assumes it's summer warmth which accumulates drops of sweat on her upper lip. Unwillingness to hear from Bosch again so soon leaves her limp. 'From Vienna?' Perhaps Czezina, with a problem about the villa.

'A Swiss stamp. I was going to ask you to save it for me.'

Switzerland? Nina has a school friend who comes from St Moritz. She's been invited there, joined the friend's family at Easter, hoping for late snow and a skiing holiday. Gabby offered the friend a break in Paris later in the year. A letter of acceptance, perhaps.

The envelope has Bosch's spidery writing on it. Rather faint.

Hubert Sanatorium, July 29th, 1951
My dearest,
Do not be too alarmed. The wretched 'flu did not get better. You probably remember that tiresome cough during the nights. After you left I developed night sweats, which is what took me to the quack. The bed rest did not work, and I started having problems with my digestion. At my next visit the doctor did some tests.

The diagnosis is upsetting. He thinks I have TB. That I have had it for some time, so it is in the later stages. He advised a TB clinic.

Hence a letter from Switzerland. I went to see the people at the Embassy. The Austrian Government will foot the bill for three months. As a special favour. I should have had a contract of employment. It seems the papers didn't get filled in.

It is beautiful here, quiet, and I should be improving shortly. The doctors tell me that with modern drug therapy — they've had an antibiotic called aureomycin since 1944 — I should be better soon. How strange that Erskine Courtling and I should both benefit from the discovery of these new medicines. Meanwhile I feel rotten. You know I don't exaggerate about such things.

I can't give you much hope of a cure. The disease has progressed too far. A respite from acute distress, and prevention of future attacks, is the best that can be hoped for. They tell me it will be at least a month before there can be any sign of improvement.

It's the end of my job in Paris. It will fall on you to pack up our things and head back to Vienna. Now you know why I didn't want you to rent out the villa. You'll have to find us somewhere to live. Ask my cousin Hans to help you. Such an ardent admirer will do all he can.

That's all I can manage for now. I'll write again in a few days.
Your loving Bosch

Gabby's hands tremble, she feels icy. Surely TB is a serious disease? How did he get it? Lieselotte or her husband Joseph can tell her more about it. She determines to find out what Bosch's chances are. Realistically.

She rereads the letter. Reluctantly. A bare three weeks of rest and she's worse off. No chance of leaving Bosch. In sickness and in health, even if it isn't a Christian marriage.

A twist of grief, of sympathy, as she remembers his glory days. Sobranie cigarette swaying in an expensive holder, his patrician air.

'Anyone can tell you're from Berlin, gnä' Frau. How come you're reading *Sturm*?' was how he introduced himself. Lording it at the *Café Herrenhof*, his acolytes suppliant around him. So many years ago, when she was a jaded housewife living in a gracious villa on the outskirts of Vienna — and bored enough to drive into the city, and its coffee houses, on her own. While her then husband Rolf was safely abroad, travelling for the IBM.

She remembers Bosch as he was then. 'Der Bosch' who pontificated to an adoring audience, who wrote anti-Nazi editorials, who paid for everyone's coffee. Who ordered einen kleinen Schwarzen — a small black coffee — for everyone because only plebs drink coffee with milk. Who jiggled his leg, right over left. Whose eyes glinted platinum as he pocketed silver coffee spoons and offered unpaid-for icons to undeserving authors, and unpaid-for wine to undeserving wives, knowing the costs would be put on his bill. It was tacitly understood that 'der Bosch' would pay for them the next time he patronised that restaurant or coffee house.

She feels his anguish, shudders for him. A Nazi death sentence on the day of the Anschluss, exiled, spurned on his return to Austria. As much one of Hitler's victims as any Jew.

The letter is folded, folded, folded. Smaller and smaller. Until she can't fold any more. She slips it into the pocket of the blouse Gemma gave her. And asks Ursula to keep an ear out for Kamilla already playing with the other children in the street.

Gabby marches along the cobbles, on to the dyke, the mudflats beyond. She's tempted to walk right out into the waves and never come back. If only the Wattengeist, the mysterious chimera said to inhabit the Watt — the mudflats — and which apparently enticed her maternal grandfather to his death, would claim her now. An end to all her problems.

The tide flows in, the warning tongues snaking her feet, playing with her. The wind picks up, the waves crest with foam and crash towards her. Seagulls scream danger.

She turns back for the shore. She's a Frisian, not a lily-livered nobody. She's brought up two girls. Gemma is about to graduate, Nina wants to go to university in the States this September. Leaving her bereft.

She still has Kamilla and Bosch to look after, she can't just leave them to manage on their own.

She forges ahead of the gathering water with its quickening pace. The battle against the sea is an easy win. Gabby sinks down on the harsh shingle of the Schwanenbruch beach. Gulls shriek their nesting sites, waves overrun the beach in proprietorial claims. The wind blows cold, it starts to rain.

An overwhelming longing to be looked after comes over her. Why did her father leave them so exposed? Why didn't he make proper provision for his children, why leave them to the so untender mercies of Onkel Wilfred and Tante Hannah? Why appoint the weakling Walter Hudwalker as guardian, far away in the States? Didn't he care about his children's future?

She realises Rolf Ferent offered protection, offered love. A decent steady hard-working man she spurned because he was too dull, too cloying. Substituting a fascinating Bosch who was no more capable of protecting or succouring than a will-o'-the-wisp.

How will she cope? She has no qualifications, no skills beyond the ones of gracious hostess and her skilful tongue. Can that be enough to keep her family from starving?

Tears well, spill, mingle with the wind. She remembers the story of the dykeman the Schwanenbruchers of long ago walled up, alive, to mend their dyke, hears his curses: is this the revenge he promised the villagers of Schwanenbruch? Is she still one of them? Has he singled the Dohlen orphans out for his revenge?

CHAPTER 14

Sussex, Summer 1951

'Welcome to Sussex, Nina!' Doly watches her secret daughter step off the bus, looking round timidly. She's only eighteen, but she's headscarfed up like a middle-aged woman. Hammer blows of guilt, dismay, alarm make Doly's voice penetrating, harsh.

'Hello, Aunt Dorinda. And Ross.' Nina stands awkwardly, a hefty rucksack on her back. Buffy trots up to sniff her, welcome her. She bends down but brushes him away, peers up at Doly furtively, clearly uncertain of her welcome.

The girl straightens. Doly throws her arms around the daughter she hardly knows, is dismayed to find the girl only reluctantly allows the welcoming embrace. Thoughtful of Gabby to send Nina over on her way to live with Rolf Ferent, but it seems there's a high price to pay.

Nina wriggles out of arm shot. 'It is most kind of you to invite me.'

Why this combination of truculence and fear? 'I'm afraid Bramlings is a couple of miles from the bus stop.' Surely Gabby told the girl she'd have to walk, that Doly only has one bicycle? 'It's a quite lovely ramble. People travel from all over to get the chance to hike in our gorgeous lanes.' The bike has a puncture again.

'That's all right. I'm used to trekking. Better than climbing those stupid mountains behind my school.'

'You didn't enjoy that?' Doly's already feeling irritable. 'Most people would think it wonderful to have those gorgeous views on their doorstep.'

'I hate mountains.'

Getting to like the daughter she gave to Gabby to bring up is going to need something of an effort. She was hardly expecting hostility at the outset. 'Well, you're in luck, then. We only have gentle hills. The South Downs.' She nods encouragingly, tries to inject warmth into her eyes. 'And this is your cousin Ross, Nina.'

'Hello, Ross.' The four-year-old and Nina stare at each other while Doly's grin is as wide as she can make it. She breathes in deep to both hide and conquer her guilt — and her irritation. Two long weeks ahead before Nina goes to stay with her 'father' in New York.

'I'm very pleased to meet you, Ross.' Nina offers her hand to the little boy who shakes it solemnly. 'You're very tall for your age.'

'His father is over six foot.' The pressure of deceit about Nina makes Doly gushy, talkative. She burbles inconsequential rubbish which is acknowledged with the occasional yes or no.

She wasn't exactly expecting love at first sight, that's ruled out by the only other encounters they've had: one wartime Christmas, and a few short days by the Wolfgangsee, during the visit which ended in such disaster. But she did expect a reasonable enthusiasm.

Nina has always made it clear she has very little time for her 'aunt'. Doly had no inkling that she'd find the girl awkward, tiresome and altogether unappealing.

'So how far is it to your house?' Nina hoists the rucksack into a better position.

'About three miles. Ross can manage there and back, so it can't be that bad.'

Nina plods on, the rucksack swaying on her back, while Doly chatters about school and holidays. 'Ross goes to Kindergarten. He loves it.'

'That's close by?'

'A neighbour drives him with her own son.'

'Lucky.'

'He already knows his alphabet.'

'Good.'

Monosyllabic replies are not encouraging. Did Gabby force the girl to come? 'Did you enjoy the Gmunden convent? A very picturesque place for a school.'

'It wasn't an Alpine holiday, if that's what you mean. The mountain towered behind the convent and obscured all views on that side.'

'Oh. But you went climbing and skiing, I take it?'

'We spent most of our time in the classroom. With religion dinned into us every day.' Nina jolts the rucksack up and down. 'The so-called holy nuns are religious bigots. They clink a rosary in their hands while making sure we feel small.'

'Really? How do they do that?'

'Acid remarks about our ugly looks or lack of education.'

Doly comes to a sudden stop, making Nina almost miss her footing in the muddy lane.

She recovers expertly. 'And slapping a cane across our palms, of course. For hideous crimes like running in a corridor, or not curtseying when we meet a nun on the stairs.'

'Really. Were you forced to stay there, then?'

'Mr Bosch preached it was an outstanding school and I would thank him once I was grown up.' Nina's naked eyebrow and eyelash look is unnerving, owl-like, predatory. 'I hate that school.'

'Well, you've left now, haven't you. So that's in the past. And what about your stepfather? Do you hate him as well?'

'He's a stupid bigot who thinks he's the world's greatest politician. Too bad no one else agrees with him.' A sudden grin. 'Not that one can blame them!'

'So you're glad to leave him behind.'

'Actually, he isn't there at the moment. He's in a clinic in Switzerland. He's got TB.'

Doly remembers her misgivings about Bosch's health during that ill-fated visit to the Wolfgansee in the summer of '49. Her instincts had been right. It explains the man's behaviour, up to a point. 'So you didn't have a good childhood?' Doly's heart flutters as she feels the guilt of abandonment.

'That would be putting it mildly.'

'I expect you're looking forward to living with your father while you go to college?'

'Who knows? I don't remember him, haven't seen him since before the war. He's got a new wife and son now.' Nina's lips purse. 'Laurence, his name is.'

'So I've heard.'

'Gemma's been to stay with them a couple of times, to get her American citizenship. She says Laura is bossy and Laurence ghastly.'

'I'm sure they'll make you welcome.' Does the girl only see life as a set of negatives?

Nina shrugs and they plod on in silence, occasionally interrupted by Ross as he chatters about the birdsong around them, identifying the different sounds.

'That isn't a chaffinch. That's a mistle thrush's alarm call,' Nina announces. 'You can't forget it. Sounds like a machine gun.'

'Never mind, darling. You do know lots of them.' Doly gives her son a friendly pat. How is she going to survive this girl's aggressive behaviour for two whole weeks?

'Well, hello there, Doly! Is this your new au pair?'

She nods, unable to find her voice immediately, dismayed to come across a neighbour while having this odd-looking girl in tow.

'Geraldine! How nice to see you. This is my niece, Nina. She's travelling from Austria to New York, via Southampton. That's given her a chance to stay with me for a couple of weeks.'

Geraldine blinks. 'Your niece? Really. I had no idea.' And tries not to stare at Nina's headscarfed head, her truculent look, her inching herself behind Doly. 'That sounds like quite an adventure, Nina. Are you looking forward to it?'

'Yes, thank you.' A low indistinct sound.

'Of course she is, it's a great opportunity. She's going to enrol at Barnard. The same college I went to, part of Columbia University. Best women's college in America. Isn't she a lucky girl?'

'It sounds wonderful.' Geraldine stares again, then whistles to her dog fraternising with Buffy. 'Walk on, Spencer.' And waves goodbye.

'See you at the fête,' Doly calls out. And starts to prattle loud aeons of praise: about her neighbours, how wonderful they are to her, how they take Ross to school, give her lifts to Midhurst and bring her home-made jam and chutneys.

Nina digs a heel into soft mud, turns to stare at Doly, her tone gruff. 'Don't you mind all this charity?'

'Charity? It's give and take, Nina. I always have a glut of plums I distribute to all and sundry, as well as many of the vegetables I grow. That's what's so wonderful about living in the country.' She blinks at the girl she knows to be her daughter but cannot feel, or accept, let alone revel in this knowledge. So far Nina has been judgmental, angry, surly and with a touch of arrogance which contradicts her obvious worry about her looks. 'I'm so lucky, Nina. I have Ross and Buffy, I'm surrounded by some of the most beautiful countryside in the whole world, I have a wonderful cottage dating from the seventeenth century...'

'I thought you rented that out in summer.'

'Two weeks between tenants, Nina. So you can enjoy my treasure.' She's given up two weeks' rent so that Nina can live in the cottage, admire Doly's little kingdom, see how well her mother has done for herself. If she ever finds out Doly is her mother. 'I think you'll find we're very comfortable.'

They plod on silently. Once home they settle down to tea, with Ross enthusiastically tucking in while Nina toys with food Doly has spent more money on than she can afford. Offered the chance to put Ross to bed Nina excuses herself, saying she needs to unpack.

Sitting in front of Doly's fire, lit because this particular week is wet and cold, Nina coughs, looks embarrassed, finally bursts out: 'How do *you* feel about the Dohlen inheritance?'

'Which one, Nina? If you're talking about money, mine's all gone.'

'I'm talking about the gene for early hair loss.'

'Feel about it? Well, it's a bit of a cross to bear. But there are worse.'

'For you, maybe.' Tone gruff and hostile. 'You're middle-aged and still have hair. And Ross has obviously escaped it. My loss is now difficult to hide. I look a fright.'

No denying that. Doly feels fury with Gabby for allowing the girl to get to this stage without having some sort of replacement. Expensive, obviously, but to leave the child walking about with straggles of hair barely covering the bald spot on her scalp is a special cruelty Doly finds hard to take.

'D'you think I should get a wig, or d'you think I should look into some sort of medical treatment?'

'I'm sorry, Nina. There isn't a cure. Didn't your mo... Gabby tell you that?'

'She tells me all kinds of stuff.' Her fingers twist in and out of a neck scarf she's brought, her teeth bite down on her lips.

Doly parries the questions, demands, wild statements, outbursts of fury as best she can.

'Gabby thinks a hairpiece is a camouflage, a courtesy to others, because if one can't get rid of a defect one should try to make it as inconspicuous as possible.'

'That makes a lot of sense, don't you think?' For once her sister has handled it right.

'So you're agreed on that.' The scarf is twisted back and forth.

'I believe any defect or handicap can also be a compensation. Just think how very minor our family problem is compared to the ghastly mutilations happening at this very moment to so many people all over the world.' Doly lights a cigarette, draws in deep. 'Or compared to other hereditary defects.'

'Like what?'

'Mongolism, for example. Cystic fibrosis. Huntingdon's chorea. Loads of much more unpleasant hereditary genes.' Doly puffs long and hard. 'One thing I would advise. Don't draw attention to yourself by tugging at your ear. I can get you out of that in the time you're here. When I say "puss cat" you'll know you're doing it and can stop.'

'What?' A frown making the young face look old. 'I suppose so.'

'And you have lovely skin. Like an unfurling rosebud. And such good teeth.'

The churlish eyes turn eager. 'I have, haven't I? And really good nails as well. So many of the girls at school have spots, and dreadful teeth and nails. Quite ugly, actually.'

Put others down a peg or two to lift one's own spirits? Not Doly's style. But she brings out her collection of hats, scarves and snoods. Shown how to tie a snood around her hair to make her look presentable Nina accepts one fairly graciously and learns to tie it. With reasonably pleasant results.

CHAPTER 15

Sussex, Summer 1951

'Let's go to Chichester,' Doly proposes the next day. She readies Ross and herself, and is pleased that Nina has worked out how to make the snood really attractive. It makes her look quite normal. They take the bus to Midhurst, then on to Chichester. And no one stares at Nina.

Doly goes to the building society, draws out scant money for lunch. 'What about looking at the Cathedral? It's the seat of the Anglican bishop of Chichester, and has really fine architecture in the Norman and Gothic styles.'

'I've had enough of churches to last me all my life.'

'It's not just a church, Nina. It's one of England's glories...'

'Could we go to a film instead?'

'What?' She hasn't enough money for a film. 'I'm not quite sure...'

'I've got some cash my father sent. I could take you and Ross.'

Doly's smile illuminates her whole being. 'What a lovely idea.'

Alice in Wonderland is on. I expect you've read Ross the story, so I'm sure he'll enjoy going to that.'

On the way back the bus is crowded. Nina and Doly are on a double seat, Ross between them. He snuggles up to Nina and she claps hands with him.

An old woman boards the bus and Doly, sitting by the aisle, stands immediately to offer her her seat. Nina stops playing, gathers Ross up and stands uncertainly, beckoning to her place. The old lady, overwhelmed by all the attention, accepts someone else's offer.

Doly tells herself she wasn't trying to point a moral, sees Nina look at her with cold eyes.

'I always got very high marks at that awful school, you know. Although it was all in German. Which I hadn't spoken for ten years when I first went there. Not since I was five.'

'How nice, Nina.'

'Top of the form in most subjects.' A shake of hardly-veiled irritation. 'The only thing I flunked was catechism. But then I did that on purpose.'

'You think academic achievements are important?'

'What I think doesn't count. I wanted to get into Barnard, so I had to do well.' She's made several tiny paper aeroplanes out of the cinema tickets. 'They credit you with two years if you've passed the Austrian Matura.'

'Do they now.' Doly grabs Ross on to her lap, kisses the top of his head, mumbles baby talk while the child squirms to get back to Nina.

'That's one thing that awful convent did for me. They're one of the elite schools in Austria, have a phenomenally high standard, so Barnard is pleased to take on any of their outstanding pupils.'

'That's what you were, is it? Outstanding?' Doly's cigarette burns red.

'In my year, yes. There was a fair amount of competition. I want to be a journalist, you see. A reporter. So I thought it was worth working hard. Anyway, what else was there to do?'

Doly turns away, checks out the other bus passengers. No one she knows. She talks to the woman sitting across the aisle. Surely the girl will take the hint?

'Even the nuns were impressed by my English essays.'

'You had been to an English school.'

'Impressed by the content.'

Ross leans away from Doly and grabs Nina's hand. She laughs, then:

'Pat-a-cake, pat-a-cake, baker's man, Bake me a cake as quick as you can,' she sing-songs to a delighted child who does his best to squirm away from Doly onto Nina's lap.

'There are other passengers, Nina. Not quite so exuberant perhaps.'

Ross and Nina subside into giggles.

Doly finds mealtimes hard to cope with. She's used to feeding herself and Ross vegetables from the garden, easy to cook and easy on the purse. Nina has a healthy appetite. She takes large chunks of the roast chicken meant to last the week, gulps her water. Didn't they teach manners at that convent?

'That was a wonderful meal, Aunt Dorinda.'

'Doly.'

'Aunt Doly. I...

'Just Doly will do. You're a big girl now.'

Nina's eyes widen, blink. She looks like a startled fawn. Perhaps donkey would be a better description. Doly wonders silently: is this really my daughter? Was she born a bore, a prig and a braggart or did she pick it up from Gabby and Bosch?

'All right. I'll call you Dorinda, then.'

After she's put Ross to bed Doly notices Nina isn't about and puts her head round the door of the girl's room. She's sitting hunched over a book. She looks up furtively, almost fearfully.

Doly feels pity welling inside, then anger. 'It's a lovely evening, Nina. Wouldn't you like to explore our beautiful woods?' Why all this charade about academic achievements? Irritation with Nina's lack of moral fibre wells up inside her. Or is it guilt that she's passed on the gene?

She shrugs that off. This pitiful being is her daughter? Oh God, oh bloody hell! Born when she didn't want a child, then so many years of miscarriages. Would the misbegotten have turned out like this as well? Will Ross?

After Ross's bedtime Doly and Nina sit around the fire, tossing pine cones on blazing logs, tickling them with a poker. Doly lights a cigarette and begins to blow smoke rings. And to talk, to relate, to inform.

'You know your grandfather sailed to the States from Germany. When he was barely sixteen, with nothing but a Mark in his pocket and the clothes on his back.'

'Really? How did he pay for his passage?'

'Worked his way over. Washing dishes, swabbing decks.'

'So why did he come back to Germany?'

'He married your grandmother. She didn't like it over there. She was homesick for her village.'

'Is that when he built that huge villa for her? The one that was sold? I'd have liked to have gone back to stay there.'

'You mean you remember it?'

'Not really. We were there before the war. I was very young.'

Doly gets the fire tongs and places more wood on the fire. It spits and crackles. She throws on a couple of pine cones. They sizzle and hiss, spread an agreeable smell of pine.

Nina laps up the stories of family history, anecdotes of long-dead ancestors, and Doly's own childhood. Her eagerness to be told more, her interest in every tale, stirs Doly into mellower mood. She finally feels a tenuous affinity with the girl sitting across from her in the fireplace alcove.

It doesn't last. Doly encourages Nina to say a few words of her own. She responds with tales of Gabby's brilliance, Gabby's worth.

'Gabby is wonderfully resourceful, you know.'

'You call her Gabby? Not Mutti?'

'Kamilla does. Gemma and I are beyond that. Thought of calling her General Smuts...' Nina looks over at Doly lighting yet another cigarette. 'After the South African general, you know.'

'Of course I know.' Does the girl think she's a nitwit because she lives in the country? 'Really? Why?'

'Well, we think she's quite like him. In spite of all his faults.' Nina pokes the fire, exploding smuts. 'He fought against Germany during the first world war and became a field marshal under Winston Churchill. Gabby fought her way through both World Wars.' A sudden grin. 'Not with guns, of course.'

Doly ignores the hectoring tone. 'You think Gabby is like a general? Because she tells everyone what to do?'

'She's able to take charge in tricky situations. Just like Smuts. He's pretty clued up. Inaugurated the British Commonwealth.'

Bloody insufferable. 'I do listen to the Home Service, Nina. Every night.' Does the girl actually idolise Gabby?

'We decided that was too much of a good thing. But she's brilliant at getting the best out of any situation, actually.'

'I do know Gabby quite well. She's my sister.'

'Haven't seen that much of each other though, have you?'

Doly's cigarette glows red.

'Just one example comes to mind. One day she finally got some money from somewhere abroad — it's been very difficult with all the problems about Korea and all that — and someone who'd come to see her tried to snatch it out of her hand. You know what she did?'

'I'm sure you'll tell me.'

'Popped it into a priceless Ming vase belonging to the tenants. With a very narrow neck.'

A large smoke ring floats above their heads. 'So that person didn't dare break it.'

'Exactly. She had it all worked out in no time.'

'Must have been difficult to get it out again.'

'Gemma borrowed some implement the workmen had.' Nina blinks, squares her shoulders. 'Vienna is in a terrible state. With the Four-Power Occupation and all. And there's very little food...'

'I do read *The Times* every day.'

'Reading what some journalist chooses to write is one thing. Living through it is quite another.'

Tendentious pronouncements leave Doly incensed, furious, but unable to protest too much. The girl is young and inexperienced, merely repeating a hodgepodge of ideas filched from home, clearly not one of them her own. Most of them, no doubt, Gabby's latest shoddy little scoops.

Above all Doly is irritated by the girl's overbearing manner, as if she were talking to a slightly feeble-minded child. All this uncoordinated effrontery upsets.

After Nina has gone to bed Doly digs out all her old diaries of 1930, when she was eighteen, Nina's age. In order to have some form of comparison. She reads avidly, finds herself at this particular age much more reserved, old-fashioned even. She skips over her many relationships since Nina hasn't mentioned a single one. It's clear to Doly that she will never be of any real use to Nina. Can they really be mother and daughter?

The next day, as Nina prattles on, Doly is reminded of the many unpleasantnesses her own memories of Gabby or Bosch bring to mind, how repulsive she always found them both.

'Gabby may not have any money now, but she's brilliant at getting deals.' Nina downs more biscuits, leaving a single one. 'Look at the way she got those old Habsburgs to pay rent.'

She should let it rest, just be gracious. Like the real her. But Doly's provoked, feels bound, if at all possible, to straighten out some of the kinks in the girl's character. In the mercifully short time left to them.

'English schools are outstanding at conveying the right attitudes to life to their students,' she begins. 'I learned that from Erksine's relationship with his boys. We have a tradition of good manners in this country, with an emphasis on courtesy.' She blows several smoke rings towards Nina. 'And keeping one's achievements to oneself.'

'You think that's different in Austria?'

'Well, we dislike prigs and grabbers. We don't approve of blowing our own trumpet.' She looks at Nina, watching her through veiled eyes. 'What we do go in for are standards of discipline and quality second to none.'

'You're talking about public school boys, I take it. Sent out to rule the Empire. You do know all that's over, don't you? America's taken on the lead position. That's why I want to live there. That's the place to make something of one's life.'

'You're saying Great Britain is no longer of any account?'

'Not just Britain. The whole of Europe. The war has changed the seats of power. And I intend to be on the winning side. I wouldn't mind if I never set foot in Europe again.'

Doly shrugs her shoulders. As if her words of wisdom could ever be anything but scraps for Nina to take with her to be churned into scum. 'So we won't be seeing much of each other, then.'

'Of course, I'll try to come over for holidays to see my mother and Kammy. Most of the liners dock in Southampton, so I hope to call on you every now and again.'

Doly has the feeling that Nina is trying hard, wants to rise above it all — but with the dice spectacularly loaded against her.

CHAPTER 16

Vienna, Summer 1951

'Welcome to Bösendorferstrasse, Bosch!'

A shrunk, emaciated man uses a stick to climb the two stories of circular marble to the two-room apartment Gabby has managed to find. By tramping Inner City streets all day for a week. It's in the centre of Vienna. At least she can forget the half-hour trek to the tram stop from the Neuwaldegg villa, the tedious forty minute jolting on wooden benches.

Bosch gathers breath for speech after several minutes' wheezing. 'This looks very cosy. You've always been good at that.'

Ignoring illness is one of Gabby's stronger traits. A tour de force which resulted in her children suffering from few childhood diseases, and those they did succumb to diagnosed by their schools. And, so far, an assured state of health for her and Bosch.

Lieselotte looked grave when told of Bosch's symptoms. Instead of a prognosis she insisted on keeping Kamilla away from other children and testing her and Gabby for possible TB. But found nothing. A concerned face gave away no more than Bosch had already written. At his stage damage already done to the lungs could not be reversed. He would be better off not smoking.

Bosch settles into the only easy chair after the hazards of the stairs. The effort of extracting the cigarette packet exhausts him. Gabby strikes a match into flame.

'The doctors think smoking might aggravate your problems, Bosch.'

'Quacks, all of them.' He takes several deep, clearly satisfying draws. No coughing, no rasping. 'Where's Kamilla?'

'Playing with the child in the next apartment.'

The right leg over the left is still. The hand holding the cigarette, the lungs inhaling smoke and expanding the ribcage, move in an unaccustomed dance of unison. 'I'd like her home. She can play here. I'll look after her.' Cough, cough. The truce doesn't last, the lungs assert their displeasure. A glow as he draws on the cigarette. Menacing silence.

Lieselotte had to be pressed about life expectancy. She finally agreed that ten more years was not unreasonable if the Swiss doctors diagnosed the stage of the disease correctly. She urged Gabby to go for a second opinion as soon as possible.

Lengthy discussions with the Austrian civil service leave Gabby exhausted with vague promises. Reinforcements in the form of a polite Hans Weiss and a belligerent János Czezina convince suave officials to reimburse Bosch for medical treatment.

'Go to the Herr Primarius, the top consultant. He's the best man in Vienna, practises at the Allgemeines Krankenhaus. No point in wasting your time on underlings.' Hans Weiss, Sobranie in a holder very similar to Bosch's pre-war one, pronounces in similar vein. The handsome face nods autocratically.

The specialist sees Bosch within a week. Takes sputum samples, listens to heart and lungs, looks grave. Motions Gabby into his office while Bosch is left to dress.

'I'm afraid your husband's is an advanced case.' He sits across a large desk, hands steepled. 'One lung is almost totally immobilised. In such cases, where adhesions have formed between the lung and the chest wall, we cannot produce a complete pneumothorax by introducing air into the pleural cavity. In earlier cases we allow the cavity to collapse the lung towards its root and so allow healing to take place in and around the cavities. In your husband's case we have to take more drastic action.'

'You mean an operation?'

He frowns displeasure at the interruption. 'What I would like to suggest is that we remove several ribs and so allow the cavities to close. This procedure often gives excellent results in the right type of case. We could even remove the affected lung and make him much more comfortable.'

'And then he'll be cured?'

'My dear lady! I am not God. Your husband is in the later stages of a serious disease. We can hope to arrest it, and to ease his breathing.'

Gabby is stunned into silence. She foresaw a gradual, but certain, improvement with miracle pills. Bosch relaxing in their living room, Kamilla playing at his feet. Good food, amiable friends who bring wine and stimulating conversation.

The consultant's thumbs press into his neck as his fingers cover lips and reach to his nostrils, hiding reactions. Breath is exploded. The knight of the knife. 'You weren't given any indication of the gravity of your husband's illness?'

'No.' Gabby's whisper disappears in a gulp. 'I was told he'd recover with good food, good nursing, not too much work.'

'By a doctor?'

'A Swiss specialist in a TB clinic.'

'A small resort, no doubt. I could schedule him for tomorrow morning, Frau Bosch. Best not to dwell too long on what has to be done. Would you like me to talk to your husband, or would you prefer to speak to him yourself?'

'It could be much worse,' Bosch maintains between puffs, relaxing in the hospital room before getting dressed. 'I certainly can't go on like this. I can hardly breathe.' Brown eyes relax into a serene, childlike trust. Smoothing out wrinkles, bringing some colour back into sallow cheeks. 'Obviously the Viennese doctors know what they're talking about.'

Did she underdo it? Gabby's halting, deliberately vague, medical references interspersed with pep talk were dismissed with an irritable wave and a demand for the bottom line. She expected resistance and finds uncharacteristic acquiescence.

'The Primarius suggests tomorrow morning, Bosch. It will save us the trouble of going home and coming back again. He's willing to find you a bed right away.'

'Good heavens, woman! Do I have to take responsibility for everything? Of course tell him to schedule it right away. This afternoon if he prefers.'

The effort ends in a bout of coughing serious enough to attract a nurse. Gabby fetches the agreement form from the Sister in charge. She waits at the bedside.

'Hallo! One thing.' Bosch leans back against a fortress of pillows. 'I want a priest. Now.' He notices the rounding brightness in Gabby's eyes. 'A precaution. One can never tell with a major operation.'

Gabby's mind lurches, unbidden, into a future scene. She sees Bosch sitting regally upright in a black car: Maria not Minerva. She is the driver, he the passenger. She drives at a sedate pace to Nussdorf. To the Heurigen, or to the Bosch family grave in the Friedhof — cemetery — there? Sharp stabs of grief, steely barbs of fear tighten her chest.

'I'll find the chaplain.' Her voice so low she wonders he's heard it.

A tall brown-garbed monk with a soothing voice walks beside Gabby. Gentle eyes smile reassuringly as she gabbles the circumstances of her husband's health. And his excommunication.

'There will be more joy in heaven over one sinner who repents than over ninety-nine just persons who need no repentance,' the gentle monk reminds her. 'This is God's way of calling your husband back to him, perhaps.'

A momentary anger at such a cruel God is replaced by the wish for practicalities. 'But if he comes through the operation, Hochwürden. How can he make a firm purpose of amendment and go back on it?'

'As long as you live as brother and sister, my daughter, the Church will welcome your husband back to the sacraments.'

Father Riesenburger's words come back to her. Defrocked now, but at the time sitting astride a motor bike he, as an enemy alien in England, was no longer allowed to ride. In wartime Lingfield. So many years ago. That was the time he told her that as long as they refrained from sexual union she and Bosch could live together, blameless in the eyes of the Church. The sacraments would be available.

Now the yielding of sexual relations to abstinence is hardly a problem.

She and Bosch haven't slept together for months. Years. Hardly at all since Kamilla's birth. Perhaps this is God's way of acknowledging the Christianity of their marriage. Chaste, like monks or nuns — or priests who have not been defrocked.

Gabby waits outside. With a certain trepidation. The monk does not take long — a mere twenty minutes to bring the lost sheep back into the fold.

'Did he tell you that you need not stay excommunicated, even after the operation? All we have to do is abstain from sexual relations.'

Bosch cackles into a cough. 'Können vor lachen, meine Liebe,' he wheezes out. 'You have to be able to perform before you're laughing, my sweet.'

When Gabby looks at Bosch again long teeth are bared in a full-bellied joyful laugh she hasn't heard for months. It turns into a cough, his eyes close. She tiptoes out.

'Gnädige Frau!' The consultant strides across the waiting room to Gabby the next day.

She's sitting rigid in an upright chair. Grasping the armrests. She stares at the surgeon, her instincts already tuned in to what he is about to say. She makes as if to get up.

'Please stay seated, gnä' Frau. The news is not good.'

'The operation did not go as well as planned?'

He sits down next to her, takes her hand. 'I'm afraid when we opened him up we had a terrible shock. Not TB at all, you see.'

'Not TB? Isn't that good news?'

'No.' He swallows, shakes her hands up and down. 'We found one lung riddled with cancer, gnä' Frau. The other is already badly affected. There was absolutely nothing for us to do but sew him up again.'

Tant' Christin' had cancer. How could the doctors have confused two such completely different diseases? 'How can it be cancer if the French doctor...?'

'Lung cancer, I'm afraid. A disease which is becoming more and more common. We never used to see so much of it.'

'But the Swiss specialists confirmed TB!'

He pats her hand between his own. 'They weren't expecting cancer. TB is by far the more common diagnosis. Even if they'd spotted it, it would already have been too late. I am so sorry, gnädige Frau. Your husband is terminally ill. He has at most six months to live.'

She tears her hand away, walks over to the window, stares out at churches which held such promise yesterday. 'But Herr Primarius! Yesterday you yourself said that several years was not out of the question!'

'Because I, like the other doctors, saw evidence of TB. I apologise for my mistake. From a practical point of view it makes no difference.'

Bosch was fifty in February. 'There's no hope at all?'

'None.' His hands are clasped behind his back. 'One thing I find hard to understand. The presenting symptoms of advanced cancer invariably include a dramatic change in temperament. Didn't either of you notice anything? Hasn't he become terribly short-tempered, even angry?'

Hindsight is easy. She now understands the change from witty sarcasm to physical abuse. She'd blamed him when she knew he wasn't a violent man, had always decried physical force used by men on women. Was she at fault for being so obtuse? 'I put it down to the stresses of the new job,' she murmurs. 'We had so many money problems.'

'Character changes are the most telling clues we have.' Vienna's top surgeon spreads helpless hands. 'Until we progress a little more. We're seeing so many cases of lung cancer suddenly. It's almost like an epidemic.' He takes a notebook out of his pocket. 'These are my own statistics, which I have collected over five years. We now find that there is some reason to suspect a correlation between smoking and lung cancer. Your husband is a heavy smoker.'

'You're saying he should stop?'

'Irrelevant at this stage. It's simply an explanation.'

Können vor lachen — you have to be able to act before you can laugh. The trusting smile, the optimistic eyes. Expectation of life. 'Does he know the prognosis?'

'He isn't round from the anaesthetic yet.'

'I don't want you to kill all hope. I'll see to it.'

The surgeon nods his way out. 'If he asks me a direct question, I will give him a direct answer. Otherwise I'll leave it up to you.'

'Well, Bosch. You're looking much better.' When a lie is a kindness does it count as a sin? Venial or mortal?

The wages of sin are a smile. Wan, slight, but nowhere near the bared-tooth snarl of Paris. 'I feel much better. Thank God all that's behind us.'

Wrinkled sallow skin has become chrome yellow which hangs in small folds from the shrunken pigmy on the bed. 'The hospital says you can leave any time you feel up to it.'

Small yellow claws insert a cigarette in the holder. 'They must think I'm doing very well. My clothes are in that cupboard. If you could get them out for me.'

The underlying threat of vomit inches up Gabby's throat. Willpower subdues it. 'I haven't prepared anything...'

'What on earth are you fussing about? I'm cured now. Just a bit of bed rest and I'll be fine.'

The motion to fling back bedding turns one tiny fold. 'I'll ask the nurse to help you dress, Bosch. I'll find a cab.' She escapes into the corridor, turns back. 'Kamilla is longing to see you.'

The young war widow upstairs lets Kamilla play with her own little girl. Gabby leans on Czezina, on Weiss, on Bosch's beloved friend Egi. Bosch ignored the forms which would have provided a pension. There is no life insurance, nothing in the bank. His worldly goods are two new suits and the shirts he bought for Paris. Schottengymnasium's old boy network is his biggest asset.

The hospital provides an ambulance. Two burly men balance Bosch on a stretcher, shoulder him up the winding marble stairs. The Weisses have supplied a bed for the living room.

'The Primarius agreed there need be no restrictions on me whatsoever,' Bosch bubbles. 'Move the bed over there,' he directs silent stretcher-bearers. A shaking finger rather than a sweeping arm. 'I'll get back to Ludwig. Let him know I'll be back in the saddle in about three months. That doctor knows his job, and he was quite emphatic. Three to six months.'

Gabby pours two glasses of schnapps from the bottle Hans Weiss brought over. 'Your health, Bosch!'

'I feel so much better. Anyway, we can't waste time like this. I need more suits. Ring up that tailor. He can come round, bring some samples with him.'

A fit of coughing sends showers of phlegm over clean sheets. Polka-dotted with blood. Gabby's shaking hands dab an inadequate handkerchief. Better used to wipe the bead-spotted forehead. 'I'll ring him right away.'

'These pillows are too high.' Gabby removes one of the pillows borrowed from her bed. 'Has Hans done his stuff?'

'You mean your cousin?'

'How many people do you know well enough to call by their Christian name, and how many of them are called Hans?'

The acid tones of the real Bosch. Could the Viennese surgeon be wrong? Being Austrian doesn't guarantee omnipotence. Bosch has changed in the short time since his operation. A terrible burden discarded, an assured expectation of continuing life.

'Your cousin has been most kind.' He's advanced hefty sums of money. There was nowhere else for her to turn. 'He seems very fond of you.'

'I keep telling you.' He pushes the schnapps away, gasps for water. 'It's you he admires. And he has a soft spot for Kamilla.'

Is Hans Weiss Bosch's idea of an inheritance? Have they discussed that he will help her raise Kamilla? Pay for her schooling the way Doly's brother-in-law has taken over Erskine's responsibilities? Parallel lives again. Is fate inherited, or is it the consequence of the Dohlen inheritance, that pesky gene?

'He's convinced she's musical. He plays the piano for her while she sings her nursery rhymes. They both enjoy it.'

Bosch's hair has receded into a marked widow's peak which is unlikely to foreshadow his future. Fine hair but it still stands, Struwwelpeter-like, around gaunt eyes. 'She has a sweet voice. Like her grandmother Kamilla. We're all musical.'

Gabby's interest in music is confined to military marches. But she has a good ear. The tinkling of false notes while Hans attempted simple ditties from nursery rhymes used in his own nursery days jarred an irritation Gabby found hard to control. But Kamilla, unlike Greti Weiss, is not a severe critic of his playing skills. Neither of them noticed Gabby leaving the apartment.

'When are you going to ring that tailor? The phone's out of my reach.'

Not before he demanded that the bed be moved.

'Herr Glauber? It's Frau Bosch here. My husband is back from hospital. He'll be up and around shortly. When would it be convenient for you to come and measure him for two new suits? And bring some samples of material, if you would.'

Bosch sits up in his throne-bed issuing contradictory orders. Though his attendants are reduced to a single one. Gabby is out, Trautl in the kitchen.

Kamilla plays beside his bed. A shoe box is filled with white table napkins. On it is laid a small doll. Covered with more napkins. Occasionally she sits the doll up.

The child, normally voluble, mumbles to the doll she's never played with before. Bosch's skinny hand hangs down beside the bed. She fills his holder with a new cigarette, flames the lighter for him.

'You're a good girl, Kammy.'

Gabby comes in to read the papers. Austrian ones, and the occasional *New York Herald Tribune*. That's always a day late.

Bosch nods an understanding head, makes biting remarks as apt as any in his fitter days.

'When is Gemma coming?' He's always liked her, pronounced her a Botticelli Madonna to convince her she's good looking.

'She's just finished her Finals. She's hitchhiking to Vienna with a friend, so she can't give a date. She'll arrive next week, perhaps.'

Nina is already in the States, enrolled at Barnard College. Gabby helped her pack with tears falling on threadbare clothes. Without trying to hold her back. Parting from Nina was a real blow. She'd hardly had time to say a proper goodbye to her. Doing without the allowance Rolf always sent so promptly is another trial, particularly now.

She puzzles Czezina by insisting on a meeting to discuss the villa tenants. Who have renovated and paid their rent on time. She does not tell him Bosch's prognosis. She does try to find out about any possible help from the government while Bosch 'recovers'.

She doesn't tell anyone about the cancer. Not even Egi. But she does encourage all Bosch's friends to visit him. Which they do. Dutifully, gladly, amiably. Encouraging his hopes. Pouring out homage in words. in words .and bringing unsuitable presents. Flowers instead of alcohol, books instead of protein.

Gabby is in the kitchen talking to Trautl, trying to magic tasty morsels out of brown bread and vegetables. There's barely enough money to buy food. Allowing for cigarettes, constant laundry, schnapps. Gabby arranges for Bosch to have separate meals — during which she keeps him company — using the excuse that Kamilla needs to sit at the kitchen table to learn table manners. Kitchen meals are bread and milk. Gabby buys meat for Bosch which he can hardly swallow.

'What is there today, Trautl?'

'Mutti! Muttiii!!' she hears Kamilla scream. Running along the corridor to the kitchen. 'Der Bogey stirbt — Bogey is dying!' She's never called him Daddy. Bosch has taught her to call him by Humphrey Bogart's affectionate nickname, positive he's just like the actor he so much admires.

A look of utter astonishment on his face. Surrounded by blood. More pouring from his mouth.

Haemorrhaging. The consultant warned Gabby that this could happen. But so soon? He's only been home for two weeks…

'What a pity. And I thought I was getting better.' A croak. He topples forward. Gabby gently puts her hands on his shrunken shoulders, pushes him back against the pillows.

Staring eyes, dropped mouth. No breath. A cigarette burning in his hand

THE BLACK COAT

THE BLACK COAT

A hard-working family man, not exactly over-burdened with worldly goods but evidently no pauper, laboured hard for many years to gain a good standing in his community. And, though he could never be mistaken for a rich man, it was clear he was not on the breadline. To make absolutely certain that no one was in any doubt he ordered a tailor to make him a fine black coat. He wore it every Sunday to Mass so that his fellow parishioners could admire it, and see that he was a man of substance.

As bad luck would have it the man sickened, of a serious illness. It soon became clear to him that he would never recover. Instead of becoming resentful he set his affairs in order, distributing his goods fairly among his heirs and even arranged his own funeral. There was just one thing he wanted for himself.

'Bury me in my black coat,' he said to his wife. 'Promise me that you will.'

And his wife agreed, assuring her dying husband that she would carry out his last wish on earth.

As soon as the worthy man died his widow had second thoughts. The good woman felt it would be a crying shame to bury the beautiful black coat along with a corpse. Why give the worms a feast when such good material could be put to so much better use? She convinced herself that that would be a crime against God Himself.

The widow buried her late husband in his shift, and left the coat hanging in his special cupboard. But she soon had cause to rue her miserliness because her husband couldn't rest in his grave. If she had thought to place a bag of sand in the coffin, things might have turned out all right, because then he would have been obliged to count the grains, one by one, and he might not have bothered the living. As it was, he found no peace in his grave.

At first the little scrabbling noises coming from the old bedroom were hardly noticeable, but when they went on night after night the widow knew something had to be done. She left the door to the room open and kept watch.

She did not have long to wait. Horrified, she watched her husband's ghostly figure float over to the cupboard and try to turn the key. He obviously hoped to open the door and put on his beloved black coat. As soon as the ghost noticed he was being watched, he disappeared.

But he returned time and again, and each time he tried to open the cupboard door and collect his coat. But he could never manage it. Eventually, wanting her peace, the widow took the black coat out to the graveyard, dug a hole in her husband's grave, and stuffed the coat into it.

Her husband's ghost never bothered his widow again.

CHAPTER 17

Vienna, Summer 1951

Requiescat in Pace. The God of mercy gave Bosch the grace to repent, offered him the promise of eternal life. But the dark side of keeping the truth from him is that he might have gone back on his reconciliation with the Almighty. Put it on hold, so to speak. Extreme unction: Gabby is desperate to find a priest to administer the final rites.

She rushes out of the apartment with no idea where the nearest church might be. The Weisses always go to the Annakirche, and she and Bosch often joined them. That's ten to fifteen minutes walk away, but she wants something nearer. Hans told her there are at least twenty-five churches within the Inner City, so there has to be one close to their Bösendorferstrasse flat. She stumbles into the confusion of narrow streets, crashes into the nearest church. A cassocked figure is arranging hymn books. Her eyes blink tears at the Blessed Sacrament hanging overhead, winking red.

'Can you come with me, Hochwürden? Right away? My husband has just died.'

An unresponsive face turns towards her. 'Where do you live?' The cassock's buttons form a phalanx of clergy from throat to hem. Christian soldiers below an unChristian face.

'Just round the corner, Hochwürden. If you could hurry — '

'The actual address, gnädige Frau?' Hymn books are slapped together into neat piles.

'Twenty minutes after death will ensure absolution,' she hears Father Riesenburger say above the roaring of his motorbike, in wartime Lingfield. 'In the case of sudden or unexpected death a priest should always be called. Absolution and Extreme Unction can be given conditionally for some time after apparent death because a person may continue to live two or three hours after death seems to have taken place. This is particularly pertinent if death is sudden. In that case Extreme Unction will avail the deceased's soul. As you can imagine, this ruling is especially important in wartime.'

Does what a defrocked priest told her years ago, in wartime England, count? He wasn't defrocked at the time. Indeed, he was the bishop's favourite. And it was Riesenburger who gave her the first instructions in the faith, Riesenburger who held out salvation.

'Bösendorferstrasse 24,' she gulps, already heading towards the door to lead him to Bosch.

'Then I can't help you.' Black back turned, cassock folds sweeping the floor. 'That's outside my parish.'

Forgive me, God, for not making him aware that he was dying. It was my sin, not his! 'But, Hochwürden, he needs the last rites!' The sharp inflections of High German ring out Lutheran bewilderment.

An almost-empty church re-echoes hollow words. Scattered faithful stare at a dishevelled, blood-stained woman shouting in a holy place. They mumble disapproval in an increasing crescendo.

Gabby runs out, home, sprints up the stairs. The most devout Catholics she knows are Bosch's cousins Hans and Greti Weiss. She's out of breath when Greti answers.

'Hans isn't at home, Gabriele. It is a weekday.'

Gabby's tearful voice pours into the telephone receiver. 'I don't know what to do, perhaps if you could ring your parish priest and asks him to come over — '

'It is always questionable whether a soul in mortal sin can be absolved after his death.'

Gabby sinks to the floor, the receiver in her lap. The rasping voice floats up to her. A lengthy treaty on the relative merits of canon and doctrinal law, on the Treaty of Worms, on the attitude of the present pope.

'Yes, of course.' Gabby puts the phone down, looks across at the unmoving figure with the wide-open eyes, dials Czezina. An atheist.

'Priests are men like all others,' his soothing, gentle voice. 'I will be with you within minutes. Don't worry about a thing.'

The doorbell shatters the stillness of the room fifteen minutes later. Gabby walks down the stairs and opens the door to Czezina with a priest in tow. An exquisitely embroidered white alb over a black cassock, hands reverently bearing a small case.

Gabby watches her dead husband anointed with holy oil blessed by the bishop, sees the oil daubed on the organs of the five external senses: the eyes, the ears, the nostrils, the lips, the hands as well as the feet. She knows that in some countries a man's loins are also anointed, is relieved to see this priest leaving out that detail.

The balm of forgiven sin sweeps over Gabby. Purgatory, perhaps. Surely not hell. Bosch wasn't a wicked man. Difficult, tiresome, overbearing. An inability to come to terms with the practicalities of post-war Austria. A dinosaur of the Vienna of the Habsburgs. But hardly a candidate for everlasting damnation.

The voice which condemned Nazi doctrine right at the start is silent. The passionate dislike for Dorinda, the impatience with Nina, his aversion for his sister Lily Bergher, making fun of his cousins Hans and Greti Weiss — all gone from that tiny lifeless body. But he lives on. In Gabby's metamorphosis from humdrum housewife to political agitator, in Gemma's conversion to Catholicism, in Kamilla, the little girl he adored.

'Requiescat in pace. In nomine Patris et Filii et Spiritus Sancti.'

'Amen.' János Czezina puts a soft hand on her upper arm and leads Gabby to a chair. 'Perhaps you should sit down, gnä' Frau. I will ask Trautl to make some coffee.'

God is good. A Father for ever. Nothing is sure in this world, but redemption is promised for the next. A desire to be part of the Church overwhelms Gabby.

'What do I do to become a Catholic?' she asks the priest putting away oil, vessels, stola. She learned the Catechism from Father Riesenburger so long, long ago. But she couldn't become a Catholic then, not without renouncing her marriage to Bosch. No barriers now.

The flick of surprise in the man's eyes is replaced by a smile. 'You take instruction. I can arrange for that in your own parish. Father Joachim is a saintly man. That's always the best from a practical point of view.'

Gabby shuts the door behind the priest and turns to face Czezina. 'That was very good of you. I wouldn't have wanted him to be deprived of the last rites. He was a devout Catholic, you know. In his own way.'

Czezina's head nods, but his eyes flicker. 'Very laudable. Now, please, Frau Bosch. Do not be offended. This last month must have been appalling. You have a small child to bring up, your resources are very circumscribed. I would like to offer my services. As a friend.'

Gabby peers at the little lawyer in a haze of gratitude and the strong desire to be on her own. 'Bosch always thought of you as a colleague, Herr Doktor. From Schottengymnasium days.'

'A great honour.' His face is moist with an oily sheen Gabby has never come across before. Mediterranean or — Semitic? Could he have survived the Nazis' final solution? 'You need legal help.'

'You mean because Bosch died here, and not in hospital?' Is that some sort of crime?

'To apply for a pension from the State.' The discreet cough which is his trademark. 'Unfortunately Bosch — your late husband — didn't make any provision for you or little Kamilla. There's no life insurance, nothing. You need help to get you back on course.'

'I'm overwhelmed, Herr Doktor.' He looks expectant. A doggy look she finds unnerving. 'And grateful, needless to say.'

'Quite unnecessary. I'll see to the arrangements, then. Herr Doktor Weiss — you wish me to get in touch with him?'

'Wonderful.' She can't face another encounter with Greti. 'Perhaps you'd be kind enough to ask him to contact Bosch's sister and her husband.'

'The Berghers. Of course. I know Markus well from Schotten' days.'

Is there anyone in Vienna who didn't go to that school? She remembers that Lothar Egartner — the beloved Egi — went to a State school. 'I've only met Lily once. When we came back from England in 1947. Bosch introduced Kamilla and me to his sister and her husband. And, of course, to Franz and Greti Weiss, the whole extent of his family.' Four years ago. A historic meeting at the Weisses' apartment. Greti's predatory looks, Hans's flittering stares. Two old maids imprisoned in a mausoleum, Bosch described them. Two more old maids imprisoned by Markus Bergher's conversion to Catholicism, he summed up the Berghers. 'You know they're over from Australia at the moment?'

'Indeed. His Jewish descent entitles him to claim restitution of his pre-war possessions. The early stages are already in train.'

'You're handling their case?' Bosch's irritation with his sister's good fortune — allowed to claim her share of their inheritance because her worldly goods were deemed to be her husband's — was alleviated by the bad feeling between the Berghers and Czezina.

'Frau Bergher felt it better to engage a stranger. A very able colleague. All their affairs should be settled within the year.' He stands, fastens a plastic cover over his hat against inclement summer rain. An odd Austrian custom Gabby normally finds hilarious but now only weird. 'The Herr Doktor has accepted a teaching post in Basle. I'm sure they'll both wish to attend the funeral and give you their support.'

Greti Weiss and Mustapha III arrive the next morning. Hidden behind an enormous bouquet of dahlias. The first hint of autumn after the safe, hygienic removal of Bosch's body to a funeral parlour. Against Gabby's ignored protestations. Which have delayed the departure of the funeral director. But not the constant reference to the 'dear departed'. As though death deprives a man of his name.

The constant bowing and kissing of hands at the slightest provocation is, at Greti's arrival, switched from Gabby to her. Though not to the dog.

'Let me assure the Herrschaften that they are welcome to visit our beautiful Chapel of Rest at any time.' A lugubrious, pestering man whose references to the sorely-missed-dear-departed-gracious-gentleman-a-great-loss-such-a-tragedy Gabby feels an unseemly urge to scream at.

Perhaps sensing unbearable sorrow he bows again. A promising grasp of his top hat. Bringing back memories of another death, another staircase, in a small North German village bordering the Elbe Estuary. Wooden, not marble, treads. High ones, which sorrowing villagers mounted in silent homage. For an old man in his coffin, lying in the huge villa he had built for his beloved wife who, though so much younger than he was, predeceased him. Emil Julius Dohlen Senior lay silent, inert, dressed in his tuxedo and, as a child of almost ten, Gabby put the book of Byron verses her father so adored under his dead hands.

'You have been told about the Bosch family crypt?'

Endless reassurances that a Requiem Mass has been arranged in the Nussdorf church where Bosch was baptised. No detail is spared. Down to the officiating priest's Christian name. Prompting an irreverent thought that at least it promises the possibility that he's a Christian.

'Thank you, Herr Schurrenfahrer. You will address all queries and all correspondence to my brother.' Greti sweeps man and hat out of Gabby's door. 'Now then, Gabriele. My brother and I are very conscious of your difficult position. We would like to offer to take on the funeral expenses.'

She hasn't even thought about those. 'That's very good of you both.'

A sharp examination of the apartment Greti has not visited before. The only relative not among Bosch's visitors. 'The wake will be held in our apartment.'

'Actually I thought...'

'You can't be expected to cope. If you need extra — er — help...' The dog begins to chew a blood-stained pillow. 'Mustapha!' Greti smacks his head. 'Until Czezina can arrange your pension for you.'

Gabby can't trust her voice. Is she a piece of furniture Bosch left behind?

'I'll send Hans round to sort all that out.'

Clearly Hans Weiss and János Czezina are under Greti's orders. What is a little surprising is that part of the schedule includes solo visits by these worthy gentlemen.

'And what are your plans, Gabriele? After the funeral, I mean.' Greti's gimlet eyes flash at her.

The purpose of the visit at long last. She's worried that Kamilla might be taken away from Vienna? That feels a little far-fetched. Gabby hasn't the energy, the will, to think it through. She doesn't really care. More worried about where Kamilla's next meal is coming from than about the long-term future.

What she needs is a large bottle of schnapps. Even Czezina only brought flowers. What's she to do with them all? The place already looks like a funeral parlour. Without the corpse.

'I thought I would take Kamilla up to Schwanenbruch. It will give us both the rest and quiet we need for our grief.'

The clear intention of a smile on Greti's face misfires. Possibly through atrophied cheek muscles. 'I'm so glad you're being sensible. Go back to your roots. An excellent idea. No point in staying in Vienna.' She clicks her tongue at the poodle which ignores her. She grabs his neckband to snap the lead in, jerks him towards the door. 'Let me know if there's anything else we can do. Lily and Markus will be with us tomorrow night. We'll see you in Nussdorf.'

The visit had an ulterior motive, the goal was achieved. What Gabby hasn't been able to figure out is what it was.

CHAPTER 18

Vienna, Summer 1951

Gabby watches the setting sun cast long shadows across Inner City streets. Two days after the funeral and she's planning her trip to Schwanenbruch. Gemma and her hitch-hiking friend, magically arriving in time for the burial, have already left for their circuitous route to North Germany. She'll meet up with them there. It's the last time she'll see Gemma before she leaves for the States.

Gemma will be leaving England reluctantly. Now a US citizen, she is only allowed to work here as a domestic or on a farm. A degree isn't a particularly helpful qualification for either of these occupations. So she'll join her father in New York, and look for a first job there. Gabby is under no illusions. It won't pay enough to help support her mother.

Gabby brushes problems away. Tonight she's longing for a bath, her bed and dreamless sleep. The clang of the doorbell startles her. Trautl is out. If she doesn't answer, her visitor might think there's been another tragedy and fetch the police.

'Hans!' It is a strange fact, but Gabby calls Bosch's cousins by their Christian names, though she's never used Bosch's once. Not only because he considered Franz too common a name. Using the surname has always seemed so much more appropriate.

Tall, nervous, stooped. With that irritating smile of adoration from afar fixed on her face. The last person she expected. The last person she wants to see.

'I don't mean… I know you must be…' He fumbles with his hat, tongue-tied and shifting awkwardly from foot to well-shod foot.

'Well, of course. Do come in.' She opens the door wide.

'…to intrude. I understand how you must feel.' He follows her into the living room. Like a little lamb. Making awkward, extraordinary allusions to Søren Kierkegaard. 'His father's death was particularly difficult for him. I thought you might like to… when you have time, of course.' He pulls a book out of his pocket, fingers it, opens it at a marked place. 'As we have discussed before, Kierkegaard, unlike Hegel, was keen on the central importance of the individual. He believed strongly in the deliberate choices each of us makes in forming our future selves. If you will permit, I would like to read you this passage.'

He tries to open the book. It drops from shaking hands. He stoops to pick it up, but instead hits his head on the edge of the table in the centre of the room.

'Do sit down, Hans. Why don't we have a glass of wine together?'

His whole body seems to tighten as he looks nervously around. 'That is extremely kind of you. I don't think I'd better. My sister is expecting me, you see. I just dropped by to give you this volume. I thought it so remarkably apt, you see…'

'Extremely thoughtful of you. I do appreciate it.' She'd have preferred a cheque to tide her over. It's what she thought Greti had intimated.

'My sister tells me you are leaving for Schwanenbruch quite soon?'

So he's the one who's worried about losing Kamilla! 'Not for several days. Czezina is looking after my affairs, but I still have to pack.'

'Well, er, of course.' A look of indecision as he stands. He bends down, picks up the book and balances it precariously on the arm of the sofa, pushes it off as he tries to move away. 'I just thought… I wondered whether… if you might do me the…' Beseeching eyes blink at Gabby, he takes a deep breath. 'I mean to say, would you perhaps have dinner with me before you leave?' He looks down at the book.

Fallen near Gabby's feet. He moves it with his shoe, bends down to pick it up again.

Taken unawares, her first instinct is to refuse. What can she do with this man for a whole evening? And why all this extraordinary attention from the Weiss siblings? First Greti calls on some mysterious errand which has never been explained. Now Hans arrives, unexpected, alone and later in the day than is considered proper. He's anxious, embarrassed, choking with unexpressed emotions. Is she being unfair? Were they closer to Bosch than she realised?

Grief must be turning her brain soft. Bosch's mocking voice dismisses grief. But refuses to elucidate. Leaving her to fend for herself.

'At your apartment?'

His Adam's apple wobbles soundlessly. 'I thought a restaurant. In town.'

With or without his sister? She dare not ask. She considers detailing how she isn't up to the harsh world as yet… Suddenly she longs for someone to comfort her, even to cosset her. She has given for years, and especially these last few weeks, without much in the way of receipt. It would be churlish to turn him down. 'How very kind of you, Hans. I'd love to.'

A rounded back retreats towards the door. 'Tomorrow, then? I'll pick you up at seven.'

The more Gabby thinks about it, the more she's intrigued. Who can she discuss it with? Both Gemma and Nina are independent of her, have left what home she could supply. International phone calls are completely beyond her means. She turns to conjecture with a Bosch who is no longer there. Feels at last the sharp pangs of grief she's suppressed with trivialities, with managing Kamilla and Trautl, with daily chores. She misses him so!

Hans arrives on the dot of seven. Flowerless, to her great relief. He towers above her. Handsome in a well-cut coat, smart shirt and tie, highly-polished leather shoes. His hair is neatly barbered. He nods like a mandarin off balance. Finally he offers her his arm.

'The *Griechenbeisl* has an excellent reputation. It's only a short walk from here.'

Bosch's puckish grin reflects from the black-framed photo on her desk. Gabby sees him wave his lordly cigarette, just a few weeks before the Anschluss and their lucky escape abroad, at the unworthy author whose book launch they were celebrating. Hears Bosch telling the young man to pocket the icon he purloined from its niche. The waiter's twisted smile — and Bosch's twisted fate. Branded a thief by the Gestapo in his absence, a judgment which, unbelievably, followed him even after the war. And was, almost certainly, responsible for his not being offered a position in Austria's post-war government.

Gabby forces enthusiasm into her voice. 'It's terribly hot and stifling in the city, Hans. Why don't we go out to a Heurigen? One with a garden. Cool new wine and a variety of cold cuts would be wonderful.' She sees him hesitate. 'I think most of them are already ausgesteckt.' The wine taverns display greenery like a flag, proclaiming to the world that the season's new wine is being served. One of the Viennese customs she adores and hasn't been able to enjoy since before the Anschluss.

'Take the tram out to Grinzing? Is that really what you'd prefer?' He stumbles on the pavement.

She steadies him. 'I think we'd both enjoy it out there.'

The strains of zither music entice Gabby towards the white clean outlines of a large Heurigen.

'None of that frightful noise, if you don't mind.' Hans can be quite decisive about some things. 'They murder music.'

It covers up the lack of conversation. Apart from zithers Hans turns down wine from the wrong grape, the smell of cooking, children playing in the street. Gabby is adamant about a garden.

The right Heuriger is finally agreed. The evening is balmy, the wine excellent, the food plentiful and well-prepared. Gabby and Hans sit at one of the wooden tables in a garden scented with roses and summer jasmine. A few other people sit nearby, not crowding them. Viennese taking their leisure. Contented gurgles, the charm of nearby church bells striking the hour, a song or two. Without accompaniment.

Gabby sips at her wine. The man across the table has not spoken for several minutes. He glances towards her, sees her looking back at him, drops his eyes. He pulls out a lighter, tries to fumble it into flame to light his Sobranie. Flick, shake. Another flick. Still no sign of fire. Or conversation.

Time crawls. A column of ants marches across the table to drink spilled alcohol. Gabby watches a cheeky sparrow alight, pick off victims one by one. The waitress's Dirndl swishes the bird away.

'You're comfortable?'

'Very comfortable, thank you, Hans.' The seventh time of asking. She welcomes the sparrow back like an old friend.

'… any idea how long you will be away?' Lamps are lit around them as twilight fades into night. The lighter flame burns bright and clear. At last.

'A few weeks I would think. Kamilla doesn't have to go back to school till the end of September.'

'But you are proposing to come back?' This time there is no hesitation, no awkwardness.

Proposing what? She looks up uncertainly. 'I'm not quite sure…'

'You'll go on living in Vienna, I take it? You're not thinking of joining your American daughters, staying abroad?' The Sobranie is lit, wafting strong odour through thick billows of smoke. Heavier than anything Bosch has been able to afford since the Anschluss.

'Move to the States? Not at all. I like Vienna, the way people live. I'm a central European, out of my depth in a country which prefers Disney to Grimm.' Strictly speaking it has turned Grimm into Disney, and made a ghastly, if dreadfully successful, mess of it.

'That's very good news.' Enormous billows. 'For those of us who think highly of you. Admire you. As I do myself.'

He's an admirer? 'You're very kind.'

'As Kierkegaard has so succinctly put it: *Though awesome in its gravity death is still the light through which great passions, both good and bad, are made apparent.*' His eyes positively blaze.

She hears him droning on, Kierkegaard this, Kierkegaard that, and has she had a chance to read the book he lent her yet?

Read philosophy, when she hardly knows where to turn for enough money to feed Kamilla? 'Well…'

'I will just point out one outstanding thought: he believes that faith itself should be considered the highest, noblest passion in a human being.'

A triumphant glare, as though he'd written the words himself.

'He makes it quite clear that no one can go further,' she hears Hans mumbling, not entirely sure. 'That is why it is always important to adhere strictly to the tenets of the Church.'

She sees Bosch's glinting eyes, his crossed leg jiggling up and down, hears his ironic voice: 'The forum internum; that's what we have to consider. Everything else is just the sinner's way to shift responsibility.'

'Bosch always felt that it's necessary to temper these tenets with common sense…' she begins.

'A man not given to tolerating fools lightly.' A slight fit of coughing, a sideways look. 'I do understand that his rather lordly statements would appeal to you, a woman of spirit, if I may say so. With style and beauty thrown in.' Several more puffs. 'As well as a superior intelligence. All the gifts rolled into one.' He smiles vaguely. 'There is just one caveat. As Hegel puts it: *When liberty is mentioned, it is incumbent on us to carefully observe whether it is not actually the assertion of private interests which is thereby designated.* I think that circumvents Bosch.'

'Well, I'm not sure…'

'And you have little Kamilla, of course. The late and only flowering of our depleted clan.'

She knew it. Kamilla is the key. With Bosch out of the way, do the Weisses feel they're entitled to an interest? Like what? Uncle and Aunt? 'I certainly think Bosch would want his child brought up in his native land.'

A trembling hand spills wine over the table, a trembling serviette wipes it up. 'It is a question of attachment, really. Those of us who feel strongly would hate to think of any lengthy separation. Even several weeks seems a long time.'

The bond between him and Kamilla is stronger than she realised. 'It's sweet of you to say so.'

He gulps wine. Mercifully down his throat. 'I don't wish to rush you in any way. You may consider me rash, indiscreet.' Another gulp. 'Perhaps you remember this passage: *To dare is to momentarily lose one's footing. But not to dare is to lose oneself.* I think that explains exactly what I mean.' He refills his glass by pouring a large stream of wine in approximately the right direction. Drowning surviving ants. 'You may consider it rather premature of me to broach a topic as delicate as this.' The stream of wine is now directed towards her glass. She moves her sleeve. 'I haven't been able to think of anything else since Bosch died. He would have encouraged me to speak.'

He's been spouting for the last ten minutes. As garrulous now as he was silent before. All those philosophical platitudes she didn't bother to listen to, instead thought about the trip to North Germany.

A wine-wet hand creeps over the table, grasps hers. 'I believe one should not hesitate where one's deepest feelings are concerned. You cannot be unaware of how I feel about you. You are my Beatrice, my

Isolde. You cannot know how highly I think of you. Have done from the first moment we met.'

Is this circuitous stuff a declaration of love? 'Well, naturally, Bosch…'

'I have become convinced that Bosch would want me to take care of you. And Kamilla, of course. I do believe he said as much to me. Not directly. But I flatter myself that I understand — understood — him very well.'

Money or matrimony?

'I hope you will allow me to be the instrument of solving your very pressing problems. Both financial and spiritual. It would be the greatest honour.'

He is a man with a wide vocabulary. He wouldn't mix up spiritual and emotional. What can he mean? She remembers his letters to Paris. Stilted, quixotic allusions couched in romantic poetry which Bosch swore proved she'd made a conquest of a man who'd never even looked at a woman before.

'I'm not sure that I quite…'

'You must, naturally, take all the time you need. I realise I should not press you so soon after your bereavement. But you are leaving us, and I feel I must open my heart up to you before you depart. Perhaps I might even hope for some indication that you would do me the greatest honour a woman can bestow upon a man.'

The hand is joined by the other one. He holds both hers in his. Her sleeve trails in spilt wine. His head approaches hers, he blinks rapidly. Is he proposing to her? What else could he mean? It would explain the excessive agitation, the visit without his sister.

A marriage proposal within two weeks of the funeral. Startling. Precipitate. Nevertheless in character. A man so shy, so indecisive, for whom, as Bosch always maintained, all life's decisions had been made by his mother and sister, would act abruptly. When he finally acts. Out of fear. Out of inexperience. Out of excitability.

'You're suggesting that we…'

'After a reasonable time.' His head nods furiously. 'The waiting will be hard to bear. But we must observe the social decencies. And of course give ourselves time to make the proper — the necessary — arrangements. Perhaps a year?'

Is he proposing out of duty? Out of a rather wooden and old-fashioned sense of chivalry, rescuing a damsel — a widow — in distress, the bereaved partner of an esteemed cousin who knew which wife to choose? 'Well, yes, I do think it will take a little time...'

'You are the most lively, most exotic, most arresting human being I have ever come across. I am longing to put everything I have at your disposal. It would be the greatest honour if you were to accept.'

Bosch was right. He's really taken with her. It explains his stares, his looking away, the mumbling, stuttered compliments, praises beyond all sense. And Bosch's sardonic grins, sly allusions. The man is actually in love with her!

'I am extremely flattered, Hans. I can't tell you how much I appreciate your — interest.'

'I may dare to hope?'

A well-off bachelor of fifty-two, longing to escape from the yoke of a spinster sister's demands, craving to get married before it's too late, showing off the prize his cousin was forced to leave behind. And acquiring a daughter whose genes are partly his.

Gabby sinks back into a sort of trance. Instead of scrimping and saving, desperately trying to make ends meet, marriage to Hans Weiss would solve so many of hers, and Kamilla's, problems.

But is that really what she wants? She hears her father's voice again: 'The hand life deals you is a given. What counts is how you play the game.' She was desperate to divorce Rolf Ferent, she feels freed by Bosch's death. Nothing but minor cards left in her hand. Still, could marrying Hans be yet another yoke? Especially as he has a maiden sister in tow?

'After, of course, the necessary arrangements have been made. *Prayer does not change the face of God*, as Kierkegaard reminds us, but it can... no, I believe he said *does*, change the person who prays.'

The emphasis on God is making her a trifle nervous, but why not encourage him? At least keep him dangling while she works out what else she could do? 'I think I understand, Hans. And I can say right away that I'm not against it.'

'So we may plan for the future? Set in train the necessary formalities?' He clicks his fingers for more wine. Just like Bosch. The waitress comes running and he points, wordlessly, at the empty carafe. 'Of course everything will have to be discussed in detail, a carefully drawn-up proposal put before the relevant authorities.'

The wine is having its effect. Gabby feels pleasantly relaxed. She's been married twice before. Whatever Hans might imagine, the authorities are not a great hindrance to the deed.

'A great many aspects will have to be gone into, discussed, laid out. But I think we can assume all will go well. Without too much loss of time or energy.'

He burbles on while Gabby tries to stop excitement making her drink too much. The idea of marrying Hans is beginning to grow on her. He is a man Bosch looked up to for his intellect. Even if his lack of worldliness was the cause of puerile merriment behind his back. Kamilla would have a father, someone willing to teach her, cherish her, a man able to provide.

'Now that the Church has decreed that a civil marriage in a Registry Office is an added necessity to the sacrament itself, you can even follow in your old traditions!'

Occasionally he actually shows a flash of humour. Raw clay Gabby can mould into scintillating company.

And so good looking.

Gabby smiles and nods as Hans talks. She picks up the occasional rambling references. Collecting the necessary papers for the legalities the authorities would need to examine, writing to Somerset House. All true, all boring, all to be seen to on her return.

'I don't expect a definite answer now, Gabriele. I don't wish to rush you in any way.'

She turns the full volume of her smile on him. 'I'm thrilled, Hans. It all feels so right, now you have pointed it out to me. I don't need time to think. Bearing everything in mind, I think marrying you is exactly what Bosch would have wished.'

They sit for another hour in the soft darkness of the garden, the smoke of the Sobranies, mellowing with wine and atmosphere. They agree not to announce their engagement until Gabby returns from Schwanenbruch. No point in antagonising the rest of the family, shocking their friends. They aren't even going to mention it to Czezina. All the 'arrangements' can wait.

PART 2

THE ROOTS OF

THE ROOTLESS

1951 – 1953

CHAPTER 1

Schwanenbruch, September 1951

Sharp marsh winds jostle with chrome yellow willow leaves to sweep in autumn. The smell of tangled seaweed blots out the reek of tobacco fumes. It chases Sobranie and Austria into salt-laden, fishy whirls which eddy fresh thoughts round Gabby's brain. Not foetid, not cramped. In the free, wide-open spaces of Land Hadeln. Which beckons with smiling Indian summer sun and gambolling clouds. Where the sailing boats glide through invisible channels in the marsh. Sailing on grass.

She can't possibly stay to bring Kamilla up in a small village in North Germany. Her father's house is no longer hers, German ways are still fighting to praise.

Gabby tramps longs walks along the dyke to lay Bosch to rest. More than twenty years of knowing 'den Bosch', thirteen years of marriage to the Bogey who shouted, begged, cajoled not to be buried in the gentle Downs of England, the craggy mountains towering over the Wolfgangsee, or the boulevards of Paris. Who asked only to defend his beloved Austria against the malign foe. In the steepled streets of Vienna.

She hears his voice, crying out in the wild wind blasting over the dyke. On stormy nights, when the weather is blustery, his cries can be heard in the shelter of Ursula's comfortable room. He rages against the windowpanes and down the old chimney. He layers the room with sooty dust.

'Don't be such a damned fool. The old fart will bore you to death, drown you in long-winded quotations from classics you've never read or ever want to read, smother you in music you have no ear for, drag you from one decrepit old church to another ancient building in ruins…'

'You're the one who set it up,' she argues along with the cold air which finds each cranny, each tiny space. 'Hans said you were the one who thought that we should marry. And now you're jealous.'

'Don't be such a scared bunny,' the bogeyman howls. And whistles shrilly down Ursula's chimney. 'Didn't I always tell you you're a witch? That you can earn your living in other ways, and make a damned good success of it?'

Can she? Is she her father's daughter? Now if she were a son… Moppel — Emil Julius Dohlen, Junior — is a son. But not exactly a chip off the old block. All the same, could she?

Vienna, September 1951

The letter to Hans announcing the date of her return to Vienna, and an invitation to a small supper, leaves the day before Gabby does. The postal services excel themselves. He's at her door on the dot of eight. Bearing flowers, a bottle of Armagnac, and a boyish grin.

Gabby greets him with fake enthusiasm. 'Hans, how delightful.' She holds the door between them. 'I've arranged a few cold cuts.'

An exaggerated bow as he removes her hand from the doorknob, brushes a fleeting kiss. 'It's wonderful to see you again. I could hardly wait for your return.'

A jiggling head instead of a jiggling knee. She leads the way to the easy chairs grouped round the coffee table. She pours sherry into waiting glasses.

He takes a sip, eyes feasting on her. 'I've been thinking it over while you were away. I know we said we'd wait a year. But why should we?

Why don't we get married sooner rather than later? You — and Kamilla, of course — need someone to look after you right away.'

Sailing on grass close to the wind. She's already spent most of the Neuwaldegg villa rent meant to last till November. Drinking her fill of schnapps, being hospitable to Schwanenbruchers she's known since childhood. Now she's returned to unpaid bills. And Kamilla's grown out of her clothes.

'You don't think people' — she sees Greti's long face bent over Mustapha, mouth twisted as she hisses the wedding date — 'would consider it, well, unseemly?'

He stands to his full height beside the mantelpiece, flicks his lighter into instant flame. 'Bosch left you without a Schilling. Czezina tells me that even if you were to get a state pension it will take considerable time to arrange. So I think it might be, well, more convenient if we pushed things forward. December, say. That should give time for everything to be seen to, don't you think?'

'Everything' presumably means arrange the wedding ceremony and the honeymoon, buy an outfit for herself and Kamilla, invite their guests. Not particularly arduous or time-consuming. A doddle compared to the complications of her life with Bosch.

'You think that will give your sister enough time to get used to the idea?' The Russian colonel who had commandeered most of their living space has departed. The Weisses' freed, enormous penthouse on top of one of their huge Viennese houses can easily be sectioned into two separate apartments. But the changes she intends to make to that tortured interior will be substantial.

The nearly-Bosch look of determination disappears. Hans sits, knees squeezed together like a vice, eyes fixed on a bald spot in the carpet. 'Perhaps a little dinner for the three of us.' Tight-pressed lips barely allow the syllables to escape.

'If you're sure…' Dare she ask if he's told his sister yet? 'Holy Moses!' her father's voice thunders in her ear. 'Ask him!'

'Sure of what?'

'Does Greti…'

'Know?' He drinks the sherry in one gulp. 'I thought we'd tell her together. As a couple.'

'Absolutely. What a good idea.' Greti was way ahead of both of them. How did she put it? 'I'm so glad you're being sensible. Going back to

your roots. An excellent idea. No point in staying in Vienna, Gabriele.'
How could she have missed what the woman was getting at as soon
as she knew Bosch was dead — and guessed what her brother had in
mind? No wonder she was delighted when Gabby mentioned her early
trip to Schwanenbruch.

Gabby pours more sherry. Hans drinks another glass.

The mulish, stubborn Bosch-look which is etched into her memory
is now once more in her present. He nods his head, smiles vacuously.
'As long as the proper arrangements are in place by December, that's
all that counts.'

THE CONSTANT BRIDE

Guta lived happily in Castle Falkenstein, her brother Count Philip's seat on the Rhine. Many suitors had tried to win her love, to ask her brother for her hand in marriage. But Guta was happy and comfortable in her brother's castle, and had no need of a husband.

It was a time of turbulence in Europe, of changing dynasties. Valiant knights left their own lands to seek followers and to win kingdoms. Magnificent tournaments were staged all over Europe to show off their valour. One of these was held in Köln, originally Colonia Agrippina under the Romans, and Cologne when it passed into French hands. It was the jewel of the Rhine and the largest German city at the beginning of the thirteenth century. Nobles from all over Europe, even as far away as England, came to compete.

Count Philip and his sister Guta were guests at the event. And Guta's eye was drawn, for some strange reason, to the young knight from England. He wore a veiled visor so she could not see his face, but he was dubbed 'the Lion Knight'. So named because his shield depicted a beautiful golden lion.

The young man acquitted himself with formidable displays of sword and horsemanship. Until eventually he was declared the winner. Guta was begged to present the laurel-wreath to him.

She took on the task, hoping to catch a glimpse of the young man's face. And she could tell that he could read her eyes as though they were an open book. For as soon as there was a chance, the young man linked his arm with Guta's, took her aside, and spent long hours in conversation with her.

Later, at the splendid feast held in the banqueting hall to celebrate the end of the tournament, the 'Lion Knight' was Guta's constant companion. He implored her to pledge him her love, and swore he would be hers. On one condition: that his name must remain a secret.

He would return in three months to claim her hand.

Guta, overcome with love, accepted the young man's offer. She waited in her brother's castle, scanning the surrounding roads from high up in the tower, hoping to catch a glimpse of the golden lion flashing on his shield.

It was a time of war. Conrad IV was a ruler of the house of Hohenstaufen, died in Italy. It was left to his son Conradin to witness the final downfall of the house of Hohenstaufen. Europe was in turmoil. Months passed. No word came from her betrothed, and Guta waited in vain. Her thoughts went from horror at his death on the battlefield to the sight of another woman in his arms.

She no longer went up to the tower. Instead she sat weeping in her sleeping chamber. She did not look out even when she heard the sound of trumpets announcing the arrival of a troop of knights. Instead, she held pearl rosary beads between her fingers and prayed for her sweetheart's safety.

There was a loud knock at her door, and her brother walked in. 'The Lion Knight has come for you, sister. He begs forgiveness for his tardiness, but it was beyond his power to change. He comes to claim your hand.'

'And who is he? What is his name?'

'He made me promise not to give away his secret. Simply to ask whether you will still honour your pledge. What is your answer, sister? Yes or No?'

Guta stood. 'I'll take him with all my heart,' she said. Her eyes are no longer sad, even her clothes are preening themselves around the happy form of their mistress. As she walked along the castle's interminable corridors with her brother he told her the knight's name. For the Lion Knight had given him permission to tell her only if she agreed to be his wife.

'He is Richard, Earl of Cornwall, son of John of England. He was elected Emperor of Germany by a majority of the College of Seven Electors.'

She was to be the bride of the new emperor. Guta held out her arms to her lover. They embraced and shortly celebrated their marriage with royal pomp and ceremony. In the triumphant castle on the Rhine which her brother renamed Gutenfels, the rock where good fortune is now the lady of the castle.

CHAPTER 2

Vienna, September 1951

Gabby buys an enormous bunch of the last of the dahlias. To hide behind when she first greets Greti. She dreads the confrontation with a woman she's depriving of her man. Unless you count the ghastly poodle.

Hans answers the entry phone he's installed, greets her formally. The ancient maid opens the apartment door into dim light swallowed up by dark furnishings. Hans kisses her hand in subdued greeting. Greti's ominous absence slows Gabby's steps towards the living room.

'Has he enjoyed his biscuit, then.' Greti is bent over Mustapha, whispering sweet nothings into his ear. She doesn't look up as Gabby walks in ahead of Hans.

'Greti! How nice to see you again.' Gabby's voice strains out of the heavy dahlias. They're her future sister-in-law's favourite flowers.

'How very good of you.' She bends closer to the dog. 'Come, Mustapha my darling. Come and see what else Mutti's got for you.' She scrabbles in the pocket of her dress, brings out a bone-shaped object.

'Let's take that smelly stuff to the kitchen, shall we?'

She grabs the flowers without looking at Gabby and heads out of the door, directing a constant stream of admonishments to the poodle unwilling to accompany her. 'Mustapha, darling. You don't want to stay all alone, without your Mutti, do you?'

Gabby sees Hans is standing by thick, dark-brown velvet curtains which obscure what light hasn't been eaten up by Biedermeier furniture. An air of condemnation, of oppression, hangs over the large overstuffed room. She's longing for a drink. No sign of one.

'Do sit down, Gabriele.'

Gabby perches on a chair three times too big for her, looks round. Immense bookcases stuffed with leather-bound volumes. Indecipherable titles peeling in old leather. Probably Latin texts. Tapestry-covered furniture of the most uncomfortable kind. Gloom and doom paintings, massive chandeliers, overcrowded vitrines. Beautiful splendid valuable antiques packed as though assembled in a warehouse.

Gabby sees how to strip out curtains, dingy carpets, stuffy coverings. How to rearrange moribund pieces to give light and space. The apartment will sparkle with light and life as soon as she's in charge. She looks forward to the transformation.

'You have some lovely pieces, Hans. And paintings.'

'My father was a collector. Particularly of books.' He opens a glass-fronted book-case, takes out a heavy tome. 'His favourites were the Romans. Tacitus, Cicero. He and I read them together.'

Gabby's speculation that they might be better than Kierkegaard is interrupted.

'Das Essen ist serviert, gnädige Frau — Dinner is served, Madam.' The maid, as dark and lumpish as the furniture, jerks her head at the dining room. 'Mahlzeit.' Gabby and Hans move slowly towards a massive table in the centre of the room. A marble-topped sideboard groaning under heavy Austrian food. Unwieldy curtains droop their funereal black. The bronze chandelier is beautiful, but half the candles are dead. They hover by uncomfortable chairs made for giants.

Greti appears and heads the table. She motions to Gabby to sit on her left. Hans takes his seat on her right.

'These Leberknödel look wonderful, Greti. Did you make them yourself?'

'Nothing to do with me. Resi's job.' The poodle is on his hind legs beside her. Not exactly dancing, but coming close. 'Here you are, my pretty one. They're your favourites, aren't they?' Pieces of liver dumpling are taken out of the soup and fed to the poodle from Greti's left hand. With which she holds the bread while she cuts it. 'So good for that lovely coat of yours.'

The sound of slurped soup. No conversation. 'And what sort of summer have you had, Greti?' Gabby narrowly avoids choking on her anxiety.

'You really want some more, don't you, darling?' Greti puts bony fingers into the soup bowl and fishes out a whole dumpling. The dog snaps hungrily.

The second course is served. Gabby chatters. About Kamilla, the North Sea, the weather. Whenever she stops, a stony silence descends. It's interrupted by intimacies directed at the dog. The woman knows about her and Hans. She's trying to pretend it isn't happening.

Gabby moves food listlessly around her plate. Nibbles. She sees Hans staring at his plate, his Adam's apple bobbing up and down. He doesn't seem able to swallow. When is he going to get round to announcing their engagement? Is he chickening out?

The maid serves coffee and Linzer Torte, clatters dishes out, withdraws. Gabby clears her throat, looks at Hans, nods.

He blinks, turns to his sister, mumbles.

'Does he want a piece of cake, then? What a little darling. Here it is.'

'Greti.'

She turns to her brother. 'Did you say something, Hans?'

'We — er — we wanted...' His voice tails off.

'We? Who's we?' Sharp and loud. He has her full attention at last.

'We, that is Gabriele and I, wanted you to be the first to know...'

'Know? Know what?' Precise staccato. 'There, there now, sweetheart. You shall have Hans's cake as well. He doesn't need it. Do you, Hans?' She grabs a slice of Torte from his plate.

'We are engaged.'

'Engaged in what?' Surly. Aggressive. Daring him to spell it out.

'Engaged to be married, Greti. Gabriele and I are going to be married.'

She's pulled the dog on to her lap. He sits, tongue lolling and grinning, hiding her face. 'What a sweetie he is, then.' Her arms are clasped around his neck. 'What a sweet, darling little Mustapha.'

'In December. We intend to be married before Christmas.'

The dog's harsh breaths are the only sound. No congratulations, no response of any kind. Not even endearments to the poodle.

Hans splutters, coughs, swallows hard. He stares at his sister with his mouth wide open. Unable, apparently, to utter another word.

Gabby feels hot and cold by turns. Should she say how she's looking forward to knowing Greti better? How...

'You are proposing to marry a divorcée?' Harsh, brittle, accusatory. Greti grabs Gabby's slice of Linzer Torte and feeds it to the dog. 'Without the consent of the Church?' The dog chews noisily.

That look of scornful pity. It's so much like Bosch's that Gabby wonders whether she's seeing a ghost. 'What are you talking about? Of course we shall be married in the Church. In the Annakirche.' A sly, superior smile. 'Gabriele is already taking instruction from our own Father Joachim.'

'Is she, indeed?' Greti's cold face is turned to Gabby, tobacco-stained teeth actually bared. 'Then she will be aware that a divorced woman cannot marry in the Church.' Her mouth twists sideways. 'If she wasn't already.' She turns to Gabby. 'I understand you and Bosch married in a Registry Office. Presumably you had your reasons.'

Gabby is too stunned to answer. What can Hans be so positive about? They've never discussed... The sombre, pedantic voice in the Heurigen garden comes back to her: *The arrangements can be sorted out by then*. Arrangements! Not a simple proposal, then. A blueprint laying down terms which include marrying in the Church, and all that that entails.

'That's neither here nor there, Greti.' Hans flicks his lighter into flame without hesitation. 'Her first marriage was never a Christian one.'

Gabby feels giddy. She and Bosch discussed her marital status from a Catholic point of view. Frequently. As well as her conversion. He always discouraged that. Because, he maintained, converts invariably go too far, become fanatics. He cited Markus Bergher as both example and proof, pronouncing him a zealot of the worst kind. Much better to leave things as they were, he said. The two of them were Catholics in spirit, and that's what matters to God.

'Actually, my marriage to Bosch was on board ship, Greti. On our way to England as we were fleeing Hitler. My first marriage was in a Registry Office. That is the point.'

The gleam of engagement in battle. 'Yes, yes. I know all that. Bosch told us. You're not dealing with some stupid ignoramus, you know. A Catholic married in a Registry Office is not necessarily married in the eyes of the Church. But any other Christian — and I understand both you and your first husband were Christians at the time — however they might be married, are deemed to have contracted a Christian marriage. Which, of course, is binding in the eyes of the Church.'

Hans rocks backwards and forwards on his chair. 'Absolutely correct. No argument. The Catholic Church insists that marriage between any two baptized Christians, as long as it is entered into with the intention to contract a true marriage, is a sacrament and therefore indissoluble. What you are not aware of is that Gabriele's first marriage was not a Christian one for two reasons. Defect of intention is the first one, to be precise. She and her first husband made a pre-nuptial agreement that it was a trial marriage.' That insufferable smirk. 'As of course you know, the three indispensable elements of marriage are permanence, exclusiveness and the couple's openness to procreation. To reserve assent to any one of these elements at the time of the marriage is a ground for nullity. In such a case the person involved is not truly intending to enter into marriage in the Church's understanding of it. Ergo, it is not a Christian marriage.'

'That will have to be proved.' Greti's animated voice. At long last in her element. An intellectual discussion, bereft of personal involvement. Both she and Hans thrive on that.

Hans interlaces fingers, moves his hands back and forth. 'In fact there would appear to be two defects of intention. One, that Gabriele married Rolf Ferent in a Registry Office so that the marriage could be readily dissolved, as accepted by both parties beforehand, and two...' the rocking intensifies 'I understand they agreed not to have children.' A defensive, nervous smile. 'The first is an intention against indissolubility — clear grounds for nullity. Furthermore, if there is a positive and deliberate intention on the part of one or both of the partners at the time of the marriage not to have children during the marriage then that is also ground for nullity.'

'They had children, Hans. Two daughters.' Her hand strays back to Mustapha.

'Well, yes, after a while, Greti. But Hans is quite right. We started out with the intention of not having children...'

'It's the intention at the time of marriage which counts.' Hans puffs smoke at the dog.

'The Church may not be so easily hoodwinked.'

'No question of that at all. Everything is in train to prove Gabriele's assertion. The papers petitioning for an annulment have gone to the Procurator Fidei already.'

Procurator what?! This is the first time Gabby can recall the phrase. Surely procurator is the old-fashioned word for prosecutor. Prosecutor of the faith? In all that twaddle about Kierkegaard, and Hegel, and free will, where did this annulment stuff come in? Another phrase at the Heurigen çbursts into her consciousness. 'So we may plan for the future? Set in train the necessary formalities?'

'I know nothing about any of that!' Greti sags down. 'And when, if one may enquire, is the wedding to be?'

Hans is still bubbling with suppressed victory. 'As soon as the protocol has been concluded. We are hoping for December. January at the latest.' He actually grins. A surprisingly puckish grin Gabby hasn't seen before. 'We can have the reception here.'

There is a wild wail. Greti is thumping the table with her fists, the dog joins in by howling in his turn. She sways backwards and forwards. 'Hans, Hans, Hans! How can you be such a stupid old fool? Have you no idea…'

Gabby, reluctantly, leans towards the hysterically distraught woman. The dog growls.

'Look, Greti. Please don't distress yourself. The last thing Hans and I want to do…'

'You snake, you strumpet, you devil's disciple! It's beyond me how anyone can fall for your disgusting charms. Men are such fools, such idiots! But you're not touching my life. Oh, no. You do exactly as you please, Hans. Throw yourself at her feet, lick her boots. What, in God's name, do I care?'

'Greti, please.'

'I want nothing more to do with you. Nothing, d'you understand? Nothing, nothing, nothing!' She waves her arms, kicks at the table. 'You understand me? I'd rather starve than take another Groschen from you!' She leaps to her feet, trips over the dog, rights herself and dashes out of the room.

Gabby is speechless. She stares at the doorway the demented woman ran through, looks back at Hans. He's standing, looking from her to the door and back again, hands trembling against his lips. How can he possibly hold out against the pressure, the moral blackmail his sister is clearly expert at?

'I'm terribly sorry, Hans. I'd no idea she felt so strongly.'

He's hunched into a smaller version of himself. 'It doesn't matter. I shall not allow this in any way to affect our plans.' Tense, pinched voice. Trembling with anger and anxiety.

'You mean…'

'Our engagement stands. With your permission, I will escort you home.' He returns to full height, digs into a pocket, brings out a small box. 'This was my mother's. I always hoped one day I might find the right woman to give it to. I would be honoured if you will allow me to place this on your finger.'

Inside the box is an antique ring. White gold, set with diamonds around a central emerald. Quite exquisite.

Tears are streaming down Gabby's cheeks. Can she accept? Is it right to deprive Greti Weiss of the only support she's ever known?

She's not going to deprive her. She will make her part of the family. The woman will come round eventually. She has no choice. And then she'll see how beautifully Gabby can transform that funereal living space into two sparkling, delightful apartments. Where she and Hans will raise Kamilla, entertain friends. And bring vibrant life into what she thinks of as the Weiss mausoleum.

God willing, they might even animate Greti.

'I wrote to the Berghers,' Hans announces. He comes to supper every Monday, Wednesday and Friday. Flourishing what is clearly a return epistle with a sardonic grin. His face, so much more handsome than Bosch's, has uncanny flashes of the dead man's facial expressions. 'A very modulated, very proper, answer.'

'Congratulations, naturally. Wishing you every happiness.'

His laugh is unexpected. And warm. 'Not noticeably. However, even though Markus is a convert, they don't quite go in for Greti's obsession with holiness.' He skims through the top page. 'A rather curious concentration on 'suitability' instead.'

'I see.' Undoubtedly disguised objections. They think she's an adventuress, a scarlet woman. 'In what way, precisely, am I not suitable?' Bosch opposed Lily's marriage to Markus. Strenuously, and on grounds of unsuitability. Because Markus was a Jew at a time when that was not — well, suitable!

'Guess.'

It's hardly expedient to voice her real suspicions. 'My German background? Or because I'm an American?'

A charming grin. 'Warm. Because you aren't an Austrian!'

'You're joking, I take it. Anyway, as Bosch's widow, officially I am. I have dual nationality.'

'I wouldn't take it literally. The other reason — of the ones Lily mentions, needless to say — is that we are incompatible in temperament. She admires and respects you, but she has serious reservations about our being able to get on.'

'So kind of her to give our future together so much thought.'

'Indeed. She's never taken an interest in me before. I am extremely obliged to her.' He takes a bulky envelope out of his inside coat pocket. 'I have no intentions whatsoever of allowing my relatives to dictate my future to me. So I thought we should annoy them even more. Visibly enjoy ourselves. Look what I've got for you.' He dangles a key in front of her.

Gabby blinks. The key to his apartment? Surely not. Too small, in any case. A safety deposit box in his bank? The rest of his mother's jewels, perhaps?

'I don't drive, but you do. You can park the car near your apartment until you move into the Karlsgasse. We can go for outings at weekends.' He places the keys, and some papers, on her desk. 'A Volkswagen. I'm told they're excellent little cars.'

'Oh, Hans. How wonderful! A Beetle!' Gabby is moved enough to entwine her arm in his. To drive a car again. The freedom, the excitement. 'What colour did you get?'

'The choice was black or black.' His eyes are on her. Drinking her in. 'Shall we go and christen her? The garage is only five minutes' walk away.'

THE BARGAIN

Before the iron age, when tilling the soil was harder work than now and ploughs were simply a piece of wood without wheels, growing crops was difficult. Until a bright farmer invented a plough which doubled the land that could be tilled. Thrilled, he told his neighbours all about it.

Then the devil heard about the new tool. He appeared to the farmers maintaining that the land belonged to him, and now that they were going to reap so much he had to insist on his half share. The farmers were upset, but knew they weren't a match against the devil. So they asked him which half of the land they were going to crop he wanted.

The devil thought himself more cunning than the farmers. 'If you divide the plot from top to bottom, and I ask for the upper half, you'll concentrate your efforts on the lower one. And if I ask you to split the land sideways it will come to the same thing. So let me have whatever grows on top of the soil, and you can have whatever grows below..

The farmers worked out how to outwit the devil. They planted root crops. When harvest time came round, and the beet and turnip stalks were turning yellow, they called the devil to take his share. He was angry at being made a fool of, but he comforted himself with the thought that even the brightest are sometimes got the better of. Next year he'd take what was below soil, and the farmers could have what grew above.

The farmers changed their tactics. They sowed winter rye followed by wheat and corn. And the crops grew, and the sun shone, and soon the farmers were ready to harvest their crops. It wasn't easy, for they had no scythes, so every man, woman and child was needed for the task. But it was done. And when they called the devil to take his share he found nothing but tangled roots. Plus any bits of straw he could glean.

It made the devil furious. He couldn't fault the farmers or find a single crumb of comfort among the helms. That's when a youth cried out: 'Look at the stupid devil!' So he ran away and has never been seen since.

CHAPTER 3

Vienna, Autumn 1951

Everything is working out so well. Gabby writes to Gemma, Nina, Dorinda, Tante Martha. She arranges for an excellent school for Kamilla, visits her dressmaker, orders two new hairdos from her hairdresser. She even remembers her catechism classes. And comes face to face with reality.

The annulment! She hasn't told Hans she never realised getting one was part of his proposal. She hasn't yet looked into it, has no idea how. What she has gleaned is that Bosch and Hans discussed the matter several times, shortly before his death. Was Bosch actually grooming Hans to take his place? Was it really his way of providing for his widow and daughter?

Father Joachim, spending hours on her instructions so that she can become a Catholic in time to offer it as a prenuptial gift to Hans, would be the ideal person to advise her. But he is a long-time friend of Hans's — and his sister Greti's confessor.

She cudgels her brains, goes to the library, can't find any references to help her. And then the answer comes as clearly as a bell. Czezina! He likes her, enjoys discussions with her. He'll be amused by the whole absurd charade. The fact that Hans is also his client, and his friend, is irrelevant. Czezina is bound to secrecy by the lawyers' code of client confidentiality. It's as safe as the confessional.

She arranges an appointment for early that afternoon. The office is near the Ring. Right by the Votivkirche, whose twin-spired towers remind her of the Nicolaikirche opposite her father's villa in Schwanenbruch. How fitting to drive over in her new car.

'Frau Bosch! Delightful to see you. Not because of problems with the villa, I trust?'

'That's all working out very well, Herr Doktor. I've come about something entirely different.' She tells him, first, of her engagement, and is delighted to hear he already knows. She goes on to explain the unexpected need for an annulment. He pushes bulky lips out in a gesture of understanding.

'Do you have the faintest idea how I would go about it?'

'Quite simple, gnä' Frau. You apply to the office of the Procurator Fidei. Right in the centre of Vienna, by the cathedral — the Stephansdom — as you'd expect. In a small alley off the Stephansplatz.'

That weird phrase again. 'Hans mentioned the Procurator Fidei. What, exactly, is that?'

'Not what. Who. The official, the attorney if you like, who administers Canon Law. The Church, you must understand, has its own Courts where it administers Canon Law. As opposed to Doctrinal Law. On which, as you know, the pope pronounces. Infallibly.'

'You mean all this is legally binding?'

'Only as far as Catholics who willingly surrender to Canon Law are concerned. But it is still a court of law. Evidence is given, and statements are taken, under oath.'

That's what Hans meant by the 'formalities'! 'You mean I just go over there? Ask them exactly what I have to do?'

'That's really all there is to it, gnä' Frau. Bureaucratic mumbo-jumbo of a distinctly Austrian Catholic kind. Entirely harmless.' He spreads plump hands to show simplicity. 'How very exciting that you and Hans are getting married. A wonderful solution.'

Solution? As in riddle? Predicament, no doubt. Prickles of irritation moisten her underarms. He's assuming her marriage to Hans is to solve her financial problems? That motivation's not much better than Greti's. 'What do you mean, solution?'

Large head on short, dumpy body. Held to one side, eyes half closed. 'An attractive, lively, energetic woman like you. An old dullard like Hans. Forgive my frankness, gnä' Frau. I have your best interests at heart. You are still in the second stage of mourning, still in shock. Are you sure you'll cope?'

'Why on earth not?' She doesn't mean to sound shrill. 'Hans is a charming, highly educated man. Devoted to Kamilla as well as to me, able to provide for us. He'll make a splendid husband and father.'

'A pedant, a recluse. Mummified — and I use the word in two senses — in that Bleak House of an apartment. Wedded to Mother Church, guarded by Sister Cerberus. You really see this as the future for yourself?'

He's genuinely concerned, or he's jealous? She knows Czezina admires her. Her wit, her liveliness, her ability to withstand the bullets of adversity. 'We are — fond of each other. Everything else is secondary.'

He picks up his glass paperweight, balances it from hand to hand. 'In that case, gnä' Frau, my wife and I both wish you the very best.'

Gabby realises she knows exactly where the Church Offices are. In the house next to the one in which her pre-war lawyer has his practice. Within easy walking distance of her apartment. At her rapid pace.

She stares at the enormous double portal guarding the entrance to holy territory. She's walked past dozens of times, never giving it a thought. No signs, no directions. A clue in stone steps grooved by faithful feet.

She discovers an ancient elevator behind an ornate grill. Like a confessional. She sees there is a slot for money. Labelled 1 Schilling. To ascend to purgatory, presumably. She drops in the coin, slips back the grill. One button to press. The lift doors close with a clang, the cage ascends. Slowly, majestically. Until it stops. Gabby slips back the door and ventures out.

A dimly lit, stone-flagged corridor. A window in the shadow of the Stephansdom. Four massive doors. No sound.

Gabby tries to muffle her heels clicking on stone. She creeps uncertainly from door to door. Procurator Fidei is proclaimed in Gothic script on the third one. No bell. She knocks. Timidly at first, then with more force. The door opens a crack, she pushes in.

A young priest with a rosy face greets her without a smile. She's ushered into an inner sanctum. An old priest with glum features listens to her story. He asks one or two questions, absorbs the answers with impassive calm.

'Applying for an annulment is a grave procedure, gnädige Frau. You have to think of it in terms of an ecclesiastic court of law. You will need to gather together documents, the names of witnesses.'

All her saliva seems to have disappeared. 'How long will it take?'

Priestly hands are placed together in prayer. Thumbs under chin, eyes contemplative. 'It all depends on how long it takes to get the evidence together, how much of it there is. Each case is different, of course. But, from my personal experience and what you tell me, I would say not too long.'

Gabby breathes in. So Hans was right. A few months. Even if December is too soon, a spring wedding perhaps. 'I'm afraid I'm very ignorant of these matters. In terms of time?'

The hands move backwards and forwards. 'Two or three years, perhaps. If all goes well.' The wide sleeves of the cassock are draped like flags at half-mast.

Gabby tries to swallow. Nothing there. She's too numb to answer, or to stand. A pitcher with water and a glass are at the side. The priest pours, hands her the glass. She drinks greedily.

Two or three years? If Hans is so clued-up on Canon Law, why didn't he warn her? And Greti? Surely she realises?

They can't know. Otherwise Hans would never have suggested bringing forward the wedding date. But tell him about it? Admit there's no way they can be married in months? Greti will, understandably, unquestioningly, be triumphant. But what will Hans say?

Gabby spends a sleepless night deciding on her next course of action. Dare she, or dare she not, confront her fiancé with the thorny facts? Would he agree to a Registry wedding, to be followed by one in the Church when the annulment finally comes through?

It doesn't seem likely. He was so emphatic about marrying in the Church that memorable night when they announced their engagement to Greti. 'You must know me well enough to know I wouldn't consider anything else,' he trumpeted at his sister.

She has to ask him. Or at least sound him out. Indirectly, perhaps. Without giving the whole show away.

Gabby buys Hans's favourite cold cuts for Wednesday's supper, opens a bottle of his preferred wine, arranges for Trautl to make her version of his beloved Sachertorte. She makes Kamilla learn all the words to Schubert's *Heidenröslein*, one of Hans's favourite songs.

He is delighted, pronounces Kamilla a mezzo soprano in the making. Beams. Enjoys the supper. Appears to have no idea that she's on tenterhooks. Coffee is finally served, Trautl retires for the night, they are alone.

'There's something I wanted to discuss with you, Hans.'

'Hmm?' The Kachelofen fire is drowsy-making.

'About the wedding.'

An irritable frown. 'I've given you carte blanche. Apart from the obligatory relatives, invite whomever you like, arrange the reception wherever it suits you. The only thing we have to do together is divide the furniture up between Greti and ourselves. I'll have to be there for that.'

'I do appreciate...'

'I'm sorry. You mean you need some funds?'

'Well, yes. But what I really wanted to discuss was the annulment.'

He stiffens, eyes shrewd, alert. 'You mean there are problems?'

'No, no. A foregone conclusion as far as the priest at the Procurator's office can tell.'

'Then why are we discussing it?' The mood of amiable languor has gone. It's replaced by nervous clicks, a shaking coffee cup. 'Why bring all that up again?'

'I just wondered, Hans. Do you consider it absolutely necessary for us to jump through bureaucratic hoops? We're civilised adults, not young things in the first flush of ardour.'

'I haven't the faintest idea what you're talking about. If we want our marriage to be a sacramental one you need the annulment.'

She drinks coffee, nods her head. 'Bosch always said what was important as far as Catholicism is concerned is not the rigid adherence to Canon Law, but to act morally according to one's own conscience.'

'An amorphous theory if ever I heard one. I mentioned Hegel's sentiments before: *When liberty is mentioned, it is incumbent on us to carefully observe whether it is not actually the assertion of private interests which is thereby designated.* Bosch was an arrogant, self-centred individual. Always bottom of the class. He simply didn't apply himself to the issues.'

'But surely you yourself mentioned Kierkegaard's views. You lent me his book.' She searches frantically through the pages. 'Listen to this: *It seems essential, in relationships and all tasks, that we concentrate solely on what is most significant and important.* Surely that could be taken to mean...'

Excitement spills coffee all over the saucer. 'You have completely misinterpreted him. Such an attitude can lead to nothing but anarchy. It simply will not do.'

'Even if, as sometimes happens, there are problems about putting strict rules and regulations into practice?'

'You just said there weren't any! What is the point of all these hypotheses? Is there some reason to suppose there will be problems, after all?'

'No, no, Hans. Nothing like that.' He isn't going to budge. If she tells him about the time scale, he'll say they'll have to wait. He can afford that. She cannot.

'All you have to do is apply.' He accepts another piece of Torte with alacrity. 'Everything will work out satisfactorily. We know all that.'

FLYING WITNESSES

After the Reformation, when Europe was plagued by strife between Christians, a fine upstanding farmer called Hake Betken was farming the rich marshland his forefathers had won from the sea. Hake was hard-working, even-tempered, beloved by his family and held in the highest esteem by his neighbours. Every year he reared excellent cattle, and every autumn he drove them to Hanover, the nearest market to Büttel, where he lived. There he exchanged his fattened oxen for a nice fat purse.

One year Hake had done particularly well. He had a good thick money belt around his waist, and was contentedly riding home on his fine chestnut stallion. He caught up with three other riders, and was delighted to recognise Willem Rassner, a farmer living in a town not far from his own. Since times were unruly, and brigands roamed the country, Hake joined Willem and the two strangers from Berlin who were riding with him.

Talk was of the uncertain times, how constant war could ruin the markets. But this year Hake couldn't complain. Business was good. And, he laughed, if you had the knack of rearing cattle you'd always have bread in your belly.

'You seem to have a flair for horseflesh as well,' one of the Berliners put in. 'I've never seen such a splendid stallion before.'

Hake stroked his horse's neck. 'True,' he said. 'If I needed to I could do the trip from Hanover to Büttel in one go. My chestnut's well up to that.'

The four men arrived at a Bremen inn by nightfall. They sat down to a meal. Hake was expecting to spend the night, but the other three nodded at each other, then turned to him.

'We thought of going on,' Willem told Hake. 'It's a beautiful moonlit night, and balmy weather. Why spend another night in a strange bed when the horses are up to going all the way home?'

'Oh, I don't know...' Hake began.

'First you boast about your horse,' Willem said, 'and then he's not even up to the trip our ordinary mounts can manage without any trouble.'

Hake's pride was hurt. His fine chestnut could outdo Willem's black nag any day. Or night.

So they set out again. Until they came to a fork in the road, and Willem argued with Hake about which would be the shorter route home. They agreed to put it to the test. Hake would go one way, Willem and the two Berliners the other, at the same pace that they were riding now. The first to arrive would discharge his pistol as a signal.

They parted, and Hake let his horse go at the usual pace. When he arrived at the meeting point, and no one was there, he fired his pistol off as a signal of victory.

At that his earlier companions jumped out of the bushes, pulled their guns on him and yelled at him to let them have his money. Hake, outnumbered, handed over his money belt and begged to be allowed to ride on.

'And get us hanged?' they laughed at him. Even when he begged for mercy, for his wife's and children's sakes, one answered with a shot, another knifed him.

Hake fell off his horse and lay bleeding on the ground. Just then a large flock of wild ducks flew over the murder scene. The dying man raised himself. 'The ducks are witnesses to this evil deed,' he cried out. And died.

While his murderers were busy hiding Hake's body his horse escaped and galloped home. He did not stop until he was outside his master's house. And there he pawed the ground with steaming hoofs and wild neighs. Hake's wife, children and servants became pale with fright. They realised that a terrible fate had overtaken their beloved Hake.

The chestnut led them to the scene of the crime. Hake's family unearthed the body, took it home in state, and buried it. The whole parish mourned their worthy neighbour, and did their best to bring the murderers to justice. It was not to be. They had fled as far away as Prague. And did not return to their own country until years later.

By now the grass had grown thick over Hake's grave, and the killers thought themselves safe. One day the three murderers found themselves back in their native land, on their way to a market in Oldenburg. Where, as it so happened, a flock of wild ducks flew over the market square. And one of the murderers joked with another saying: 'Look, there go

Hake Betken's witnesses!'

Some of Hake's old neighbours from Büttel were standing nearby, and wanted to know what the strangers meant. At this the three men panicked, and tried to run. They were soon caught, and taken to Bremen where they were brought to trial before the Archbishop. There, under torture, they confessed to their terrible crime. And were hanged for it.

CHAPTER 4

Vienna, Autumn 1951

Gabby gets up early, reads the paper, looks at her post. A letter from Frau Czezina congratulating her on her engagement. Inviting her and Hans to coffee after Sunday Mass. Saying she would also invite Greti.

Gabby wonders how she could have missed the obvious confidant. Czezina is the man to approach for a solution. His legal mind might just come up with something which will cut through all the red tape. She makes an appointment with a puzzled secretary.

'How very nice to see you again, Frau Bosch. And so soon.' Sallow skin, deep lines from nose to mouth, alert suspicious eyes.

Preamble of weather, state of health, political situation. Czezina leans back in his chair, on the tip of overbalancing. Gabby's chatter becomes faster and faster. His silence quells her.

'I have been to the office of the Procurator Fidei.'

Vacant eyes engage. 'There's a problem? From what you told me you have a cast-iron case. Two, actually.'

All her breath is expelled. Her life is a constant battle. 'Open and shut, yes. But these things take time. Rolf Ferent is the main witness. As you know, he lives in New York.'

'The Catholic Church is universal, gnä' Frau. There are Jesuits even in America.'

'Not speedy ones, it seems.'

'A matter of years?'

She manages a nod.

'In what way can I help?'

She sniffs. A lace handkerchief twists round slim fingers. 'You've known Hans since you were at school together. Would you say that if I spell out the facts he'd consider a civil ceremony while waiting for the Church to grind to a decision?'

The laid-back stance is replaced by an upright back. 'Marry outside the Church? Hans Weiss? Speaking as devil's advocate, I consider that impossible.'

'No chance at all?' The delicate lace tears. She stares at jagged edges.

'It would be utterly wrong of me to encourage you to hope along those lines. I'm very fond of Hans Weiss. But that doesn't blind me to the facts. He uses the outward forms of religion as scaffolding for life. He's rigid, stubborn, inflexible. He misses the essence of humanity.' He takes in her mute, white face. 'You must forgive me for being blunt. I hate to see you throw yourself away. You are so full of life, gnä' Frau. He is a fossil.'

She blinks sparkle back into dry eyes. 'That's really what I thought. You see — well, without beating about the bush — I doubt whether we'll have a, well, how can I put it? A physical relationship. More like brother and sister, wouldn't you say? In which case we don't really need the sacrament of matrimony!' Men, she's found, are such romantics. Women are the pragmatic ones.

'You are missing the point, gnä' Frau. Herr Doktor Weiss is concerned with convention. His understanding of the Church's teaching. How it looks, not how it is.'

'That's a straitjacket, not a religion.'

Czezina's eyes close with amused agreement. 'Why not just forget it all, gnä' Frau?'

Throw the love, the adoration, of a good and decent man in his face?

Deprive Kamilla of a father, herself of financial security? Do without a handsome escort, companionship, intellectual stimulation? Opt for scrimping and saving, a pitiful widow mouldering into old age? Is it likely that another man, someone capable of supporting her in the style she'd like to become accustomed to once again, will propose to her? Czezina is as hopelessly impractical as all the other men she's known.

'But I can see you aren't going to.'

Gabby knots the remains of the lace together, dabs at her nose. 'I'm very fond of him, you know. You haven't taken account of that.'

His pencil stabs the blotter with muted blows. 'There might be a way out of your impasse. You believe in individual conscience, don't you? The forum internum which tells you the difference between right and wrong?'

'Bosch always said that was more important than clutching at the forms of religion. Hans maintains it's replacing the infallibility of doctrine with personal wishes.'

The man across the desk raises two eyebrows. Like little horns. 'I thought he was a fan of Kierkegaard's.'

'Of course.'

He rubs his pencil between his palms. 'Weiss has left all the "arrangements" to you?'

'Absolutely.' She can feel her heart thump. He's found a loophole?

'Then I think there is a way out.' He stands, walks over to the window, built-up heels clanking across the floor. 'My idea does involve an element of deception. A white lie, one might say. Although *you* know the essence to be true.'

'Tell him I refuse to go in for this pantomime of marriage in the Church? That if he truly cares for me he'd agree to a Registry Office ceremony? Moral blackmail, in other words?'

'That could misfire.' He turns against the light. Dimmed features surrounding eyes which reflect his desk lamp. 'Tell him you've applied for the annulment. Then, at the appropriate time, announce it's come through.'

Her nose smells the sulphur as he strikes a match to light his cigar, her eyes are temporarily blinded by bright sunlight as Czezina steps from the window. Her fingers feel the hard steel of her chair, her ears hear the Votivkirche bells peal loud. Joy at deliverance.

'Expedite matters by assuming the outcome?'

'Why not?'

'But, surely, there will be questions? The priest who's going to perform the ceremony — '

'That's the whole beauty of it. Why would there be any reference to an annulment? The priest will ask you whether you've been married before. And you will answer that you're a widow, produce Bosch's death certificate. There's no reason in the world for him to delve further.'

The more she thinks about it, the more she and Czezina discuss the implications, the more right it seems. Why let these barren formulae, which miss and even frustrate the actual doctrines of the Church, stand in the way? Why force a man who's been deprived of emotion, condemned to act like a clockwork automaton, to make such decisions?

She will act for him, take full responsibility. Hans will be married in the Church, his conscience crystal clear. Happiness for them both, the right decision for Kamilla. All she actually has to do is — nothing! Except tell Hans that the annulment has come through.

Gabby immerses herself in outward forms. A wedding outfit, a bridesmaid's dress for Kamilla. She books two weeks' honeymoon in Florence, the reception for forty people at the *Hotel Sacher*. She writes letters to relatives, collects together necessary documents. Birth certificate, registration card, Bosch's death certificate, their marriage licence.

She glances down at the details of the licence. She's so startled that spittle drops unheeded, spreading old ink.

Marital Status: divorced.

Why didn't Czezina know the certificate would spell that out? What can she do?

Forget the whole scheme, come clean, trust Hans to do the right thing? Impossible, with Greti and the Berghers waiting to pounce. He'd never manage it.

The person she has to show the documents — Father Joachim — is a simple man. Not in the first flush of middle age. He's so compassionate, so unworldly. He has recently received her into the Church. It must be possible to — well, satisfy his bureaucratic requirements without alerting his suspicions. But how?

She hears her father's voice again: 'Decide what you want to do, then do it.'

'Trautl!' she calls. 'I'm going out for an hour or so. Keep an eye on Kamilla.'

She rushes through Vienna's streets at top speed, dispersing adrenaline which charges energy through her whole body. She walks around the pond outside the Karlskirche several times before she knocks at the presbytery door.

'I'm so sorry to bother you, Hochwürden. I had to come at once, there's so little time left.'

Father Joachim ushers her in, calms her down. He has a mild form of dropsy. The constant nodding of his head suggests affirmation.

'My marriage licence.' She swallows hard. 'Until I looked I'd quite forgotten. Lost in the Blitz, you know. Burnt in an incendiary bomb fire.'

Mild, untroubled eyes. 'No need to distress yourself, Frau Bosch. It's always possible to send for a duplicate.' Nod, nod.

'I know, I know! But there's only a fortnight before the wedding. I'm not at all sure a copy would arrive in time.' Genuine tears to wipe away.

Nods turn to constant trembling, leaving still kind eyes. 'I'm afraid I do need some formal evidence.'

She sits for a while. Silently. While the priest explains his reasons.

'What about an affidavit from the Chancellery, Hochwürden? My late husband was a member of the Diplomatic Corps. They know me personally. Someone there will be happy to help us out, I'm sure.'

The trembling turns back to nodding. Mild eyes blink acquiescence.

CHAPTER 5

Vienna, Winter 1951/1952

The authorities have dragged their heels over a pension for Gabby. She has no problems persuading a guilt-laden Secretary of Affairs to write an affidavit out for her. On imposing notepaper displaying impressive Austrian insignia, signed by high-ranking officials.

She takes the precious paper round to Father Joachim, together with all the others. 'I've written off for a copy as well,' she tells him. Truthfully. 'But just in case it doesn't come in time, I've obtained this affidavit. Will that do?'

He reads it carefully. And goes on nodding.

Greti, Mustapha at her side, opens the door of her apartment to Gabby. She invites her in as though the outburst against her never happened.

Rooms are allocated to Greti and Mustapha, Hans and Gabby. Terms of cohabitation are secured, the silver, china, glass, paintings, figurines, photographs are all split up in an atmosphere of icy restraint. The furniture is labelled, to be placed in new positions by removal men.

There's less than two weeks to make changes to the decorations. Gabby confines herself to choosing colours to redecorate the walls, orders new curtains, has the carpets cleaned and adds two comfortable armchairs which can be sat in without incurring permanent injury.

The Berghers, still living in Switzerland, will be attending the wedding. The Czezinas have offered to act as witnesses. Kamilla has preened for hours in front of the small mirror in Gabby's flat. She won't be doing that for much longer. She'll have a full-length mirror in her new home.

There's one last small hurdle, one final piece of bureaucracy before the wedding can take place. The bridal instructions which Father Joachim will dole out to them, that vital preparation which the Church insists on before she will allow Catholics to marry. Another couple will join Hans Weiss and Gabriele Bosch in Father Joachim's study in the presbytery.

Hans picks Gabby up from her apartment. The Annakirche is only a short walk away. She's full of pleasant anticipation, she's happy, chattering like a magpie, beaming at the lull in the freeze, the melting snow.

Hans is monosyllabic, morose. He walks slowly through slush-covered streets, steps over puddles. Gabby puts it down to pre-nuptial nerves. A bachelor in his fifties. Not a surprise. She's wondered what will happen about the intimate side of their marriage. She brushes that aside for another day.

'I'll just run through the documents,' Father Joachim nods at both couples settled on hard-backed chairs. 'Then we can have our little lecture.'

He questions the young couple in a monotone. The responses, rehearsed, already known, are ticked off on a piece of paper.

The priest turns to Hans. 'Johann Theodor Weiss. Catholic. Bachelor.'

'Correct.'

Nod, nod. He turns to Gabby. 'Gabriele Dohlen Bosch. Catholic. Widow.'

She nods. Somehow uncomfortable. There is a tremor in the priest's voice she has not heard before. The voice drones on — more words which are not her date of birth, the name of her parish, or her marital status. She's answered all that. She assumes a kind of social babble to show the end of this stage and the beginning of the next.

Father Joachim looks up, directly at her, the nodding more pronounced.

'Why don't you tell him about the annulment?' Hans's tetchy voice beside her sharpens her into attending. She swallows, clears her throat, stares at the priest.

'Tell him that yes, you were married before, but that your first marriage has been nullified.'

'*Were* you married before?' Father Joachim frown-puzzles his eyes.

What has made him ask that question? She cannot answer. All the saliva has left her mouth, she can hardly breathe.

Gabby can't face Father Joachim, can't face Hans Weiss. She looks, instead, at the young couple's faces. They're gawking at her, mouths agape. She turns back to the priest, manages a nod.

'You were married before your marriage to Franz Bosch, Frau Bosch?' Father Joachim's gentle voice sounds no reproach. His nodding head encourages an affirmative answer.

No sound. She cannot speak.

The priest may be old, and infirm, and unworldly. But he reacts quickly. 'Don't worry now. We'll talk about this later. In private.' He motions the two couples to relax while he intones the full marital instructions.

Gabby hears nothing but the droning voice, pattering rain against a window. She closes her eyes but is still acutely aware of the man sitting, bolt upright and tense, beside her. She prays for the earth to open up and swallow her. It refuses to budge.

Father Joachim ushers the young couple out, says a word or two to Hans and asks him to wait outside. He turns to Gabby.

'Why not tell me what it's all about, my daughter?'

He listens without making any interruptions. There are no expressions of pious incredulity. Nothing but the silent nodding of his head. As though he agrees with her.

'I believe you came to your decision in good faith,' he tells her. 'Do not grieve. The question I asked is simply a prescribed form. Age takes its toll. Normally I would not have questioned you further. But in your case I…' Old lips move without sound for several seconds, his eyes blink.

Even in her state of shock Gabby wonders why. Like many holy people Father Joachim finds it hard to anticipate sin. His reaction seems so out of character.

He clears his throat, his eyelids working overtime. 'I felt obliged to read up the guide rules.'

It's neither here nor there why he delved more deeply than either Czezina or she had anticipated. He did, and she has to cope with the consequences.

His eyelids calm down, his eyes shine sympathy, his hand is warm. 'God be with you, my daughter.'

Will He be? Did she commit sacrilege, the unforgivable sin?

Vienna's church bells peal out the hour. Did she mistake the Votivkirche bells? Were they a warning rather than the peal of victory?

Hans is waiting outside the presbytery door, his handsome face composed like a stone mask. They walk, unheeding of slush and the day's suddenly freezing temperatures.

'I believe you owe me an explanation.'

She tries, stumbles over words, chokes. She knows she cannot explain how a sinner feels to such a righteous man.

'You've betrayed my trust, you've abused my confidence.' His teeth are chattering. 'You snaked your way into my affections. It has to stop. I never wish to set eyes on you again.'

Elegant shoes plough through a muddy puddle, dirty water covers his trouser bottoms. He turns his back and hurries off without a backward glance.

There's only one person she can turn to. Only one other human being she can discuss the matter with. The one who landed her in this mess.

She doesn't blame him. He did his best to think of a way out and it misfired. But she needs someone to talk to, someone who will not pour scorn or preach pious sentiments. A man of the world.

'Herr Doktor?' The secretary reluctantly puts her through. 'I simply have to talk to you.'

'My diary's full for the day. I could come round this evening, on my way home?'

She should have realised he already knows. Hans rang him at once. Berated her for a witch, a sorceress, a woman without scruples, an unfit companion. A she-devil.

'You're surely not still contemplating marriage to that shrivelled shell of a man, are you? I warned you before, and I'm warning you now: he'll never marry you. All this twaddle about the Church is simply an excuse.'

'That doesn't make sense, Herr Doktor. If he didn't want to marry me, why did he ask me?'

'Look, Frau Bosch. Herr Doktor Weiss has many admirable qualities. And so do you. But you are incompatible! A withdrawn, inhibited man and a gregarious, vital woman. How can you expect that combination to work?'

'For those very reasons. We are complementary, Herr Doktor! I would go so far as to say we need each other.'

'You're determined to pursue the matter? Talk him round?'

'I was wondering whether you'd help me.'

'You want me to act as intermediary? Plead your case?'

'I won't be able to get near him. What with Cerberus barring the door, and the Furies backing her, I haven't a chance.'

'I see. I do feel responsible. If it weren't for me you wouldn't be in this position.'

'Same position, different reasons for it. You think it's a lost cause?'

The gloomy brow gives way to amusement. He downs a glass of schnapps, then another. Then he outlines his plan. He'll visit Hans at home. He understands he's taken to his bed, is indisposed. So he'll visit the invalid.

Czezina spends the next ten days visiting Hans Weiss and reporting back to Gabby. And when they've finished discussing Hans and his recalcitrance, as the dapper little lawyer puts it, they have a little chat. Politics, books, ideas. The sort of things Gabby so much enjoyed discussing with Hans. But Czezina is a married man, and Gabby isn't out to wreck marriages. Her sights remain firmly on Hans Weiss.

There are trickles of change she hears about through Czezina. A strong letter from the Berghers, condemning Gabby as a wicked woman, oozing sympathy, have the opposite effect. Boredom with bed rest, an eagerness to hear reports of Gabby's whereabouts and intentions, make it clear that Hans is willing, if not eager, to resume relations. At last he allows tentative admissions that his conduct might have been somewhat harsh, precipitate. Concessions that Gabby's intentions might have been good, that she acted for what she saw to be the best intentions, were grudgingly entertained.

'He says he's going to get in touch,' Czezina reports. With a doom-laden face. 'You're sure you want this? You're such an attractive woman. Any number of men would be delighted to marry you.'

She knows it's true. Two husbands, a new fiancé, admirers in Schwanenbruch. The fact that she has no hair has not discouraged any of them. It isn't what they're interested in.

But it's Hans she's after, Hans she wants to marry. Because, she tells herself, he's related to Kamilla, and will be the right father figure for her. And he's the right companion for herself, whatever anyone else may say.

Nor does she want to live with the idea of having been jilted. If anyone is going to call off the engagement, it's going to be Gabby herself.

He rings on Sunday. After the ten o'clock Mass he attends with Greti in the Annakirche. One which Gabby has decided to avoid until relations are resumed.

'Hello?' His voice is hesitant, slurred.

'Hans! I heard you weren't well. Are you better now?'

'It's so good to hear your voice.' Some seconds of fumbling as she hears coins pressed into a slot. A precaution against Cerberus. 'I thought, perhaps, that we should meet.'

She invites him to come over.

Hollow cheeks, black under the eyes, his handsome features drawn. But his relief at seeing her again is incredibly touching. There's nothing as intimate as an embrace. He kisses her hand, his spaniel eyes unable to leave her face.

'Come in, Hans. Do sit down.'

There is a long, self-pitying account of his illness. He can't restrain himself from recriminations. Her profuse apologies bring acknowledgements of her good faith. He's been to see Father Joachim.

'He says we could solve the whole problem by applying for an annulment and, while we're waiting for it to come through, marry in a Registry Office.' Hans's ineffectual flicks do not produce a flame in his lighter.

Gabby offers him a box of matches. She makes no allusion to the fact that it's what she's wanted all along.

The Sobranie glows red. 'There is, of course, how shall I put it? A slight impediment.'

She knows that. There's no way of knowing whether the annulment will actually be granted. As the priest at the Marriage Court has already mentioned to her. Likely, but not assured.

Hans rambles on for several minutes. He quotes from St Augustine, St Paul. Brings up examples of holy men whose lives, she is fairly sure, do not parallel his. When stripped of all the verbiage — the allusions to cohabiting — she gathers he's talking about avoiding marital relations: sex!

'Live as brother and sister, d'you mean, Hans?' A state he is, after all, intimately familiar with.

He looks down at his feet. 'You could put it like that.'

She pours them both another drink. Downs hers. 'Well, you know, Hans. I don't think that's the important part of our relationship. I don't see any problems with that. None at all.'

His smile is positively beatific. Gabby has just one reservation. Which she doesn't voice. He does know, does he not, that their Christian marriage, when it finally takes place, is only valid if it is consummated?

MANNA FROM THE SEA

MANNA FROM THE SEA

The twin-spired church of Schwanenbruch boasts a most impressive altarpiece which is famous throughout the whole county. It's a beautifully carved triptych of unknown origin. There is no record of where it came from, nor any clue as to who the master carver was. The three beautifully and intricately decorated panels now form the altarpiece of the St Nicolaikirche. People come from far and wide just to get a glimpse of the wonderful piece.

One story attributes its appearance to a devastating Christmas flood nearly three hundred years ago. At that time the skill of dyke-building was still in its infancy. The dykes were narrow and steep, and didn't form much of a barrier against quite ordinary winter gales. The mighty North Sea would wash over them, and even breach them. So sea water flooded the nearby fields and villages quite regularly.

But when gales and storms turned into hurricanes, and simple floods became flood tides, the dykes proved no barriers at all. Such overwhelming seas could produce flood water reaching up to the roof tops. Even the churches, built on the highest land, might be flooded right up to the altar. But the biggest danger was never the flood itself, but the returning flood waters. The great charge of water gushing back to the sea will sweep away anything not nailed down or made fast in some other way. Whole houses might be lost, barns might be carried off, and smaller objects such as cupboards, beds, cattle, or bales of hay and straw would have no chance at all. And whatever did not sink, but managed to float, might reappear on some far-distant shore a long time afterwards.

The villagers claim that a severe flood tide struck the far side of the Elbe. The waters burst into a church, dislodged the altarpiece and carried it out to the turbulent estuary. The wooden triptych floated on the waves until the sea calmed down and deposited it on the southern shore of the river.

It so happened that the Schwanenbruchers were lucky enough to find this great work of art on their shingled beach. They claimed the ancient right of salvage and carried it back to the village. The villagers soon realised that the heavens had sent them a pearl beyond price. They proudly set it up on their altar, replacing their own indifferent altarpiece with this outstanding one. Then they unfolded its great panels to display the carving in its full glory. And there it still stands to this very day.

CHAPTER 6

Sussex, June 1952

All week Doly busies herself with things she does not do. Expecting something in the post. Not knowing what. Finally, a letter from Bobby Hudwalker announcing a visit in October. Nice enough, but it's not what she's been waiting for.

She wanders out. Sunshine followed by the soft English summer rain she loves. Her eyes roam the roof; still keeping out the wet. Her mind conjures up the image she's never been able to forget, the broad Sussex tones she thrilled to quite a few years ago.

'Peter Jennings. Brand new firm, old-established family. There's a few in Midhurst can give you references,' she hears him say. Clear, standing straight. None of that deferential tone so common before the war.

She checks the tiles on the roof which the young builder she christened Piers hammered home five long years ago. Thoughts of him will not be tamed, will still not let go. The planned unplanned meetings in Midhurst which they became so expert at. The trysts in the woods, the heavings in her marriage bed. All in the past, fading to grey.

He was so eager for her to write. Which she did, faithfully. Strange never to have had word from him during his five years in the Services. They knew each other so well, so intimately.

She cycles to Midhurst while Ross is at school. She's magnetised to the cottage where she knows Piers's mother lives. The lamp behind the old glass circles a light in her heart which is still not extinguished. Window boxes ablaze with colour bring red to her cheeks. The brass knocker resounds with Piers's shutting of the door. Even the street itself brings back emotions she's tried to bury in the soil while planting spuds. Feelings which resurface with every balmy breeze, with every lark rise.

She leans her bike against his parents' cottage wall, inhales. Her heart is beating, her breath short.

'D'you remember me?' His voice is lower, but the inflections haven't changed. Soft, country tones.

Her breath deserts her, her heart flutters, thumps. Is that what she's felt — sensed — all week? His presence in Midhurst? Asking after her?

'No.' She needs time to compose herself. To stop herself rushing into his arms. That would never do.

His smile is the same, his looks so very different. He left a boy and has returned a man. There isn't a spare ounce on him. Cheekbones prominent, eyes hollowed in burning darkness, nose sharp, chin leading.

'You aren't changed none, Dorinda. My mother tells us your little boy be called Ross.'

His smile the same, his look, his voice. But something's changed: an edge to his tone, a hardness she doesn't remember from before. 'How has it been for you, Piers?'

'A girl in every port.'

Maybe a girl, or even many, but she knows, senses, none who matter. Obvious from his tone, his look, his leaning towards her. She understands. Both of them unable to shake the past. Shackled by the present.

'Will you come in and 'ave a cup o' tea?'

His father is out all hours working on the railways. His brothers work on nearby farms. His mother smiles amiability. And puzzlement. But not rebuke. 'Oi did seen you with yer little boy, Mrs Courtling.'

What can she say to that? 'I often pass your cottage. Such a lovely spot.'

His mother's eyes have the serenity of a son restored. 'So good to 'ave Peter back for a bit, though 'im don't seem to 'ave much leave. I do wish 'im did settle down with some nice girl.'

Doly swallows lukewarm tea. 'Will you stay on after your seven years?' He joined the Navy to see the world. Before settling down, he maintained.

'There be another two years ter go. Time enough fer deciding then.'

The clock on the mantelpiece chimes twelve. 'I've got to rush. Ross will be back by one.'

'I be seein' you out.'

Six hours to go before Ross's bedtime. Too much and too little. The lawn gets a special cut, the house a going over. A vase full of lilac. Burning fir cones. Whether old passion will lead up or down can't be foretold. But he is back. And one-time beloved husband Erskine chose to leave — for reasons of his own. No hindrance now.

The knock on the kitchen door is soft. His individual smell is strong on his breath, his hair, his clothes. He's wearing the old brown donkey jacket of so many years ago.

'Come and sit by the fire. I thought you might be cold after the south of France.'

'I like it well enough. You might put these 'ere in t' fridge for a hour or so.'

Three bottles of Goldener Oktober. He remembers her taste. 'I can't wait that long,' she dimples at him. 'I'm thirsty. We'll open one now.'

No strangeness to wear off. No tension to relax. The right wine to go with them. A happy-making wine donated by a generous spirit.

Ross sleeps upstairs. In the tiny room beyond Doly's bedroom. They use the small bed in the spare room instead of her double bed which was the marriage bed of long ago. And fall into the rhythm of past loves. Lyrical.

He slides, naked, into her. Wet, waiting, glistening with the joy of it. His lips are on hers, his teeth are sharp against her tongue, his bones nestle into her flesh. Melting there.

She opens like an unfurling bud. Straining to raindrops, longing for April showers followed by sun. Will his seed inside her to turn to fruit?

His thrust is deep and sure. He comes in one long spurt, flooding her, spreading inside her. He lies against her for a time, stiffens again.

She arches her back, raises her legs and twines them around his neck. He fills her, teases until she begs. He kisses her mouth, her throat, her breasts and then pulls out. She is beside herself. He thrusts back again.

Much harder. And faster.

They come together in one long, gushing stream of blending intoxication.

'You'm a beautiful woman.'

It's poetry to say that to her. 'This is the way I want and love you.' She cups his bony head, strokes damp hair which is no longer boyish but short-stubbed Navy cut. 'All others are incidents.'

They stay entwined all night. Sleep comes late. And awakening comes early.

'That there dawn chorus be louder'n storms at sea.' He's up at five. A fleeting kiss. 'I be off again termorrow.'

There's nothing now to separate their separate lives. Golden weft and platinum warp are free to weave tight the links of a special love, to form a strong fabric which can weather any parting, any time.

Doly's whole life is here, in Dramlings and the surrounding woods. It is her home, her sanctuary. Piers's is roaming the wide oceans. Where he's as free as the waves to come and go as he pleases. And he pleases to come to Dramlings.

Doly is steady as she goes. Ready to accept what appeals, to reject the false. There are no second chances in the game of love which involves a young life. Her first responsibility is to Ross. The rest is as and when she chooses. No bars of any kind.

'Look after yourself.'

The desolation of parting must be transformed. She walks him to the end of her drive, turns into the woods. Listens to the rain dripping from rhododendron leaf to leaf. Different sizes reverberate different tones. Which go back to the beginning of time and she is there to listen to them. She has the ear for what sounds right in all creation. She has the sweet desire to be part of it.

THE UNHAPPY SOLDIER

At the time when the French marched victorious through Germany the local women and children had to defend themselves as best they could. Their own men had fled in disarray, and the victors rode triumphant through the land, plundering and looting without hindrance.

A widow, living alone, saw a French soldier riding proudly into her village and towards her house. She had just finishing shelling a good catch of the tiny local shrimp, one of the finest delicacies of the area. So she smiled at the soldier and, not speaking his language, merely pointed at her laid table and inclined her head.

The man nodded and sat down. The woman fetched the dish of shrimp which always colour a delicate pink when boiled. And she surrounded this with the dark rye bread of the district, which makes such a good accompaniment to shellfish.

The soldier took one look and turned much pinker than the shrimp. He took her plate and smashed it against the wall. For, to someone who's never seen shelled shrimp before, they might well look like a can of worms!

CHAPTER 7

Vienna, Summer 1952

It is only now that the strain of her deception is over, and she no longer has to suppress her feelings of guilt — or the dangers of damnation — that Gabby blossoms. She's not immediately aware of this herself. She merely feels a gaiety, a freedom from oppression. And realises with a pang that Bosch's death has released a novel sense of freedom in her. And that she's not averse to it.

A new life with a good conscience. Following Czezina's advice was a mistake, and she is never going to repeat it. Virtue, if not its own reward, is better than sin. She applies to the Marriage Court for an annulment. She doesn't actually care whether she gets it or not. She can sleep, she radiates bonhomie and sees it reflected back to her in every face she meets.

Czezina, whose job as mediator is long complete, still appears on her doorstep almost every evening. On some excuse or other. He stays for a drink or two. Professor Abel, a recent widower and a friend of

Bosch's before the war, invites her to a talk on neo-Nazism. The painter Weiler invites her to his latest show. Lothar Egartner is keen to conduct her round the newly-reconstructed Austrian mint. He isn't married. And his housekeeper not only doesn't share the general admiration for Gabby, she's positively hostile. Gabby laughs to herself. Egi certainly isn't on her list of possible future husbands.

A friend she and Bosch cultivated in Paris — a successful entertaining academic called Professor Schlech — calls unexpectedly. He survived the war as a professor at the University of Vienna much as Hans Weiss survived it as loss adjuster in the insurance company in which he still works — by keeping the lowest of low profiles. Professor Schlech is now teaching at the Sorbonne. He visits Vienna from time to time to see his mother. He's not married, has no siblings. He's one of those men who fill the need for single men at the best dinner parties. Which means he's much in demand.

'Gnädige Frau! It's probably not seemly to say so, but you look radiant.'

'How nice to see you again, Professor Schlech. What is unseemly about being on top form?'

'A recent widow, gnä' Frau. But I do understand. Herr Doktor Bosch was gravely ill. You were beset with problems. You may be without a husband, but you have a life. That much is clear.'

'Of course I miss Bosch. He had one of the sharpest tongues in Vienna. I've learned to make do with what's left.'

'A tragic loss.'

'And relatively young. But I have to survive. And, believe it or not, I'm engaged to be married again.'

'Dear lady, that is excellent news! For yourself and little Kamilla.'

'A cousin of my late husband's. A family friend from the moment we came back to Vienna.'

'Herr Doktor Weiss! It was always obvious that he admired you enormously. Well, well. I never thought he'd have it in him to ask for your hand.' He kisses it again. Presumably to make the point.

'How long are you staying? We must all meet. Perhaps a dinner at my apartment for you, Dr Weiss and his sister Greti. Have you met her?'

'Indeed. A very learned lady. Enormously erudite.'

She isn't matchmaking, though getting Greti off her hands would be an excellent idea. Bosch always maintained that Schlech is, if not a practising homosexual, a man's man. And one who finds it quite unnecessary to live with anyone else.

The dinner party is an enormous success. She follows it with another, inviting Czezina and his wife. She also meets Professor Schlech for coffee in the city at frequent intervals.

Meanwhile a reformed Hans Weiss heaps gifts upon her. A fur coat to withstand one of the coldest winters on record, a diamond brooch, valuable prints he picks up in the Saturday Naschmarkt flea market, a hefty deposit into her bank account for 'extras'. The date for the civil ceremony is fixed for July.

Gabby wonders at the delay, but not unduly. The honeymoon will be a mere weekend in Venice. As Hans has already had his two weeks' holiday. The apartment has been refurbished, though some of the changes have been, if not exactly reversed, remoulded in some subtle way.

The wedding dress, a restrained affair as is seemly for a widow remarrying, will do as well for a civil ceremony as for a Nuptial Mass. The winter of penance turns to the lilac spring of disembodied passion. Words, books, concerts in the Musikverein, the Opera.

One lone, small grass snake to mar the paradise. While dressing for the opera Gabby realises her diamond brooch is missing. A burglar would have taken more than one piece of jewellery. Trautl? Gabby sends the girl out to fetch milk before the shops close. She roots through her drawers. And finds the brooch nestling among the maid's underwear.

'What is my brooch doing in your drawer, Trautl?'

Recriminations, accusations, the vilest of foul language. It's no longer possible to leave the girl in charge of Kamilla. Gabby breaks the news to Hans when he comes to fetch her. He gives Trautl a month's wages, tells her to pack her bags and leave immediately.

Which means Gabby is without a maid, and so without anyone to look after Kamilla when she wishes to go out. Not too important. The wedding is a mere three weeks away.

Gabby writes once again to relatives, to acquaintances. New wedding date, no flowers this time please. She buys a reckless hat for her new life. Sets it at a rakish angle and walks briskly across town to pick Kamilla up from her Kindergarten.

The child skips home and in through the front door of the apartment house ahead of Gabby. She makes for the letter boxes in their neat rows because she's longing to receive a letter. Metal grills show whether it's worth unlocking.

Kamilla tugs at her arm. 'Look, Mutti. I think there's a letter for me.'

'No, Kammy. If you want someone to write to you, you'll have to write to them. And you haven't, have you?'

She's surprised, because the post for the day has already been. She unlocks the door, sees an envelope without a stamp. And Hans's handwriting. Why write and ask someone to deliver by hand? Why not phone if he's been delayed for tonight's supper?

She smiles as understanding gets through. Hans must have phoned when she was out. No Trautl to answer now. She slips the envelope into her handbag, follows Kamilla up the stairs.

No letter heading, no date, no address. A sheet of white letter paper. The writing is crabbed and tight.

I have it on good authority that you are conducting a liaison with Professor Schlech. Needless to say I am appalled. When I consider that I have already forgiven your attempt to deceive the Church authorities – even to commit sacrilege – and the compromises I have already undertaken on your behalf, I am completely at a loss for words. Except to say that our engagement is at an end. Irrevocably.

Thin letters biting into the fabric of the paper. No signature. No name. Anonymous. And yet it can only have been written by one person. This time there is no question of bad luck, of an old man not trusting himself to remember the rules. No question of someone else writing the letter, either. Greti would not be able to forge her brother's handwriting, or his words, to this extent.

'What are we having for lunch, Mutti?'

Kamilla is tugging at her sleeve. Bringing her back to the unpalatable present.

'How would you like to play with Brigitte, Kammy? Perhaps have lunch with her?' The amiable young war widow with a little girl Kamilla's age, living in the flat above, is always glad to earn an extra twenty Schillings.

Gabby needs time to think. To sort out this latest wreckage of her life.

She walks to the Stadtpark, strolls along empty paths between beautifully tended flower beds. This time there's nothing to blame herself for. Czezina was right. There is nothing to be done. Except to get out of Vienna.

She heads for the Ring, watches the traffic speeding past. She has the car! She can drive herself and Kamilla up to Schwanenbruch. And sell the diamond brooch to raise the necessary cash for the rest of the summer.

To hell with being a lady, handing back the loot. Hans Weiss owes her.

IRON JOHN

Iron John was a giant of a man, as strong as a bear and as crafty as a fox. But one day he was caught with his hand in the till, and taken to court. The punishment meted out was that he should be shackled to a post, with his head and hands gripped in the stocks. And that this punishment should be in full view of his neighbours, in the centre of the square in front of the church.

The shopkeeper Iron John had robbed happened to pass by that day. He began to laugh at John, to taunt him, and to call him names. The shackled man could stand no more abuse and lost all reason. With an enormous roar he tore the stocks, together with all the tackle, out of the ground, and chased after the nagging shopkeeper.

The man, horrified, felt his legs give way under him with terror. Until he realised he was right by the inn, and that the innkeeper had recently built a trapdoor through which he rolled his beer barrels and his cheeses. An ordinary man could also crawl through, but Iron John wouldn't be able to follow him there, encumbered with the stocks and tackle. The fleeing man opened the trapdoor and slid down.

Iron John was now powerless. He stood above the man he'd wronged, unable to get at his victim except with the curses and stones he cast down on him.

CHAPTER 8

Schwanenbruch, Summer 1952

'But surely, Gabby, you must have done something!' Martha Bender's schoolmarm voice is accusing a pupil of cheating during end-of-term examinations.

'Nothing. Absolutely nothing at all. My relations with Professor Schlech were entirely proper.'

'You didn't give the impression...'

'Impression? Impression? I enjoyed the man's company. I invited him to dinner with Hans and his Cerberus. And with the Czezinas. All right, I met him a couple of times in the *Sacher.* Where he introduced me to friends of his. I think we even went to *Demel's* once. Trying to rediscover the great confections of the past. We didn't manage it.'

'Manage what?' Headmistress frown. Once a cheat, always a cheat.

'*Hofzuckerbäckerei Demel,* Tante Martha, the coffee house famous for its pastries. Their cakes still look wonderful. Mouth-watering, enchanting. But when you taste them they're more like cardboard than cakes. Perhaps they've lost their pastry cooks or something. Maybe the Nazis dragged them off to concentration camps.'

'It's that sort of attitude which gets you into trouble, Gabby. Why can't you just behave yourself? Then you'd have been married to Herr Doktor Weiss ages ago.'

Ursula welcomes Gabby and Kamilla like a favourite niece and great-niece. She's provided them with two bedrooms, centrally heated against the North Sea cold. Which strikes even in summer. There's a bathroom but no kitchen. Ursula cooks for them and sleeps downstairs.

Gabby is lavish with the cash the brooch released. She didn't sell it to the jeweller Hans bought it from. She found somewhere less fashionable, in the Mariahilferstrasse he doesn't frequent. Why should she care? She's never going back to the tyranny of being his fiancée, even if he were to ask on bended knee.

She finally realises what Czezina tried to point out to her. She hasn't been free since Bosch died: she's been occupied. By benign powers maybe, rather as Vienna has been occupied since 1945. But she's been kept down a good deal more subtly than the Four-Power jeeps patrolling the streets of the city night and day can manage. She's been controlled by the past, by outmoded attitudes to women, by guilt.

Not any more. Never again. She's a vibrant thinking competent human being, who has foolishly allowed herself to be shackled by bygone prejudices she has no right, or intention, to tolerate again.

She pays a visit to the tobacconist by the church and buys cigars. She goes on to buy a bottle of her favourite schnapps and retires to her room in Ursula's house. Takes out a pad, a sharpened pencil. She writes down the pros and cons of her predicament. Her chances of finding a job.

PROS:	CONS:
Intelligent	Woman
Well-read	No qualifications
Determined	Child to raise
Good health	Forty-six years old
Quick learner	Never had a job
Courageous	Bad at numbers
Socially adept	Never in business

Gabby sits tapping the pencil against the bottle of schnapps. She hears the St Nicolaikirche peal out eleven. Not as clearly as when she lived in the Villa Dohlen. Which reminds her of her father's portrait. And that it still belongs to her. To her alone. A bargain she struck with her brother Emil long ago, before the war, hinting at irregularities she suspected — suspects — but cannot prove. The portrait is hers.

The holy German lunch hour starts at noon on the dot. There's nearly an hour before it, for the new businesswoman Gabby's just invented. She straightens her stocking seams and her skirt, grabs her handbag and marches down the Osterstrasse to the church, turns right to the house her father built. She rings the front-door bell.

A young girl she's never seen before opens it.

'Yes?'

Perhaps she should have worn a coat rather than a cardigan.

'Do you have business with the Council?'

'Gabriele Dohlen Bosch.' No smile. A business encounter. 'Herr Fosse, please. I won't take up much of his time.' Past conditioning betrays her into defensiveness. 'I have to see him right away.' But she uses a determined tone. A loud one.

'You have an appointment?' The door is already shutting in her face.

'Well, no. But he does know me. I wonder whether you'd be kind enough to ask…' Already floundering, dithering. She knows she has to do better than that.

Footsteps resound on the hall floor. 'Frau Bosch! Come in, of course.' Friedrich Fosse turns to the young girl. 'This is Frau Bosch, Fräulein. One of Herr Dohlen's daughters. This used to be her home.'

The girl's scowl remains in place. But the door opens wide.

Herr Fosse leads her to her father's old study. She can see right away that it's been painted in the wrong colours. Fosse sits in her father's old chair, facing her across a modern desk, looking down on her. She's perched on the edge of chrome and plastic. Jaw up. Resolute.

'I'll get right to the point, Herr Fosse. My father's portrait.' She points to it above his head. 'I left it in the villa, like everything else.'

The genial, avuncular nod of the respected burger. In charge of an important office. 'The sale was completed in spring 1938. Fourteen years ago.'

'March 11th, 1938. I sailed for England on what turned out to be the night Hitler marched into Austria. And I wasn't able to return to

Germany because of my anti-Nazi activities.'

Geniality is replaced by the busy tidying of papers on an immaculate desk.

'My funds were frozen. And, as you know, eventually taken over by the Nazis when America entered the war. As enemy property.' A smile of victory is permissible.

Eyelids blink a cover for his eyes. 'A terrible time. You know that if there were anything I could do, I'd do it. Your father was a great man. He helped my parents when no one else would help them.'

'I had no idea, Herr Fosse.'

'I owe him a debt I would love to repay to his family. I've often thought about it. But there's nothing I can do. Appropriated funds are a matter for the Federal Government.'

Gabby's smile broadens. 'Indeed. I am applying for restitution. Today I'm concerned about the contents of the villa. They were not part of the sale.' She unclasps her handbag.

She can see the ignorant-little-widow-look reflected in Fosse's eyes. 'Fixtures and fittings, surely?'

'The movables, Herr Fosse. Paintings, furniture. It was agreed they were to be left until I could arrange to pick them up.' The handbag yawns wide. 'This is the original agreement.'

Pebble lenses are placed before surprised eyes. A podgy hand reaches over the desk to take the paper. Crackled into the correct position for bureaucratic reading. 'I see. The chair I'm sitting in. The painting over my head.'

'Exactly. My father's portrait. I'd like to have it.'

The protestations are voluble. It fits so well into the villa. Where would she put such a large painting. What can she do with it?

'That, dear Herr Fosse, is for me to decide. I'm sure you don't want me to bring a case against the Council.'

'That will be quite unnecessary.'

'I am prepared to sell you the remaining furniture for a reasonable sum. As for the painting, I'm willing to accept a photographic copy for the time being. While you have an oil copy made. My time scale is next summer.' She smiles. No longer hang-dog, apologetic. A smile of triumph. 'Deal?'

'And if I don't agree?'

The smile stays on her face. 'I will lodge a complaint. I'll make it part of my case against the Federal authorities. Which will deprive the council of their offices while the case blunders through lengthy legal proceedings.'

He nods as he hands back the contract at the precise moment the Nicolaikirche bells rings out the midday hour.

'Holy Moses!' she hears her father roar. 'About time.'

A small, penniless, middle-aged woman with no qualifications has done her first business deal. In the house her father built. She feels his strength run through her, remembers the day her mother died. Neither her mother's gene, nor her father's money, is what it's all about. Forging her own destiny. *That* is her true inheritance.

'A glass of schnapps to seal our agreement?' Herr Fosse rummages in the cupboard behind him.

Gabby pulls out a packet of cigars, offers one, lights up herself. She raises her glass to the portrait of her father. Amen.

The letter from Hans Weiss is delivered two weeks after Gabby's arrival in Schwanenbruch.

The translucent airmail envelope sits on her windowsill. It's propped against the morning sun shining into her bedroom, proof positive that he can't do without her. She twirls it. Sunbeams catch the dust and hold it suspended. The message inside is as harmless as a buried manuscript — unless she sets it free.

She holds out for ten days. When another letter joins the first. And as she's about to set it in front of the other, obscuring more light, several words become legible and stand out.

It is possible I acted somewhat hastily. ....out of...

Out of what? Jealousy? To get back at her for her deceit? Because he trusted his informant more than he trusted her? And that informant, she finally worked out, was Trautl. Furious at being dismissed, telling all kinds of tales. Which doesn't excuse Hans for believing them.

She tears open the envelope.

My dearest heart, my Beatrice,
It is possible I acted somewhat hastily. Which, I believe, is quite out of character.
Do please forgive me. Let us at least be friends. I hope you will accept that I would
not have been so cavalier had I not, very recently, had occasion to see evidence of
your — well, let us call it dissimulation. No more of the past, I give you my word it
is over. And I am a man of my word.

Needless to say I do not write to reprove you. I merely try to find excuses for a man who cannot live without you. An admirer who thinks so highly of you that he cannot believe he is the only one to pay you court, yet one who knows his court is circumscribed by prohibitions a good Christian must observe.

I cannot help myself but to try to win you back. The whole of Vienna is dead without your presence, silent without your voice. My ears can hear no music, my eyes see no paintings, all my senses are dulled. I am like the enchanted prince. I cannot function unless you break the spell.

Allow me one more chance. Let me provide for you and sweet little Kamilla, as we planned. Let me give you the comforts and joys you so richly deserve. Forgive me as I forgave you, and let us speak no more of it.

And if you cannot find it in your heart to agree right away, at least please send some sign. Answer through a messenger, send me some hope. Don't let true love wither into despair.

Your obedient, adoring, exasperating

Hans Weiss

An excellent photograph of her father's portrait hangs above her bed. 'What shall I do?'

'Nothing at all!' she hears him say. 'Let him sweat it out. You have the advantage. You know his strengths and his weaknesses. Which means he's at your mercy. Keep him there.'

She makes another list. The pros and cons of marrying Hans Weiss.

> She's vivacious, younger than her years
> She's middle-aged, fading looks
>
> Small child to bring up, related to Hans
> Kamilla brought up in occupied Austria
>
> Outstanding hostess skills to put to use
> She can use these skills to earn money
>
> She has no qualifications, no prospects
> She can manage without qualifications
>
> He is intelligent, cultured, handsome
> He is a bore and sucks her dry

She is poor, he is well off
She would be free to emulate her father

He belongs to her, she can mould him
Loss of freedom to do as she pleases

Her pride vindicated, opponents crushed
There are other ways to do that

Position in society assured
Forced into religious bigotry

Gabby turns the options round in her head for another week. She tosses
the first bouquet of flowers onto the compost heap, hands the second one
to Ursula. She walks along the Braake, on the dyke, gazes out to sea.

Then she remembers what was once a curse, but is now an advantage.
She and Hans will be married in a Registry Office, just like her marriage
to Rolf Ferent. If it doesn't work out there's the option of a divorce.
Because they won't be married in the Church until the annulment
comes through. So there's no real commitment until then. She has the
Church's word on that.

Dear Hans,

*I have given your letters careful thought. You must already know that there is no
foundation whatsoever for the accusations you brought against me. There was not —
there never has been — a liaison between Professor Schlech and myself. If you were to
look into his way of life more carefully, you will see there never could have been.*

*In any case, I thought I'd made it clear. Such matters are not of paramount
importance to me. I am as content with the state of celibacy as any postulant applying
to enter a convent.*

*Gratifying though it is that you miss me so much, I do not intend to return to
Vienna until the autumn. Perhaps we will see each other then.*

As ever
Gabriele

It isn't only strengths which make a relationship. The weaknesses
of both parties are just as important. Hans is a mature man with the
outlook of a child. He is hers to mould, to shape, to control. He's the

frog she will turn into a prince, she is the beauty to his beast. She is his destiny, his fate, his duty even.

And then there are her weaknesses. She doesn't quite believe in herself, it would be so easy simply to allow Hans to see to her financial needs, he would provide a father-figure for Kamilla.

Hans Weiss arrives in Schwanenbruch within the week. He takes a room at the *Elbfluss Haus* and is there for the whole village to see.

He woos Gabby even more ardently than before. Flowers, chocolates, expensive restaurants. Gifts for Onkel Wilfred and his family, and for Tante Martha. A tour round the Villa Dohlen amid much admiration. The Tiffany windows are pronounced exquisite, the original kitchen, bathroom and hall admired. The new offices are examined in silence. The handsome head shakes over the council officials' ignorance and their lack of taste.

Gabby is the chauffeuse as they tour the area in the Beetle, Kamilla is bored restless on the back seat. But both of them have to be there while Hans goes Wattlaufen in Duhnen, on trips to Neuwerk, tours the fishing harbour in Cuxhaven, arranges boat trips, takes them on expensive excursions to Hamburg.

Hans is particularly taken with the St Nicolaikirche, its magnificent organ, and the many other splendid marsh churches and their treasures. He spends hours in musty interiors. Gabby escapes on pretext of Kamilla while the child plays and she enjoys a glass of schnapps and a cigar.

The introductions to her relatives are more of a success than hers to his. Onkel Wilfred is red-faced benign, Tante Martha eruditely impressed.

This time it's different, Gabby tells herself. This time the marriage really will take place. She's looking forward to it. Immensely. Though Hans hasn't, as yet, mentioned anything about dates.

'Why don't we all drive back to Vienna together?' Hans likes to start the day early. He arrives on her doorstep on the dot of seven. 'That would be so delightful. We can call in on Heidelberg. There's a church there I'd love to see again.'

Gabby sighs. Yet another church to be examined to the last tombstone. When all she wants to do is enjoy herself vegetating in Schwanenbruch.

'It will give you time to arrange the civil ceremony. I thought

October. That's a lovely month for a weekend in the Wachau.'

Is he implying that the honeymoon trip is more important than the marriage?

He can see she's still hesitating. 'It will give you a decent amount of time to get everything ready.'

This time relatives and friends will be informed after the event. The authorities have already mentioned, with puzzled frowns, that they do not need to be shown documents more than once.

Hans, in full flow, stops in the middle of the main street. Forcing the Cuxhaven bus to screech to a halt. 'I thought this time we should arrange a much more personal reception. In the Karlsgasse.'

'Your apartment, you mean?' His, or the two together? Anyway, far more work than booking the *Hotel Sacher.*

That pitying look has not been abandoned with the new fervour. 'I only live in one apartment in the Karlsgasse. You've made it look so splendid. It would be a great pity not to show it off.'

Not strictly true. He's sharing his apartment with his sister Greti. The apartment may have been designated into two parts, but they are still together.

Hans only has two weeks he can spend in Schwanenbruch. Which were prised out of his employer on the basis that, in December, he was indisposed. He persuaded his superiors at the insurance company that he badly needs a holiday.

Valiant efforts to persuade her to return to Vienna with him right away are side-stepped. Doly and Ross will be arriving in two weeks, Gemma and Nina shortly after that. Gabby attributes her feelings of relief to the need for more seaside breezes.

'Another month, then? You'll be back in August?'

Vienna is hot and dusty in August, Schwanenbruch always swept by cleansing air. She agrees reluctantly.

CHAPTER 9

Schwanenbruch, Summer 1952

Doly has renewed the comfortable berth with Rula's daughter Anna. In the second house from the dyke, next to the house her father was born in. Small, stone-built, two up two down. No running water. An outside toilet. She shares one upstairs room with Ross. It's cosy, rural, and within her means. And much more comfortable than the garden shed at Dramlings.

Tante Martha paid for the trip. She clucks over Ross and Doly with approving smiles. Until she finds out Doly spends her evenings at the *Schleuse Inn* and doesn't get home till the early hours. Often accompanied by married men, and after Ross has had his breakfast.

Schwanenbruch is a small village. With gossips to match. Not always female ones.

'Liesl!' Doly recognises the matronly walk, but not the cold look. The frank eyes she used to look into are laced with embarrassment. 'So wonderful to see you.'

The hug is peremptory and as distant as Lieselotte's arms can make it. 'I can't stay long. Joseph is…'

Doly is there at most one month of summer. 'Surely he can spare you for half an hour?' Nothing changes: Joseph's distaste for her is as it always was, as Nazi doctrine dictated. Lock the skeleton back in the cupboard.

'I'm only home for the weekends. Joseph quite reasonably expects to see something of me.'

One cannot possibly have any quarrel with an honest opinion honestly put. Though she knows Joseph spends weekends hunting. And Doly's determined not to be riding in anyone's Jim Crow car. The Nazi influence hasn't disappeared with the end of the war. Not in Germany, nor anywhere else. Eugenics in the 1930s was not confined to Germany, and it's still around.

She tries another tack. 'Don't you miss your girls, Liesi?'

'I've tried to explain. I have a career, and you're the one who made it possible, so you should be applauding me.' She stares at Doly, blinks. 'I like my job. And I spend every week-end with the girls. Because I can afford to pay someone to do the household chores.'

Three daughters, and she's not even there to bring them up? How can doctoring compensate for that?

Tonight Doly leaves the *Schleuse Inn* before it closes, as soon as she sees the moon rising over the sea. It sparkles diamonds into her eyes. She sleepwalks to the end of the stone jetty, nearer to the ships plying the Elbe. Is Piers's among them? She strains hopeful eyes throughout long nights when sleep is as elusive as Piers's love.

Why all this restless urging when she knows how to wait? Is it really anything new to her to be so very alone? The things she could never say to anyone else she can say less and less. She can barely even think them. She will keep faith with the spell she's fallen under. Her constant and abiding love for Ross, for Piers, for Liesi — and for her little haven in the Sussex woods.

And the greatest of all loves is charity. She will keep faith with that as best she can.

'You can't be serious.' Gemma's long strides along the Braake are hard for Gabby to keep up with. 'A woman like you, courageous, vibrant, clever, the one who made what deals could be made about the two villas — you're still set on marrying that wizened old bore?'

'He's fifty-two!'

'He's ancient. And thinks of women as chattels he can move around.'

'What rubbish, Gemma. I'm very fond of him. And Kamilla will have a steady decent childhood. Like my marriage to Bosch gave you.'

'How can you even mention Bosch in the same breath as Hans Weiss?'

'Hans is much more stable.'

'The man is moribund. And he's let you down. Twice. I wouldn't trust him if he were the last man on earth.'

'The first time was my fault.'

Gemma's young face is contorted. 'How can you be so blind? Can't you see what this nonsense about annulments is all about?'

'He's terribly devout...'

'Really? In that case he must have known you can't get an annulment in a few months. He even suggested shortening the time!' Gemma's blazing eyes sweep over her mother. 'You must have worked it out by now. He was using the Church as a cover to get out of marrying you.'

That somewhat shocking thought, one which, in fact, did insinuate itself during nights when sleep eluded her, has now been given substance. 'Of course not. Even Greti didn't know, otherwise she'd hardly have worried about our actually getting married.'

'That's another matter. She was probably too shocked, too horrified, to think properly at the time.' Gemma slows down. 'You say she was quite pleasant when you were getting the apartment ready?'

'Well, yes, that was some time later...'

'She knew as well.'

A small slight prick insinuates itself into Gabby's mind. Father Joachim is Greti's confessor. Did she, by any chance, mention she'd been uncharitable about Gabby, was sad that an annulment would take a long time, alerting the gentle priest to circumstances he had no means of knowing before?

Entirely possible. If so he must have wrestled, hard, with his own conscience. Would it be right to act on information received in the confessional? How would he avoid doing that? Was reading the 'rules' his way of avoiding the issue?

'I do see that pious Hans reminds you of Bosch physically, of the past, and I can sympathize with that.' Gemma's tone has softened. 'His mannerisms are so similar to Bosch's, and that's terribly misleading. Just one thing I want to emphasize: he'll never be anything but a pale imitation of Franz Bosch. I think, deep down, you already know that.'

Gabby can't deny the touch of Bosch. Cantankerous, stubborn and testy but with none of Bosch's irony or flair. Hans does have a courtliness, and the occasional desire to please, which was entirely absent from her late husband's disposition. 'I don't know why you're quite so set against him, Gemma.'

'There's something fishy about the way the priest asked you whether you'd been married before being married to Bosch. There wasn't any hint on paper, was there? So what on earth made him ask that?'

'I didn't say he did. I said I wasn't really listening...'

'But Hans chipped in, saying why don't you tell him about the annulment. That means he must have asked whether you'd been married before. You're sure someone didn't put that priest up to it?'

'What an incredible idea!' So Gemma has worked it out as well. The old man was certainly not one to probe such an unlikely scenario. She remembers he said: 'Normally I would not have questioned you further. But in your case...' Precisely why was her case different? 'So who d'you think it was?'

'Pretty obvious, I would have thought. Greti, or the Berghers.' Gemma stares at her. 'The fact is that Hans was the one who brought up the annulment which he must have known you couldn't have got. You have to face the fact that he lied, Gabby. To himself as well as to you, probably. He may not have told an untruth, as such, but basically he must have known you can't get a marriage annulled in a few months.'

If Gemma could work it out, why hadn't she? What stopped her from knowing exactly what Hans was playing at? 'Lied? Hans is as honest as the day is long!'

'I see no reason to assume that days are honest.' Gemma looks through the microscope of analytic thought. 'Of course a religious bigot like Hans Weiss knows the Church takes years to do anything. Everyone knows that, but I decided to look into it and read it up in one of those pamphlets they have at the back of Catholic churches.'

'I'm sure he doesn't read...'

'It was his way of stalling you.'

'You'll be telling me next it was he who alerted the priest!'

Gemma looks pensive. 'That's a possibility, I suppose. It would have had to be anonymously, of course. Not really likely, he was too busy fooling himself. But it was Hans who brought up the annulment.'

She simply can't remember exactly who said what and when. She does remember Father Joachim's gentle voice. 'You're terribly hard on him, Gemma. And he's very presentable.'

'More to the point is that he's got the lolly. I'm not being spiteful, but that's why you're even thinking about it again, isn't it? If you could rustle up a job, or any other way of making money, would you go near him?'

If Gabby had feathers she would preen them. 'Of course I would.'

'Why?'

'I like his company. He's a cultured intelligent man. A presentable escort. And he enjoys spoiling me.'

'I don't believe I'm talking to the woman who defied Hitler, who watched the war-time dog fights instead of cringing in shelters, who found us a brilliant house in exchange for playing chess. You want to turn into a boring Viennese housewife, whose main concern is whether her husband's meal pleases him?'

'You're exaggerating, Gemma. You don't understand...'

'I do. You haven't grasped that the war has changed the position of women. Not only that. It's changed the way women think about themselves. For ever. They had to do men's jobs, and did them just as well as the warring men. And they're not going to forget it.'

'You'll be telling me that women are men's equals, that...'

'Of course they are. I'm in what used to be termed a man's field. I'm a computer programmer and very good at it. And I can tell you this. My boss is a misogynist, but even he hasn't been able to find a man to replace me, though he's tried hard enough.

'If you want to earn your own money, Gabby, you can. You don't have to submit to some boring old fart for a few glad rags.' She slows a little, softens her expression. 'I know you don't believe me. The generation gap, I suppose.'

A PROMISE KEPT

There's a small hill near the village of Rahden. The locals call it the Chapel Mound. It is surrounded by the meadow they call the Chapel Field. Because many years ago there wasn't just a chapel here, there was a thriving convent and a large community of nuns. Until the number of sisters dwindled to just two ancient nuns left from the old order.

The villagers of Rahden were not keen to support the two old ladies The feeling was strong that contributions to the nuns' welfare were definitely on the high side. Bearing in mind the lack of return. So the village elders made it absolutely clear to the Holy Sisters that an early departure would be appreciated.

The two old nuns begged to be given just one more year in which to sow a crop which they could harvest. The villagers did not like to seem churlish and to refuse such a simple request. So they granted it. Graciously.

The two holy nuns were, however, as prone to human frailties as any of their more worldly sisters. And, true to the inheritance from their mothers, bountifully supplied with female wiles.

The two old ladies bought their seed. They planted the whole mound with acorns. And, in so doing, laid the foundations of the Westerberger Forest. A crop which will take a good fifty years to come to harvest.

If the nuns had not died in the meantime, and the walls of the convent had not fallen into disrepair, then the two old women would still be enjoying their right of tenure. In the ancient convent, on the densely wooded hill surrounded by the meadow now turned to oak forest.

CHAPTER 10

Sussex, September 1952

'You're living alone, well beyond Stedham, aren't you, Mrs Courtling?'

Doly sees red but calms it down to pink. What has that to do with what she's here for? Doctors should stick to their last just like cobblers. 'A lovely spot. Have you been out there?'

'I was thinking about emergencies. You've had no nausea, no problems of any kind?'

'Nothing at all. I feel wonderful.' Will the scars on her legs, long vertical cuts to prevent possible blood clots, give away that she had a difficult birth with Ross? Doly wraps her coat round herself protectively, pats the bulge in her abdomen. Boy or girl? What does it matter. Piers's child at long last. Joy unrestrained.

'I don't wish to be indelicate. Will the father — will you marry the father?'

'Is that a medical question?' This doctor is one of those brisk, middle-aged women who can only see the physical side of things. She wears a white coat, starched so stiff that it crackles as she picks up her pen to write.

'I didn't mean to pry. It's just that you're so far out, there'll be no one to help you…'

'Good of you to be concerned. No need to worry.'

The doctor's eyes quiz over glasses. 'And you've missed three periods?'

'Since June.'

'Left it quite some time to come to see me.'

'I wanted to be sure.' Doly feels the hot prickle of irritation running sweat down her back. 'Pregnancy isn't a disease. And I don't like to bother you for nothing.'

'Pregnancy at over forty has a substantial risk factor for intrauterine foetal demise or stillbirth. It is not to be trifled with.' The doctor is writing something on a prescription pad. 'Right then. Bring a sample in as soon as possible. Then we can test to make sure.'

A surge of fury coursing hot blood through veins. 'Sure of what?'

'That you are actually pregnant, Mrs Courtling.'

'Hardly necessary.' Doly rubs her bump affectionately.

'I'll prescribe something in case you have problems.' The doctor's nostrils dilate. 'It would be wrong to damage the baby in any way, of course, but at your age… Well, it could be a false alarm.' That dead blink behind pebble glasses. Magnifying it.

'Why would you think a wanted pregnancy alarming, Dr Wells?'

'Of course that isn't what I meant.' The pen scratches deep impressions on innocent paper. 'What is your year of birth?'

Testing her! 'I believe you have all my details. In the notes you've been reading.'

'Just making sure they're accurate.'

'1911. May I remind you: other women have borne children well beyond forty-one.'

The pen stops writing, the doctor looks up. 'You mean you want it?'

'Want him or her? I'm absolutely thrilled.'

Glasses are pushed up the nose, notes read again. 'You did have several miscarriages when you were much younger, Mrs Courtling. And Ross was born abroad, I understand. Were there any difficulties then?'

'None at all.' The wretched woman will rush her off to hospital if she's not careful. Who knows what they'd get up to there. Childbearing is a natural process and she's going to make sure the medical profession doesn't interfere. But she does have to make sure they're alerted and available.

'Perhaps it would be best if you could let us have a sample of urine now. And blood. We'll need to look after you properly, you know. You and the baby.'

'I'll bring them in another day. I'm late for picking Ross up from school.'

Vienna, Autumn 1952

'You're not serious, gnä' Frau?' Czezina is pacing his office. His hands plough through his hair, his eyes are wild. 'You can't believe it will work!'

'Why not? Hans and I get on so well in so many ways.'

'Because you play up to him. He's as stubborn as a mule. Obstinate, unyielding, bull-headed, intractable.'

'He'll go through with it this time. There's no comparison.'

'You think he's going to stand up to a new onslaught from Greti and the Berghers? At the moment he imagines he's come to a final decision. But when he's supposed to act on it, he'll back off. A different excuse, but he'll find something.' The sigh is deep. 'Not through malice. Through terror. Just like a horse which won't leave a blazing stable.'

'You're completely wrong.' Gabby crosses one leg over the other.

'You sound positively smug. Want to tell me what evidence you have?'

She uncrosses her legs, settles back into her chair. 'There was all this nonsense about Professor Schlech. So I thought, why not test him out? I told him that there was nothing — absolutely nothing — between Schlech and myself. Or any other man except Hans himself since Bosch died.'

'Quite. So?'

'But I did have a liaison I wanted him to know about. Before he hears of it from someone else.'

'You told Hans Weiss you've had an affair?' Czezina's mouth literally drops open, saliva trickles down his chin.

He's clearly scandalised. By the admission, or by her foolhardiness in telling Hans?

He swallows, wipes his mouth. 'And he didn't run off in horror?'

'Certainly not. He was very nonchalant, very matter-of-fact.'

203

'If I might ask — when was this?'

'Ages ago — over ten years. During the war. A young man I met when Bosch was interned. In London during the Blitz. Christopher Hyllier managed to get Bosch released by finding him a job.' She did think it strange that it took a year, longer than many of the other refugees who'd been interned. But Bosch was given a job in a physics laboratory, trusted by the British. That had to be Christopher's doing.

'You told Hans all that? And he accepted it?'

'Yes. I told you I was sure this time. He's a completely different man.'

The lawyer stands, crosses over to the window dominated by the towers of the Votivkirche. He stands motionless so long she wonders whether he's forgotten her. 'Two reasons why it will never work out, gnä' Frau.'

'You're still not convinced?'

'Not remotely.' His shoulders heave up, down, up. 'I repeat: it will never — it *can* never — work out.' His thick lips are rounded as though he's about to whistle. 'Your character, and his. Nothing you say or do can make any difference to either of you. One last warning, so that my conscience is clear. He will produce another last-minute bombshell of some sort. Some outlandish reason why he can't go ahead. I wish I could convince you.'

'You only see the worst, the problems, Herr Doktor. Like all lawyers, I suppose.'

Gabby is called to give evidence at the Marriage Court in early October, ironically just days before the civil wedding date. As she leaves the office of the Procurator Fidei black clouds obscure the autumn light, threaten torrential rain. She scurries through cobbled shortcuts but she can't escape. The heavens empty, drenching her. Wet, cold, somehow depressed she fumbles with the heavy front door of her apartment house.

Inside she shakes the water from her head, her face, her clothes. She looks idly at the letter box she emptied earlier that morning. Blurred white of — something. An advertisement? Her throat constricts. Or a note?

Suddenly she knows exactly what it is, feels herself gag. She realises Czezina was right long before she opens the letter cage to take the piece of paper out. Even before she recognises her fiancé's handwriting.

It can't be true. It simply can't!

She pushes the note into her coat pocket. Hiding it. She plods up two flights of stairs, nauseous and breathless. She unlocks her door, crashes it shut against the outside world. She's alone in her snug, warm apartment. Yet she feels so cold.

She takes off her wet coat. Pours herself a drink. Sits down.

Yesterday I was told something quite unforgivable about you. I am not in a position to divulge what it was, or the name of my informant, but on this occasion there can be no question of its truth. Do not attempt to get in touch with me. I have no intention whatever of seeing you again.

You have utterly destroyed my happiness.

No signature. No date. Empty space.

That's exactly what he is. A null, a zero, a shell of a man with no substance. How could she have fallen for it all a third time? Why didn't she listen to Czezina? Or to Gemma?

She's been an idiot. Never again. She isn't sorry, or worried, or in any way apologetic. This time she knows it is a ruse. Whatever trumped-up rubbish he's dreamt up, this time he won't get away with it.

A small, short stab of conscience. Has he found out she sold the brooch?

That would still be a pretext. Why shouldn't she? She has to live on something. And it was hers.

What, then? Wild theories tumble through her mind. She runs a cold bath, deliberately makes herself shake, suppresses all thoughts about Hans. This time she's fighting back.

She rubs herself warm with her bath towel and rings Czezina. His secretary, hearing her tone of voice, puts her through although he's with another client.

'Herr Doktor. When can I see you?' Even she doesn't recognise her voice. Tense, brittle, hard.

'It's happened again, hasn't it?'

'Yes.'

'I'm in court all afternoon. I won't get through till six. Come and see me then.'

Gabby busies herself throwing everything Hans gave her into a rubbish bin. Until she's startled to see the time. She has to fetch Kamilla from her Kindergarten. She's already fifteen minutes late.

She grabs her coat, rushes out. There's one lone teacher who's stayed behind with a fractious irritable child.

'I'm terribly sorry, Frau Sundermann. I simply forgot the time.'

'Are we going to the Prater right away, Mutti?'

'What are you talking about, child?'

'Apparently you promised Kamilla a ride on the Riesenrad, Frau Bosch. She's talked of nothing else for days.'

She and Hans went to see *The Third Man*. They'd never, in all their years in Vienna, taken a ride on the splendid Ferris wheel which is such a feature in the film. They saw an opportunity to try it out and entertain Kamilla at the same time.

'Oh, dear.'

'You promised, Mutti. You and Onkel Hans. You promised me we'd go today.'

The small face is turned up to her, the eyes beseeching. 'You are quite right, Kamilla. It slipped my mind. Onkel Hans won't be coming with us. But a promise is a promise. You and I — we'll go for a ride on the Riesenrad.'

She turns back to the teacher, thanks her profusely. And takes Kamilla's trusting hand in hers, smiles at her smiling face. She promised her. She did. And promises should never be broken.

Gabby arranges for Kamilla to play with Brigitte. She sets out for her appointment with Czezina, feeling more serene than she's ever been for a meeting with him.

'I hate to say I told you so,' he greets her. Affably enough. 'The poor man cannot help himself. I'm sure he adores you. It's obvious he can't manage without your company. He'd like to get married. He just can't go through with it.'

The same discussion they've had a hundred times. 'What is there to go through with, Herr Doktor? No carnal intercourse, after all. We were going to live as brother and sister!'

Czezina's small plump fingers spread out. 'Once your annulment is through, gnä' Frau. What then?'

'But what revelation is he talking about? There's nothing. There *can* be nothing.'

'Quite right. A fabrication of some sort. An excuse, however tenuous.

Something without essence. A mirage, if you like.'

'Very well. I'm perfectly willing to listen to what he has to say. But we have to meet. I insist he tells me what it's all about. In person.'

'Please do believe me, gnä' Frau. He won't see you, he won't explain. And when, eventually, he can't manage without you any more, he'll arrange a meeting and evade the issue. What you have to face is that he will never marry you. Never.'

'I'm no longer interesting in marrying him, Herr Doktor. I merely insist on my right to know what he's accusing me of. His greatest hypocrisy is to hide behind some "secret" he's not able to divulge. I refuse to settle for that.'

'He'll take to his bed, decline to see you, get his sister to do his dirty work for him.'

'Very likely.' A small slight lifting of the corners of her mouth. 'But he'll see you.' Soft, soft voice.

'You will forgive me, gnä' Frau. I will not be the go-between again. For your own sake.'

'I'm not asking you as a friend, Herr Doktor. I am instructing you. As my lawyer.' No anxiety, no fear, no tremor in her voice. 'If he prefers, he can let me know through you. I am prepared to settle for that.'

'I am his lawyer too, gnä' Frau. Long before I was yours. Again, I'm sorry to refuse.'

'You're adamant?' He's frowning. Her responses worry him. He nods. Gabby feels power run through her. Right to her fingertips. 'In that case I have absolutely no option but to force the issue.'

'Force it? How can you possibly force it?'

'I would have expected you to have worked that out by now, Herr Doktor.' Emphasis on the k.

His bloodhound nose is twitching. Aimlessly. 'I have no idea.' His eyes are blank, but he can't conceal the sweat of anxiety. 'But surely you must realise…'

Czezina has never seen the portrait of her father, of his eyes. If he had, he'd recognise the expression in Gabby's. The smell of fear spreads in the stuffy room. 'I'm waiting for you to enlighten me.'

'All right.' Gabby nods. 'It's actually very simple. I shall sue.'

He scrunches up the papers on his desk. 'For goodness sake, gnä' Frau! Sue whom? For what?'

Her trump card. The ace her father would have played at just the right time. 'For breach of promise, Herr Doktor. Hans can't deny he promised to marry me. Unless he has some cast-iron case — and I know very well he can't have — he'll be in contempt of court. And the laughing stock of Vienna.'

Czezina cajoles, flatters, expostulates. Creeps hands towards her. She rises to leave.

He sees he can't change her mind. 'You won't get anywhere like that, you know! The Austrian courts are set against women in the first place. You're also a foreigner, a woman married outside the Church. A self-confessed adulteress. They'll make hay.'

He still underestimates her. Gemma was right, it can only be because she is a woman. 'What's that to me, Herr Doktor? As you say, I'm a mere woman. A widow of no account. I have no standing, no job, nothing.' She tries to stop the triumph welling through. 'I have a reasonable case. And absolutely nothing to lose.'

'But what can you possibly gain, gnä' Frau?' He's back to his concerned friend role. Exasperated, polite, but on her side. 'You can't imagine you'll get significant damages?' The wail of worry.

'You really think I'm after money?' An overwhelming realisation of victory makes her feel tall. 'I want the truth. The judge, however great a misogynist he may be, will have to allow my lawyer to question the learned Herr Doktor Weiss. On oath. And he will be forced to answer.' Her hands slap the arms of her chair. 'Not money, Herr Doktor. I want my moral rights. Basic justice. An explanation for the breaking of a solemn promise. And the acknowledgement that Johann Theodor Weiss has acted like a coward.'

His pencil tattoos the desk. 'If you get to court. You'll need someone to represent you.'

How strange. He hasn't even spotted the danger to himself. He put the idea of pretending to have obtained her annulment to her. An unethical — illegal — suggestion. Which is bound to come out in court. 'There are other lawyers in Vienna, Herr Doktor.'

She sees the danger has been recognised. Coal eyes smoulder. Can she win against such odds? The smile around her lips flickers on and off. A neon light advertising her stock-in-trade of charm. Misleading even Czezina.

'Just one more plea to leave it all alone, Frau Bosch. I alerted you to problems about re-renting the villa only last week. Where will you get enough money to live on, let alone to fight a legal battle?'

Gemma's words swirl round her head. 'A woman like you, vibrant, clever…' She remembers how she confronted Herr Fosse. She had the nerve, the wit, the determination to claim her birthright from the Schwanenbruch Council — her father's portrait, strong and proud. Her features reassemble into determination, the conviction of success.

The Dohlen Inheritance — the *real* Dohlen Inheritance, the one that counts: the determination to win against all odds. She is Gabriele Dohlen Bosch, Emil Julius Dohlen's heir. It's time for her to act on that.

CHAPTER 11

Sussex, October 1952

'Welcome to Dramlings, Bobby.' Doly heard the taxi turning in her drive. She's halfway across the lawn to greet the American sweetheart of her Riverside Hall years. When they were lovebirds in New Jersey, and sometimes in Paradise, Pennsylvania. Paradise! She thought so then, though now she knows where real paradise is. Her eyes smile, her arms outstretched in welcome.

'Doly. You're a sight for sore eyes.' Paunchy, middle-aged, hair on top thinning to baldness. She wouldn't have recognised him if he weren't walking across her lawn. Gingerly. He's used to asphalt sidewalks. More used to the inside of cars.

'How long's it been? Twenty-two years? A generation ago, by golly.'

'I guess that's true enough. I've never even had a sight of Ross.' He stops on sodden lawn. 'Say, this is a real cute place.' He's a tall man. Hudwalker men are often six-footers, like her one-time guardian Walter — Huddy Fuddy, as they dubbed him. Huddy Daddy Tante Martha thought she'd said. Either way a good description of a preaching, boring do-gooder, thin and gaunt. Still preaching to the remnants of his congregation.

So different from Bobby. He's burly with height, grizzled and deep-lined. He squelches on, then squeezes sideways into the small front door, stooping under the lintel. 'Piece of old England, right?'

'Tudor, yes. People were shorter in those days.'

'Not enough protein. Sure thing.'

'Your bedroom's just off this room. Let me show you where to put your case.' Doly walks to the door leading to the small room off the living room. Eight by six. A single bed, an upright chair. She backs out to let him in.

'Say, this is great. Get a load of these walls!' He fingertips playfully over stone decorated in cream eggshell paint, not whitewash. That reflects what light there is with a low ceiling and a small window. And it's easy to keep clean.

'You wash in the kitchen. The toilet's outside. I'll show you when you're ready.'

The mechanical smile shows he's used to a softer life. He hands her a bottle. Chanel No 5. Almost the size of a half-bottle of wine. Which she could have put to better use.

Does she look as middle-aged to him as he does to her? She's forty-one, after all. And her belly is swelling, perhaps a little more than necessary because she can hardly wait for Piers's child to grow to maturity inside her.

She knows she hasn't worn as well as Gabby. The constant hard outdoor work has sun-creased her skin and thickened her frame. She's obliged to cover her skimpy hair with a National Health wig. Not quite up to Viennese standards.

'So where's the little guy at? Where's Ross?'

'It's a school day, Bobby. He's at a pre-prep Kindergarten.'

'Kinda young for that, ain't he? Thought I'd be seeing him running around. Plenty of space on that brilliant English lawn you got there.' He hauls his suitcase on to the bed. 'Leastways I brought him a present.' He opens the case, hauls out a large dump truck, and a horse with a cowboy on it. 'Bet he's a handsome kid, with you for a mother.'

'An English gentleman.'

The low infectious laugh she remembers. 'I'll bet my bottom dollar.

Haven't lost your sense of humour none.' He closes the case, backs into the living room. 'You got a drink for an old friend?'

'My very own brew.' Commercial alcohol's beyond her means. She offers home-made wines in recycled beer bottles. 'A glass of elderflower champagne to welcome you!' Two dull, chipped glasses, not spectacularly clean. The opened bottle gushes the sparkling liquid.

Bobby drinks. Manfully. 'In a class by itself.' He holds his glass out for more.

'Headier than you'd expect.' She pours for both of them, feels twenty years lift off her shoulders. Refurbishing dull eyes.

'Cheers.' He squashes beside her on the narrow sofa. 'Great place you have here, Doly. But where in hell is it, for chrissake? Why are you tucked off the beaten track this way? Can't see a single neighbour.'

'It's how I like it, Bobby. No traffic noise, no fumes, no rat race. Wonderful walks. I can pot the occasional rabbit or wood pigeon.' She strokes the Jack Russell terrier panting beside her. 'Buffy fetches for me.'

'You don't get lonesome?'

'I have Ross. Living here means I can bring him up in peace and quiet.'

'If I can put in my two cents. No greenbacks neither.'

'Money is the root of all evil.'

'And makes the world go round.' His eyes take in the shabby furniture, the worn rug, her dowdy clothes, her figure. 'You don't even have wheels. The school has to be miles off. How in the world d'you pick Ross up?'

'I don't, Bobby. Neighbours drop him off at the bottom of the drive. He walks the rest of the way.'

'That a fact? How far's that?'

'A few hundred yards maybe! Along the track you must have noticed in your taxi.'

'The potholes, right. And he's not yet five?'

'Shank's pony is a damned good horse, my father used to say. Remember how we walked everywhere? What fun we had?'

He puts an arm around her shoulders, hugs her to him. 'I remember, Doly. Sweet stolen kisses behind old Fuddy's back. Out-running and out-gunning the Ugly Sisters.' He takes an experimental bite at her right ear.

She gets up and pokes the fire. 'How are they?'

'Ma and Pa Fuddy? Doddering. Still preaching. Ugly sisters Gertrude and Hildegarde looking after them. Ferociously.' He pulls her to him, plants a wet kiss, rubs her belly. 'I guess there's someone special now?'

She nods, unable to discuss carrying Piers's child. But she's over the moon with the happiness of it. Even though the father won't be around again for months. Maybe years. 'Not really. I prefer to be free.'

'Hello, Mummy.'

Small feet are silent across muffling grass. Accusing eyes shift from Bobby to her and back again.

'Ross, darling. This is Bobby Hudwalker. I told you about him, remember? He and I went to Washington together. That's the capital of the United States.'

'Washington DC,' Bobby puts in.

'Of course. And we took other trips to explore that great country. He came and visited me at my school. Now he's come all the way from America to visit the two of us.'

'Your Uncle Bob I guess, Ross. Been looking forward to this here meeting for a good long time.' A giant above the slight figure. Which shrinks into the nearest wall.

'I've got to do my homework.' Ross rushes past them and up the stairs. They can hear him clattering across the ceiling.

Bobby stares after the boy. 'Cute kid, even in that terrible outfit. What in the world happened to your sense of style, Doly?'

'You don't think it fetching?' Bobby's always been good for a laugh. Boy does she need one now.

'Short dark-gray pants with some stiff kinda coat...'

'A blazer.'

'You gotta be kidding.' His eyelids are closed by an enfolding frown.

'No, honestly. It's the uniform they wear at his school. Ross goes to a posh preparatory — '

'Posh? What in hell is posh?'

'Schools for the middle and upper classes. Dressing them in a school uniform avoids class distinctions.'

'If they're all posh, how come there are distinctions?'

'Posh and posher!' Doly laughs, seeing the funny side, remembering Bobby was used to no class distinctions in the States. Though Riverside Hall had its own way of discriminating, substituting money for class. 'Making them wear unbecoming gear discourages envy. Some people get annoyed with kids from Ross's type of school.'

'That a fact? I hope he has decent togs for weekends.' His eyes roam the room. 'This don't look like a gent's house to me, Doly. More of a done-up hut. Where's the posh in that?'

'Bothy. Actually a shepherd's cottage in Tudor times. Now it's very fashionable and pricey.'

'Snob stuff. I never reckoned you'd turn into one of them.'

'I'm not. I take everyone as I find them. The Courtlings are an old county family. They have their traditions. Iain Courtling pays enormous sums out of his Army pay for Ross's education. To make sure he has the right start in life.'

'You reckon that's the way of it?'

'There are many different accents in England, Bobby. And you're judged the moment you open your mouth. The right school makes sure that when Ross opens his, he doesn't sound like a village child.'

'There's something wrong with that?'

'Not wrong. Different.'

His eyes dull.

'They teach him the social graces. I can't deny him that.' Doly buys cast-off uniforms, and her own clothes, from the second-hand shop in Midhurst. Surreptitiously. Though she's seen her neighbours — stockbroker-belt wives, county landowners — eye some of them with recognition. Tant pis.

'So the US of A didn't get democracy through to you none?'

'What choice do I have, Bobby? I have to do my best by him. He's the son of an Army family Englishman, he'll live in England. I have to educate him for that the best I can.'

'I gotta meet this guy, this English gentleman. You wanna introduce me to him?'

'His father, you mean? No. I never see him. I'll introduce you to Ross's Uncle Iain if you like. He's coming over tomorrow. On leave from abroad.'

'This is Major General Iain Courtling, Bobby.' Doly greets her brother-in-law, recently promoted to this high rank, without much enthusiasm. He uses that upper middle class sneer towards her which she finds distinctly unattractive. 'My friend Bobby Hudwalker, Iain. From Detroit. My former guardian's nephew.'

'How d'ye do.' Cold eyes swivel from her to Bobby and back again, his nose twitches. He clearly draws the wrong conclusions.

'Just fine and dandy. So what's with you?'

The Major General's neat hairstyle is turning a distinguished grey. What's left of Bobby's pepper-and-salt locks tumble into merry eyes. He wears a T-shirt under his open shirt, no tie. Jeans. Suede slip-ons. Simply not done, Doly grins to herself.

'You're from Detroit, Mr Hudwalker? From the Middle West?'

'My folks are from there.' He looks at Iain Courtling, slits his eyes. 'My old man worked in the auto industry. A fitter. You heard o' that?'

'Cars, of course. Henry Ford, the modern assembly line and mass production. The beginning of affordable cars for the masses. Just like Hitler's Volkswagen. Of course we've heard of that.'

'Long before the jumped-up corporal. He copied us! Good money to be made. But my dad didn't work for Ford, he worked for General Motors. Pontiac, Michigan, not Dearborn.'

'Really?' The eyebrows lift.

'Now I live in New Orleans. Best place, seeing I'm a song writer by profession.'

'Indeed? How very interesting.'

'Didn't used to pay that much, but suits me down to a T.' An explosive laugh. 'Not a Model T, you understand!'

'Very droll.'

'I have a seller on my hands right now. New singer giving my latest tune a try. Doin' pretty good there.'

The monocle held to the right eye drops. The officer's stick under the Major General's arm swirls round. 'Fancy a game of badminton?'

'New one on me. Show me the ropes and I'll lead with my chin.'

'Jolly good show. You can help Ross and me put up the net.'

Bobby's wild hits get lost in long grass and nettles. Ross searches enthusiastically. Doly watches the uneven match. The Major General's 'jolly bad luck, old man' while standing by the net and smashing soft shuttlecocks aren't quite playing the game. They're driven with vicious spitefulness straight into Bobby.

The change is sudden and abrupt. Bobby's eye clicks in. His aim turns precise, shuttlecocks whistle through the air, land in the court and out of reach. He wins the last game.

'Excellent timing. Tea's ready. Ross is responsible for our very own strawberry jam. He picks wild strawberries on the railway banks. Much better flavour than the cultivated ones.'

'Red jam for a red house, I take it.' Iain's shooting laugh leaves Ross staring and Doly exchanging looks with Bobby.

'Do you like Bath buns, Uncle Iain? Uncle Bob got them for us in Midhurst.'

'Bald as a Bath bun, eh?' Bobby spreads ample butter and jam for a filling, pats the whole thing. 'Bun in the oven as well.'

The Major General's eyes swivel, his nose actually twitches. A trickle of disastrous barbed remarks pour out, which Doly and Bobby parry as best they can.

'Say, buddy, you got a problem?' Bobby's good humour suddenly gives out.

'Not me, old man. Never come across anyone as extraordinary as Dorinda here, that's all. Makes a chap restless.'

'Extraordinary?' Bobby is standing two inches taller, six inches wider. Belligerent.

'Beautiful, of course. Wonderful mother. Must dash, Dorinda m'dear. 'Bye now, Ross. See you on my next home leave.' His batman is waiting by the car. Dust flies.

Ross at school on Monday morning leaves the field clear for Bobby's advances. It's been a long time since Doly's double bed has heaved and shuddered with urgent needs. A form of friendship as far as she's concerned. Nothing more nor less.

'I've brought you a record of each of my songs, Doly. Pristine. Cut them myself. Some day they'll be real valuable.'

'That's so sweet of you. I'll enjoy listening to them. While I'm rocking the baby to sleep!'

'The kid you're having: what kind of a guy is the father?'

'He's in the Navy, away at the moment. Always off for months at a time. Years, actually.'

'Another British Forces officer? How does a girl like you get involved with that type?'

'Not an officer. A simple seaman. Nothing at all like Iain Courtling, if that's what you're thinking. He's from around here, from Midhurst. Salt of the earth, no side to him at all.'

'You going to marry him?'

Doly moves away, sits on the edge of the bed which shook with Bobby's passion, but not hers, moments ago. 'No.'

He takes her hand, spreads the fingers, kisses her palm. 'I've never really loved anyone but you, Doly.'

'We had good times, didn't we Bobby?'

'I'm having a good time now, a great time. Quit this stuffy little cottage. Come back with me to New Orleans. That's one great town. I'll make you happy, sure thing. The pair of you. All three.'

'You're sweet, Bobby. But the roads from Dramlings lead nowhere in particular.'

'Is that a no?'

'Maybe. I need time to think, Bobby.'

CHAPTER 12

Vienna, Autumn 1952

Gabby is fully aware of the extent of her problem. Her one-time fiancé, the erudite Herr Doktor Hans Weiss, is a respected and well-known figure in Vienna. He and his sister live in a prestigious house in the Karlsgasse, one of the classiest streets in Vienna. They own several large properties which bring in substantial rents. And she is about to sue Hans Weiss for breach of promise. She knows Hans can afford the best lawyers but, of course, she's clear he will instruct his buddy Czezina.

Undoubtedly a good lawyer — shrewd, diplomatic, quick. And he knows Gabby inside out. He represented her after her pre-war lawyer Otto Venn made such a hash of her case against Blenkindorff, he also helped her find the right tenants for the villa.

Even right at the beginning she often went to him privately, for personal guidance. Czezina was, they both knew, smitten with her. But, poor like so many after the war, his marriage was one of monetary convenience, one he had no intention of giving up. Neither of them was under any illusions. As for Gabby, she would never have considered Czezina a suitable match even he were free.

Her task now is to find the right lawyer willing to represent her for the breach of promise case against Hans Weiss, using criteria relevant for her. Which may well be irrelevant as far as others are concerned.

She has a solid case. Naturally she realises that the course of justice has a large number of obstacles to overcome. From her point of view expense is the least of them, though she doesn't even have the proverbial bean. The pertinent question is: who is going to risk representing an impecunious widow, an American pariah? Who'll be brave enough to take on a case the press will pounce on? There's enormous fall-out potential for any unwary lawyer.

Gabby's heels grind into the cobbles of fashionable Kärntnerstrasse. Sparks flash from her speeding shoes. The Viennese have a genius for making shop windows sparkle with sparse goods. Even if she had money to spend there's virtually nothing to buy. She ignores tasteful window displays of the most expensive garments in Vienna, her nose like a pointer's, aimed towards the Stephansplatz in front of Vienna's splendid cathedral now glittering its new roof. Her eyes search beyond the massive building to the alleys leading off behind the grand Stephansdom.

She's looking for Otto Venn's office. The man — he must be getting on for seventy — handled her divorce from Rolf Ferent, now nearly twenty years ago, as well as the ill-fated Blenkindorff affair when she and Bosch returned from England in 1947. It was Venn's bungling of her case against her gardener which had prompted her to change to Czezina. Blenkindorff had, after all, purloined virtually all her furniture and other goods left in the villa during the war. It should have been an open-and-shut case.

So why choose him? Why settle for the lawyer who bungled an obvious case of burglary?

Several excellent reasons: because he's old-fashioned enough to understand the sort of case she wants to bring, because he is bound to feel obligated to her, because she knows he holds her in high esteem. He remembers her glory days before the war, not the impecunious widow of the present.

Gabby heaves against the heavy door leading off the alley, climbs two staircases because the lift will only work if you have a key, and knocks on another solid door.

'Herein!'

An old man's voice quavering come in. Evidently Venn no longer has a secretary. He's seated behind an enormous desk in an equally enormous room which she remembers being exactly as it was years ago. In particular she can see that the decorations haven't been touched. They have yellowed into mournfulness.

'Do you remember me, Herr Doktor Venn?'

His tortoise neck telescopes cautiously out of a stiff, too-large collar. Thirty seconds tick by as his brain cells sort through the past. 'Frau Ferent — I mean Frau Bosch! How nice to see you again.' The neck draws in a little, starched shirt a withdrawing shell. 'You've found more evidence against your gardener, gnä' Frau? Blenkindorff, wasn't it?'

The old man's office is in an ancient house in the same alley off the Stephansplatz as the office of the Procurator Fidei. She always finds it amusing to think that the official who represents the Church in matters of Canon Law has the same title as the official who represented the public interests in the courts of the Inquisition. And, in her irreverent way, she imagines that her experiences trying to get an annulment from first husband, Rolf Ferent, is in many ways similar to trying to prove one's innocence to the Inquisition courts. An eighty per cent chance of the negative.

Gabby had an excellent case against her old gardener. It wasn't difficult to prove he made off with her furniture and valuable effects while she was a fugitive from Hitler and living in England. A case Venn mismanaged by failing to keep up with new laws. Blenkindorff was convicted without a problem, and is in prison now. But the stolen goods remain in his family's possession because Venn hadn't read the new laws and therefore did not ask for restitution. The old pre-war lawyer hadn't realised that special laws were passed to deal with offences perpetrated during the war. Which means Gabby has no means of getting her property back.

All that is neither here nor there now. This time Venn is the perfect man for her. He out-ages Czezina by twenty years or so and retains old-fashioned attitudes. He also commands respect. And he's known to be a rich man. Because remuneration will not be his primary concern, he's unlikely to be overwhelmed with work and guilt will ensure full attention.

Gabby explains her visit. There's clearly no problem about other clients intruding on Dr Venn's time: there are no phone calls during the hours she spends in his office. Gabby doesn't give it much thought, but decides he probably only has the few clients who haven't died off — yet. She's offered coffee — an order telephoned with great ceremony to *Demel* — to sustain her throughout the long story. Eventually Venn asserts he understands the situation. He professes to be appalled by her former fiancé's behaviour and is delighted to offer his services. Gabby is aware that it's almost certainly his last chance to play the white knight rescuing his queen.

'We shall have to ask for substantial damages.'

Gabby sighs. She's made a terrible mistake. Again. Two exhausting hours wasted on an antiquated charlatan. Can she manoeuvre him to do what's necessary? She's not trying to win the case, after all. She's intent on embarrassing Hans Weiss before the whole of Vienna — to show that his behaviour has been appalling, cruel and denigrating. 'It's not the money, Herr Doktor...'

'Fifty thousand Schillings at the very least.' He holds up a shaky hand to signify he hasn't finished yet. 'Otherwise, gnä' Frau, they will offer to settle out of court!'

Doing her own share of underestimating.

'The problem is that you have no idea why your former fiancé called off your engagement. If he stands up in court and produces some valid reason...'

'That is my point, Herr Doktor. There is no valid reason. I've told you how it was he who brought up the question of an annulment — I'm sure the priest had no intention of mentioning such a thing — which suggests Herr Doktor Weiss already knew I couldn't have obtained one in the time. Which in turn suggests that he already knew the wedding would never take place.'

'Indeed. I am fully cognizant that a man like the eminent Herr Doktor would undoubtedly be aware that the time scale would be years, not months.'

'Exactly. And I've told you that he accused me of having an affair, and that he eventually admitted he was completely mistaken and apologised.'

'Another stratagem.' Smiling would be to overstate his expression, but there is an undercurrent of amusement. 'I understand.'

'So it's not unreasonable to suppose that Herr Doktor Weiss might, once more, have made assumptions which are incorrect.' She sniffs. 'I think he is simply imagining — or fabricating — improper behaviour on my part.'

The notes are made in a broad, decisive hand. In the old Gothic script which Gabby dimly remembers using as a child but no longer writes in. Long angular letters become squiggles which, she judges, even its writer may not be able to decipher.

The old man looks up, eyes almost completely obliterated by wrinkles. 'We will have to accept that your attempted fraud against the Church authorities will come out in court. That will damage your case substantially.'

It's true she lied to Hans, but even the priest said he was sorry he'd felt obliged to ask her whether she'd been married before. Morally speaking, that holy man had soothed her, Gabby was within her rights. She clings to that.

She knows Venn is a practising Catholic. Is he unable to schism between Church and law? And it's the fourth time the obvious has been agreed. Fortunately it's irrelevant. 'I take your point, Herr Doktor.'

'It will count heavily against your character, gnä' Frau.'

She sips more coffee while longing for a schnapps. 'I accept that. I'd like to emphasise again. What I'm concerned about is getting at the truth. Nothing else matters. The thing I'm after is your cross-examining Hans Weiss under oath. I'm entitled to know the reasons he broke off the engagement. He will have to produce some which stand up in court.'

'You will be hazarding a great deal of money. Do you really wish to run that risk?'

Her only cash is the furniture money due from the Schwanenbruch Council for the sale of family effects. She'll have to find a way to raise more, somehow. 'I understand that. I consider it money well spent.'

Venn's obviously got time on his hands and is delighted to spend it with her. He's polite, forbearing, remembering the past. Perhaps looking for some excitement in his life. 'I will be honoured to represent you, Frau Bosch. And my fees can wait until you can afford to pay them. I'll lodge the papers with the judge tomorrow morning.'

CHAPTER 13

Vienna, Autumn 1952

'Gnädige Frau! This is an unexpected honour.'

The estate agent who is now handling the rents for her Viennese villa isn't one of Gabby's favourites. The Middletons — such brilliant tenants — have been recalled to the States. Michael Dorndiener uses unctuous, high-flown phrases to explain the problems of the market, the aftermath of war, the difficulties…

'Yes, yes, Herr Dorndiener. I know all that. What I would like to suggest is that I try to find a new tenant for the house myself. I have some contacts you don't have, you see.'

Professor Schlech introduced her to interesting acquaintances. Protestant ministers of religion, high-powered military personnel, diplomats from the Chinese Embassy. The Four-Power occupation will not go on for ever. Vienna is, once again, becoming a significant staging post between East and West and people have to live somewhere. Numbers of high-ranking foreigners must be looking to house their families. A villa on the outskirts of the Vienna Woods has to be an ideal location.

'Gnä' Frau! I have no desire to speak out of turn…'

'You wish me to take it out of your hands, Herr Dorndiener? Or shall we make a deal? I'll undertake to represent your agency to a prospective tenant. No need for them to know the house belongs to me. You can mention Herr Ferent as one of the owners, and his former wife as the other.'

He isn't arguing any more.

'If I'm successful, we split the commission.'

'But you are completely inexperienced, gnä' Frau — '

An older dinosaur than Venn. With no redeeming disadvantages. 'I speak English, Herr Dorndiener. And French. Fluently. I know the right people socially. I simply steer them in your direction. In any case, you've just given me a long lecture saying there's no market for a house like this. And you've had plenty of time to find a new tenant. I can hardly ruin anything for you.'

It's almost too easy. Within two weeks three foreigners are queuing up for the house. A Frenchman and two Americans. They're all about to work in Vienna for several years, and want to bring their families. They are delighted to find someone they can negotiate with in their own language. Especially the Frenchman, who goes so far as to refuse to even attempt to speak German, or to engage directly with Austrians or Germans.

Gabby conducts a Dutch auction between the two sets of Americans. She reports back to Dorndiener. He calls it a fluke, eyes rounding at the figures. What Gabby fails to do is to secure her commission. He very much regrets. She's not on his staff. Company policy.

The buzzing of the telephone. Gabby picks up on her way out. 'Herr Doktor Czezina.' Her tone is ready cooled for the expected call.

'You will be surprised to hear from me directly.'

'I rather think that that might be considered irregular, Herr Doktor.'

A rattle of phlegm doing duty as a laugh. 'We have always been friends as well as lawyer and client. We have never stood on formal ceremony, gnä' Frau.'

It's Venn who's taught her that silence is more menacing than the best-chosen words. Gabby's about to end it by replacing the receiver.

'I really urge you not to go ahead with that case. Such an enormous amount of money down the drain. And what will you achieve? What can you gain?'

'The truth, Herr Doktor Czezina. I'm willing to settle for the truth. Hans Weiss can write, or phone, or meet me in person. But I'm determined to be told — explicitly — his reasons for calling off our engagement. I am entitled to that, and I won't settle for less.'

Volumes of words pour out of the handset. She turns it away from her. When there's no end she cradles it. Gently.

Letters. Registered letters. Couriers delivering letters. More phone calls which she ends by replacing the receiver, gently, courteously. She teaches Kamilla to answer the phone, instructs her to say her mother is unavailable. The child is an apt pupil.

A note from Otto Venn to say the preliminary hearing is set for October 16th.

A large bouquet of flowers arrives with a flourish. The card is signed Hans Weiss.

More phone calls from Czezina. Kamilla plays her part to perfection.

The next call is from Hans Weiss himself. 'Hello, Onkel Hans. Mutti is resting.'

More flowers, a formal letter of invitation to a dinner at the *Griechenbeisl*. A follow-up phone call. It is two days before the hearing. Gabby accepts the dinner invitation. Hans must be ready to talk at last.

Hans Weiss is noticeably thinner, greyer, bowed. 'So good of you to do me the honour.'

A cursory nod. 'We should get on. Frau Meintner can look after Kamilla until ten. Then she has to get home.' Pumpkin-coach strategy is another Venn pearl. Has the lawyer noticed what an apt pupil she's become?

Neither of them is able to do justice to the excellent food. Preambles, excuses, evasions from Hans. Meanwhile Gabby folds and refolds her serviette, taps her shoes, stares at the pictures on the wall, a restored icon in the niche where the absence of the original caused so much trouble for Bosch. She remains defiantly silent. Coffee is served.

'Thank you for dinner, Hans. You know I have to get back.'

His lips look dry. He swallows, coughs. 'There is one last matter we need to discuss.'

She's too tired to summon up the pretence of a smile. 'Really? What?'

'The hearing...'

Cat and mouse is a game she and Doly have honed to perfection since early childhood. 'Set for the day after tomorrow. First session in the afternoon.'

'You told him all about it. You discussed intimate private details with a stranger.'

'Herr Doktor Venn, d'you mean? Of course I told him everything. He's my lawyer.'

'Not Venn. Czezina. Something private, something you entrusted me with, and you blurted it out to Czezina. You have no decency, no sense of decorum, no shame. Why not broadcast it t-t-to the whole world?'

The stuttering is new to her. Bosch mentioned he knew how to trigger it. Another acquired skill. 'I'm not quite sure I follow you, Hans.' Told Czezina what?

'You t-t-told someone in your and m-m-my employ about your inti-ti — intimate relationships.'

'You mean we discussed the fact that you broke our engagement yet again? For the third time?'

A trembling hand covers his mouth. His eyes examine the weave of the tablecloth. 'You t-t-told him about England. About the war.' The same phrases seesawed up and down, again and again. A gramophone needle caught in a record groove.

She frowns. She really can't make out what he's getting at. The marriage licence scam?

'When Bosch was interned.' His voice down to a whisper whose meaning she can hardly decipher. 'About the m-m-man who found a j-j-job for him.'

The affair with Christopher Hyllier! He can't be serious. How can that be his reason for breaking off the engagement? She told him about that! Intentionally... 'You knew about that, Hans. I specifically told you.'

The contortions of face and mouth threaten a heart attack. Gabby signals for more water.

'You t-t-t-told *him* about it. An outsider, an underling!'

'You are telling me you broke off our engagement because I told my lawyer, in the strictest client/lawyer confidence, about a relationship I'd mentioned to you?'

He nods. Slurps noisily.

'I see.' A turn of phrase. It is not a reason which would ever have occurred to her. Because it would never have dawned on her that Czezina would betray her trust. 'That really is the reason?'

'Isn't it enough?'

'In that case I should change my accusation from you to him. From breach of promise to breach of client confidentiality.'

He stares at her. 'You c-c-c-...' He sips more water. 'You can't do that! Czezina told me in confidence.'

'The fact is, Hans, he had no right to tell you. None at all. I promised that I would withdraw my case against you if you told me what you were accusing me of. I understand you have, and I am a woman of my word. Czezina will hear from Venn tomorrow.'

She rises, picks up her handbag. The waiter is ready with her coat. She sweeps out before Hans can pay and join her.

'I have to see you immediately, gnädige Frau.' Czezina's voice is pressing on the phone.

Gabby agrees to drive over to his office. Later that day. She has some urgent business before then which cannot be put off.

Czezina stands as she is ushered into the room. Torturing an inoffensive fountain pen.

'You can see I was absolutely right.' His forehead is glowering in concertina folds.

She expected apologies, grovelling, flattery. But an attack?

'A trumped-up nothing. Weiss was never intending to go through with it. He finally found his excuse. Even I did not work that one out. But I knew he'd come up with some pretext or other.'

'Judgments of that sort are neither here nor there, Herr Doktor.' North German syllables slice soft Viennese away. 'My concern is that Hans Weiss was told about a conversation you and I had in this office. In a lawyer/client exchange.' She sits, crossing her legs. The peal of victory from the twin towers of the Votivkirche.

'That is my point, gnä' Frau. I told him *nothing*.'

Lawyers may be slippery, but this is absurd. 'You're telling me Weiss lied? Impossible. The man's a stickler for morality.' Apart from the insignificant breaking of solemn promises to her, that is. 'So how did he find out?'

Czezina's palms are spread in supplication. 'Not lied, no. He was in this very office, endlessly discussing — well, he came to consult me.'

'About whether he should go ahead with the marriage. Consulting you when he should have been talking to me.' No response is obviously an affirmative. 'So?'

'In the course of the discussion — more of a monologue, really — he mentioned his feelings, his problems, his worries. He was not sure whether he would be the right man for you.'

'It would be nice to know why.'

'As you wish. He was worried about marrying what he termed a Jezebel, a scarlet woman. Someone who had a liaison with Bosch while married to Rolf Ferent. Furthermore, a scarlet woman who made eyes at *him* while still married to Bosch.'

What an array of virtues for a future wife. 'Hans Weiss said I showed interest in him before Bosch's death? You can't be serious.'

'I am. When I protested, he said he could prove the kind of woman you are. And then he told me about your affair with the Englishman while Bosch was interned.'

'I see. In what way did that give you permission to betray my trust?'

'That's it, you see.' Oil oozing from shining hair. 'Believe me, gnä' Frau, I did nothing of the kind. My fault was to underestimate his perception, his sensitivity. He saw by my reaction — by the way I was not surprised by what he'd told me — that I already knew. From which he deduced, quite correctly, that you had already told me. His logic was impeccable. But his deductions put me in an untenable position.'

'You're saying he worked out I told you and, because of your body language, assumed he was right?'

'Yes.'

'And that he used that as the trumped-up reason for breaking our engagement?'

'Exactly. Then he left without in any way alerting me to what he proposed to do. It was as much of a thunderbolt to me as to you.'

Gabby watches the dark eyes fog expression. 'I can see that might exonerate you from my reporting you to the law society. At least on that particular point. What about your client Hans Weiss? Aren't you betraying his trust right now? And rather graphically at that?'

The clear bright spark of victory is obvious in his erect frame. 'He gave me his permission, gnä' Frau. I insisted on that.'

This man's the most accomplished liar she's ever come across. 'I only have your word on that.'

A smug head inclines towards his desk. 'Ask him. You know he's fanatical about the factual truth. Lies of omission may not be quite as vigilantly censored.' He returns to his desk, the fountain pen in halves, hands blue with ink. He wipes them with his handkerchief. 'I've tried to be a friend to both of you. Now I wash my hands of the whole affair. I never wish to discuss that relationship again.'

It was Czezina who started the domino slide of broken engagements. With his suggestion about deceiving the priest. Which she now realises, with hindsight, that he, too, must have known might not work. The law society wouldn't take kindly to that piece of information, those facts. But she won't pursue it. For now.

Did he also alert Hans? Was it Czezina, not Greti or the Berghers, who's been trying to stop the marriage all along? He has a clear-cut motive. It would show him capable of handling Markus Bergher's lucrative restitution case. He might still get his hands on it.

'No fear of that, Herr Doktor. At any rate not with me. I'm leaving Vienna. Kamilla and I are sailing for New York in mid November.' She opens her handbag, takes out the keys of the VW Beetle. 'Perhaps you'd return these to Herrn Doktor Weiss. The car is parked in the Karlsgasse. By his front door.'

She's off to make her fortune in America. Vienna is moribund. The Four Power Occupation has broken the city which withstood the Turks twice, and even the Russians, though not the Nazis. The city which is coping with the Four-Power occupation right now. But there's no Stahremberg to save her.

TJEDE PECKES

In the early part of the sixteenth century Archbishop Christopher of Bremen stood at the borders of Land Wursten, intending to subdue the Frisians and to make them subject to his bishopric.

The Frisians had other ideas. Their bells clanged storm alert throughout their lands, and Tjede Peckes was elected the people's standard bearer. Everyone, including women and girls, was armed. A small nation was intent on fighting for liberty, convinced that Christmas, due in a few days' time, would see their cause vindicated.

The Archbishop assembled a host of thousands. The Frisians knew only too well that the situation was grave. Warning fires were lit far and wide, and Tjede Peckes carried her standard to every part of Land Wursten. She called on both men and women to fight, she encouraged them with the words: 'See, the flames rising high are a sign from God. The foe has forced his way into our territory, but I know the Almighty has chosen me to lead you to victory. Long live liberty!'

The peasants were glad to follow their standard bearer and ready to die for the cause of freedom. The peasant army didn't have a leader, but the white cloth unfurling in the dusk of a winter's night was like a spirit leading the way. And Tjede Peckes was the one carrying it.

They knew they barely had time to rescue their comrades in the next town. Tjede, raising her flag high, bore down on the unsuspecting enemy like a whirlwind. Those who didn't flee were killed, and every house was set on fire. The conflagration painted the whole sky red.

Tjede didn't rest on her laurels. She followed the fleeing foe, laying waste the towns and villages in her path. Her flag flew high, encouraging the Frisians to ever-greater deeds of valour.

News of their triumphs went before the Frisians. The Archbishop rallied his troops, enlisted more men and had his standard painted with the skull and crossbones.

Tjede Peckes was undaunted. She called on her fellow men and women to stand firm, to fight for their rights. She ignored the advice of experienced men who warned that their troops were no match for a trained army. Raising her flag even higher, Tjede rushed to the attack.

The peasants' enthusiasm gained them early advantages. They broke through the serried ranks of the Archbishop's men. But they hadn't taken his cavalry into account. He ordered his riders to attack from the rear, and Tjede and her people were surrounded.

Undismayed, believing in her cause, expecting a miracle any second, Tjede continued to fight. She did not see one of the Archbishop's men raise his sword with both his hands. He cracked her skull in two. Tjede sank down on to her native land and died for freedom.

Her death spelled the end of the battle. The Frisians surrendered.

CHAPTER 14

New York, Winter 1952/3

'How you've grown, Kamilla.' Moppel's wife Rachel is unable to have children. Her eyes are soft as she offers to adopt Kamilla. Gabby has no intentions of giving her up.

'How are you both?' Gabby holds Kamilla's hand. Firmly.

'Can't complain none. Business done picked up since I married my beautiful Rachel. She's my treasure, my lucky star.'

Gabby cannot deny that Rachel is good looking, with one of the finest heads of blonde hair off the silver screen. The Boadicea of Long Island.

'Isn't her hair wonderful? It's long enough for her to sit on!'

Not Boadicea, perhaps. Rapunzel's fairytale tresses. What can Rachel see in Moppel? The prince rescuing the damsel isolated in her Ellis Island tower? She hasn't been told, but she's sure Rachel is of Jewish descent, part of the flotsam and jetsam from the wreck of Europe. Moppel was her chance of instant American citizenship.

'So you've really come to the good ol' US of A to find a job, right, Gabby?'

Which is Moppel-speak for he isn't about to support her.

'What kinda qualifications d'you have to offer?'

His world is beer in the fridge, cards with the neighbours, dogs in the living room. Onkel Wilfred and Tante Mary cloned.

Speaking French and German and being an outstanding hostess are hardly attributes needed in New York City. 'I can cook, look after children, run a household.'

'You mean you're lookin' out for a job as a domestic?' Moppel and Rachel gape in unison. 'No way that's suitable, Gabby!'

'Kamilla and I have to eat. And I'm tired of living on a shoestring. Domestic jobs attract a higher rate of pay than secretaries.'

Rachel is outraged. 'You speak three languages fluently. You spent two years studying at the Royal Friedrich Wilhelm University in Berlin. And you want to be a cook-housekeeper?'

Gabby remembers her father started out sweeping floors, admittedly at an earlier age than hers at present. 'Want, no. I've tried applying for office jobs. The United Nations, the International Atomic Energy Agency, other worthy bodies in Vienna. None of them want to know.'

'And Kamilla? What are you going to do with Kamilla while you're waiting on other people?'

She's going to take a big gamble. Will the child be tempted away from her if she allows her to live with Moppel and Rachel for the time being? Surely not. She's Bosch's daughter. And hers. 'I can find somewhere she'll be welcome.'

Rachel crouches level with the little girl. 'How would you like to stay with Uncle Emil and me for a while, Kamilla?'

'I want to go with Mutti.'

'You can play with the dogs. Minx and Manx. They're lovely little dachshunds.'

'I don't like dogs.'

'You'll love Minx and Manx. And we'll drive round in our beautiful white Lincoln. We'll buy ice cream and take you to Coney Island. That's just like the Prater in Vienna.'

'I'll teach you to make paper planes.' Take-over eyes glint at the prize. Moppel has always had an affinity with children. 'How's about

it, Gabby? Why not let us take care of her for the time being? Give you
a free hand.'

That innocent, roly-poly smile. Eyes wallowing in deep wrinkles.

'For a month or two, perhaps.' She's not giving up Kamilla.

Gabby walks up Park Avenue. Dressed in muted brown, shoed in
sensible Oxfords. She puts on her glasses, looks for number 1048.
Manhattan blocks seem longer than she remembers them.

The name plate is recessed into the wall behind thick glass. Shocking
gold which, she realises, is the genuine article. She feels like Judy
Garland in Easter Parade:

> For we'll walk up the Avenue
> Yes we'll walk up the Avenue
> And to walk up the Avenue's what we like

A Lord & Taylor mannequin answers her ring. White from choker
to tennis shoes. Curious, but then Americans tend to be. By Central
European standards. 'Mrs Kley?'

'Mrs Kley only sees people by appointment.'

Gabby pulls out the form the agency gave her. 'I do have one. For
ten-thirty. Gabriele Dohlen Bosch.'

She recognises the smile specially reserved for children and imbeciles.
She qualifies for the latter. But by the time she realises she's turned the
gun on herself it's too late.

'I figured.' A Shirley Temple smile, tossed curls to match. Not
entirely white. Peroxide blonde. 'The new hired help. You want to ring
the doorbell down in the basement?'

The smile is not confined to children and imbeciles. It includes the
lower orders. A real bonus.

Mrs Kley is formidably slim. And tall, even without the four-inch
heels, mummy-wrapped skirt, make-up to compete with Hollywood
and marshalled hair. 'You're a new arrival from Europe?'

Is she asking whether Gabby's ever been to the States before? 'I
arrived on Saturday.' She who hesitates misses the pearly job.

Mrs Kley half-closes her eyelids. 'You have connections in this
country?' Clearly not even a second's equivocation escapes her.

'I'm staying with my brother. In Seaford, Long Island.'

'And where can we get references?' She's firing straight from the slimmest hips Gabby has ever seen.

'Walter Hudwalker and his family live in New Jersey. Before he retired he was Head Teacher at Wyckoff Grade School. His daughters teach there now.'

'Anyone else?'

'My bank manager and lawyer in Vienna. But only for character references. I've never actually had a job before, you see. I'm a widow. I have a six-year-old to bring up. She's with my brother at the moment.'

One phone call to the Hudwalkers and the Kleys can hardly wait for Gabby to start. They must have got old Fuddy Duddy, whose apple pie appeal can't be bettered. They certainly can't have been talking to ugly sisters Gertrude or Hildegarde.

'Well now, Gabriele. You take your meals in the kitchen with the cook. And you sleep on the top floor. Your hours are from seven-thirty in the morning till five-thirty at night. Week-ends you may have off. So you can spend time with your family.'

Are they planning to direct her free time as well? 'And the salary?'

'You live in, a freshly-laundered uniform will be provided every day. $50 a week wages on top of that.'

She'll be well paid. She can save all but fares out to Long Island, and the occasional bottle of bourbon, America's cheapest equivalent to schnapps.

The biggest surprise is the bedroom. Gabby expects to acclimatise to grime-laden city air, to answer to her first name, to endure the white uniform. But to be relegated to a cubby-hole on the top floor? With nothing but a narrow bed wedged tight under an airshaft window which doesn't open?

The growling, knocking central heating pipes run along the ceiling. There's a bare light bulb, no chair to sit and read, no table to write on. Barely enough room for her small suitcase under the bed.

Exhaustion brings early sleep the first and second nights. On the third a headache demands action. She could spend time in the kitchen with Sadie. Amiable, but addicted to listening to the incessant sound of soul music. With sing-along at full throttle.

Television in the nursery is a Kley-ordained alternative. Neither Mickey Mouse nor Donald Duck were ever favourites of Gabby's. She opts for Sadie's singing, and plans to add one friendly ingredient.

Gabby hauls herself up the four flights of stairs, pulls out the bourbon she bought on the boat and takes a swig. Then she clatters down to the kitchen with a cheerful grin. And waits for the hallelujahs to end.

'Hi, Sadie. You got a couple of minutes?' The cook's prejudices brand Gabby an untouchable. But surely not undrinkable with?

'Sure, Gabrielly. Go right ahead. I just served dinner.'

Gabby's smile has charmed ambassadors, even — on occasion — the IBM's chief executive, Thomas J Watson. Sadie is harder to please. She's as tough and globular as an unshelled coconut. 'I bought this on the boat. Johnny Walker. Want to join me in a nightcap?'

Sweat beads on the round face enlarge, coagulate, then eddy down dark-brown cheeks turned to a pallid umber. The wet under Sadie's armpits turns snowy white to transparent grey. Soap bubble eyes defy Satan with a Bible held up to prevent the sight of evil. A quaking body bursts from the rocker.

Gabby recognises a serious mistake. Which she can't reverse. She takes another swig as she watches Sadie undulate past her, the capacious lungs of the righteous puffing upstairs.

The stern upright figure of Mr Kley preaches into the kitchen on rubber-soled shoes. 'I guess we had no idea you have a serious alcohol problem.' The voice of a funeral director, reassuring and kind. 'We have the children to think of. Here's a month's pay right now. We expect you to leave tonight.'

The wages of alcohol — a $200 cheque — are welcome. Though not on a par with stripping out of the uniform, away from the tiny room with its clattering pipes, and out into the remarkably unstuffy air of Park Avenue. The subway to Grand Central Station, the ride back to Moppel's place, are both exhilarating rides to freedom. Gabby giggles all the way to the bank.

Gabby returns to the agency she used before. They aren't bothered by the Kleys' reactions. And they take on board that Gabby would prefer a room she can turn around in.

'We have just what you're looking for, Gabriele.'

Gabby subdues her distaste at the use of her Christian name by people she employs. She swallows resentment: she needs another job.

'You do?'

'With a family from Indiana. They're living in a small town in Connecticut. You can take Kamilla with you, if you like.

That sounds like a good solution. It will be good to have Kamilla with her again.

CHAPTER 15

Sussex, Winter 1952/1953

'I thought I was pregnant again this summer.'

Faith has taken up Doly's Christmas invitation and is installed in the little downstairs guestroom at Dramlings. If she has a problem with the size of the room she hasn't mentioned it, just asked if she could leave some of her clothes in her suitcase, and park that in the living room.

'Really, Doly?' Faith's eyes open wide. 'You got a beau?' Her nostrils broaden as her eyes squint at Doly, blink, return to staring at the huge log blazing in Doly's enormous Elizabethan fireplace.

The two women sit, companionably enough, on the little sofa facing the log fire crackling chestnuts. One of the dozen bottles of wine Faith bought in Midhurst that day is open between them, their glasses full.

Doly's shoulders are so much more solid now. The slight young girl has gone for ever. She shrugs. 'An old friend I see now and again. Nothing binding.' Her shoulders sag, then perk as she drains the wine from her glass, pours herself some more. 'I never even knew there was such a thing. The local doc called it a phantom pregnancy. No one knows why it happens.'

'You mean a growth?'

'A sort of fluid which feels like a pregnant womb. No morning sickness, but a swelling belly which feels soft, not hard. Wishful thinking I suppose.'

'You really wanted another child? Without marrying the father?'

'I wanted his.'

'But I thought you said…'

'He or she would have been a part of him. The father's abroad most of the time, you see.' She drains another glass. 'I would have cherished such a gift.'

Another cigarette, more wine. An embrace as Faith puts her arm around her. For auld lang syne, nothing more. But Doly knows her heart isn't in it and, truth be told, neither is Faith's.

Doly sits, sipping her wine, relishing the treat. She's startled to think that she no longer wishes for anything. She reflects that if she had her life to live over again and could choose between the tough trek and having the moon and all the good things in life except the moon, she'd know exactly what she'd want.

Not to cry for the moon.

Sussex, 1953

Miss Tilletson lives at Wellick House, about ten minutes' walk down the track from Dramlings, then turn right on to the path leading to the woods. Her beautiful Jacobean mansion is set in a deep little hollow of stream and wild rhododendrons. Miss Tilletson uproots these and plants exotic shrubs as though her life depends on it. Which, almost certainly, it does. She's eighty now. Her face and body are like the crackling rust of last year's beech leaves holding on until new growth pushes them off.

'I can't see to drive the Mini,' she tells Doly who, out walking Buffy, calls now and again to make sure the lone old lady is still mobile. 'Why don't you have her? Name of Agnes after my great-aunt. You'll find her sturdy enough to pick up bits and bobs for you and me.'

'I couldn't take…'

'You'd be doing me a favour. I'll pester shamelessly if I need a lift or would like a drive.'

The little red Mini is a godsend. It ploughs back and forth from Midhurst as though it could find its own way. And it passes the cottage Piers's mother lives in whenever Doly goes shopping.

She comes across his parents from time to time. His father is failing rapidly, his mother at the end of her strength. She's confused, and says she's had no real news of Piers except that his arthritis is no better. Because one leg is shorter than the other and that puts a great strain on his whole body.

Doly never even noticed he had a problem until he pointed it out one time, when he was barefoot. She thought he was limping because he'd hurt himself. He concealed it so cleverly with a built-up shoe and she had no idea. And noted that other people also have hidden physical problems.

He's heart-achingly self-conscious about it. Appearances no longer matter to her at all. She's ashamed they ever did. He's always said they don't matter to him. In other people. She knows exactly how he feels.

Beauty is a two-edged sword whose slashes she avoids by shunning her reflection. What's hard to understand is why something so fleeting was ever important.

There's no news about his coming home.

'I want you to have a keepsake of him.' His mother — who can't remember the name Dorinda — presses a diamond ring on her finger. Just like that.

Driving back after taking Ross to stay with his father over the Easter holidays, Doly is startled to see Piers cycling towards her in the lanes from Stedham.

Strange to have known him so intimately — on and off — yet never to have had any word from him. She waves and drives on. She doesn't push in where she's not wanted.

Next time she's in Midhurst she avoids the cottage his mother lives in. She parks on the street at the other end of town, but she still comes across Piers while shopping in the High Street. Entirely by accident.

'Happy Easter, Piers!'

'Can't very well be happy, can it?'

She knows his father is losing force. She fights the urge to throw her arms around Piers's neck, to drink in his smell, feel his lips. 'I'm so sorry.'

She feels powerless, something an exchange of platitudes can't improve.

Eyes naked with want stare at her. 'I need you.' Piers's voice hoarse. 'Come back to Mum's for tea.'

She's near enough to feel his scorching breath. His suffering is mingled with the scent of a brown jacket steeped in heather. He's dragoning across to her, grabbing at her with fingers so thin they look like claws.

'Yes.' She doesn't hesitate though already behind with chores for the new tenants arriving next day, and dead beat as well. 'I'll come back. First I have to dump the shopping in the boot. And park properly, in the car park.'

She pops into the Angel for cigarettes, and to freshen up. Then she knocks gently on the back door of his mother's cottage.

He's there, alone. Both his parents are at the hospital. He embraces her in a sort of anguish. She feels overwhelmed, consumed. The cottage is a tomb which even true love can't bring to life.

'Let's go back to Dramlings.'

Doly brings the car round. He climbs into the Mini, face closed and tight. His hand is heavy on her knee as she negotiates lanes she knows so well she doesn't need to look.

What is there to say? They opt, instead, for physical frenzy. As though the twisting turning sweating heave of bodies intertwined could change the paths of death. Mouths greedy for a suck of life draw back at last. The taste of oblivion.

They wake to the early morning din of partridge and pheasant flying high. A beautiful dawn lights the sky in spun sugar spirals streaked with slate. On which are writ the ballads of life and death which no man or woman can escape. And yet their beauty is not changed.

'I'm glad you came,' Doly whispers in his ear.

She's talking to a stranger. His face is already closing in with pain. Shutting her out.

Doly searches for a card for his birthday. She finds one with a path weaving through rhododendron woods and scribbles *Every good wish* because she must not say *Happy Birthday*. Then she writes the real message below: *When next you are in Midhurst.*

It isn't right. She throws it away and spoils a second, a third card. All end in the waste basket. Until the right words come at last: *Every good wish for the road.*

She's gardening when she sees him cycling up her drive. Wobbling from side to side. He is quite drunk. A garble of words which defy interpretation.

'Please don't apologise.'

'I aren't apologisin'. Explainin'. My dad's illness has been hell. It's fair done me in. Didn't seem right ter drag yer under.'

His need for her is urgent. And irresistible. The au pair Tante Martha sent will look after Ross. 'Shall we meet your mother at the hospital?'

His mother is waiting in a small courtyard outside the ward. Piers lights a cigarette, his hand deliberately touching Doly's.

'Hello.' His mother who can't remember the name Dorinda.

'Say Doly,' he coaxes her. 'Yer be able ter remember that, won't yer?' He smiles down at her as though she were the child. His tenderness makes the worn face, strained with age and loss, soft and happy.

They leave her to her grief, drive back along lanes overhung with trees losing their leaves. The constant, inevitable changing of the seasons. Winter has a frosty beauty of its own. Denuded, stark, essential.

'Let's stop ter get a bottle o' Scotch. Wanna come in with me?'

Doly is puffing away money she can't afford. 'No. I'll wait here.'

He comes back with champagne. The genie of tears in a bottle. Which will not do for Ross at Dramlings.

'Shall we take a trip to Iping Common before we go back? For some fresh air? The young girl staying at the house can give Ross tea.'

He takes her hand as they walk up the chalky trail she's often roamed for comfort. It's never let her down. 'I've walked this path for years. From long before your time,' she murmurs. Leaning against him, walking in step on uplifting cushions of heather.

He sucks in heathland air, gathers it into his chest in great lungfuls. Dried plumes of wild ling are inside him, are part of him. And of her.

There's a little hollow beyond a mound which is insulated from the world. They slide into a double bed of earth-coloured gorse and bracken. His hands reach for her, tear off clothes. His fingers find her, tease her open. They're part of the earth, the leaf mould which enriches next year's growth, wet and pervasive.

'You be leanin' against gorse. Don't it hurt?'

'I'm used to it.' She welcomes the prickles which foretell a larger one.

'You be so solid. Salt o' the earth. You'm never do change.'

Afterwards they go home to a prosaic supper shared with Ross and

Sabina. Rabbit pie, baked potatoes, tomato salad. Love apples from the autumn garden, squelchy with frost and brimming with flavour.

'Dramlings do feel so good, so true.' His munching jaw juts angles into her heart. 'You be the one as be home and dry. I did lose my anchorage. Dunno where I belong.'

She sees his face lined like the runnels which slide down the rain-soaked windowpanes.

'Love? Oh yes, Piers. I love so many things. The fire and the rain. The clock ticking. And you gliding over me. My body, my mind, my house.'

'It would be good to have a place of me own.'

Is he asking her whether he can stay? To share Dramlings and Ross with her? Her paradise, her treasures, all she holds dear? Her limbs stiffen away.

'Come nearer. You aint afraid of me, be you?' He draws her to him. Grabs her tight.

'No. Wary of being overheard upstairs.'

Sweet hands stroke round her, hold her. His soft lips whisper, suck. His strong legs are around her own, her waist. They stagger to the narrow guestroom bed and make it wide with joy.

A long time later Piers clears his throat. 'No need for us to get back to town tonight.'

'Right. I'll straighten out this room. Can you make do with the sofa and leave before Ross and Sabina come down?'

Her reward is that sudden surging happiness on his face. And the river runs through her yet again. Gentle and rough, turbulent and clear. Still the same force she's got to know every time it decides to flood through her territory. Leaving its traces. She tastes it on her, in her. She is no longer herself. As though another's river bed makes her land for richer, for poorer.

It has. It does. The golden lava which knows no bounds.

CASTLE WOLFSBURG

Wolfsburg was a fine castle built high on a hill dominating the surrounding lowlands. It was the seat of the most distinguished family for miles around – the Wolffs of the Wolfsburg. Their standing gave them the power of life and death over their neighbours. The rack and gallows stood outside the castle gates as a grim reminder of their might, for all to see and be afraid.

The Wolffs, being the bravest knights and the largest landowners attending the nearby church, had certain privileges. One was that Sunday service would not start until the lord of Wolfsburg was seated in his pew. The incumbent pastor did not view this as a great burden. The present Knight Wolff was a model church goer, and never late.

Until one particular Sunday. The congregation of farmers, farm workers and their families had been sitting in their pews for more than an hour. It was a sunny day, and the time was read on the sundial fixed to the church's outside wall.

The pastor realised his flock was becoming restless. Children cried, feet shuffled, boots began to beat a tattoo on the stone floor. So when the sundial showed another hour had passed, and still the noble knight Wolff had not appeared, the pastor was convinced something dreadful must have happened to his lord. Perhaps he'd been taken ill, or some other terrible mishap had taken place.

The stamping of feet grew louder, the infants cried piteously, and the pastor went outside once more to check the time. Another hour had passed, so he scanned the surrounding area for sight of Knight Wolff and, with nothing to be seen on the far horizon, decided to begin the service.

He walked slowly towards the pulpit, opened the Holy Book and began to read the first words of the day's Gospel when they died on his trembling lips. For there, inside the opened church door, stood the

244

mighty Lord of Wolfsburg, his face puce with rage.

He wasn't ill. Nor had any mishap overtaken his family. He'd been out hunting and, excited by an enormous bag of deer, had forgotten about Sunday service. And it wasn't the chase after game, or the speed with which he galloped to church when he realised he'd forgotten his God, which brought the blood to Knight Wolff's face. It was fury with the pastor who dared to question the privilege which was his due. With malice aforethought.

Knight Wolff threw a look of hatred towards the altar, charged up the aisle, tore his dagger from his side and pierced the holy man's breast with it. Blood spurted over the alb, flowed down the pulpit, spattered the altar. That was how justice was done. Cruel, terrible justice.

Since that day the curse of Heaven has lain on the Wolfsburg and its heirs. The family died out after Knight Wolff's murderous revenge.

The weapon used for the evil deed stayed in the church for many years, guarding the crypt in which the Wolff family lay. Until that, too, fell into disuse. The stones in both church and churchyard disappeared without trace, sold and dispersed throughout an indifferent world.

CHAPTER 16

New York, Summer 1953

Mrs Bluefield meets Gabby and Kamilla at the station.

'I'm doing the school run. You can sit in back, Kamilla. Going to be kinda crowded.' She turns to Gabby. 'I'm Petulia, Gabriele. Guess we should be on friendly terms since you're going to be part of the family. Can you cook?'

'I love cooking. Petulia.'

The Bluefields are delighted with the results. They house Gabby in charming chintz next to minor chintz for Kamilla. Both bedrooms look out on the Bluefields' manicured garden. Birdsong, serenity, nodding maples. The idyllic scene marred only by a curious mound of recent vintage.

'Are you building a swimming pool?'

Mr Bluefield's laugh overwhelms his family's. 'Swimming pool? That's real cute, Gabriele. Coming from Europe I'd have thought you'd have guessed. That there's our shelter.'

Gabby tries to remember American geography. 'You mean because of earthquakes?'

'Why no, Gabriele. We don't have 'quakes in Connecticut. You're thinking of California. We have the future in mind. Protection from attack in case of nuclear war. This here's our very own haven. A real priority. Lemme show you around.'

The shelter is vast, and underground. The mound simply protects the entrance. A generator for lighting and refrigeration, tins of food, air-conditioning, furniture. A large container filled with gasoline. An arsenal of weapons. To repel neighbours not as farseeing as the Bluefields.

'You think there are going to be nuclear attacks on New England?' Gabby keeps her voice level. But wonders whether all Americans are mad. Or just the rich ones.

'Maybe not direct ones. On New York City, sure thing. The Russians developed an atomic bomb in 1949.'

'You're thinking World War III is around the corner.'

'You bet. You've recently arrived from Europe, Gabriele. I guess you don't know the situation in the Far East — in Korea — is very grave. The Russians could invade at any moment.' Milton Bluefield taps his nose. 'We need to keep in mind what happened in Nagasaki, Gabriele. Here's what we want you to do. You and Kamilla join us for Russian classes. Beginners' course. We've already achieved grade two.'

'You want us to learn to speak Russian?' They're not only determined to survive a nuclear attack, they're clearly entertaining the possibility of a Communist invasion.

'That's about the size of it. Let me spell that out for you. If the Russians do take over here, they'll need people who can liaise between them and the American people. We plan to be the interpreters. The whole family is learning Russian to that end. We need you to be a part of that. I guess we have to say it's a condition of employment.'

'The agency didn't mention that.' Gabby hides surges of fury behind seeming stupidity. Comparisons with pre-war Vienna don't show the Bluefields in a shining light. Not even a red one. A muddy tone of yellow.

She doesn't want to know the colour of collaboration. Even if she did, the price is low. $150 a month. All found for her and Kamilla. In two chintzy rooms with a view.

Not even the efficiency of the local library keen to supply Gabby with any reading material she likes to order can compensate for the distaste she feels. She stays the month she agreed, pockets her wages of collusion and escapes back to New York.

A sitting duck for an atom bomb. Considering the alternatives available, it's a risk she's happy to embrace.

The agency, though not overly sympathetic, does find Gabby a new job. A simpler one. As companion for ninety-two-year-old Mrs West who lives in a Manhattan hotel. Gabby is to be housed in an adjoining room, not banished to servants' quarters.

There are no cleaning duties, nothing onerous. The main requirement is that Mrs West not be left on her own during the day. That her lighter, cigarettes, pills and alcohol be removed at night. Discreetly.

Mary Beth Burnett is one of Mrs West's three daughters. 'My mother has recently had several bereavements. She's lost her husband and three sons in the last two months.'

'That's really terrible!'

The daughter's blue-rinsed curls nod. 'Two of my brothers were on a hunting trip. Their car ran off the road. My father had a heart attack. And my eldest brother's been sick for a long time. Cancer.'

'I'm terribly sorry.'

'Sure. What we need you to do is make sure Mom takes these pills.'

Gabby stares at an array of bottles. Is the old lady sick?

'We have to make real sure she doesn't find out the truth. The schedule's written out for you. You need to keep to it religiously. Some of these tranquillisers are dangerous in the wrong dosage.'

'But, surely...' Gabby tries out. Appalled the old lady is being cheated out of legitimate grief. Possibly feeling a worse one — that her sons are not visiting her — instead.

'There's a problem?'

'I mean to say. Shouldn't she be told about these deaths?'

'No, ma'am.' Blue rinse curls shake vigorously. 'It would kill her if she finds out.'

It isn't Gabby's business. If she doesn't play ministering angel they'll find another one. 'I just make sure she takes her pills at regular intervals?'

'And see she doesn't set fire to her room.'

'Perhaps you'd like me to take her for walks?'

'That won't be necessary.' An embarrassed, sideways glance. 'We also need you to check she doesn't drink too much.'

Gabby's eyes clear. She thinks she and Mrs West might hit it off. A certain fellow feeling.

Mrs West smokes a great deal. The pills not only tranquillise, they fuddle her so she's liable to forget her cigarette is lit. She might put it down somewhere and leave it to ignite.

'I guess it's good to have you around.' Mrs West is not a great talker, and tends to repeat herself. 'My sons no longer even come to visit with me,' she tells Gabby over and over again. With tears in her eyes.

Gabby allows more drinks. She keeps the old lady company with watered down whiskey. She even develops a taste for bourbon. In the absence of schnapps.

Life is pleasantly dull, cash is accumulating in the bank. Mrs West takes her 'vitamin' pills without dissent, asks for more drinks, allows Gabby to stub out unsmoked cigarettes. Until the day another of her daughters — she favours purple over blue rinses — calls. And decides the combination of hotel and Gabby is too expensive. She will take Mrs West home with her.

'But that won't cause a problem for you, Gabriele. My sister's looking for a companion. Maybe you'd like to take over there.'

Mrs Seton does not favour rinses. Her hair is a uniform blonde. And, though evidently in her sixties, she's still a great beauty.

Her schedule is regular. She rises around noon, consumes iced orange juice and consults her diary for the day's events. The first few hours are devoted to applying make-up, seeing her hairdresser, choosing clothes. And talking to the beaux — that, apparently, is the correct term — who phone in hopes of arranging dates.

The number of Mrs Seton's admirers is exceptionally large. They come for cocktails followed by dinner prepared by Gabby. Nothing too daunting, and there's only one problem. The hotel apartment Mrs Seton chooses to live in includes a tiny kitchenette for making coffee or boiling eggs. Gabby is expected to cater for dinner parties of four or six.

She's used to handling greater predicaments. Except for one tiny complication. Mrs Seton insists on planning the menu. That involves several hot dishes, far more than the single burner can manage.

'No problem, Gabriele. We'll purchase an electric saucepan.'

Gabby is presented with a brilliant modern artefact which has a minor drawback. It blows the fuse. Regularly. Mrs Seton overcomes this insignificant obstacle with grace and dignity. She orders fuse boxes by the dozen — since she has no idea how to rewire a fuse — from a bewildered hardware store clerk.

The phenomenal success of her dinner parties encourages Mrs Seton's culinary ambitions. She buys a rotisserie. With dramatic results. The whole hotel is plunged into darkness. And despair.

Handymen are summoned by an outraged Mrs Seton. The rotisserie is pronounced the culprit, the damage repaired. And the hotel is short-circuited again the following night.

Mrs Seton pronounces the management ridiculously incompetent. She instructs Gabby to light candles for expected guests. The doorbell rings just as Mrs Seton is enjoying her first Manhattan. She signals Gabby to answer it.

A formally dressed stranger strides past Gabby. 'Turner Carlton, Mrs Seton. Manager of the Carlton Apartment Hotel. I sure am sorry to intrude, but we have to talk.'

Mrs Seton is seated on her chaise longue. Majestically. She flings a filmy scarf around her neck. 'I'm expecting company, Mr Carlton. Maybe if you could make an appointment with Gabriele here...'

'I won't take up more than a minute of your time, ma'am. I have to ask you to dispose of that rotisserie right now.' He walks over to the kitchenette and disconnects the offending kitchen ware.

Mrs Seton rises. The scarf is flung across the room. In the absence of a glove. 'If you can't accommodate me here, Mr Carlton, I shall remove to Palm Beach.'

There is no contest. The manager bows, the rotisserie clasped firmly to his bosom. He retires backwards out of the room.

Mrs Seton packs boas, jewellery, fur coats, sequinned dresses and a suitcase full of make-up. And leaves Gabby looking for yet another job.

CHAPTER 17

New York, Autumn 1953

The Billingers are different. Uncannily normal. Gabby is able to communicate with them. They hand their two children and their household over to her with relief. And complete trust.

The house runs smoothly. The children get to school on time and enjoy their meals. They consider Gabby weird, but not antagonistic. She's invited to family parties because they enjoy her company.

Bud Billinger's brother Clinton is a frequent guest. He enjoys talking to Gabby about Europe and finds her fund of stories fascinating. On her advice he applies for a job at the Atomic Energy Commission. And, to her surprise, he gets it.

'I'm off to Europe in two weeks!' he tells Gabby. Excitement is evident in the flushed face and eyes startling into enthusiasm. 'I kick off at the Atomic Energy Commission in London. For training. And guess what? They're considering opening a branch in Vienna! The International Atomic Energy Agency they're going to call it. That'll take a while. I'm helping to set it up.' His grin spreads wide.

Pangs of homesickness overwhelm Gabby as she thinks back to solid grey buildings only five or six storeys high, cobbled streets, the sound of church bells, the clanging trams. No neon, no billboards. 'So you'll be living in Vienna shortly?'

'Right. You think I'll enjoy it?'

'I think you'll love it, Clinton. I wish I could be there to show you round, introduce you to people your own age.'

'I guess he'll meet them, Gabriele.' Clinton's brother doesn't feel the same enchantment with Gabby's stories. 'He'll have the local girls dancing all round him.'

'Sure thing, Bud. Thing is, I'll need to find accommodation first. You know a good agency, Gabriele?'

It's never struck her so forcibly before. There must be dozens of Americans looking for flats, apartments or houses in Vienna. Gabby looks out of the Billingers' window, across Central Park. She sees the magnificent Manhattan skyline silhouetted against the clouds. An exciting, exhilarating city. Right for her father even when it was in its infancy. But not for her. She is a central European by temperament. She can admire, enjoy, take part in the freedoms the United States offers its citizens. But she cannot feel at home.

Longing for Vienna has been haunting her days and nights. She has to return.

'I've decided to go back to Europe myself next summer. New York gets too hot for me from June onwards. I'm hoping to book a passage then.'

'That mean you're leaving us?' Sarah Billinger's mouth curves downwards. 'We sure will miss you, Gabriele. I guess you're the best housekeeper we've ever had.'

'And I've enjoyed being with you. Come and look me up in Vienna.' She's genuine about it. She likes them, and turns to Clinton. 'I'm going to be looking for a flat for myself. Why not get in touch when you've finished your training? Write to me care of my lawyer. Doktor Venn's office is just off the Stephansplatz, right in the centre of the city. I'll see what I can find for you.'

'Doctor? They call lawyers doctor in Vienna?'

'We call everyone Doktor at the drop of a piece of Apfelstrudel. Any graduate is entitled to the form. Including doctors of medicine and philosophy.'

'Lesson one!'

Why hasn't she thought of it before? She found a new tenant for the villa. She can as easily find other flats and apartments for people to rent. Viennese landlords are looking for foreigners to circumvent the Viennese rent laws, foreign newcomers are desperate for accommodation. She's in a unique position to introduce the two parties to each other, to settle any differences. She's trilingual, good at smoothing over complications and she can act the guide and mentor. Maybe she can even sell her Viennese villa herself.

Visiting Emil and Rachel in Seaford that weekend she explains her plans.

'Why, that's a really great idea, Gabby!' Her brother is so overcome with delight he banishes Minx and Manx to the kitchen. 'I've never felt comfortable with you being a domestic. Real estate is much more in your line. Following in our father's footsteps.'

He's right. It's part of her inheritance. The glow of assurance brings words tripping gaiety off her tongue, a straightening backbone to a drooping posture. 'You think I can pull it off?'

'You'll need to work at it. Establish yourself.'

'What about Kamilla, Gabby? Why not leave her with us until you're settled?' Rachel adores looking after the little girl. Kamilla basks in the undivided attention lavished on her.

'What d'you think, Kamilla? Would you like to stay with Uncle Emil and Aunt Rachel for a little while?'

The child looks from her mother to Emil and Rachel. 'What about Onkel Hans?'

He's sent letters and presents to Kamilla. Frequently. He's written to Gabby as well. The same tortuous, formal letters he wrote when she and Bosch were in Paris. 'He'll go on writing to you, I'm sure.'

'Who's going to teach me singing and the piano?'

Gabby is surprised. She was unaware that Kamilla actually misses Hans, and even the music lessons she professed to hate. Though there's no mention of Greti. Or Mustapha. 'Perhaps we can ask Uncle Emil to arrange piano lessons for you, Kammy.'

'Sure thing. Be glad to.'

'When will I live with you again, Mutti?'

'Soon, Kammy. Very soon. Let's make a date in Schwanenbruch next summer, Rachel. Bring Kamilla over. If I've been able to make a go of it, Kamilla can come back to Vienna with me. If not, I can always come back here and earn myself more dollars.' She pulls Kamilla on to her lap. 'What d'you think, Kammy? Would you like to spend a year here?'

The child's feelings are guarded since Bosch's death. Her emotions are only expressed in her singing.

Kamilla nods. 'I can play on Uncle Emil's boat. And fly his paper aeroplanes.'

Letters from Hans aren't just back to their pre-engagement style. They're more numerous, lengthy, erudite.

Missing Vienna as she does, even missing Hans, Gabby eventually replies. She's overwhelmed by his response when she tells him she will be returning in the autumn. The card accompanying the bouquet of flowers confirms what she's already guessed.

My dear Gabriele,
I hope you will not allow the past to jeopardise our relationship. There is so much we have to give each other.
In case you are worried about Kamilla's schooling, and her music lessons, you know I will be happy to see to those. And, though I have returned the car to the garage, I realise you will need another one. We will choose it together.
In friendship, Hans

Is she courting disaster by reading his letters, even contemplating a response to this last one? The man can't help his nature. That's actually why she took to him in the first place. His interest in Kamilla, his intellect, his generosity. And his desire to remain unmarried.

It isn't like her to bear grudges. Why shouldn't they resume their platonic relationship? There will be no question of an engagement, or a future marriage. Why shouldn't they simply be friends?

The letter telling Hans Gabby sees no reason not to meet when she finally returns to Vienna opens a pent-up dam, an avalanche of flowers, chocolates, books. More letters. Even a phone call to Emil's house while she's working at the Billingers. A request, relayed through Rachel, that he be allowed to visit her in Schwanenbruch.

'It sounds as though he can hardly wait to see you.' Rachel is baffled and disapproving. 'I take it you're not even considering seeing him again.'

'He's Bosch's cousin, Rachel. I can't deprive Kamilla of the few relatives she has.' Gabby refuses to be drawn further. When both her brother and his wife remind her of the way Hans behaved, the disgraceful way he treated her, she shrugs. Her relationship with Hans is between the two of them. She's never going to discuss it with anyone else again.

THE SCYTHE

It was at the time when peasant farmers living on their lord's estates were duty bound to help him get his hay harvest in. The whole group sharpened their scythes for the appointed day. And a young boy of the village, wanting to prove his mettle, begged to be allowed to join his elders.

The men laughed, and pointed out to that he didn't even have a scythe. So he went to the smith and begged him for one. The blacksmith smiled, agreed to make him one and handed it over with the words: 'No need to sharpen it. But be sure to bring it back tonight.'

The workers walked over to the fields they were to mow, and the young boy went with them. When the foreman saw the young lad he laughed at him, and told him to get back to feeding the pigs. But the boy begged until he was allowed to join the mowing gang. And when the swathes were allocated he was given the last, most difficult, one.

As the mowing began the foreman had to concede that the boy was giving the older scythemen a run for their money. In fact they had to work hard to keep clear of him and not fall foul of his swinging blade. Even the foreman had to work harder than he liked.

During the midday break the young lad took his ease in the meadow, while the older men marvelled at his skill.

The foreman, meanwhile, was plotting a way to put him down a peg or two. He hid the whetstone used to sharpen the blades in the longest swathe. When work started again he allocated that one to the youth, content to wait until the young lad would hit the whetstone and blunt his scythe.

The youth knew very well what was going on, but he went on working. When he came to the whetstone he didn't stop. Instead he cut it right off its shaft. And it still didn't blunt his blade.

He went on mowing behind the loathsome foreman, right on his heels, so that he couldn't ease off. The man worked on, determined not to give way to a pimply youth, glad it was Sunday the next day. And returned home to bed. From which he never rose again.

The other mowers marched back to their village, and the youth returned the scythe as he had promised. The brawny blacksmith took it back and melted the blade down again.

'That scythe has mowed enough,' he said.

PART 3

REAL ESTATES

1954 – 1956

CHAPTER 1

Sussex, Spring 1954

Doly comes across him again in Midhurst. Months later. 'This be my first weekend off since October,' he almost yells at her, the sharp angle of jaw and chin cutting through. 'I did go through one hell of a trip. Week in week out, and I got vicious with it.'

No word for months, and then he greets her with verbal abuse? That will never do. 'Well, don't take it out on me.' She picks up her shopping bags and is about to walk away.

The briefest silence stabs her back. 'It be very, very nice to see you again.' His voice is already warmer, with that slight quaver which wants to ask for help but doesn't know how.

There's certainly been nothing these past months for Piers to be happy about. Leaving him would be like leaving a drowning man. He's so absorbed in his anger at his father's sickness and death, and his pervading grief, that he doesn't focus on her, on them. Even to the extent he did before.

He stands aside, then suddenly: 'Let's git away tergether. Jest the two on us. A sea change.' Eyes which don't ask, only demand.

It's the Easter holidays. Ross is with his father for three weeks. Doly sees an ad for an exchange flat in the south of France. She suggests to Piers that this might be a place for a holiday. After he's spent time with his family.

His eyes cloud, then open. 'Something 'ere you might take a look at.'

They're standing outside a newsagent's window, looking at the small notices. Two people wanted for a private yacht cruising from Dartmouth to Cannes and back, needing a crew. Two weeks. The offer is for a free passage in return for cooking and help.

Doly thinks it a wonderful idea. Though Cannes would be the last place she'd consider if they had the cash to pay their way.

The trip itself will be a reminder of jaunts long past. With Lieselotte, her bosom friend who was not then occupied by husband Joseph. Doly also thinks back to the time when she went by herself until she met a grizzly bear who licked clean the plates she didn't wash.

She sees herself and Piers standing together at Cannes overlooking Mediterranean waves instead of the Elbe froth she'd prefer. Because there are no yachts going to the North Sea.

'That sounds a good idea. Ross won't be back for another two weeks.'

He shuffles, humps his shoulders, moves away from her. 'Not too sure as I kin make it after all.' The foot drags slow. The eyes recede.

Doly's anger erupts into strength. She grabs his shoulders. Shakes. 'What *do* you want?'

He stands, sways, suddenly looks so pale she thinks he'll keel over. She hasn't realised her own strength. Which isn't at all like her. An impulse she's ashamed of. Suddenly she understands it isn't physical. Their relationship is threatening to become too consuming for him, too personal.

She has no intention of forcing herself on anyone, let alone Piers. 'Best if I push off home now. By myself.'

He shrugs.

She leaves it for a couple of days, runs into him in Midhurst again. Is he lying in wait?

But there's no improvement. Quite the reverse. It's the end of just another interlude. As if he were slowly coming to that part of a magic spell which can never last beyond midnight.

He'll disappear again soon. On his bicycle made for one.

There's no point fighting it. She has to grab at happiness where and how she can. 'You were quite right. Let's not bother to go abroad. This is the way I want to love you. My real life is at Dramlings. Has been for nearly twenty years. Everything else is just a passing incident.'

A happy two weeks passes in the twinkling of an eye. They stalk the woods, crush the gorse, chase each other to the millpond. He leaves the night before Ross is due back.

The next time she's in Midhurst she sees his mother who tells her Piers is abroad again. Spain this time.

She needs a more constant friend.

Dear Faith,

I've had a wonderful idea. Why not join Ross and me in Schwanenbruch this summer? Come in late June. Then we can celebrate your birthday.

Stay as long as you can. It'll give us a chance to rehash old times. I wish I could offer you the hospitality of my father's villa, the one I've so often told you about. Sold long ago, but I'll be allowed to show you round. And you'll enjoy the village, the marshes. Meeting my old friends and relatives. We'll have a ball.

Book your passage to Hamburg and I'll get the train and meet you there. There's a queue of people waiting to look after Ross. Means we can take a few days in the city for ourselves.

All my love, Doly

CHAPTER 2

North Germany, Summer 1954

Doly has always been attached to camaraderie. The shoulder to shoulder togetherness she enjoyed with Lieselotte before Joseph took over, the schooldays with Faith in Paradise, Pennsylvania. And, of course, in Oklahoma when she was carrying Ross. Doly thinks of all her genuine friends in this way: Lieselotte, Bobby, Faith, other Riverside Hall friends, fellow students at Barnard. Even Tante Martha. She hopes everyone she knows locally will merge in amiable gatherings. A few weeks shared, a joy to all, in which one summer will gather together the essence of the past. Schwanenbruch delight wrapped in candy floss.

'Over here, Faith!' Doly runs to meet her friend and hugs her. It's so good to feel the strong hands, to bask in the warm smile, to be with faithful Faith again.

'Doly, honey. You look real swell. The picture of lil' old Mom and apple pie.' She stands away and grins. 'Surprise, surprise! Guess who I met on the trip over?'

Doly's eyes shine. 'One of the Riverside Hall girls? Barnard alumnae?'

'Not even close.' The low, vibrating laugh which always gets to Doly. 'Your sister! You didn't write me she'd be on board.'

Gabby's back? Doly's gay mood turns to anxiety. Will she have brought a fistful of dollars to flaunt where it's not wanted? 'I'd no idea, Faith. Maybe she wrote to Dramlings and I'd already left.' Damn! 'How did you come across each other?'

'I saw her in the bar and did a double. I knew right off Gabriele had to be related to you. You're so alike.'

Gabby buys her wigs from a top hairdresser on the Kärntnerstrasse while Doly makes do with National Health. Which makes a difference. 'You think so?'

'No one could miss you're sisters.' Faith's frown is deep. 'A strong family resemblance somehow. So I went over and introduced myself. We had a great time together. Sharing drinks, smoking cigars. She's a real trouper.'

Gabby is tripping down the gangplank, waving, just the way she did, so long ago, when she and Doly were both pregnant. This time it's Gabby who's springing the surprise.

'Hi, Gabby.' Doly is dumbfounded. Why does her sister always push in? And have the two of them been talking behind her back, out of turn? 'Where's Kamilla?'

'Marvellous to see you, Doly. Faith told me you're already here.' Gabby arranges for her bags to be collected by a porter. 'Kamilla's staying with Moppel and Rachel for a year. While I find my feet.'

'You mean you're coming back to Europe for good?'

'Back to Vienna, yes. I think I've worked out how to swing it.'

Doly hooks her arm through Faith's. 'I've booked us into a nice little hotel. You won't mind sharing a double room, will you?'

'Very cosy.' The throb of Faith's voice. 'Might be real handy in this climate. Say, d'you folks get any summer up here? It's kinda chilly for end June.'

'We have other ways of keeping warm,' Doly laughs. 'You off to the station, Gabby?'

Gabby and Faith exchange looks. 'I thought I might stay in Hamburg tonight, Doly. If that doesn't put you out. I've already arranged to see the Dieners — you remember, some distant relatives of Bosch's. We could get together in the evening.'

'We're celebrating Faith's birthday tonight.'

'Exactly. Faith and I thought make it a party.'

Doly shrugs. 'I've booked the restaurant. They have live music and a dance floor. Not quite your style, Gabby.'

'Say, the more the merrier, right?' Faith's boom sweeps hesitation to the winds. 'Let's get to the hotel, unwind. I wanna pretty up.'

'This is some treat, Doly. Sharing a room like old times. And your sister's swell. A darling simple girl. The stories she told me about working in New York!'

'Simple is about the last adjective I'd apply to Gabby. She's entirely incalculable. She has a real kink in her nature, you know. Go easy.' Doly tries to keep anxiety out of her voice. Or is it fury, hate even?

Faith's laugh shakes the windowpanes. 'So, you set to mosey on down? I could eat a horse.'

Gabby's already at the bar, sampling her first drink. She signals the barman for two more. 'I told them to change our table to one by the window, Doly. They tried to fit us in some small hole by the service door.'

Gabby in full flow intimidates the waiter. The music is loud and jazzy, the drinks strong. Gabby waxes eloquent and confidential. Faith hangs on every word.

Doly focuses on the music. The violinist is a youngish man who reminds her of Piers because he's skeletal — and absorbed in his playing. She lifts her glass to him, smiles. He nods, polite and distant. She persists, beckons him over. He ambles from table to table playing his violin. He reaches Doly's at long last and asks her what she'd like to hear.

'D'you know *Petronella*? That still something you play around here?'

'Of course, gnädige Frau.'

He doesn't call her Fräulein. The Mom-look Faith mentioned must be obvious to everyone. She's not settling for that. As Doly listens the familiar tune turns the dingy dance-floor into the sparkling parquet of the Blue Salon in the Villa Dohlen of 1925, the hotel dining chairs to gilt, and she's ghost-dancing with Lieselotte. She sees pieces of clothing tossed over their heads, their shoes kicked off, their stockings stripped until only their short dresses cover them. Almost twenty-ninesix years ago, and Doly still hankers after that friendship. Which, she's loath to admit, eludes her.

She's going to prise Lieselotte away from Joseph this summer.

Somehow. They'll ride on the Watt just the way they used to. She'll leave Faith to Gabby if that's what they're both so bloody keen on.

Doly drinks, smokes, toys with her food. She kisses the violinist on the mouth when they say goodbye, and is satisfied by the look of stupefaction from Faith, from other diners. Gabby's eyes film.

CHAPTER 3

North Germany, Summer 1954

'You really seem to dig my sister, Faith.'

The strong arm is heavy around her small shoulders. The soft squeeze of her breasts is comforting. 'Not feeling neglected, are you, Doly? It's you I came to see. Gabriele's just good fun for a holiday. There's no past between us — and no future, either.'

She doesn't convince Doly, who feels she's sharing her room with a complete stranger. And assumes, huffily, that if Faith can gamble away an old friendship with one Atlantic crossing she can as easily gamble away something more valuable.

Things do not change for the better. Doly is baffled that Faith is so taken with her sister and her endless stories that she might as well not be there. She makes a desperate attempt not to feel aggrieved about the company of two turning into a gooseberry crowd. Worse, Faith is short with her, calls her childish. Doly gives up the idea of a happy holiday, but she's appalled at Faith's attitude.

'So let's go back to Schwanenbruch tomorrow, shall we?' Gabby's question is rhetorical.

'I can hardly wait to see this incredible village you two babble about for hours. It sure will take some living up to!'

'It can stand the heat,' Gabby purrs. 'Now, Faith, you'll have to book yourself into the *Elbfluss Haus*. You can't possibly stay with Doly and Ross, their place is unbelievably primitive. No flush lavatory, let alone a bathroom!'

Surely that's the cue for Faith to say she and Doly have spent days riding over the prairie, nights in the same bed, that they camped out under the bright stars of an Oklahoma sky?

The tight, embarrassed smile of a stranger as Faith turns to her. 'What d'you say, kiddo?'

'Gabby's quite right. Sharing a room with Ross and me is bound to cramp your style, Faith. We'd better book meals at the restaurant while we're at it. We don't want to make the relatives feel obliged to feed us.'

'Really, Doly. You never see the point. They'll be so disappointed! Of course we have to accept the invitations — '

Gabby is putting her damned oar in again. 'I've known them just as long as you have. Why would you know best?'

Her sister's flat palm bangs the table in front of her. 'I've known them five years longer, actually. And maybe I'm better than you at reading between polite smiles?'

'Please yourself.' Tautological. She never considers anything else.

Gabby arranges to have their bags fetched from Schwanenbruch station. She grabs Faith's arm, points out landmarks. Doly hangs behind as their voices bubble excitement. They pass Anna's house and she ducks into it to greet a Ross who isn't there.

Two frowning figures are walking back towards her. 'Where did you get to?'

'I dumped my coat. This is where I'm staying, Faith. Isn't it great?'

'Wowie! How old is this place?'

'My father was born here in 1836. My mother was born next door. Much later, of course. She was the eldest daughter of my father's best friend.' Doly always feels the pain of her parents' death, even after all these years. Then rallies, pride overtaking pain. 'They're supposed to be two of the earliest houses in Schwanenbruch. A reasonable guess is early twelfth century.'

'That sure is something.'

Gabby urges them on. She greets all and sundry, volubly, as they pass them on their way to the centre of the village. 'Here we are, Faith. The Villa Dohlen is on your right. Our father built it for our mother in 1908. She was too homesick to stay in the States.' Gabby turns to her left. 'And this is the famous St Nicolaikirche. If you like beautifully carved altar pieces, this one will blow your mind. And there's the famous Klappmeyer organ as well.'

'Klapp, klapp!'

'Really, Doly, not everyone's a philistine.' Gabby draws breath while Faith marvels at the church. 'I'll take you to a service on Sunday. You can choose between Protestant and Catholic. They use the place for both.'

'God, Gabby! Not a sermon at this time of day.' But she can see Faith revels in it.

'Fancy a ride across the mudflats, Faith? Lieselotte's father will let us have the horses. If we plan for the weekend, she'll be able to join us.' Gabby doesn't ride. She's afraid of horses. One plus.

'And we can take Buffy along.' Doly is leaving Ross with Anna. It's only fair to offer to exercise the terrier puppy she's given her as a present, and named. And it reconciles Doly to her sorely missed English Buffy left with Miss Tilletson.

Lieselotte and Faith saddle up while Doly insists on riding bareback. They race over the Watt until the tide begins to turn. Doly lags behind, partly because she's unsaddle sore, partly to annoy the others because she's risking the flood tide swirling and rising around her horse's legs.

Buffy stays with her, bounding with glee. A lashing wave sends him hurtling against the hard pebbles and boulders guarding the Schwanenbruch shore.

He lies there, panting. A rusted nail deep in a boulder is splashed with his bloodstains. Doly calls to the other two already on the grassy marsh. Her waving arms semaphore an emergency. They walk their mounts back without undue hurry.

'Buffy's hurt! We have to get him to a vet.' She's almost sobbing. Why are they dawdling? Can't they see the puppy's been hurt?

Lieselotte's face is stern. 'You know perfectly well how dangerous the flood tide can be. We have to see to the horses first, Doly.'

Doly, dismounted, leaves her horse to find his way to the marsh, holds the terrier in her arms. He's limp, his eyes closed. 'He's injured! We have to get help for him — '

'They're valuable horses, Doly. My father — '

Tears are pouring down her cheeks. 'Are you saying the horses come first because they're more valuable in terms of money?'

'Give me the dog, Doly.' Faith holds out a determined arm. 'I'll give you a leg-up back onto your horse and we'll all ride over to the vet. There has to be one near Schwanenbruch some place. We'll drop you off with Buffy and see to the horses.'

'The puppy's just stunned, Doly. Don't panic.' Lieselotte's voice is infuriatingly calm. 'I don't think there's anything to worry about. After all, pebbles make a reasonably soft landing.'

'Pebbles?' Doly's screech overpowers the wind. 'He was bashed against some metal in the rocks! He's cut — bleeding!'

'Let me see.' Lieselotte sighs, dismounts. Her fingers feel the small body. 'Right. A sucking wound. We've got to seal it.'

'What does that mean, Liesi? Will he die?'

Lieselotte's mouth shuts tight. 'I've got it under control.' She puts thumb and forefinger on either side of the wound, pinches it shut, winds her scarf around the small body. 'When he breathes air is sucked into the chest instead of into the lung, so it doesn't inflate. I've seen to it.'

They process slowly to the vet, drop Doly off, ride on leading her horse.

'I'll give you a ring at the *Elbfluss Haus* as soon as I know how Buffy is,' she calls after them.

They wave goodbye. The waiting, the smell, the harsh remembrance of German medicine. The vet's smiling face. 'There, what did I tell you? He'll be back to normal in a couple of weeks.'

Doly rushes for the telephone and rings the *Elbfluss Haus*. 'Frau Bosch, bitte!'

'Hello, Doly. Is that you?' Gabby's slightly slurred voice.

'Buffy is going to be all right! They've stitched up the wound. He's got a couple of broken ribs, but he's round from the concussion already. They don't think that amounts to much. I'm bringing him back now.'

'What? Oh yes. Wonderful news.'

She's already half-tipsy by five in the evening? 'Can you put Faith on, please.'

A long wait while the phone dangles on the hook. Doly can hear the familiar inn noises in the background until at last heavy reluctant footsteps near the phone, accompanied by a flurry of giggles, meaningless words, Faith's guffaw.

'Faith? Is that you, Faith?'

'Sure thing, pardner. Glad the little dog's pulled through OK. We're kinda...'

'I'll be able to join you in an hour or so.' Maybe it's all her imagination, a high-strung reaction to worrying about Buffy, but surely the little dog is entitled to a little more sympathy than that?

'Why don't we play a game everyone can join in?' Faith has taken to German beer in a big way. She's in gregarious mood. 'A word game. One person goes outside while the others choose a word. Then she's asked to come in, to pose questions to try and guess what everybody thought of.'

There isn't even a pause for breath, or a chance for anyone else to choose another game.

'Or we could play arm-wrestling. Though none of you weaklings would stand a chance against an Oklahoma cowgirl.'

Gabby orders another round of drinks. 'I vote for brainwork. If we must play games.'

Doly lights up another cigarette.

'You go out and finish your smoke, Doly. Meanwhile we'll think of something, then call you in.'

Faith can't even cope with her in the same room. Doly meanders out into the corridor and realises they're calling her back almost at once. She stubs out her cigarette and notices Faith's eyes following her hand. 'Let's see. I'm going to ask Faith. Something connected with smoking?'

'It would be very dangerous if it weren't available!'

'For goodness sake, Faith.' Lieselotte's look is severe enough to rival Tante Martha's. 'You're giving the game away!'

'Ashtray!'

Faith whirls from hot crimson to puce, her contorted face approaching Doly. 'You listened at the door, didn't you?'

'She can't have done, Faith.' Lieselotte pours Doly a drink and offers it. 'She was much too far away. And we were whispering.'

'You did, didn't you?' Faith's accusing finger is within an inch of

Doly's nose. 'You can't just play the game, can you? You've always got to come out on top! At least admit it.'

'If you say so.' And Doly lights another cigarette and walks out of the stuffy atmosphere. She breathes the damp still evening air, sits down on a park bench which holds quite different memories of long ago. So many flirtatious young men, callow, warm, crazy for a Doly with a svelte figure and billowing red hair. And a Lieselotte whose aim in life was to escape her father and come over to be with her blood sister.

She allows the chiming of the church bells to call her back into the glorious past. Which, at the time, she thought so flawed.

Dear Diary,

To say that I'm disappointed cannot express my desolation. In my anxiety about Buffy I assumed Faith would be waiting for news of him. All I heard was indifferent slurring, indistinct muffles of hardly suppressed laughter, when I expected to share. I rode my horse along the dyke and imagined no breach. But I was wrong. Storm clouds had already formed, and a few short days were enough to turn a long-time relationship into a flood tide cascading over the defences.

The Faith I invited to spend time with Ross and me was different. I no longer wish what cannot be. But to feel Faith's spite is to feel gigantic breakers rolling over the dyke. And they're strong enough to breach the weaknesses made by mouse holes and neglect.

She accepted my invitation to show her my roots. Then she panicked, took a spade and cut not merely tentacles but the tap root. Turning my lovely Schwanenbruch into a brothel of schnapps-soaked relationships. And when I urged her to keep faith she turned on her heel.

Why throw away the precious gift of sharing? She and Gabby can be with each other anywhere. If that is what they wish. I've always kept faith, stuck to enduring friendship.

When Liesi arrived from Hamburg to join us, I saw her close her eyes as Faith came into the room. Though I have always made it clear where my deepest feelings lie. Why are you so remote, Liesi? Don't you remember our blood sisterhood, our shared childhood? Don't you want it to last until one of us dies?

She offered me cash. Surreptitiously, so Joseph wouldn't know. I'm not something that can be bought and sold like a sack of potatoes. But the hurt in her eyes when I pushed her hand away was worse. Suddenly I felt at home with her again. Nothing else mattered.

The ghost rider galloped through the storm and begged his people to reinforce the new dyke again. Too late. The sea saw its chance, found the flaws, swept away both worthy and unworthy.

In spite of Faith's foolishness I felt a softening towards her. But she's withdrawn from me entirely. I cannot help her avoid her own disaster. It will steal on her when she's by herself, late at lonely night. When there's no one, nothing. Except memories which can't be changed in truth.

Late that evening Doly tries again to join the now enlarged group of Faith and Gabby, Onkel Wilfred and Tante Mary, Erika, Lieselotte and Joseph. They're all assembled at the *Schleuse Inn*. She sits disconsolate as the laughter flows in and out. As though she, like Buffy — not being of monetary value — was expendable.

The visit she longed for as a homecoming is proving a disaster. She goes outside to contemplate the sea, sits on a jutting rock, her favourite spot for looking seawards and feeling in port.

The moon is still young, will-o'-the-wisp fireflies play across gentle waves. The clean North Sea breezes caress her face, embrace her with their permeated smell of fish and seaweed. A promise of rich harvests from the deep.

Gabby and Faith join her, insist she sits with them on the bench outside the inn. They sit in uncomfortable silence while Doly fumes. Why so determined not to leave her alone? Why spoil so entirely the trip she's been looking forward to?

She pulls out a packet of Players. 'Cigarette?'

'No thanks, Doly. I've brought my Luckies.'

'I'll say goodnight, then.' She realises she has to give way. If this must be farewell to a long-cherished friendship it's no use spoiling the holiday for everybody else. Let Gabby and Faith find their shortcut fling at happiness. After their own fashion.

The summer is almost over. Faith Bowler has long since sailed back to the States, Doly has returned to England. Gabby enjoys the tranquil solitude after they've gone. She's retrieved her strength, recharged her spirit. It will soon be time to tackle Vienna, to turn her plans into reality. She summons up the memory of her father's decisive voice and practises an imitation.

The walk beside the Braake is her favourite. She sweeps hands through gilding corn wind-singing along the earth-packed track winding through it. Sweeping willows are swishing branches in tune like batons. She's reluctant to make out a human voice among the soughing, to acknowledge a figure waving to her.

A man. Who would be looking for her? A phone call from the States? Has something happened to Kamilla?

'Grüss Gott, Gabriele. I thought I would surprise you.'

The very last person she expects, or wants, to see. 'Hans! What on earth are you doing here?'

'Perhaps I should have written I was coming. My two weeks' holiday was due. It's been so long, I couldn't wait for you to turn up in Vienna. And I began to worry you'd change your mind. So I found a driver to bring your new present to you.' He dangles keys in front of her. 'The latest VW. I know you like Volkswagens, particularly the Beetle. And your favourite colour is blue.'

He burbles on, as excited as a small child. How he's missed her, how Vienna is dead without her, that he misses Kamilla. That he will pay all expenses, make sure the child has the best of everything — if only Gabby will return to Vienna. Permanently.

Surely he isn't proposing again?

'I don't think I can accept..'

His head nods eagerly. 'Naturally I would never expect you to consider our previous relationship. I know I don't deserve that. But surely we can be friends?'

Friends. That is exactly what she'd like. An escort, a companion several times a week, a fairy godfather who will provide for Kamilla. And someone who will leave Gabby to start her new life as an independent woman.

'When were you thinking of coming back?'

'In a week or two.'

'Wonderful. I've read there's a special exhibition of Nolde's paintings only a day's drive away. It's a rare opportunity to see the complete retrospective. And there are so many other marsh treasures still waiting to be explored. Why don't we spend the rest of my holiday together? And, when it's over, you can drive us back to Vienna.'

THE RHINE MARKSMAN

Siebold was a rapacious robber baron, a cruel hunter, a godless womaniser. He celebrated each successful raid with a huge banquet. Paid for by the victim of his thievery.

Many a strong man had tried to curb this fiend, to slay him in battle. Among them was the greatest marksman of them all, Hans Veit of Fürsteneck. But Siebold had got the better even of him.

The hall was filled with richly-dressed women with painted faces, drunk men, the discordant sounds of a band of musicians who assumed the greatest noise produced the best tunes to dance to. The choicest cuts of meat were bitten into, then thrown away. Wine flowed freely, love-making became a common spectacle. Until big Siebold roared for silence.

'Noble ladies and gentlemen, honoured guests. After you have had your fill of food and drink I, your esteemed host, will be pleased to find some entertainment for you. I can't reproduce the Roman Coliseum, or the wild beasts tearing Christian captives limb from limb, but I can show you one of the most ferocious animals in captivity.'

Tittering women pretending fear slid their arms around their partners' waists and hid behind them. The men raised their tankards and cheered. The wide portals leading out of the hall opened, and a dishevelled man in coarse sackcloth, his hair and beard unkempt, stood before them. Two guards held his arms, there were chains on his feet.

All eyes were fixed on the closed lids and haggard face of the prisoner. Suddenly he raised his lids, and two black cavities showed he had no eyes. Just holes where they had been.

'Behold the best marksman on the Rhine,' Siebold shouted out. 'His fame made him feared along the length and breadth of the land. Just like me. And when we met in mortal combat, I conquered him.'

'I lay prostrate before you,' the prisoner agreed. His voice loud and vibrant. 'My shield was battered, I was bleeding from many wounds. And still I did not cringe from the death-blow I knew was rightly mine.'

Siebold's cruel laugh rang out. 'I did not want to finish him off! Not when I could have some sport at his expense. So I had both his eyes taken out. The eyes of the greatest-ever marksman on the Rhine are preserved in my collection of rarities.'

'My eyes may be murdered, but they can hear your scorn,' Hans Veit called out. 'There is no chivalry in your stronghold of terror.'

'You shall have a final test of your marksmanship.' Siebold, sure of himself. 'My servants tell me you boast that, even blind and guided only by sounds, you can hit a given mark with an arrow. If you can prove yourself, I'll reward you with freedom.' His voice is raised in triumph. His assembled guests cheer.

'Undo my shackles,' Hans Veit demanded of his guards. 'I cannot shoot unless my legs are free.'

'Unbind him!'

'Death is more dear to me than a fettered life,' the blind man said. He flexed the crossbow put into his hands, a look of sweetness passing over his face like fleeting sunlight on a rainy day.

The guests stood away from the table, worried that the arrow might go astray. Siebold held up one of his goblets. 'I shall strike this silver goblet with my sword. When you hear the clang, shoot!'

Within seconds he tapped the goblet with his sword and tossed it from the table.

'Shoot now!' he roared. And immediately an arrow pierced his mouth.

The blind sharpshooter stood silent, black eye cavities gaping. He heard Siebold's terror-stricken friends stampede from the room like a herd of wild animals. Leaving only his servants to say the last prayers over their master's dead body.

CHAPTER 4

Vienna, Autumn 1954

'So you are back in Vienna for good, Frau Bosch?' Herr Dorndiener is sweating fat behind his estate agent's desk. Glowering guilt for the commission he refused to pay Gabby. It wreathes a transparent shroud between them.

'Like the proverbial bad penny, Herr Dorndiener.' Now that the Four-Power occupation of Vienna is openly discussed as coming to an end, many Americans are planning their move back to the States. Gabby is determined that *her* occupation, judged by the mores of her time, will also come to an end. She has to — is going to, she corrects herself — find a buyer for the villa before the present tenant leaves.

'There still aren't any outright buyers around, Frau Bosch. And your present tenancy agreement can be cancelled within a month. You can imagine what the psychological effect would be if that happened. We should guard against that at all costs.' The same smile which promised her a commission. 'I've had the offer of a Leibrente. Why not take that, and be rid of the place?'

'And what, exactly, is a Leibrente, Herr Dorndiener?' She'll check it out with Venn. Two opinions are always better than one.

The smile twitches in the corners of his mouth. 'The problem is a shortage of capital. So the buyer is offering a small monthly sum until you die.' He interprets the lack of response as a lack of understanding, spreads out his arms in an expansive gesture. Warm and comforting. 'A sort of annuity, in fact. An excellent solution for you, don't you think?'

'Indeed. I understand precisely, Herr Dorndiener.' Her apprenticeship in the States taught her more than she realised. Her body language conveys this with a pleasant, though determined, nod. 'But how will that solve the problem for Herr Ferent? Are you suggesting a small income in Austrian Schillings is going to be acceptable to him?'

He shakes his fountain pen which, apparently, isn't producing enough ink. He writes some figures on a piece of paper. 'Joint ownership is always a problem. Perhaps you could buy him out? Something in the region of three thousand dollars would be fair, I think. If you could come up with that…' He pushes the paper across to her, puts down the pen. His hands wring uncertainty.

Gabby shuts her handbag with a loud snap, her voice equally short. 'I wish to take the whole villa off your hands, Herr Dorndiener.'

His hand is already on the telephone. 'You're confident Herr Ferent will accept your offer? Then we can close the sale.'

Gabby stands. 'No, Herr Dorndiener. I have no intentions whatsoever of paying you commission to undersell my house. And to find $3000 for you in the process! I mean I shall be marketing the villa myself. As from today.'

The telephone receiver clatters back into its cradle. 'We need not be quite so hasty, Frau Bosch.' He stands to bar her way to the door. 'Naturally, if you would like to try to find a buyer yourself, I would be delighted to employ you as one of my staff.' He opens a file drawer, pulls out a form. 'Some references, perhaps?'

'Always learn from your mistakes,' she hears her father say. 'That's the way to turn a sow's ear into a silk purse.' She won't be working for Dorndiener. Or anybody else. She's registered *Dohlen Real Estate* as her trading name, funded an impressive letter head as well as compliment slips, both on excellent paper, from the commission she earned finding Clinton Billinger's apartment. And opened a *Dohlen Real Estate* banking account with the money she accumulated in the States.

She's in business within a week. Colleagues of Clinton's, friends of theirs, ask her to help them out. Eager to do business with a fellow American.

Viennese property laws are convoluted in archaic German no foreigner can hope to understand. Which ensures that Gabby's business thrives on a small scale. Discussions with Viennese landlords open up a world of two markets — black and white. Only the white shows on Austrian documents. The black part is paid in hard currency. In solid greenbacks.

Her new clients, whom she invites for drinks to initiate them into the glories of Vienna, soon net her a buyer for the villa in Neuwaldegg. Gabby agrees to sell for a reasonable price provided payment is partly in dollars. Rolf Ferent's share is transferred direct.

More city properties become available. Gabby uses her share of the villa cash to persuade a tenant in a substantial apartment house to abdicate the rights to his apartment to her. It is, she feels, in a very symbolic location, in one of the gigantic eighteenth century town houses lining the Prinz-Eugen-Strasse. Opposite the walled gardens between the Upper and Lower Belvedere castles, the one-time residence of Austria's famous general, Prinz Eugen. He left his native France to help Leopold I of Austria to fight and vanquish the Turks.

Her apartment has gracious reception rooms. The kitchen and bathroom are Austrian sub-standard, but her guests will only see the separate toilet she pays to have transformed to modern standards.

There is one snag to her apartment, the reason she can afford it. The access is through an impressive front door but, though there is a lift to other apartments, her visitors have to walk through a courtyard brimming with pigeon mess, then climb the back staircase originally built for servants. A metal spiral affair which is not easy to negotiate.

Gabby sells the staircase, though not the pigeon shit, to prospective clients, all foreigners, as one of the curiosities of Old Vienna, and therefore priceless. They ooh and ahh in a very satisfying way. The pigeons are a pest most large cities are prone to and are easily dismissed.

And by the time her guests have been treated to belegte Brötchen — open canapés topped with shrimp, smoked eel and other exotic fare, together with an excellent wine — her guests are lulled into agreeing anything she might suggest. Which, she makes sure, is always to their advantage as well as hers.

'The best business deals are always those in which both parties are satisfied,' she hears her father say. And silently agrees with him.

Vienna, Summer 1955

May 1955 sees the signing of the end of the Four-Power occupation. The Staatsvertrag is signed at the Belvedere, just up the road from Gabby's apartment, the modern cradle of present-day Austria. It echoes, Gabby senses, her initiation into her new life. Just as Austria's occupation by the Four Powers is now virtually over, so Gabby is freed from her past occupation by men, by the mores of her time. She is, at last, reliant only on herself. Relishes it, can hardly believe it took her so long to get to such a blessed state.

She has two bedrooms, a living room almost as large as the one in her former villa, an office, a reasonably imposing entrance hall. And all within ten minutes' walk of the city centre.

The rent itself is relatively low. Pegged by Austrian rental laws which have suddenly turned from negative to positive for her. She — and her heirs — are entitled to live there until they choose to leave.

'Gnädige Frau! What a pleasure to see you again.' Otto Venn rises, unsteadily, as Gabby gushes into his office. Negotiating the threadbare carpet.

'How are you, Herr Doktor? I hope the arthritis is better now?'

'There's always an improvement in the summer.' The wince across his face shows in white lines from nose to mouth. 'And how can I help you?'

'I would like to discuss my business plans with you, Herr Doktor.'

He nods. 'You are a remarkable lady, gnädige Frau. I have learned not to be surprised. But are you sure I am the right man for you? Someone younger, perhaps?'

'You are the perfect representative for me, Herr Doktor. If I may briefly explain.' Gabby sits down, pulls a sheaf of papers out of the briefcase which has replaced her handbag. 'I have thought hard and long about what I can do to earn my own living. You know my history. You will appreciate that I am not intending to remarry.'

'A very wise decision.'

'I have thought carefully about what I can do. I am not young, I have no qualifications, and I have a young child to look after. The options are somewhat limited.'

'Indeed.'

'I've concentrated on my talents rather than my defects. I am bilingual in English and German, reasonably fluent in French. I am very used to dealing with people who are, shall we say, in the higher income brackets, on an equal footing.'

'Very true, gnä' Frau. But that is not a commercial skill.'

'I rather think it is. The sort of people I want to deal with are diplomats, executives of the large international companies, church leaders, opera singers. They are the people who are going to form my future clientèle.'

The lined face hardens, the arthritic limbs move in an uncharacteristic fidget. 'Clientèle? What did you have in mind?'

The word does have other connotations. Surely he can't be misconstruing her intentions? 'Real estate clients, Herr Doktor. I intend to find apartments for foreigners in the higher income groups.'

Relief trembles his head up and down. 'Vienna already has several good agencies...'

Gabby's dissembling smile is artificial. But still effective. 'Of course. But I am prepared to offer a much wider service. I can discuss clients' requirements in English and smooth over problems arising from different cultural expectations. I can assure you, Herr Doktor, that anyone who could charm Thomas J Watson of the IBM, or keep Franz Bosch from quarrelling with the Austrian Government, can handle such assignments standing on her head.'

Gabby's hand lies idle in her lap. She is relaxed, confident. About to engage the right lawyer for her purposes.

He's too polite to scoff. 'You sound most persuasive. How can I help?'

'You, dear Herr Doktor, are complementary to me. You embody the courtliness foreigners associate with Vienna. All the virtues of a bygone age without its inadequacies.'

A twisted smile. 'You mean I'm old-fashioned. Moribund. A left-over from Habsburg times.'

'You are amiable, gracious, honourable. In all the best senses of those words. Apart from meetings with prospective clients or their representatives, what I'd like you to do is to draw up special contracts.

For me to use when dealing with Austrian landlords. The local byelaws, of course, will not come into that.'

'You mean specific contracts aimed at foreigners?'

'Exactly. If you would word them so that non-Austrians can follow them. I'd like to translate them. And then I'd like you to vet the translation.'

Old eyes take on a new lease of life. 'I'm beginning to see what you have to offer, Frau Bosch. I think you're right. You have the germ of an excellent idea.'

'Thank you, Herr Doktor. I'm using my maiden name for the business, by the way. Gabriele Dohlen, chief executive of *Dohlen Real Estate*.' Not rentals, she suddenly realises. Real estate. Her unconscious is already ahead of her.

Gabby calls on embassies and consulates — including the Far Eastern ones — in person. She offers her services as a freelance translator specialising in real estate contracts. She hands out beautifully printed cards at the American Embassy and various official agencies. She calls on Protestant ministers anxious to protect their Anglo-Saxon flocks from the terrible consequences of having a popish landlord.

Her services are almost immediately called on. And appreciated. Within three months she has enough work to cover basic costs. And her telephone never stops ringing.

CHAPTER 5

Sussex, Spring 1955

'Have you thought of selling?' Roger Quinnel, a frequent guest, a sterling friend and Doly's stalwart solicitor, squints at Dramlings bathed in the rosy tints of winter evening glow. 'I think you might get a fair price for it.'

'The agents have been here before you, Roger. Very fair indeed. But I'm not selling.'

'You're surely not intending to go on living in that ghastly shed every summer, are you?' He looks around to see whether Ross is within earshot. 'You can't expect the boy to put up with that as he gets older.'

Doly puffs away contentedly. She's been proved right. The despised cottage has come into its own. It retains Ross's innocence, and idyllic surroundings for his childhood. She's not giving it up.

'I'm not sure that's a disaster as far as Ross is concerned. He's free from the ratty greed and petty lusts most children are caught up in.

Bobby Hudwalker was here again the other week, you know.'

Roger nods. He's urged Doly to consider Bobby's proposal of marriage seriously.

'He pressed a ten bob note into Ross's hand as he left. You know what he said to me? "Uncle Bobby gave me this piece of paper, Mummy. Could you look after it for me? I don't know what to do with it." Now, is there any other eight-year-old you know who wouldn't have any idea that it was money? And quite a lot of money at that. Or any other child who wouldn't want to spend it on some rubbish?'

'The Princess might never discover the Frog King among the brambles, Doly.'

Earth-worn hands light another cigarette. Determined lips blow smoke rings into the still air. They laze towards the chimney, circle it. Joining thin smoke from deadwood logs. 'I've had an idea, actually. I'd like to build a self-contained wing on to the side of Dramlings. Then I can rent out the original cottage for the whole year for a steady income.' Doly ruffles peahen wings. She knows she's doing well. In spite of insignificant plumage. 'If Erskine hadn't mortgaged the place, I could have done it years ago. But there's still life in the old mother bird. I'm determined to leave Ross a treasure.' Her eyes dance amusement. 'A Rembrandt, so to speak.'

The solicitor blinks that aside. 'A wing, eh? Brilliant idea! You've managed to accumulate the capital? Found someone to stand by you?'

'I'm going to ask my brother. He's doing very well now. And he owes me. It was his stupidity which lost us Castle Bath. And the East Side People's Baths as well. His stupidity, his greed, and his negligence.' She doesn't mention the derisory sum Moppel paid her for her share of their father's Schwanenbruch villa because, in her innocence, she simply asked for what she needed at the time together with the fees for Lieselotte studying medicine in Berlin. He was the businessman, he knew what he was doing and allowed her to throw away her birthright.

'I really wouldn't count on your brother, Doly. Why not sell up and find yourself another place? Leave Dramlings to the stockbrokers who have to commute to the city. You have the option to find something much cheaper, possibly even better. In the West Country, say.'

Nicotine-stained fingers pull a stray weed out of her cardigan. 'I'm staying here, Roger. I love the woods, I love Dramlings, I love the neighbourhood.'

'And what about Ross's education, Doly? What if he doesn't pass the eleven plus?'

'Iain Courtling is taking care of that. Ross is down to go to Seaford College, in Petworth. The Greenells along the road are sending Sam. They'll drive both boys over every day.' She straightens, opens the front door. 'This is where I want Ross to spend his childhood. And this is where we stay.'

Dear Faith,

How appalling that my brother was so rude to you when you were simply representing my interests. I can only apologise on his behalf.

It's been my misfortune to observe, time and again, that the majority of people can't enjoy birds without hating cats. Studying birds may well be a deserving pastime. Lace it with sentimentality and it's a disaster. When a healthy cat has pounced his kill the pitifully mangled birdie corpse is dissected in gruesome detail, earnest bird-lovers wallow in an orgy of moral indignation. Worse still, they call on the God who created both birds and cats to be witness to their cause.

Impassioned funeral wakes and caveats of hellfire and brimstone are used to show that birds are a species apart. Not like those terrible cats. Yet creation needs predators as much as prey. Making apparently worthy sentiments as grooved as any other fanatic diatribes.

We have, in our time, sprung all sorts of cats on each other. Never a gory one. Not even when, living close together in our youth, our growing pains were as catty as they come. Or more recently, when a cat of a ginger colour came between us.

I like to think that our various meetings can be seen in that light. Anything else would presuppose incarceration in a cul-de-sac relationship.

I know you understand the thoughts I write. But it's always better to be together, even in silence. If you've a mind for another interlude at Dramlings, book your passage and visit Ross and me. The whole cottage is ours over Christmas. Why not come then? Remember we had a ball your last visit. Let's repeat good times.

Your loving Doly

Sussex, Summer 1955

'I sure am sorry I couldn't talk your brother round, Doly. Has he seen this place?'

'He's never bothered to visit.'

'So he has no idea of the conditions you live in during the summer?'

Doly's puffs are satisfying. Faith has brought a whole carton of Lucky Strikes. 'He disapproves of everything I do. Why add fuel?'

'I'd let you have the money like a shot, Doly. But I haven't got it.' Faith leaves her chair and sits down beside Doly on the narrow couch. 'Why not let me take care of you both? Sell the cottage, come and live in the States with me. Ross is an American citizen, after all!'

Doly edges away. 'No, Faith. I'm staying put. The roots of the rootless cling tenaciously. This is Ross's true birthplace, and this is where we stay until he's ready to fly the coop.'

Faith Bowler's arm is across Doly's shoulders. Her lips brush her cheeks. 'I can't make a living here, Doly. My career is in the United States.'

'I didn't ask you to.' Doly stands, rattles the poker. A shower of red and black.

'You mean you don't want me?'

'Want you?' Doly is surprised. She's never given Faith Bowler any thought as a fixture. A like-minded friend who helps her out when she needs it. As she would help her. Is that now conditional? 'We've always had a close relationship, Faith. Which doesn't mean I want to live in your pocket. Ross and I — '

'That's it, isn't it? Ross and you. He's everything to you. No one else counts.' She swallows hard. 'You used me when you needed me. Now you have what you want I'm expendable.'

Why this extraordinary diatribe? The rolling eyes, the raised arms. Not like the Faith Doly remembers. 'That isn't the way of it at all, Faith! Of course I value your friendship, love to have you come and visit us. But...'

'Different if I were Lieselotte, right?'

'I'm in love with someone, Faith. I haven't mentioned it because there's no chance of a permanent arrangement. He lives abroad. We meet in intervals of years.'

'So there's no hope for me? None at all?'

'You're a true friend. And Ross's godmother. We love you very much and we will always welcome you.'

Faith's features settle into a landscape of despair. She arranges for an earlier passage home, packs her bags, refuses to embrace, even to wave. Flurries off in tears.

Dearest Faith,

I'm sad you left us in the mood you did. I never thought you would. Our worlds are separate. And must be so. It has been, I suppose, my understanding that we are free to experience adult life without the ties of a shared youth. I thought you, of all people, would know and understand that.

In spite of everything, I sit around companionably with you. In spirit. Because the only right thoughts of you are written, not physical, love. Which has grown habitual, the way love does. Without diminishing it.

I know my monthly letters must seem a meagre crop. I still hope they reach the innermost you. And that you enjoy them in the spirit in which they are sent.

Maybe your hand will spank across the paper again like the regular ocean-going liner it used to be. I hope so. I'm waiting for the recorded music of your words. When the ebb is lowest, the tide begins to turn. May it set in soon.

My love as always,
Doly

Dear Doly,

When one evening we come together again we're going to have almost as much undigested history under our belts as on that first evening. We shall come together, I believe, quite as fresh. Freshness seems an attribute of those who count on nothing from life and love greatly its swinging doors.

The woman who puts her heart into a letter is a fool. Better, if she must put her heart somewhere, that she send it as a contribution to the New Yorker. *There she will at least get a rejection slip and the statement that contributions are never accepted.*

But if she posts off a letter to a friend she may receive only silence in return. Human beings are interested primarily in themselves. Personal contact arouses interest of the moment and brings vanity into play, so that in conversation between humans there is often some approach to mutual interest. But let a woman receive a letter from a former conversational intimate, and she's under no obligation to keep up appearances, her natural interest is undisrupted. The problematic, the distasteful, the boring, the alter ego, each becomes a mere scrap of paper. The waste basket is handy and uncritical.

The fool, on the other hand, has certain compensations in the lilt of her bells. Since her tastes are low, she can agree with the old slogan: She's off because she's out. Her bells toll for no one. And while they jingle there grows material for another letter to another princess she cannot put her trust in.

But, dear friend, the solitary candle gives a lovely light. The cap and bells go well therein. And tomorrow is always another day.

Your bell hopping friend,
Faith

Something has clearly gone amiss. Not just with their relationship, with Faith herself. Another psychotic interlude? Nothing to be done at this distance except write. Doly's letters remain unanswered for weeks.

Madison, Wisconsin
Dearest Doly,
It's been months since I've written. And the reason has been good. Very good. So I was thankful to have your letters forwarded to me.

My doctor in the asylum is a very wise man. He has no goatee beard or Viennese bedside manner. He resembles any American businessman or practical scientist of early middle age. Short and stocky, approaching heaviness. He chews a cigar and holds conversations to facts. He is hard, but in no way brutal. And his excellent advice is to get back to work as soon as possible after my release from hospital.

I continue to appreciate his wisdom. No one in Madison knows my story.

'Stone walls do not a prison make' — but they make a damn good imitation, I do agree. Fortunately my walls actually were of stone. So I could still, in a sense, have a field day with red Triassic sandstone, sometimes conglomeratic, sometimes shaly, sometimes clay galled. The floor of my period of solitary confinement was a very interesting crushed contact metamorphic limestone, rich in diopside or some closely related pyroxene and pyrite. Ordinary ward floors were of crushed marble without the contact minerals. It still amuses me to recall how the doctors in charge rather bashfully confessed to me that they'd never before had a geologist as a patient, and that half the time the authorities were pretty much at sea as to the factual content of my conversation.

The mind is a queer thing. In my particular derangement I remember the rocks. I can say that the red sandstone was as I have stated above. Further, my judgment of people was not very different from my normal one.

Your new friend Pete who fell from Faith. But remains a solid rock.

Pete. Of all the names that Faith could have chosen that is the weirdest.

Sussex, Autumn 1955

Doly sees the cottage at Bepton for the first time that summer. On one of her solitary expeditions. Piers has spoken of it, never invited her.

He's in the garage which is also his workshop. On home ground doing what he knows how to do. She savours the joy of a glimpse of his old face again. Which, during long absences, has grown blurred and indistinct. Still silent, still grave. And sadly gathered in.

She stares at the box hedge clipped to perfection. She's always suspected, now she knows. There's someone else then, to make him take such pains.

She knows what's inside the cottage without being invited in. The plan of the house is inspired by one they loved to visit together and discussed in detail. The staircase is fitted with a fine-chiselled balustrade. The surround and mantel in the living room carved into a magnificent fireplace.

'There,' he says. Spotting her, coming over, sweeping his arm. 'Our land do include this field and it do go back to the woods.'

Our. He must have a certain happiness then. Specially with such words spoken of their own accord. Is the cottage hers? And the land? Perhaps it's shared.

He invites her in. And assures her there's no one else in the cottage now. She was evicted from this paradise by some outburst of temper, apparently. He wants to meet up with Doly later. In the dark.

Her heart is touched by his look of exile and homelessness when she sees him waiting for her. Oh, yes, she knows only too well. A lover's quarrel is a cross to bear. But emptiness weighs heavier.

Doly thinks back over their lives so deeply intertwined for over ten years. Lately she must have been the third party who has increasingly come between the unknown companion and Piers. And he looks so immensely drawn and skeletal. But whatever the incident, or the past, they do not discuss it.

Knowing about it does throw some light on their whole relationship. In particular his present unhappiness, their real need for one another. And their lack of contact.

In what seems no time at all he's gone again.

CHAPTER 6

Vienna, Autumn 1955

Candy-stripe border on light blue. Gabby recognises the writing on the airmail envelope from the United States. Not as even and vigorous as it used to be, but unmistakable. Keeping no secrets between its upright strokes. Rolf Ferent is sixty-seven and, forced to retire from the IBM, has moved to sun-drenched Florida. What can he want with her?

Dear Gabriele,

I write to tell my dear wife Laura passed away June 30th. You already know we retire to Florida only two years ago. Poor lady did not have much pleasure here. Her leukaemia already was advanced when we were in New York. The doctors try hard to save. She die of blood transfusion.

My son Laurence and I will be coming shortly to Europe. First we stop in New York to see Nina and husband Warren. Then we go England, to visit Gemma and family. I see first time our granddaughter Marina you already know. Afterwards we go continental Europe. I like to take Laurence Switzerland. Maybe we transfer to live in Lausanne. Is good opportunity for Laurence to learn French.

After Switzerland I like show Laurence Vienna. I cannot take where we used live in Berlin, is wrong side of wall, and Hungary not possible. Vienna at least will show a little of my past to him. Perhaps I introduce Laurence to you? Also we would enjoy to meet your daughter Kamilla.

Yours sincerely,

Rolf Ferent

Gabby's nose twitches curiosity. Not only because she would meet the second son the gypsy predicted for Rolf, at that time so eager to have a son. Naturally Rolf never knew his first son was stillborn. As far as he knows he only begat one son.

Actually seeing Rolf again is not remotely what she's interested in. It's much more personal: she's burning for a chance to cross-examine him. He's the key to an unsolved jigsaw. He must hold the missing piece.

Why did the Church turn down granting her an annulment? The Procurator Fidei refused to discuss the matter with her. He pronounced the Church's decision final, and not to be challenged. Or even questioned.

Gabby refuses to let sleeping sins rot. Did Rolf misinterpret the Jesuit's questions? She intends to finesse out the truth. A welcoming letter invites Rolf and his son to afternoon Jause at her apartment.

'Rolf! How nice to see you again.' She'd have spotted him anywhere. Spicy aftershave smell of the five-o'clock shadow man who shaves twice a day. Top-drawer American tailoring, crisp white shirt.

The years since she's seen him have effected only subtle changes. Black hair with distinguished streaks turned uniform grey. And scantier. Facial lines deeper, the flesh paler, gravity-concentrated in the lower half. The walk a little less springy. Same mournful smile, same submissive eyes. He was middle-aged when they married.

Her looks will have changed much more. Only now does she realise she must have been beautiful. Wearing the right hairdo. The plus side is she always had to fight to look good. Ageing has merely changed her armoury.

The doorbell rings on the dot of four. She opens it to a huge bouquet of roses. A box of chocolates for Kamilla. Surely he doesn't think…

'And this is Laurence? How d'you do.'

'Hi. Where's the TV?'

Kamilla is eight to Laurence's eleven. And still remembers the English she learned as a toddler. 'We haven't got a television. We'll play cards in my room. I'll teach you bezique.' He follows her, pliant as warm plasticine in her hands.

'I was so sorry to hear of Laura's death,' Gabby assures Rolf. Genuinely. 'You must feel terribly drained.'

'Is loneliness is so terrible. Of course, you already know what is like.'

Bosch died four years ago and has become very remote. Though she does miss his clever tongue and ready satire. But she's never felt lonely. She is a brilliant hostess, has a host of friends, a real liking for her own company. Besides, her job is taking up most of her day. 'Indeed.'

Gabby sees little of Rolf in Laurence. A shock of straight blond hair toppling into sly eyes. A truculent stance. Polyp-muffled tones which phlegm loud demands. No sign of reticence.

'You have very beautiful apartment, Gabriele.'

'Thank you. I need some more furniture, but it's coming along.'

They can hear that Kamilla wins the card games. Hand after hand. Laurence appears and grabs a delicate Meissen figure from the mantelpiece.

Rolf's hurry to stand trips him into the table. He whitens with apologies. 'Give to me, Laurence.'

'When are we gonna eat, Dad?' Fat boy appetite.

Rolf runs his hands through his son's hair. He backs away. 'You remember you promised be polite boy, Laurence.'

'I'm hungry.'

Gabby's best hostess smile seats them around her beautifully laid tea table. Lace tablecloth, delicate china, silver cake forks. She switches on her kitchen kettle, brings in the Dobosch Torte which she remembers as Rolf's favourite.

'Is that a cake? Looks kinda weird.'

'Is special Hungarian cake, Laurence. Is my favourite even as boy. You will enjoy — '

A delicate china cup and saucer are swept aside by an uncontrolled arm. 'Can I get some ice cream and a glass of coke?'

Kamilla's nimble fingers rescue the china. 'We don't eat ice-cream for tea, Laurence. And we don't have coke in this apartment. Would you like some raspberry juice?'

'I'll take some cake.' A plump, unwashed hand grabs the dainty pastry fork lying on his napkin. He digs it into the Dobosch Torte's caramel topping. Which flips up.

Rolf tries to wrest the fork out of his son's hand. 'I do for you, Laurence — '

His left hand has already removed the brittle topping, flung it aside. A sudden, unsuspected dexterity grabs the cake knife and carves a chunk of torte. Which is grabbed by his right hand and pushed into his mouth. 'Yucky!' he howls, spitting it out.

Gabby sits frozen into speechlessness.

'I brought Hershey bars, Laurence. Maybe you eat.' Rolf's suit is spattered with Dobosch filling, his eyes avoid Gabby's. 'I will clean, Gabriele.'

Kamilla is the one in full control. She brings a dampened teacloth and a tray.

'No ice cream, no TV. What kinda place is this?' The Hershey bar wrappers are on the floor. Laurence is sprawled across Gabby's tapestry sofa.

'You're quite disgusting, aren't you?' Kamilla grabs sticky hands, wipes off the worst. 'I think you should wash in the bathroom.'

He follows like an obedient little dog. To Gabby's astonishment. And relief.

Rolf flutters around the battle-scarred tea table. 'I think we already stay long enough.' He looks for the raincoat they brought against turbulent weather. Rolf's destiny.

'There is one thing I meant to ask you, Rolf.' No chance of a finesse. Full frontal attack.

He turns. Suddenly an old, bowed man. No wife, no job, unable to control his son. What will he do? 'Ask.'

'You were requested to testify before the Marriage Council of the Roman Catholic Church. About my application for an annulment of our marriage.'

'Is correct.'

'What did you say, exactly?'

Rolf bends down, uses a paper serviette to clean cream from a burnished shoe. 'I say is real marriage.'

She hears Laurence approach and changes to German. 'What do you mean, a real marriage? You know we agreed it should be a trial one. We even agreed that we wouldn't have children in the first place!'

'You put on coat, Laurence.' His feet dance round his son. 'Is not correct to make childrens illegitimate.'

Gabby subdues her longing for a schnapps. 'I don't follow you. An annulment has nothing whatever to do with the law. It is a Church matter — Canon Law. It would merely mean that the marriage was not Christian in the eyes of the Catholic Church. It would have no effect whatsoever on its legal status.'

'I say put on, Laurence.' Rolf's voice is a repetitious, persistent drone. Laurence puts his right arm through the left armhole. Rolf patiently reverses it. 'It was Christian marriage, Gabriele. We both were christened at time.'

'Not sacramental as far as the Catholic Church is concerned. Because, you see, we agreed that we might not have children.' How did she manage seven years with this moron? 'And we discussed that, if either of us felt it wasn't working out, we would divorce.'

Rolf's eyes refuse to abdicate his rights. 'I not think you divorce once you have the childrens.'

'That's beside the point, Rolf! It was our intentions — my intention, if you prefer — before the marriage which is the issue.'

Laurence is dressed. 'I no like to say our girls illegitimate. Therefore I say not true.'

Why argue? She's found out what she wants to know. She realises, of course, that it was deliberate. A man who was very capable of interpreting the small print in an obscure article about getting American citizenship for stateless Gemma's advantage would have no problem making the distinctions between Canon and civil law.

'Was very nice tea party, Gabriele. You have lovely little girl. Laurence a little unruly is. Death of his mother make him upset.'

He showed Kamilla photographs Laurence had taken. Of Laura's corpse.

As Gabby and Kamilla return her beautiful apartment to its proper state Gabby rethinks her opinion of Rolf. He's brighter, sharper than she'd credited. Worked out his cover, and took his revenge.

She can't blame him. Her behaviour was appalling. Rolf doesn't even know the extent of her deceit. An irony that he should worry about Nina's legitimacy. Which does confirm that, however sharp he may be, he doesn't begin to suspect she's not his daughter.

Rolf's brother Bandi refused her love. Because his love for his brother was greater. And the reason? She remembers what he said word for word: 'To paraphrase the Bible, Rezsö is a prize greater than diamonds. And that is rare. Believe me, very rare. Take him while you have the chance, Gabriele.'

Didn't he know what he was doing to his brother? That he was throwing him to the lioness? True brotherly love would have refused her, but also discouraged her from marrying Rolf.

She's being unreasonable. Beautiful young women — and, she now realises, she was definitely one of those — are hard to predict, even for a mother choosing a wife for a son. Who would have guessed that the retiring modest young Gabriele, who thought herself ugly because she has no hair and a gene which has a fifty-fifty chance to affect any children, would become an outstanding hostess, a political agitator, a woman able to win against all odds? And, if the progress she's making with her company continues, a very rich woman in her own right?

She's being unfair to Bandi, judgmental. He was a handsome bright sexually vibrant young man. Fragile and flawed. Temptation takes many forms. He chose the lesser evil. Which does him credit.

CHAPTER 7

Sussex, Spring 1956

Bramlings, April 20th, 1956

Dear Pete in good Faith,

I was thankful to hear back from you last month. It startled me that I didn't recognise your writing. I was so greatly moved. So I looked at old photographs to put you back into a pair of dungarees. They used to sit well on you once. Have a look at these snaps we took in Tulsa in 1932. Remember? I suppose you still feel too seedy to care one way or another.

Come and recuperate here, with Ross and me. Not that the enclosed snaps are any inducement. You said you wanted to see my new hairdo and this is what the camera did with a self-release. Which doesn't do me justice at all. It missed out on a bevy of freckles and wrinkles.

Well, since I've put myself into recruiting vein I wish you'd let me know when you'll give it a try. Please be sure to do something about it.

As always, in the same friendship,

Doly

Madison, June 6th, 1956

Dear Doly,

My friends have, almost without exception, been very kind about my episode in the asylum. I am fairly certain that had a person whom I knew to be insane turned up in the same room with me I should have been thoroughly frightened. The chances are, too, that had I met anyone whom I knew to have been once insane I should never have been able to remove my fundamental distrust.

These are average reactions, interesting and rather sad illustrations of ignorance faced by the active unknown. Considering them, one is forced to admit a certain practical advantage in the cloud of secrecy with which past insanity is swathed. Even though the secrecy is, in the large view, part of a vicious circle. Facts are the only true literature.

So I don't know my friends any longer. Though only as compared with the present did I ever know them. They, I suppose, do not know me either. So, as usual, the breaks are even. And the years have made men of those of us who have it in them.

Your friend Pete

Bramlings, September 15th, 1956

Dear Pete,

I thought it wasn't any of my business unless you wanted to make it so in your own good time. So when you first wrote news of your illness I deliberately shut my mind to the causes. And they came to me regardless, uninvited and without evidence. It's only a year ago now, and we've let other matters rest for many years. But the unwanted knowledge has bothered me more than most.

Emotionally it was at first a certain anger that you should have been left to suffer so much hurt, that your share of that should be so great. Then I came to see, as I can see you do, that the hurt was necessary for healing to take place.

Be healed, my friend. All internalised experience is shaped by our own view of it. The rest can be borne. That is much to be thankful for.

You say: The years have made men of us. I say: It takes a woman to be a gentleman. And my Onkel Wilfred topped us both. When he reached out for an ashtray and dropped the ash on the carpet, he said: 'I almost made it.'

I would like to qualify your statement that facts are the only true literature. It depends a good deal on the handling of those facts. Cover, for instance, half of my face in the enclosed photograph and it's dead serious, whereas the other half smiles the beatific smile. So I suppose there's more than one facet to most things.

Have, dear Pete, whichever you want.,

Doly

Doly can't get Faith out of her mind. Was she responsible for her mental breakdown? Surely nothing in Faith's letters suggests such a possibility. She's always been volatile. But something, somewhere is nagging at Doly. Has been for a few weeks. She can't put her finger on it.

She helps Ross get ready for school mechanically, jumps at the slightest sound.

'You haven't packed my apple, Mummy!'

'Sorry, Ross. Here it is.'

The child scampers off to school. Doly waves, feels faint. Is she sickening for something? She goes back to bed.

'Mrs Courtling?' The postman is knocking at her door, calling her. 'Registered letter for you. All the way from America.'

She grabs her dressing gown, forgets to button it. The postman's an old friend and keeps his eyes on the letters.

'Sorry to get you up. If you'll just sign here.'

Her fingers are busy, her eyes soft. Madison, Wisconsin. It has to be from Faith. Maybe she's coming over again. But why registered? Has the dear girl sent tickets for her and Ross to visit? She feels a flutter of pleasant anticipation.

Law Offices Nate and Keiller
6226 North Henry St, Madison, Wisconsin
Dear Mrs Courtling,
It is our painful duty to inform you of the death of Miss Faith Bowler. She was found in her room by her landlady. Apparently she died in her sleep. We understand Miss Bowler has been unwell recently. The coroner's verdict brought in death by misadventure. He told the court he suspects Miss Bowler may have become confused, having inadvertently taken the wrong selection of pills together.

Some weeks ago Miss Bowler came into our offices. We drafted a new will for her. She appointed us her executors. Since you are the sole beneficiary we enclose a copy of it.

We appreciate that you live abroad and may not know US procedure. Probate will take approximately six months. We anticipate that, after funeral and legal expenses, there will be a disbursement amounting to some $5000. Please inform us at the earliest opportunity where you would like the funds sent.

Very truly yours,
Dwight Nate'
Nate & Keiller

The letter flutters out of Doly's hands. She stares at the field of waving corn, sees the taller Oklahoma kind. She and Faith walked through golden fields, it seems, only days before. How did she manage to fail her? Why?

Poor, dear Faith. The one who stood by her when Nina was born, when Ross was born. She's laid down her life. Unrequited love for Doly? Or despair brought about by an illness medicine was unable to cure? She'll never know.

Doly cries hours into the night. For her friend, for herself. The channels of communication across the wide ocean, the empty prairies, failed them. Forever passing each other. Ships in the night.

Faith would have wanted Doly to build her wing. Whatever she felt, whether betrayed or simply unloved, her testament was recent, and unequivocal. Doly is her sole heir. What better way to show her love of a dead friend than to build a monument to her? A living one.

Piers is abroad. She would have loved the opportunity to let him do the work for her. His mother gives Doly the name of a friend. He'll build her a wing which is in harmony with the rest of the cottage. Same stone, same roofing tiles, same style. On to the side of Dramlings where, long ago, there was a shed. Housing the water pump and outdoor lavatory. Long replaced by running water, flushing toilet. Lately even by electric light.

A living room with a traditional fireplace, a picture window over the fields. Facing south-west. A small kitchenette off it. A tiny bathroom. A downstairs cubicle for Ross to sleep in. An upstairs attic bedroom for Doly. Such bliss. The plans finally passed by impersonal planning officers. Who had to be talked round.

Piers's friend is out of work. He's young and strong and willing. As soon as the plans are approved he begins to build. Doly moves into the wing she's dreamed into existence within three months. And purrs contentment.

CHAPTER 8

Vienna, Spring 1956

'This is a good piece. Very nice indeed.' Hans Weiss walks past the chest of drawers Gabby has just acquired, moves slow fingertips over the wood.

'One of the landlords I deal with was determined to refurbish. He's on the right track. Most of his stuff was dreadful old rubbish. He was letting the lot go to a house clearer. This one piece caught my fancy. I offered him three hundred Schillings. He jumped at it.'

Hans takes out a drawer, turns it upside down. 'See this? Smooth bevelled joints. Solid wood.'

'A genuine antique?'

He peers into the hole left by the drawer. 'Not exactly Chippendale. But not rubbish. Good quality Biedermeier.'

'You sound a little disparaging.'

Hans is still prodding, examining his fingers after running them along the wood. 'Well, you know, this stuff was made in the early part of the nineteenth century. For the bourgeoisie, substituting Gemütlichkeit for style. Which means it was rather looked down on.' The pitying tone of a master instructing a particularly stupid pupil. 'I would have thought it would be right Unter den Linden, for you. Or perhaps up the Kurfürstendamm. Biedermann and Bummelmeier were bourgeois characters satirised in a Berlin journal.'

The early nineteenth century is a teensy bit before Gabby's time. But let Hans have his fun. He's got plenty to teach her. *I know nothing about furniture, but I know what I like stuff*, you mean?' His vast knowledge is a treasure trove. 'You know so much about these things. I simply never connected the two.'

'Prices are going up all the time. You could do worse than collect the period. Provided you're choosy.' He taps. Knowledgeably. 'So-so condition. But I know an excellent restorer. Would you like me to introduce you?'

'Would you, Hans? That's marvellous.'

'Most people can't be bothered to learn. You, on the other hand, might do quite well.' His normal withering look is replaced by something nearing respect. 'You should talk to Greti. She's the real expert on period furniture. And china. That's how she spends her time — looking for auction bargains. She goes to every single one the Dorotheum runs. I always tell her that's her real home. She deigns to eat and sleep in the Karlsgasse. And uses it as a repository.'

That's why the place is crowded out with antiques. Gems, admittedly. Gabby's told herself before that Greti is no fool. She was surprised that, after her first outburst about the engagement, Hans's sister remained calm and collected. However many times Gabby and Hans got engaged.

Gabby worked out the reasons later. Greti obviously realised that Hans would never marry her after that very first evening. When she calmed down, this highly educated devout Catholic who wolfs down Aquinas for breakfast and Newton for the midday meal must have known that annulments take more than a couple of months. And she would have grasped that Hans and the Berghers knew that just as well as she did. And so did everybody else in Vienna, a Catholic city ruled by the Church until the Anschluss. Gabby was the only dupe, a Protestant sucker.

Why did Greti encourage the charade? Why bother to prod Lily and

Markus into righteous horror to give it substance? Why give Gabby a free hand with refurbishing the apartment?

Because she wanted to use her as a free stylist! She plundered her mind for what she could find, then spat out unwanted knobs and valueless trinkets. She must have laughed herself silly. The time has come for Gabby to finesse some return on that investment.

'Hallo, Greti. Gabriele here.' She knew there'd be a pause, didn't plan to wait for a response. 'I wondered whether you and Hans — and Mustapha of course — would like to come to Sunday lunch with Kamilla and myself. It doesn't seem fair that we always go to you.'

'How very thoughtful.' Civil, calm, modulated. A tremor in the voice. Pleasure, a scent of sport? Or simply lack of breath. She smokes as much as Dorinda. 'What about Kamilla's singing lesson?'

'Well, Greti, I've thought about that. You know how ignorant I am about music. Would you do me a really big favour?'

'Favour?' Cerberus bark.

'Only if you think it might amuse you. Come to the Dorotheum with me. They have a sale of pianos next week. Perhaps you'd help me pick one out for my living room. Then Hans and Kamilla can have their lesson here.'

Kamilla no longer enjoys her hour with Hans. The weekly dirge of the piano played indifferently, merged with the music of composers who died hundreds of years ago, leaves her longing to escape. Even after the lessons she's subjected to outdated philosophy combined with the history of music, leaving her dangerously bored. She enjoys modern music, sings pop songs in the bath. Gabby doesn't sympathise with pop, but understands the reluctance for unknown, outdated composers. Her musical preference is the military marches she enjoyed as a child. But Kamilla's sentiments are fair enough.

'It is true that a piano in the apartment will help Kamilla practise properly,' Greti intones. 'No more excuses.'

'Exactly.' Gabby relies on Kamilla's reluctance to shelve that problem. 'Come over right after Mass.' All four attend Sunday Mass at the Annakirche in the Annagasse. Somewhat low key, no singing, mumbled Latin with the priest's back to the congregation. In strict adherence to the old traditions. The Weisses do not favour the new rites. They're appalled at the vernacular used in most of Vienna's other churches. Even in the Stephansdom.

'Are you free tomorrow? We can look at what they have to offer. If we find a good instrument, I'll help you bid at the sale.'

The Bösendorfer's tone is mellow. Its case goes well with Gabby's vitrine.

Cordial relations have been resumed with both Weisses. Gabby is aware there's always a price. In this case bombarded ears. Kamilla's infrequent practising of the scales Hans considers necessary is still cacophonous. Gabby buys earplugs and removes herself to her office.

Her collection of antique furniture increases. Steadily. Her source is landlords keen to sell 'their old rubbish'. She has the good pieces restored, keeps the best for her own apartment and sells on the rest. An excellent sideline. Netting as much income as the commissions for the apartment rents themselves.

Another bonus falls into Gabby's lap. Unexpectedly. During a Sunday lunch at the Weisses.

'Of course, the youngest daughter was banned from the family after that.' Greti strokes the most recent Mustapha into submission.

'Youngest daughter?'

'Yolanthe. Kamilla, Christina and our mother Theresia's sister. She married a workman. A builder, can you believe. She insisted she was in love. Quite absurd.'

Gabby's ears turn into antennae. Sensitive ones. A certain fellow-feeling with a Bosch relative cast out into the cold. She must engineer a way to meet this rebel.

'She lives somewhere out near Grinzing now. Her husband eventually owned a factory. Then he built them a fancy villa around the turn of the century. Which consists of terraces and conservatories. Terribly bourgeois.'

Shades of Emil Dohlen, then. Does Yolanthe's husband have the same flair as her father? It would be fascinating to meet him. 'She and her husband still live in Vienna?'

'He died. She lives in that huge place all by herself. Ambrustergasse. A lower class area.'

No mention of Yolanthe's married name. Not even a mumble. How is she going to find out? 'So Kamilla is the sole representative of the younger generation of your family?'

Greti's eyes narrow. Hans trembles his legs excitedly. 'Exactly. There's no one else.'

'Yolanthe doesn't have any children?'

'She had just one child, I think. A little boy who died. That's why we must make sure Kamilla gets a decent all-round education.'

Education? Is that what's going to ensure the survival of the Bosch clan? Strange idea. In her excitement Gabby steps on Mustapha's foot. High-pitched and frenzied, the barking succeeds in removing both him and Greti from the room. 'I'd love to see a family tree, Hans. D'you have one, by any chance?'

'You mean you haven't seen it?' A massive, leather-bound tome. With beautifully scripted pages. Giving all the names Gabby could possibly need.

Vienna, Summer 1956

The old lady is as suspicious as Greti. And surprised, but eventually intrigued.

'You really have a daughter by Franz Bosch? I have a great-niece?'

'I'd be delighted to bring her to meet you. There are so few family members left.'

Explorations into the state of the summer, how dusty Vienna is, that Yolanthe finds it hard to cope with the Föhn blowing migraines from the Sahara.

Gabby assumes she's muffed it. Bosch's relatives are a rum lot.

'Bring Kamilla out to tea, Frau Bosch. The apricots are just ripening. She'll enjoy that.'

Yolanthe Dengler is seventy-five. The youngest of the four Leopold sisters. What amazes Gabby is that Bosch never even mentioned her.

'It's wonderful to think that Kamilla has a great-aunt,' she burbles. 'She has so few relatives from her father's side.'

Leathery old lady features remind Gabby of Bosch. 'I can't hear all that well, you know. Speak up!' An ear trumpet is applied to her right ear.

'Who is that in that wonderful portrait?' A blooming girl under a hat with ribbons. A hint of slant eyes, peachy apricot skin, mocking bud mouth, long black hair. Pure Kamilla. Gabby can't take her eyes off what is clearly a family portrait.

'You recognise your daughter. But not me.' Wizened skin, hair devoid of colour, no rose in her cheeks.

'Oh, dear.'

'I was beautiful. Which meant I had far too many suitors. Yet I chose to marry my true love. My family relied on me to make the best match. They disowned me for daring to marry a workman.'

'They actually threw you out?'

'Without a Schilling. Alfred was a marvellous man. Far too good for them.'

'And you had no children?'

'One boy. He died of scarlet fever when he was ten. An only child.'

'How very sad.'

'I'm ten!' Kamilla's apron is bursting with apricots she picked from a tree so loaded with fruit its branches reach the ground.

'I can see you are, Kamilla. You don't know what this means to me, Gabriele. To see a little one of my own flesh and blood. My husband's family are delightful. Really sweet. But there's no one I can call my own.'

Gabby feels good about it. She takes Kamilla to visit the old lady every two or three weeks. And is surprised to find Kamilla loves it there. She pesters to spend time with Tante Yolanthe rather than with the Weisses.

PART 4

HOME TRUTHS

1956 – 1970

CHAPTER 1

Schwanenbruch, September 1956

'It's simply wonderful to see you all here. I do appreciate your coming such distances. I'm touched and honoured to have my whole family gathered together.'

'No need to make a song and dance about it, Gabby. Moppel and I are Schwanenbruch fixtures every summer anyway. Nothing to do with you.'

Gabby blinks as she ignores her sister's barbs. 'We all know der blanke Hans starts fuming by end September, so it's good of you to stay and celebrate my half century with me.' She raises her glass of sparkling wine. Known locally as Tchampagne. Real champagne is something she can't afford as a general rule. Yet. 'Here's to all of us. Especially to Marina, my first grandchild and the latest in the Dohlen bloodline.'

'Hip, hip, hurray!'

'A glass in your hand is a lot safer than that baby, Gabby.' Doly stands behind Marina's head, squirming her round.

Gabby, losing confidence, hands the child back to Gemma. 'And now I'd like to tell you my plans for the next half century.'

Doly cackles. 'Wouldn't count on anyone but Marina making it. Apart from Gabby, that is. Oldest and youngest.'

'I'm not talking about living that long. That's not the point. You all know I've started a new career late in life. It wasn't easy, but I'm getting there. *Dohlen Real Estate* is building nicely, but I need a few more bricks.'

'C'mon, Gabby. It's no big deal. You get a little commission from renting apartments. Kinda what I do, but on a smaller scale. No need to make a meal of it.'

'Yes, there is, Emil.' Gemma hoists the baby on to her hip. 'Gabby's running in the Grand National in spite of several handicaps. And leaping over all the hurdles. That's real achievement even if she's not the eventual winner. Though my money goes on her getting first place.'

'Thank you, Gemma.' Gabby turns to her brother. 'It's not a competition, Moppel. Why shouldn't I feel good about coping against heavy odds? It shows it can be done.'

Doly's puffs come thick and fast. 'With a bit of luck thrown in. Not all of us owned a big house to sell after the war.' She drinks her sparkling wine, holds her glass out for more. 'Some of us have to make do with a small cottage. Even though that's a gem.'

'I'm not belittling anyone, Doly. All three of us started with silver spoons in our mouths. We lost them through others' greed and our own stupidity. Now we're all solvent again. I want to toast each of our futures, to wish you all the things you wish for yourselves. My particular dream is to buy back the Villa Dohlen and turn it into a family home any of us can visit whenever we like. A place to recharge our energies.'

'C'mon, Gabby. How in hell are you going to raise that kinda dough?'

'Why in hell shouldn't I is a better question, Moppel. Our father made good, and built the place. It's the bricks and mortar which represent the Dohlen inheritance, though I now know the inheritance which really counts. And it wasn't the fortune which he left us and we lost.'

'So what's the big deal?' Emil pushes his hat down over his bald head.

'Our father's spirit: the nerve, the nous, the belief in providence — call it what you like — which is what made his fortune.'

'So you reckon you've got that?' Doly puffs several perfect smoke rings.

'I reckon I have the spirit to have a go, yes.'

'You're saying you're going to become a millionaire and make more money than he ever made, right?'

'I neither know nor care about that. What I do care about, what I intend to do, is to buy the Villa Dohlen back for the family, and restore it to its former glory.'

Moppel's laugh gurgles round his belly. 'You got any idea how much that would cost?'

'Money is secondary. Perception is what counts.'

Doly's giggle froths wine bubbles on thinning lips. 'The latest philosophy from big sister Gabby. Amen.' She leans back against the wall. Closes her eyes.

'That's just a lot of hooey, Gabby.' Moppel wipes his bald head.

Gemma raises her glass. 'Wrong again, Emil Dohlen Junior. I'm drinking to the future of the Dohlen Inheritance now in my mother's competent hands. She's managed a start, which is great. She has the guts to go on. To Gabby, whose life begins at fifty!'

The sound of breaking glass turns all eyes on Doly. Face ashen, beads of perspiration standing out. 'I'm so...' She doubles up, her head on the table.

Not another damned trick to get attention! Doly's shenanigans are beginning to be more than Gabby's good resolutions can cope with. 'What on earth — '

'She's gone all blue! There's something really wrong.' Nina and her husband Warren, sitting on either side of Doly, swivel her body to lay her on the bench they've been sitting on.

'No...' She pushes them away, grabs the table. Heaves, vomits, sits huddled over herself.

Gabby gapes at her sister, appalled. Is she really ill? Her breathing hisses. A locomotive valve letting off steam. 'We'd better call Lieselotte.'

'Get the manager to ring the duty doctor, Gemma.' Nina is by Doly, her hand on her forehead. 'Her skin's all cold and clammy. We need some blankets. She's shaking with cold.'

Gemma sprints for the phone. 'Joseph Miessmann's the local GP, isn't he? And Lieselotte's home at the weekends? I'm going to call both of them over. This looks really serious.'

'Tell them it's an emergency. Her pulse is racing.' Joseph Miessmann arrives within ten minutes. He doesn't take long to come to a decision. 'This is a medical alert. I've rung the ambulance to take her to hospital at once.'

The family cluster round. Joseph sees Doly into an ambulance and stays with her. They turn to Lieselotte.

'What is it, Lieselotte? Food poisoning?'

The tired eyes are curiously vacant. 'Unlikely. Those symptoms fit any number of acute illnesses. It could even be a heart attack.'

'Because she smokes so much, you mean?'

Lieselotte's head is in her hands which scour her hair. 'That wouldn't help. But I don't think that's it. Another possibility is a peptic ulcer perforation, or peritonitis brought on by a burst appendix.'

'That can be seen to, can't it? They can operate?'

'Provided she gets there in time. The nearest emergency department is in Hamburg, an hour's drive away.'

'You don't think it's any of those, do you?' Gemma's eyes scan the rapid blinking, the hesitation.

'No. I think it's a recurrence of what we call chronic relapsing pancreatitis. She's had bouts of these symptoms before.'

'She's been ill before?'

'She has attacks of terrible nausea. And chills and a rapid heartbeat.' Lieselotte's fingers comb through her hair, pull at it. 'I've seen her doubled up with pain, warned her to get medical advice. She brushed me aside. The trouble is that the periods between attacks can be symptomless, so she assumes it's all over.'

'So what causes that?'

'That's hard to say. Alcoholic excess can do it. That isn't a great threat in Doly's case. Maybe smoking is a contributory factor. Once the pancreas is diseased, repeat attacks make it fibrous, scarred and calcified. The periods between bouts get shorter and shorter. I think that's what the trouble is.'

'But why tonight?'

Her hands pull back her head. 'I've gone on and on about diet. Given her recipes. Lots of carbohydrates, not much fatty food or alcohol. She probably gorged herself tonight, possibly drank more than she's used to. That could set off a serious attack.' Tears are beginning to cluster. 'That's why I'm still here. I wanted you to know what could be going on.'

'You mean she could die?' Gemma asks. The harsh, bare word ricochets from table to bench. Clattering the glasses.

Lieselotte tousles back her hair, wipes her eyes. 'It can't be ruled out. She'll need surgery even if she recovers, and careful dietary management after that. Not exactly Doly's style.'

'You saying Emil and I should be at the hospital?' Gabby is already up, looking for her handbag.

Lieselotte's face is as long as one of her father's horse's. 'They won't let you see her until she's stabilised. But there could be bad news. I'm off to Hamburg now. Can I offer anyone a lift?'

'If it's that serious, I think all her blood relatives should be there. You take Emil and Gemma, Lieselotte. Leave Marina with Jonathan, no point in their coming. And I'll follow on in the VW with Nina.' Gabby's determined face is peaky.

'Why don't I come with you as well?' Gemma's frown is puzzled.

'Someone has to go with Moppel, Gemma. You know how hopelessly impractical he is.' Gabby's eyes signal red for stop.

THE SILVER LAKE

The Silver Lake lies between marshy land and hard rock. Once upon a time a fine castle stood on the rocky side. And one evening a nobleman was passing by, and since the sun was almost below the horizon, he begged for shelter there.

A somewhat grudging woman opened the door to him. Tired after his long journey, the nobleman retired almost immediately. And when he rose the next morning, he could not find the silver gauntlets that he had taken off the night before. He asked the woman who had opened the castle doors to him what had happened to his belongings.

She denied all knowledge of them. And he, realising that he could not get his stolen goods back, shook the sand from the land around the castle from his feet. And cursed the great edifice and all its inhabitants.

Almost immediately water began to well out of the marshy land. It rose higher and higher. Until finally the whose castle began to sink. As the nobleman watched he could see nothing left except a chair on which the silver gauntlets lay. And even the wooden stool, with its valuable cargo, sank. Leaving a lake permanently coloured silver.

CHAPTER 2

North Germany, September 1956

'It doesn't take journalistic genius to work out you want to be alone with me. Gemma's twigged as well.' Nina is in the passenger seat of the Beetle. Staring ahead. Tense. 'What's going on?'

'Quite right. I want to talk to you. On our own.'

'Now? Why?'

'Doly could be dying, Nina. Not because Lieselotte says so. I'd expect her to be emotionally involved. Because of Joseph. He's hardly a Doly fan, and he thinks it's serious.'

'Let's cut to the chase. There's obviously something you want me to know about Dorinda before she dies. Why me?'

'Very perceptive. Because it concerns your relationship with her.'

'I hardly have one, Gabby. The only time I've spent with her was when I stayed for two weeks just before I went to the States. You sent me, remember?' Nina laughs. 'Not a resounding success.'

'You didn't get on at all?'

'Gemma is much closer to her than I am. They hit it off. She sees quite a bit of her, apparently. And they live in the same country. I'm much closer to Emil.'

'I'm talking about a biological relationship.'

Nina's hands are knuckled on the dashboard. 'Biological? What's that supposed to imply? We're both her nieces.'

'You've never felt any particular affinity to her? Close to her in some special way?'

Nina's right hand is pulling at the fingers of her left one. Irritably. 'Temperamentally, you mean?'

'If you like.'

'Holy Doly? No. Her brand of sentimental hypocrisy gets on my nerves. Just like it does on yours.'

'That's how you see her? As a sentimental liar?'

'If you want my honest opinion, yes. Look at the way she squandered all her money, then accused Emil of being responsible for her poverty.'

'Not entirely unreasonably. He did accept a ridiculously small sum for her share of the villa.'

'She was the one who set the price! Not particularly admirable that he accepted, I do agree, but it was a deal she was a party to, just like he was.'

'Given that, he could have helped her out when she was really down on her luck.'

'We're discussing Dorinda. Remember the way she led Erskine one hell of a dance, flirting and maybe worse, then felt aggrieved when he left? And she's got virtually no income, yet smokes away a good portion of what money she has. She bums around instead of getting down to it.'

'She has tenants. And her own way of skinning the cat. She lives the simple life out in the country, grows her own food...'

'Don't start about the glories of Sussex and surviving on bloody nature. All that crap about how she's managing on practically nothing. What she does — and I have to admit she does it well — is exploit guilt. Neighbours, relatives, friends. She could earn her own bloody living, get a job. I do. Gemma does. You have!'

'She's given Ross an idyllic childhood, Nina. Living in unspoilt country, far away from city fumes, an excellent school, the right friends.'

'At the price of always being the poor relation. It's her ex-brother-in-law who foots the bill for the education, the neighbours who ferry him to school.

'Actually, it's Ross I feel sorry for. Living in that revolting shed for years, dressed in second-hand cast-offs, forced to accept charity from all and sundry. While his mother smokes away money and passes judgment on other people.'

'You're being a little hard on her. You've just heard she's really ill.'

'She brought all that on herself as well. She abuses her body with incessant smoking, drinks herself silly whenever she get a chance. If you want to know the truth, I find her really tiresome.'

'Then what I'm about to tell you will come as a terrible shock, Nina.' Gabby crashes the gears. 'You have absolutely no idea what it could be?'

'Something to do with Dorinda which affects me, obviously.' Nina's quick brain flashes through possibilities. 'Did she know Warren's father, sleep with him, something like that?'

'An entertaining possibility. Not anywhere close. But she did know a number of men. In the biblical sense.'

'Hardly a state secret. So?'

Gabby misjudges her distance from the curb and jolts the car. 'Sorry.'

'Shall I drive?'

'I'm all right. You know you were born in the States.'

'I always thought it very clever of you to arrange that.'

'In 1932. In a Manhattan hospital, after a car crash. Dorinda was driving the car.'

'Emil told me. Time and again. Because it was when you were both in hospital, after the crash and just after I was born, that you all drew tenement house names out of a hat, and Dorinda bagged the best. Then gave most of them away. All history. So?'

'Emil told you about that, did he?' Gabby stops the car and puts her hand on Nina's knees. 'You're quite fond of him, aren't you?'

'He's been decent to me. Nicer than my own father. When Warren and I wanted to get married, he didn't look down his nose at him. Rolf actually went so far as to engage a private detective to check Warren out!'

'Not Rolf, Nina. It was Bandi as a matter of fact.'

'Really?' She stares at Gemma, blinks. 'How d'you know that?'

'He told me.' Gabby puts her hand on the driving wheel, grips it hard. 'There's one thing Emil evidently didn't tell you. He didn't know. No one except Faith Bowler knew at the time.'

'Who? Who's Faith Bowler?'

'A friend of Dorinda's from Riverside Hall and Barnard College days. Summa cum laude graduate.'

'Really? Doly's got a degree?'

'No, no; Faith. Doly left before finishing the course. Faith Bowler was a really good friend of hers. Stood by her. The point is that Doly was pregnant at the same time that I was. We were both about to give birth.'

'She was pregnant?' A short pause. 'Surely she wasn't married in 1932…'

'People do get pregnant without being married.'

'Right. Sure. But I thought she had all these problems? Several miscarriages?' Nina rolls down the window, gulps at the air. A reporter sniffing out a story. Her own.

'That was later. Probably because of Erskine's faulty sperm. You know he had that blood-poisoning thing. Which they didn't cure until antibiotics became available.'

'You're telling me Dorinda gave birth to a baby after the car crash as well? That she's got a son or daughter somewhere, father unknown? Well, that isn't an enormous surprise, except I didn't think she was that fertile.' She gulps more air. 'But what's it got to do with me? You saying I know him or her?'

'Quite right. She did have a child. A daughter. Born within hours of the crash.'

'Just like me, you mean. You sure kept that hospital busy!'

Gabby opens her window, fans air across her face. 'My baby died, Nina. A little boy. He died because I was penned into the car by the accident.'

Nina is gripping the dashboard, staring ahead.

'The impact started the birth process. He was throttled because he couldn't get out, couldn't breathe.' She looks at Nina. The changeling who became a beloved child.

'And Dorinda had a daughter. A live birth.' The brittle voice of journalism.

'Yes.'

'You're saying you managed to swap babies, somehow?'

'Not swap, no. My son was already dead. We swapped identities. Not too difficult in the general mayhem, and we did look quite similar.'

'So I'm Dorinda's daughter?' She swallows. 'Not yours? Not even Rolf's?'

'I felt you had to know. It isn't right to keep it from you for ever.

Everyone has a right to know their biological roots. We should have told you sooner. Somehow it never seemed to be the right time.'

'And now is?'

'I don't know about the right time. It is a time.'

Clenched fingers unwind and drum on the plastic dashboard. 'You're really telling me that Dorinda is my mother, not you?'

'I'm telling you what happened, Nina. Because that's the way it was.'

'But you and I — we've always hit it off.'

'And always will. You may not be my biological daughter, but you were always the daughter I felt closest to. The God you don't believe in works in mysterious ways.'

'I think we can just stick to you and Dorinda, Gabby.'

Gabby hears the bitterness, the anger, the helplessness. Will they ever go?

'And my father? Not Rolf, presumably?'

'Not Rolf, no. That much I can prove. Doly refused to tell me who he is.'

Nina gets out of the car, breathes the fresh wind blowing from the Elbe. 'I know Rolf always tried to do his best for us. But he never felt like my father, somehow. I put it down to not seeing him for so many years, during the war and later.' Nina stares at Gabby now also out of the car. 'D'you know who he is?'

'No, Nina. I don't know. I can make an informed guess. It would be utterly irresponsible of me to put ideas into your head.'

'I can't believe Dorinda was foolish enough to get pregnant before marriage in the early thirties. I've read they banished unmarried mothers into lunatic asylums!'

'She was desperate for love. She mistook the physical for the emotional. She still does. And she was very beautiful, reckless, highly sexed. She had any number of admirers.'

'So she might not even know who my father is?'

'I don't think she actually had intercourse with many men. She was, you won't be surprised to hear, quite a cockteaser.'

'So he was someone special?'

'Not necessarily. I strongly suspect that your father was her first lover. An older man who knew how to get his way.' Gabby takes out a handkerchief, wipes her eyes. 'Dorinda was wild and careless of her reputation. That didn't mean she slept with all and sundry. She liked leading men on, mostly very young ones. People assumed she slept with them because of the way she behaved socially.'

'So if she doesn't recover I'll never know who my father is?'

'For certain, no. Let's deal with that if it happens.' She takes Nina's hands in hers. 'I have never regretted bringing you up, Nina. You have always been pure joy to me. I hope you won't allow it to ruin our relationship.'

'I suppose I can see Dorinda didn't have much of a choice. It must have been quite ghastly for her — for both of you.' She stops, puts her arm around Gabby. 'And you lost your little boy. I'm so sorry. I know you always wanted a son.' She leans out of the window, breathes in more air. 'And I'm really glad you took me on. I'll always think of you as my real mother, Gabby.'

THE MOVING TOWER

Towards the end of the thirteenth century the tiny hamlet of Wanna did not have its own church. The villagers, whether they liked it or not, had to join the congregation of the much larger settlement of Süderleda.

Time passed, and Wanna's population increased. In fact the village became two communities: Osterwanna to the east, and Westerwanna to the west. And, everyone agreed, the two villages together could boast enough inhabitants to form the basis for a joint church. It was also agreed that the building material should be the stones used for the old, neglected chapel in Süderleda. What was not nearly so easily resolved was which village should have the new church within its walls.

After much discussion it was decided that the old sandstone crucifix, at present adorning the gable end of the old chapel, should be taken down, attached to a stake and stuck into the ground. Then, after sundown, prayers were to be offered up to Heaven to place the stake, with its cross, in the place where the new church was to be built.

As the fateful night approached the people of Osterwanna could not sleep. Whether it was that they didn't believe in miracles, or whether they were worried that Heaven might decide against them, was not clear. What was definite was that they decided to help Heaven make its decision. As soon as the midnight hour struck a party of the strongest Osterwanners crept, noiselessly, to the old chapel. They loaded the cross on to a wagon and drove it over to their village. Then they rammed the stake into their soil and went to bed. For well-deserved rest.

It was never made explicit how the villagers of Westerwanna became aware of what their neighbours had been up to. But somehow they found out. They waited patiently until they guessed the Osterwanners were sleeping the sleep of the just. Then they crept over to Osterwanna and hauled the cross off to their own village. And, just in case the sleep of the just became fitful, they thoughtfully provided a couple of watchmen to guard it. After which the rest of them went to get their beauty sleep.

Next morning the Osterwanners were up at sunrise. And astonished to find that not only had the cross disappeared, it was now in Westerwanna. Their faces were long with disappointment. But they were not foolish enough to think that this was due to heavenly intervention. However, it was decided it would not be politic to question God's judgment, and the church was built in the place where the cross was found.

Which isn't quite the end of the story. Many, many years later, when the time came to build a fine wooden tower for the joint church, an Osterwanna cabinet maker was entrusted with the job. And he worked hard, and completed a beautiful tower within the time allotted.

Then a group of Osterwanna men helped to mount the tower on to a cart, and to transport it to Westerwanna. For some strange reason the wagon broke down just before they reached the church. Which misadventure was taken for a sign to mean that the tower should be erected on the east side of the church, facing Osterwanna, rather than on the more usual western side.

CHAPTER 3

Hamburg, September 1956

'Nina! How nice of you to come all this way.' Doly's private room is deluged with flowers. 'They say I have to stay in for a couple of weeks for some very boring treatment. While they get me back to a semblance of normality.'

'I've come to say goodbye, Dorinda. Warren and I are flying back to the States tomorrow.'

The room is already reeking of smoke. 'Hand me that packet of cigarettes, will you?'

'Aren't you supposed to take it easy on those?'

'I'm not supposed to be thwarted. That could set me off again.' Doly takes out a cigarette, lights up, inhales deeply. 'No point in denying oneself life's pleasures. Mine are limited.'

'You have Ross. And Dramlings.'

Doly puffs contentedly. 'And my little Buffy dog. And the garden. I've always counted my blessings and I'm very lucky.' That half-child, half-woman look. 'And you, my dear? I haven't had much chance to get to know you. Are you happy?'

'I am now. Warren and I are very much in love.'

'I'm delighted for you.'

Nina is surprised to see innocence mingled with pride, to realise that, almost certainly, Doly gave her up from motives of the truest mother love. It can't have been easy for a woman with Doly's personality. Perhaps a Wolderich Lappe forced himself on her.

'Tell me about your childhood, Nina. All right, was it?' She blinks. 'Except for the war, of course.'

'You know perfectly well it was bloody awful. I couldn't stand Bosch. Or he me. If it hadn't been for Gabby…'

The smoke rings float towards Nina. 'As bad as that?'

'And I understand I have you to thank for it.'

The coughing is extensive. So prolonged that Nina begins to wonder whether she should have come. After all, the past can't be changed. 'D'you want me to call the nurse, Dorinda?'

'No. It will pass. Just hand me a glass of water.'

'You're not supposed to drink! That's why they've got that nasal drip going — '

'I'm not supposed to choke to death, either.' She sips the water. 'So you've been told. I take it Gabby spilled the beans.'

'She thought I ought to know.'

'Because I might have died. What a weird way to view life. Well, I can't undo what she's put in train. And whatever you say about Bosch, Nina, Gabby has been a wonderful mother to you. Better than I could have been in the circumstances.' Tears trickle down. 'You get on so well.'

'That, I suppose, is why it's been such a shock.'

'I don't see why it should change what you already have. What I can tell you is this. We hated Tante Hannah when we were children. We blamed her for everything that went wrong. Hating a non-parent is good therapy for life's vicissitudes.'

Nina laughs. 'That's a new one on me. Thank Bosch for being a bastard.'

'It's the better option.' Doly sighs. 'One thing, Nina. Keep our relationship to yourself. It won't help if others know. And you'll really upset Rolf Ferent. A decent enough chap.' She drops the glass, leans back on her pillows. 'Call the nurse, Nina. That water hasn't helped.'

Nina joins Gabby, Emil, Gemma and Liesi in the waiting room.
    'Another crisis, I'm afraid. She drank water when she wasn't supposed to.'
    'Typical.'
    'Is she really going to make it, Lieselotte?' Nina is pacing up and down, nerves showing.
    'She's actually quite strong. And now they've got her round from the attack, and she's here in hospital, I would think she'll be fine. Eventually. Of course, she'll lengthen the time she has to stay in hospital, and the time she'll take to recuperate.'
    'Same old Doly, whatever the circumstances.'
    'Not a surprise. Most people never change, and Doly definitely belongs in that category. Should we alert Erskine? And what about Ross? Will Erskine and his new family be able to keep looking after him?'
    'If she survives the next twenty-four hours she'll be fine. She'll kill us if we let them know, make a fuss. My vote is wait, and make sure she takes at least two weeks in Schwanenbruch to get over it.'
    'Won't that mean she stays longer than she planned for?'
    'I can write to Erskine and say I've invited her to stay on, so she gets a really good holiday, can rest up from that constant gardening.' Gabby looks round the room, blinks. 'No point in all of us sitting here being glum. One of us can stay and fetch us when there's news. The rest of us can go to the cafeteria. I need a drink.'

THE CHANGELING

A young couple were working in the fields and laid their recently-born son to sleep in the shade of a hill. They didn't know that the hill was inhabited by a tribe of imps. While they were away an imp came out, dragged the child into the hill, took off his clothes, put them on to an imp child and took him back to the spot where he had found the human baby.

When the parents returned to pick up their son they knew right away that the big-headed being was a changeling, but what could they do? They took him home and did their best to raise him.

By the time he was seven he was no taller than when he was born, and could neither speak nor walk. The parents began to worry, realising that something was very wrong. They consulted a wise old woman living in the village.

'There's nothing wrong with that child,' she told the sorrowing parents. 'He can walk perfectly well. Make a millet pudding, put it on a chair and leave him to it. Watch what he does.'

The parents followed the old woman's advice and watched the child through the window. As soon as he thought he was on his own he ran over to the bowl and polished it all off.

'He can talk as well!' the old woman told them. 'What you must do now is milk the goat straight into the pipe bowl and butter the tinder box. Then you'll see a wonderful sight.'

When the imp saw what they had done he jumped up and down and screamed:

> 'I'm as hoary and old
> As the witch foretold
> Yet I've never come across such antics!'

The parents answered:

The outraged parents whipped the changeling for as long as their strength held out, and demanded that he return their child. But the imp laughed at them. He spent his time playing tricks and pranks, and refused to obey them in any way.

The parents, realising nothing else would help, decided to take the boy to be baptised. They hoped that the holy sacrament would tame this child which wasn't theirs. The father caught the imp, locked him into a willow basket and shouldered it. He was determined to take the little devil to church whether he wanted to go or not.

The way to the village led past the very same hill where he had lost his son. As he walked by, a myriad voices called: 'Rossab, where are you? Rossab, where have you got to?'

The being in the basket cried out: 'I'm being taken to be baptised!'

The father found himself surrounded by the most terrible shrieks and howls. The racket went on and on, until he couldn't stand it any more. He took off the wicker basket, threw it at the hill, and ran home.

The next morning the parents found a handsome young boy in their barn. He was tall and strong, and looked like the father in his youth. So they recognised their son.

The boy was a joy to them from that moment onwards. He already knew how to cobble, and tailor, and shoe the horses. And he turned into a hard-working, God-fearing man.

But though the imps returned their son, they kept the willow basket.

CHAPTER 4

Sussex, Summer 1957

'Well, you two. This is a pleasant surprise.' Doly, between tenancies, suggested that Nina and Warren might like to spend a month in Sussex, living in the main part of Dramlings. A holiday in England. Getting acquainted. With Doly, not Ross. Who's gone to spend the summer holidays with his father and Erskine's new family. Now in Somerset.

Which suits the young American couple's plans. Warren has managed to arrange two major commissions in London and southern England. Nina intends to use the opportunity to research the family problem before having any children of her own. An investigative journalist, she feels there must be a solution somewhere. The trail has led to a Harley Street doctor.

Doly has invited the two young people to breakfast in her little wing. They sit at the table under the window overlooking a splendid expanse of fields sprouting wheat and ringed with tall elms. A spectacular panorama Doly never tires of. She's serving the young people bacon from a local farm, eggs from a neighbour, toast made from bread bought in the village, a friend's chunky marmalade and English tea strong enough to stand a spoon up in. Warren leaves his untouched and Nina wonders how to get rid of hers gracefully. She's longing for American coffee.

'We're finishing work early this week, Doly. Taking the weekend off.' One of Warren's cameras is at the ready. 'I'll start with a couple of shots of you.'

'You can find a much better use for your film in the woods. The kingcups are out down by the millpond. Not quite over yet, I hope. One of our glorious sights.'

Warren isn't a nature photographer. His job is working on assignments dictated by Time Magazine, his passion is shooting unusual buildings. In England that's primarily historic ones. He's hired a car, makes polite noises and drives off, leaving Nina to spend the day 'getting to know' Doly. The unspoken intention is to investigate her paternity, press her newly discovered mother to tell her who her father is.

'So, how are you feeling these days, Dorinda? Is the pancreatitis under control?'

'On and off. I mainly stick to my own spuds and vegetables. But a woman has to have the occasional fun.' Doly lights a taper from a flaming log in her fireplace, the fire lit because even damp summer days need its warmth to keep comfortable in a dank stone cottage. She puffs at her cigarette, motions to Nina to leave the table and sit in the chairs half-circled round the crackling logs. 'Let's talk about you. I hardly know you.'

Time spirals lazily. An hour, two. Buffy starts barking, jumping up and down.

'He needs his exercise, poor little chap. Let's go for a walk in the woods.' Doly leads them across her lawn, down her drive and straight into the rhododendron woods virtually on her doorstep. They scramble along narrow paths in Indian file, up river and down dale. They wade through a jungle of bracken and enchanting wildflowers. The dark leaves of wild rhododendrons contrast with the white of oxeye daisies, the air resounds with bird calls.

'Well, Nina? What d'you think of my little kingdom?'

'Enchanting. But how d'you cut your way through all these briars and brambles?'

'I don't need to cut my way out of anything. Simply use a walking stick to push the brambles aside. No trouble at all.'

'Reminds me of the days when Gemma and I first came to England. We used to go looking for birds' nests and pick wildflowers, build bracken houses on the common. What d'you do with yourself for entertainment?'

Doly's earth-stained hands move through flowers rich with pollen, crush soft leaves. 'I grow my garden, clean my house and contemplate the beauties around me. Which can't be bettered anywhere.'

'Not even in Schwanenbruch?'

'Not any more.'

Doly leads them to a large log in dappled shade, the earth around it speckled with cigarette butts. 'Let's sit on this log while I have a smoke.'

'Great idea. It's good to get to know you better. I'm sure you understand there's one thing I'm burning to know.'

A slight nod, a brief smile. 'Who your father is.' The smoke curls skywards. A still day on which Doly can hear the leaves grow, shooting furled buds into oak and ash. 'You think it's relevant after twenty-five years of blessed ignorance?'

'I sure do. I guess you remember well enough?'

She doesn't take to that haranguing, journalistic tone. Nor the implicit suggestion. 'Hardly a question of buying hats in Piccadilly.'

'I wasn't suggesting any such thing. And I'm not prying, Doly. I'm sure you understand my natural curiosity. Everyone likes to know their biological roots.'

'You mean if I told you who it was you'd track him down.' The puffs come hard and fast.

'Track isn't quite the word I'd use. But, yes, I sure would like the opportunity to meet him, to find out where he lives, what he does, whether he has other children.' Nina grabs a dead stick, slashes at stinging nettles growing nearby. Buffy pants eagerly for her to throw the stick. 'I'm not trying to be rude, or to judge you, and certainly not to antagonise you, but does he even know I exist?' The weeds wilt at her attack. 'I'm only asking because I need to know who I am. So far in my life I've made completely wrong assumptions. I really think I have a right to know.'

'You've lived successfully for twenty-five years without knowing. You've done well, qualified as a journalist, had a decent education courtesy of an honourable man who thinks of you as his daughter, and who, according to Gemma, is particularly fond of you. You've lived with him through your college years, until you married. Why shatter all that?'

'Agreed. I didn't say I'd ever tell Rolf Ferent. I can't see any advantage in that for either of us.'

'Once you know who your biological father is, your relationship with Rolf Ferent is bound to change.'

'That doesn't make sense. I've known he wasn't my father since our trip to Schwanenbruch. It hasn't changed my attitude to Rolf. It's not that close a relationship. Don't forget I didn't see him during the war years and for some time after. 1938 to 1951, to be precise. World events, his living in the States, conspired against that. And I'm married now, that too has an effect. What possible difference could my knowing who the actual father is...'

Nina stares at Doly who moves a little sideways. She stands, grabs Doly's shoulders, turns her to face her. Keen eyes, almost as blue as Gabby's, show a journalist's understanding, betray a nose for the truth which will be hard to counter. 'What you're saying implies I know him, doesn't it? That's why it's a problem. Are you saying Rolf knows him too?'

Doly twists herself loose. 'I can tell you have the makings of an outstanding journalist! A real hound-dog, smelling a good story, not letting go.'

'That is my job, you know. So who is he?'

'You've lived quite near him for part of your adult life.' She watches her daughter's changing features, the pleasure at the chase, the delight at the kill. Not each other's sort.

Nina stands tall, looks Doly up and down, her eyes sharp and gleaming. 'I'll ferret it all out, of course. But I have to admit I'd prefer it if you were straight with me.'

Definitely not each other's sort. There's something about Nina she doesn't take to. But it's probably safer to tell her the facts. 'You've never felt some sort of pull?'

'To whom?'

'Obviously one of the middle-aged men you know.'

'Why would that even occur to me?'

Good to know that Nina's bloodhound expertise can't come up with any immediate answers. Or even a pertinent question. 'Gabby was out of her mind with grief at losing her baby. Especially as he was a little boy. She so much wanted a son.'

'Really. She didn't go into motivations when she told me. Didn't explain how you managed to fool the authorities, either. So I'd appreciate it if you got to the point.'

A long silence while Doly puffs, stares across the woods. 'A question of circumstance. Hard to believe now, but we looked quite similar then. Same height, same body build, family resemblance made stronger by the undressed eyes. How could the medics know who was who? Two young women taken to hospital after a car crash. One had just given birth to a stillborn son, the other about to give birth a couple of weeks prematurely. So we changed names in the ambulance, duped the hospital staff. Left the hospital together. And Gabby took you back to Vienna.'

'I understand you still had hair. She wore a wig.'

Doly's eyes turn to marble about to hit another marble. 'So what? Not stated on the passport. And Gabby's choice of colour reinforced our similarities. Strange to think how that used to infuriate me. Now it just seems irrelevant.'

'Auburn suits her, you know.'

'The fiery temperament, yes.' Doly stares at her daughter. 'Funny how you're her favourite, how well you get on.' Garden-worn fingers grab a dead stick. She throws it for Buffy, who sprays loose earth in the chase. 'One of the reasons I agreed to let her have you was that your genes and Gemma's are so very similar.'

'That bloody early hair loss, you mean.' Nina scrabbles at unoffending plants. 'Or are you saying that Rolf Ferent is actually my father? Gabby maintains he can't have been.'

'I always liked Rolf. But, no, I didn't seduce my sister's husband.' She watches Buffy's antics, feels her heart softening with love for him. 'You're his brother's daughter, Nina. Andrew, not Hugo. We travelled together on a boat bound for the West Indies. A shipboard romance.'

'You mean *Bandi* is my father?' Nina gasps, mouth hanging open. 'And he's known all along?'

'He had no idea I was pregnant, let alone the circumstances of your birth. All he knew was that Gabby had sailed to the States to have her baby, and that she returned with a little girl. How could he possibly have known that I had one at the same time, and that Gabby's baby died?'

'Didn't they all know about the car crash? And what happened?'

'About the crash, yes. But they'd no idea I was pregnant. I spent the pregnancy in Oklahoma, with my friend Faith. No one, except Faith, knew anything at all.'

'But both of you were pregnant. Surely the crash got reported in a paper somewhere, mentioned that?'

'No. It was Independence Day. Manhattan was crowded, there were probably a lot of crashes. And no one in the family saw a police report or anything. They just accepted our account of it all.

'As I said, I lived in Oklahoma, with Faith. I arrived in New York the day your mother's boat came in, drove there in my little Ford. I went to meet her, on my own. In a manner of speaking.' She laughs as the scene comes back to her.

'Gabby must have known.'

'Only when she saw me, when she got off the boat. I'd rung Moppel, heard he was due to meet her. As soon as he knew I was in New York he asked me to go instead. Bowed out, as usual.' Doly grins. 'Quick thinking made it clear that was a bonus. I thought Gabby could help me decide what to do.'

'That's why she was in your car?'

'I was giving her a lift to our hotel. Right near the hospital. Another car came towards us in the middle of the road. I swerved, and hit the hydrant.' Doly blows several smoke rings. 'I only met Bandi one more time. When he came to meet the boat in Cuxhaven, in Rolf's stead, to take Gabby and her new baby back to Vienna. Because IBM's president, Thomas Watson, needed Rolf for an important business deal at that time. So that's the only time I saw Bandi again — and that very briefly. Can't see how he could possibly have worked anything out.'

Nina's eyes are glowing. 'You're saying my father is Bandi? Really? That's wonderful! He and I get on extremely well. He gave me a horse when we were still in Lingfield, you know. He's always been real swell with me.' She hugs Doly. 'You're right! I think both of us sensed something.'

'I'm glad.' The reason Doly prefers Gemma to Nina is because her father is Rolf!

'You said you don't want anyone else to know. I respect that. Except for Warren, obviously. But I would really like Bandi to know. How d'you feel about that?'

Doly inhales several times. 'Be careful of Rolf Ferent, Nina. He's done his damndest to be a good father to you. It would crush him to know what really happened. Especially if he found out that he lost the son he'd hoped for, and that you're his brother's child.'

'Bandi is very protective of him. Neither of us would dream of telling him. You've heard Rolf's married a rich widow? Mary has adopted Laurence. She rules him and Rolf with a cat-o'-nine-tail tongue. Rolf's whole life circles her words of wisdom. He's loving it.'

'Third time lucky, then.'

'If you can call being hitched to a termagant lucky, then he's won the jackpot. I thought his second wife was Medusa personified. This one is something else.' She grabs the returned stick from Buffy's jaws. 'Mind you, no one's all bad. She boxes Laurence's ears.'

BLACK MAGIC

Once upon a time a farm labourer was working for a landowner living in Schwanenbruch. The young man not only owned the sixth and seventh books of Moses, he was also able to make good use of them. He was an avid fisherman besides. He set his nets, his fish traps and his eel baskets in the deep drains surrounding his employer's farm. And he was always certain of his catch. Until a time came when he found his eel baskets empty every morning.

The young man knew very well that it wasn't a lack of eels which was causing the problem. It had to be a thief. Someone as partial to the tender meat of eels as he was, someone who was robbing him of his catch before he could collect it for himself.

The young man shared his bedroom with a boy who was also in the landowner's employ. 'Well,' he said to the boy, 'I've had enough of catching fish for others to eat. Want to come along with me and catch the thief?'

The boy was curious to know how the young man would set about this task and agreed to go along. That very next night he woke the boy at around midnight. 'Come on,' he said. 'We'll see who that thieving varmint is.'

As the boy was dressing, he noticed the young man take a book out of his trunk and begin to read. Then he shut the book very carefully, put it back in the trunk, and strode confidently out to where he'd lowered the fish traps.

As the two of them approached the spot they saw a man standing stock still in the moonlight. He must have heard their feet squelching in the mud, but he didn't move at all. He seemed to be stuck in the earth.

'Right,' the young man shouted out. 'Now we know exactly who it was who keeps stealing my eels!' His voice was quite loud enough for the whole neighbourhood to hear. 'Come on, let's go home!'

The boy was surprised at this. He asked the young man why he didn't give the thief a good thrashing.

'No need,' the young man told him. 'He's already undergoing his punishment. He has no option but to stand there until I release him from the spell. I'd better go home and free him now. Unless I do he'll turn to carbon with the first rays of the rising sun.'

The boy watched the young man open the book he'd read before. But this time he read it backwards.

Next morning the boy was eager to satisfy his curiosity. He crept back to the spot where he knew the thief had stood. He had gone. So the boy knew that the young man really had broken the spell and set the thief free. And from that day onwards the eel traps were safe from thieves.

CHAPTER 5

Garden City, New York, Autumn 1957

Nina and Warren are frequent visitors to Garden City. Where Andrew Ferent, known as Bandi, now lives with his wife Anne.

'Well, Nina. So you and Warren had a most successful trip to England. Did you visit with Gemma and her family?'

'We stayed a week or so with them. She's got her hands full with three children under two. But she seems to be loving it.'

Bandi smiles benignly. 'Maybe you and Warren soon will be parents. To this I very much look forward.' He stares out into his garden. 'And how did you find your Aunt Dorinda?' His eyes betray his guard. 'You visited her?'

'Indeed. Well settled, I think.' Nina keeps her voice even, calm. 'She adores Dramlings, the woods around her, the English country life. Thinks she's doing the best for Ross, giving him the sort of advantages money can't buy.'

'She always was much taken with nature. She still has money problems?'

'By other people's standards, yes. But she thinks she's in clover. Enough for the basics, though nothing for the inevitable can of worms.' Nina looks at the man she now knows to be her father, and also knows he can have no idea. 'Why don't we go for a short stroll, Bandi? There are a couple of family matters I wanted to discuss.'

'Trouble with the delightful Mary?'

Rolf's third wife, married after his second one died of leukaemia and leaving him to bring up his son Laurence on his own, is a harridan all Rolf's relatives do their best to avoid.

Bandi stands, puts his hands on his wife's shoulders. 'Show Warren your little treasures, Hasi. Especially the photographs. Nina and I won't be long.'

'Don't leave your little Hasi for long, will you, big Hasi?'

An odd endearment, Nina thinks. What's so fetching about a hare? Even if it does have a harekin diminutive? Nina signals to Warren about to ruin the ruse, since Anne is not a favourite in-law. He flaps his hands behind his ears. To show he's joined the Hasi clan.

Bandi is nearly sixty, but his body is still erect, his strides long. 'Rezsö isn't happy with his new wife?'

'She's a fiend, Bandi. The archetypal virago. But he adores her. She gives his life purpose, I suppose. Not sure what she does for Laurence, but her iron fist is felt physically as well as spiritually there!'

'My hands always itch when I am in Laurence's company, but they are tied. So Mary's tactics may not be such a bad idea.'

Nina laughs. 'You may well be right.' She looks at the man who is her biological father, is impressed. Six foot in height, almost bald, a little on the heavy side, but fit. He's having trouble slowing his pace to hers. 'I want to talk to you about Dorinda, Bandi, not Rolf. Something I think you should know.'

'I see.' Nina has to run to keep up with him. 'I wondered for a long time, but had no way of finding out. I spoke with Gabby a couple of times, but she's much too clever at avoiding issues she'd rather not delve into. So Dorinda told you she had a child before she married?'

'You've guessed?'

'That I have a child by her? It was always a possibility. I tried hard to approach her. She brushed me off. Naturally I assumed she'd have let me know if that were the case.'

'You and she have a daughter, Bandi. Born in New York after that car crash.'

His eyes scan passing cars traffic-cop style. 'And what did she do with her?'

'That's the incredible part. Prepare yourself for something of a shock.'

'Why should I be shocked?' A light goes on behind his eyes. 'You are saying I am acquainted with her?'

'Yes. She's closer to you than you think.'

'What do you mean, closer?'

'Dorinda gave her to Gabby because Gabby's baby was stillborn. Because of the crash. Gabby took her back to Europe with her.'

Bandi has stopped by a building, leans against the wall. 'What you are saying, Nina?'

'Precisely what you think I'm saying. I am that baby. Gabby and Doly swapped identities in the hospital. They got away with it because they looked very alike, there was the muddle of the car crash, and both stuck to their stories.'

He leans his back against the wall, breathes deep. 'The strange thing is that, perhaps subconsciously, I always fantasised something like that. Perhaps I sensed it when I picked you and Gabriele up when the liner docked in Cuxhaven. Gabby was exceptionally defensive, drank more than usual even for her.'

'Not surprising.'

'Also I saw the way Dorinda looked at you as I carried the cot. At this time my thinking was she has the feelings of an unmarried woman longing to find the right man, to settle down.' His pace is slower now. 'But I could hardly guess about the baby swap.'

'Audacious, clever, incredible. I know. I can't get over it.'

'You still are young, it will pass.' He puts his arm around Nina's shoulders. 'And I always had a special place for you in my heart. I think you know this.'

'So you guessed I wasn't Gabby's?'

He shrugs. 'Not at all. I never thought it through. Somehow I always had a special affection for you.' He embraces Nina, holds her in his arms. 'What a wonderful surprise. My only child, my special daughter.'

'I suppose I did notice that as well. Now I understand about the horse, all those presents.' She blinks. 'I've only told Warren. I'm sure you understand he had to know.'

'Of course. And that is very good. I think it could kill my poor brother if he found out. He tried — tries — so hard to be a good father.'

'I know. Fatherhood is being a good provider. And he did his best, in spite of Gabby. What's always been hard to take is that he can't cope with the family problem. It doesn't seem to worry you. Even that tiresome Bosch didn't care, couldn't give a damn. I have to give him that.'

'Rolf has no tact, no finesse. But he sent money for your maintenance throughout the war. Knowing that only part of it was used for your and Gemma's benefit.'

'He knew about that?'

'He is not stupid, not intellectually anyway. And he wanted to make sure you and Gemma didn't starve.' He kicks at an inoffensive pebble. 'Unfortunately the just tend to be exasperating.'

'I also have some brilliant news to report. Now that you know your genetic line is involved.'

'More good news, you mean.'

She links her arm in his and pulls them on. 'I've looked into that tiresome genetic defect. I haven't found anyone who knows how to stop it being passed on, but I have found a way to cure it. Rolf's — and your — grandchildren won't have to put up with its consequences.'

'You always have been a clever girl.' He laughs. 'Now I know why. When you say cure — you mean you know how to make your hair grow?'

'Not mine. Not anyone over puberty. It's an autoimmune disease you see, brought on by a deficiency of certain vitamins and proteins. An inability to synthesise these substances adequately. Leading to an inadequate supply of whatever makes hair grow.'

He chortles, fingering his own almost bald head. 'And the cure?'

'Megavitamin therapy. An affected child, given a course just before puberty, stands an excellent chance of keeping their hair until middle age. Maybe later. Which is what counts.'

'Ah, puberty. So there's no hope for me?'

She laughs. 'Guess not. Nor any of the other billions of men who'd rather keep their hair. I'm told that's an over-production of testosterone. A completely different ball game.'

'So, congratulations, Nina. I wondered what was holding you and Warren back. I hope you'll start a family soon. Give me some grandchildren I won't lay claim to.'

CHAPTER 6

Sussex, Summer 1964

Doly, limbs deliberately exhausted from working in her vegetable garden all day, lights the fire. She sits back in the chair bought second-hand for five bob. Which only she and Buffy are allowed to use. A brilliant buy: small enough to make her comfortable, soft enough to cosset her.

Her favourite pastime is sitting, face to the window, watching the sun pink away the day. Red sky at night, Doly's delight. Her navel is covered so she contemplates nicotine-stained fingers while she reflects on her good fortune.

She has her home, her garden, her dog and cat sleeping beside her. Keeping her company when Ross is out. Which is, now, often. He exercises horses for their rich neighbours, as well as helping out at the local riding stables. After school and during the holidays when he's not in Somerset. A choice of occupation Ross adores and turns to bronze if not to gold. Which means he's out from dawn to dusk. Sometimes later. Arriving back starving for a meal. Always the same question: 'What's for pud?'

Ross has grown into a strong, healthy young man. He takes after Erskine: tall, his own blonde hair, but much bulkier than his father. Strangers find it hard to believe he and Doly are mother and son.

Naturally Doly no longer needs a babysitter or help with Ross, it's now her son who helps her out. The pancreatitis attacks, particularly the one in Germany which left her more vulnerable to further attacks, have weakened her. She finds the summer vegetable gardening and harvesting hard work. Ross isn't around to help her then. He spends most of his holidays with his father and his two half-sisters. They get on well.

Doly has offered English lessons in exchange for help in the house and garden. Helga is over for the summer. She's a pupil at the Cuxhaven school Doly and Gabby attended, the school where Tante Martha taught English. The arrangement works out well for all of them.

'He who has sufficient has enough.' Wise old bird Onkel Wilfred.

Tonight Helga has borrowed Doly's bike to go to the village, meet other young people at the village dance. Doly is content to wait for the girl to come back. She dozes. Is startled into wakefulness, a cigarette butt burning in her hand. She stubs it out, but is reluctant to put on the light. She stirs the fire into life, sinks back, Pusscat on her lap. She twirls yesterday's *Times* into spillikins and lights another cigarette. Where is the girl?

Pusscat, disturbed, stalks off. Buffy's barking is high and excited. 'Quiet, boy. What's got into you?'

He's too old for games. He leaps up, clawed paws skittering across bare floorboards, charges at the back door.

Doly's comfort is disturbed. 'Need to pee? Not like you at all, old man! Must be your bladder getting weak.' He's old, he won't live much longer. A giant hurt.

Barks turn from annoyance to frenzy. Doly throws off the rug draped round her lap. The back door is wide open, the night already dark. Buffy barks furiously, the moon flits through shifting clouds. Why is Helga so late? A new boyfriend?

Doly sees two figures by the beech hedge, struggling. A tiny flash. Reflected moonlight? From some sort of metal? Earring, bracelet, blade of a knife? Doly's throat feels tight.

'Let me go!' Muffled, but Doly recognises the staccato sounds of German intonation. Stolen kisses with a young man she's met, or a stranger attacking her?

'Is that you, Helga?'

'Ahhh…'

Doly's legs scissor towards the hedge. 'Go, boy!' she howls at Buffy as she runs. White patches of terrier are ahead of her, the barks turn to growls. His head shakes from side to side as his teeth fasten on something. A trouser leg?

'Fuck off!' Not one of the village lads she knows. A male voice Doly doesn't recognise.

A thump, a kick. The figure dissolves into the hedge. Doly catches Helga doubling up.

'Put your arm around my neck, my girl. We'll get you inside.'

Blood is welling sticky, Buffy is barking around their feet. They hobble in. Doly eases Helga on to the floor. Puts cushions behind her head.

Trembling fingers remove the clutching hand. Blood is oozing through her blouse below her left breast. A wooden shaft is sticking out. Calm anger brings a choice. Remove the knife or leave it in?

Helga pulls it out herself. Blood-stained liquid bubbles as the girl's stentorian breathing flashes Doly's memory. The little dog impaled on the mudflats of Schwanenbruch. Lieselotte's assessment. 'A sucking wound. Air sucked into chest instead of lung. So the lung won't inflate. We have to seal the wound.'

Hand pinched over the laceration, handkerchief wound tight round the puppy's body. That saved his life.

Doly rushes her hand to Helga's wound. Squeezes it together. 'You have to be really brave, my dear. Hold your hand here, and hold it tight. I'll get something to strap it up.'

A clean handkerchief over the wound, sticking plaster to anchor it, Helga's arm laid over to apply pressure.

She has no phone. Her tenants are away. Can she manoeuvre Helga into the Mini?

'Mrs Courtling?' Fred Hawkins' quavering voice. He digs her garden, snares rabbits in the woods at night. 'I did 'ear Buffy barkin' like billyo. Be you all right?'

'Thank God, Fred. There's been an accident. My summer guest — Helga — she's badly hurt.'

His face comes round the door. 'Knew somethin' rum be goin' on. Buffy did sound frantic like.'

'Could you rush over to Wellick House? Get Miss Tilletson to phone for an ambulance.'

'Be right off.' She hears him turn, the gravel flying under foot. Thumps in the night.

She bolts the door which is always kept open, stays beside Helga, holds her hand to comfort her, supplies drinks of water. And prays.

The ambulance takes thirty long minutes to arrive. Not bad considering where they are. The ambulancemen take over efficiently, transport Helga to Chichester Hospital. Doly follows in Miss Tilletson's Mini. Is enormously relieved to be told all will be well.

Dear Doly,
What a terrible thing to have happened. And what a relief that Helga is all right. After all, I feel responsible telling her parents she would be safe with you.

Now I don't want to play the heavy aunt, and preach, but if you insist on living in the wilds all by yourself, you really must have a telephone. With your permission I will order a line to be installed.

Your loving Tante Martha

The line is brought along the lane, down the drive. At a substantial cost which is beyond Tante Martha's means. But not, any longer, beyond Gabby's. She rings her aunt still living in Cuxhaven.

'Please let Doly assume that you saw to it all, Tante Martha. I don't want her to feel beholden to me.'

Martha Bender clears her throat. 'If that is your wish, I will honour it. Doly writes that Helga didn't know this boy. He's someone who's been watching her, some local who has a problem. He followed her to Dramlings after a dance at the village hall. It could have been Doly or Ross! They can't go on living in that isolated place.'

'This sort of thing's more likely to happen in a town than in the country, Tante Martha.'

'Doly must sell the cottage — '

'She won't. Her whole being is wrapped up in Dramlings. She tells me she needs a new roof. I've bludgeoned Moppel into pretending he's footing the bill for it. She'll never take it from me.'

'Very good of you, Gabby.'

'I can afford it. Perhaps Ross has had too sheltered a life for the modern world. Maybe you could suggest a stint abroad? After he finishes school this summer. I understand he wants to study modern languages. He could take a couple of years in Germany, to learn German. Or go to the States to make his fortune... He's a citizen, after all. He can get a job there, get to know the States and something of the world beyond Dramlings.'

Sussex, Autumn 1964

Doly is in the garden with Fred. Deciding where to plant asparagus. The shrilling phone rings are an insult to birdsong. There's no law to say she has to answer them.

Late that night the phone rings again.

'Bet you can't guess who.'

She would recognise Piers's voice from a single word. A single syllable. 'No idea.'

'I did come back last week.'

'Piers; how nice to hear from you.'

'My mum told me about the attack on the girl that be staying with you. Said as she's gone back 'ome to Germany. And as Ross be gone abroad.'

'Helga left as soon as the hospital gave the all clear. I think that means that Bramlings is off the list for English lessons!'

'Rum thing to be happening. If I get my 'ands on him...'

'He's under medication, Piers. And Ross is abroad as well. Decided to take a gap year; staying with a family in the Tyrol, helping with farm chores. And picking up a smattering of German at the same time. He's loving it.'

'Thought I be comin' over and give you a little sympathy.'

'How very charming.'

'Around noon tomorrow be all right for yer?'

Doly's pants have ants crawling all over them. Weeds fly by the bushel from the flowerbeds in front of the cottage. She recognises the figure wheeling a bicycle at the top of her lawn. He's still the only person she can make out at any distance.

'Like the new roof?' she asks by way of greeting. Replacing the tiles he fitted for her so many years ago. 'A present from my brother in the States. He's turned over a new leaf.'

'Do look good enough to keep you dry for life.'

'Fancy a drive through old haunts?'

October noonday sun has a crystal brilliance. Like eyes which shine their sadness before the tears pour. Lanes slippery with autumn-painted leaves lead to Lurgashall. Noah's Ark for a drink and a sandwich, flittering chat, local happenings of the past year. The man who attacked Helga was jailed for six months.

'I'd give 'im summat more permanent.' Piers's hard mouth which shows no mercy. 'Sorry I weren't about.'

'Trevor wanted to go and sort him out. The police warned against it.'

'You mean she did 'ave a local boyfriend? Be the one who stabbed her, right?'

'A would-be boyfriend. She's a young girl, Piers.'

'And Ross weren't around neither.'

Is he implying that Ross should be with her, shouldn't have left? 'He's seventeen, Piers. The Frog Prince has been woken up by Princess Sally. He's a full prince now.'

'Princess Sally?'

'Sally Glover. He met her at the riding school.'

'You'll soon be on your lonesome, then.'

Chit-chat of non-essentials. No mention of Piers and his life. No emphasis on Doly's either. The chance meeting of strangers.

'Let's go and sit in the church.'

The cool interior. Such blessed calm. His hand holds hers and makes it warm. They let the peace sink in while sitting in a pew and just absorbing.

'Ross and Sally have decided to get married as soon as he's back from abroad next year. They're thinking of where they'll want to live.'

'We could go lookin' at that cottage we saw in the woods.'

Already bulldozed out of recognition. The Mini meanders on. Through Upperton and the place for sale there. And then Doly's latest discovery. Snare's Wood. A gorgeous cottage nestling in woodland. Hansel and Gretel in the garden of Sussex. Which she knew all along would draw Piers. As it does her. Their kind of place, crooked and secret. They talk of Ross and Sally living there. Love's young dream. Which slipped Doly and Piers by. Like the ghost rider on the mudflats of Germany, riding grey on grey, invisible against the mists of rising foam and battling wind, decaying bodies and advancing years.

Having allowed the way of strangeness to wear off, able to face each other in the intimate way they always come back to, they return to Dramlings.

Departing tenants say goodbye as they draw up.

'Meeting that one and they shutters do come right down,' Piers says, with that instant intuition.

'Sometimes I strike lucky. This time it wasn't so good.'

'Easy to tell them don't fit in. Where you likes a place the place do like you.'

Now rest content to be liked, Doly tells herself. A precious jewel to be hugged in bleak moments. With a lonesome cup of tea by a cosy fire.

'Let's go for a walk.'

Buffy to heel, they amble through Moors Valley, down to the water garden, along the river, back through the woods. They drink the two bottles of Moselle Bobby left on his last visit. And experience that fleeting mellow gentle feeling of togetherness.

'All right to stay the night?'

Doly is taken aback. With so much else on her mind to be lifted up and out. 'If you wish.'

'Be good to 'ave a larger bed this time.' Friendly, impersonal, demanding. All intertwined.

Not very much later they fall asleep. The next morning they go to work. Cleaning the cottage for the next batch of tenants. Scrubbing down walls, doing each room out in turn. Methodically and thoroughly.

A brief walk over Iping Common. Doly drops Piers off at his brother's place. To meet again some time. Next week, next month, next year. Not having come close enough to Piers to know.

MOUNT JEDUT

Many years ago enormous flames, reaching high into the heavens, could often be seen on the topmost part of the Jedutenberg – Mount Jedut. Strong, powerful figures stood by the fire and stirred the flames. The forebears of the farmers and smallholders living on the North German lowlands looked out from that hill top because it gave them a wonderful view of the River Weser. There they kept watch against a constant danger threatening from the North. For the pirating Normans rowed up the Weser on their speedy boats and brought death and destruction to the settlements and farmsteads along the great river's shores.

As soon as the watch caught sight of Norman boats in the Weser estuary they lit mighty logs. The leaping flames were a warning to the whole neighbourhood. They gave the marsh dwellers the chance to flee inland. Some sought refuge behind the high walls of their church, others fled right into the church and up into its tower. Here they were safe from the spears of the Norman robbers and murderers.

Mount Jedut lent its name to enormous stones called Jedutensteine. They were set up as watchtowers in different parts of the lowlands. And, because Mount Jedut was the place where the call to vengeance, as well as the call to flight, was heard, Jedut became synonymous with revenge.

In the case of murder, the relatives would carry the corpse up to the top of the hill. The head of the victim's family would put his spear into the streaming gore and hold his bloodied weapon to the four winds. The terrible, dreaded cry of Jedut Jedut Jedut would peal across the land. Demanding revenge.

It was the signal for the kinsman's neighbours to hurry off in all directions and look for clues which might lead them to the murderer. If he were found he was dragged to Mount Jedut. There he received the death blow from the dead man's nearest of kin.

CHAPTER 7

Vienna, 1968

'My name is Miles Havering, Mrs Bosch. I'm in charge of housing.'

Gabby's business-suit smile welcomes the distinctive card. OPEC: the organisation of oil producing exporting countries headquartered in Vienna since 1960. Its members have been a rich source of clients for Gabby's real estate business.

Dohlen Real Estate lands glossy illustrations on all high echelon desks. At the International Atomic Agency, the United Nations refugee agency, the UN Industrial Development Organization and any other United Nations organisation Gabby can track down. Her favours are indiscriminate. Newcomers are as enthusiastically courted as entrenched global empires, for the mutual development of establishment status. Financial rough diamonds are often higher in carats than stones already cut and set.

Word of mouth, top resource of garrulous Vienna, promoted Gabby's business. Her brilliantly promulgated trademark of honesty and fair dealing flocks foreign clients to her. Her office is an elegant suite of seventeenth century rooms adjoining her apartment. Glittering chandeliers, tapestry hangings, Persian carpets; the office is the design team's showcase. Gifted restorers revitalise and gild war-worn town houses and villas, transform humble flats. Facsimiles of Vienna's Franz Joseph days are the most popular. Colour schemes can, if preferred, be chosen by clients' wives. Though discreet suggestions are given in case of catastrophic design choices.

Gabby's receptionist Irmgard is a carbon impression of IBM charmer Viktoria Scheiderbauer, the girl who bewitched IBM staff in pre-war Vienna. The 1968 vintage is a soupçon headier. Less Dirndl, more miniskirt, opera-box pretty, obliging, discreet. The rest of the staff consists of older women. They're fluent English speakers entrusted with all but the most important clients. Gabby enjoys flattering these herself. When she isn't abroad, that is. Or negotiating the deals which stratosphere her business.

'How nice to meet you, Mr Havering.' Unmistakable Eton plummy drawl, Jermyn Street shirts parading as Carnaby. He reminds Gabby of her war-time lover, Squadron Leader Christopher Hyllier, without the wooden leg but with that stiff Eton-collar hesitancy which makes it hard to make friends in Vienna.

'Personal meetings are always better than the telephone. Don't you agree?'

What does he want from her? Old Spice lightnings her back to Blitz-streeted London. The Connaught's plush carpets softening the constant background of anti-aircraft booms. Deep velvet curtains obliterating search lights.

'You're not looking for anything specific?'

His over-her-head glance at the portrait of Yolanthe, so like Kamilla, brushes past to the shifting silk drapes and gilt mirrors. Approval is etched into assessing features. 'Vienna has so much old-world charm. Absolutely delightful; enchanting.'

His suggestion of coffee at the ever-useful *Sacher* is accepted with alacrity. It's no surprise that Miles is suave, educated, politically astute. The unexpected bonus is the fascination he shows for her stories. So often told, her family can hardly bear to hear them again. But Gabby feels compelled to tell them.

'We went through difficult times right after the war. When my husband was still alive.'

'It must have been ghastly to come back to chaos.'

When Miles himself was barely at prep school. 'It was strange. Funny how quickly perceptions change. In 1938 Vienna, people were persecuted for being Jews. In 1947, when we returned to a shattered city, Jews were the favoured ones, the returnees who found it easy to get restitution. While Bosch, who spent his money on his newspaper, who risked all to avert the holocaust and lost everything to bombs and looters, was denied anything at all.'

'It does seem weird.' He glanced at her with slitted eyes. 'What about you? You mentioned you owned a house, furniture, all that. Did you get compensation?'

Gabby's laugh is harsh. 'Mine consisted of choosing from confiscated furniture stacked in a huge warehouse. Surrogates for my lost effects.'

'Doesn't sound remotely adequate.' He clicks impatient fingers at the waiter. 'Perhaps coffee isn't the right drink for this occasion. I like a good glass of wine. What d'you recommend?'

'Austrian wines are excellent. But they don't age well. So I wouldn't order Austrian here. That's so much better at a Heurigen. I'd recommend Grosslage Johannisberger Erntebringer. A great Rhine wine. Provided it's true Johannisberger.'

'There are substitutes?'

'Bereich Johannisberg takes in the whole of the Rheingau. I suggest one of the true vineyards. Klaus. Or Vogelsang. The *Sacher*'s cellars will have some.'

'You sound very expert. Is wine one of your hobbies?'

'Not really. The glories of Johannisberger were drummed into us as children.'

'I smell another excellent story. Tell me.'

Gabby smiles, settles back into her chair. 'The vine, you see, is said to have been planted by Charlemagne.'

'You mean the emperor? He had time for planting vines between conquering campaigns?'

'He took time off between them, at Castle Ingelheim on the banks of the Rhine.' Gabby settles back in her chair, relishing a fresh audience. 'One early spring day he was looking at the snow on the surrounding hills, and he noticed that one side of the Johannisberg melted more quickly than the other.'

'Johannisberg's the name of the mountain?'

'Indeed. A spot like that, he thought, might grow something better than grass. And as the best wine he'd ever tasted came from Orléans, he sent a rider over. To remind the citizens that their great ruler had not forgotten he'd tasted some of the best wine in their city. And to ask them to send him some plants.

'The vines were duly sent and planted. And Charlemagne, though always on some campaign or other, sent messengers to find how the plants were thriving. After three years, when he was staying in his northern capital Aix-la-Chapelle, the wine-making season was in full swing. So he set out to taste the produce of his new vineyard.'

'You're certainly giving me a completely different picture of the Charlemagne of history!'

Gabby laughs. 'Perhaps. Anyway, the vintners were delighted to give him a taste of their brew. They offered him the golden drink from a golden goblet. And the king's eyes grew soft with pleasure. Which is how one of the greatest German wines was born.'

'A delightful story.' His blinks are so rapid his eyes look closed. He sniffs as though sampling incense and exotic spices.

'There is a sequel. It is said that every spring, when the vines are flowering, the luscious scent from the flowers wakes Charlemagne from his sleep in his grave at Aix. He rises up and rides to the Johannisberg on moonbeams. And when they form their silver bridge across the waters of the Rhine, Charlemagne can be seen wandering from one side of the great river to the other. To bless his vines.

'At first cock crow he returns to his grave in Aix-la-Chapelle. Where he sleeps until the scent of the grape flowers wakes him again the following spring. For a repeat performance.'

The waiter brings a bottle, uncorks it, pours. Miles lifts his glass. 'Whatever it tastes like, it's always going to have a special flavour for me now!'

'Prost.'

The wine flows, the conversation quickens. Giving Gabby the pleasure of re-roasting old chestnuts for an eager, pristine listener longing for as much as she can provide. She's in her element.

'One of my stickiest moments was when the official came round for the ground rent for the villa I owned then. Unsaleable at the time, needless to say. I had this wad of cash my husband had just sent from Paris. To pay off urgent debts, and to feed my girls.'

'You mean he saw it in your hand?'

'I'd just opened the letter.'

'So he grabbed hold of it, I take it? Leaving you with nothing?'

Gabby twirls the glass in her hand. 'I didn't have long to find a solution. But I couldn't just let him have it.' She sips a little. 'I raced across the newly restored parquet of my living room, up to the marble mantelpiece. That was one of the few things the Russians left intact. The American tenants had just furnished the place. I slipped the money into the neck of their Ming vase. They were moving in the next day, you see. Part of the Occupying Forces. There was no way the collector could touch their property.'

'Couldn't he simply have confiscated some of your goods?'

Gabby's eyes glitter into the past. 'He paled and became extremely angry. Insisted he'd serve me with a subpoena within days because he knew I had the money and was withholding it from him.'

'Rotten luck. Bet you found a solution.'

'I wasn't worried. Courts always take their time. I knew I'd be in Paris within weeks. As it happened, by the time the case was actually brought I was a widow. I had less money than ever.'

'You had to rely on the court's lawyer?'

'I decided to represent myself.' The eyes across the table are pale pools of English sky. She can smell the scent of new-mown grass after April rains. Oh to be in England.

A warm, athletic hand reaches across the table. 'You have legal training?'

'A reasonable portion of common sense. Was the court likely to condemn a sorrowing widow with a small child, an American national, for a petty sum?'

'Courts are hardly noted for extending sympathy.'

'Maybe not courts. But judges are human. This one was old. I wore a filmy veil to remind him of the women of his youth, and told him my story.' Gabby grins. 'Only slightly embellished.'

'Delivered in just the right way!'

'That's how it turned out. The judge reduced the amount of money by nine-tenths. Which is what I said I could pay.'

Gabby finishes her wine and stands. She seldom mixes business with pleasure. There are always exceptions. The relationship with Miles Havering might benefit from her social evenings. 'I'm having a little party on Saturday, Mr Havering.'

'Do call me Miles.'

'Miles, of course. A number of people I'm sure you'd be interested to meet. Max Weiler…'

'You mean the painter?'

'And Professor at Vienna University. Indeed. You said you were interested in modern painting. Weiler is highly esteemed in Austria but hardly known outside.'

'I look forward to meeting him.'

'And Hans Fronius will be there as well. Actually. I like his work even better than Weiler's.'

'Nothing's going to keep me away.'

Miles Havering is an instant success with Gabby's circle. Business hasn't diluted her hostess talents. She avoids competing with Vienna's famous Sachertorte and other sugared delights by offering savouries accompanied by Johannisberger specially imported from Schloss Johannisberg itself. Belegte Brötchen — quite ordinary open sandwiches but with a Gabby twist — are served with the wine. Not only topped with exotically smoked, imported Cuxhaven eel and other North Sea delicacies on tiny ovals of Viennese bread, but now the added attraction of the best osetra caviar. They make a voluptuous combination, creating highly satisfactory envy among prosaic rival hostesses. An invitation to one of Gabby's parties has become a Viennese status symbol.

'Where did that supercilious young man come from?' Hans Weiss is the lone survivor of Gabby's guests, a long battle with Miles Havering ending in narrow victory. Due to forces outside Miles's control. He has a dinner engagement at his boss's house, a palatial residence Gabby has found for him, and name drops to similar chief executives.

'Adam Colesworth, you mean?'

'You know perfectly well I'm talking about Miles Havering. I haven't seen him before.'

'Isn't Greti expecting you? You always insist she gets upset if you're late.'

He lights another Sobranie with unusual precision. 'Your belegte Brötchen are more filling than they look. It must be the smoked eel.'

Gabby is prepared to allow Hans the time she takes to finish her schnapps. Then she's intending to spend the evening by herself reading the *New York Herald Tribune*. She's not in the mood for Nietzsche or petty jealousy. 'I don't want to throw you out, Hans, but I do have business to catch up with.'

He coughs, splutters. 'You're having dinner with him, aren't you? You arranged it when I went to the bathroom?'

The flattery of full-blown jealousy doesn't make up for its pervading green. 'He told us he had to leave because he was having dinner with his boss, Hans. But what if I were?' No need to remind him they aren't married or, indeed, committed in any way at all.

'You seem to be neglecting your daughter. I'm told Kamilla is going out with someone quite unsuitable.'

Gabby blinks, acknowledges Hans's deft change of subject. Greti's spying doesn't rule out accuracy. But arguing with an unwilling Kamilla won't deter her. She doesn't enjoy studying music in backward-glorying Vienna. A huddle of musical history, a cuddle of composers who died hundreds of years ago, a fuddle of outdated philosophy. Gabby doesn't blame her. The opportunity to change her studies rather than marry herself out of a corner might be a good idea.

'You seem to have forgotten that Kamilla is of age. She's entitled to do as she pleases.'

'Always some trumped up excuse.' Hans stands, his chin trembling, his legs looking as though they are about to give way under him. 'You're getting at me because I haven't changed my will. That's what it's all about, isn't it? You think I'm not treating you properly. Or providing for Kamilla.'

Somewhere in Gabby's mind a memory stirs. Of what? She's mentioned to Hans several times that it would be nice if he left some of his estate to her, and so on to Kamilla. Or directly to Kamilla.

'I won't deny that I think that would be a good idea, Hans. There's no one after you and Greti; neither of you have children and Kamilla is your nearest relative. But I do assure you — '

'Always the same. Everything has to be done your way.' He grabs an envelope from Gabby's Louis Quinze writing table, scribbles a few words with Gabby's fountain pen.

Which she restrains herself from rescuing. Is he finally going to do something about a will? Ask her to accompany him to a lawyer? Surely not Czezina...

He finishes writing, hands her her pen.

I leave half my estate to Gabriele Dohlen Bosch. Hans Theodor Weiss. May 21st, 1968.

His hand is trembling, he sways on his feet. 'The pharmacy on the corner's still open, isn't it? Let's finally get it over with. Get it witnessed.' He stumbles as he walks towards the door. 'After that, perhaps Kamilla and I might be allowed to spend some time in your company.'

Gabby is dumbfounded. What's got into the man? Has jealousy changed his character?

CHAPTER 8

Sussex, 1969

Doly telephones Piers's mother out of the blue. Hardly expecting him to be there. Just to have news of him.

He comes to the phone. 'Right you are. I be comin' out, give you an 'and.' He helps again with the chores. Carries the basket heavy with bedding and towels to the launderette for her. They sit while filthy sheets are washed, spin dried. A strange place to be together.

Then home — Dramlings — through pelting rain. Much more relaxed and easy in one another's company than the last time they were together. The wary weariness of the past few days suddenly slips away, his tension lessens.

The things discussed now have an added warmth of old affection. It's wholly unexpected to find themselves drawing the curtains, shutting the door on the outside. Doly relaxes into bliss. To have this private world of theirs one more time. Like angels in heaven, or the garden of Eden come to Dramlings.

'I do give you one guess,' he chortles down the telephone a few weeks later. 'I
be stayin' at Bepton. My place now. Why not come on over for tea?'

She's left him? That other, unnamed she? Or is she dead?

What does it matter? Doly drives over and feels the long round trip
voyage is within sight. It seems right, after such a stormy passage, that
the old familiar past should be journey's end.

Piers is tranquil, composed. 'Being with the family don't work for me.
I doesn't fit in.'

'Not with any of them?'

'One sister-in-law preaches at me. T'other do think on nothing but
money.'

'Perhaps they're envious of your life abroad. And make you feel it
when they think you're dependent on them.'

'What's there as they can be jealous of? Anyway, soon as I knew Bepton
were mine they asked me back fast enough. Better that way around.'

Diamonds of silence sparkle light into the gloom.

'Should have thought afore going on at me. It do mean as apologies
need to be on a grander scale.'

Not that he's good at those himself. And he knows very well that
the return of the native came too late in life for a suitable job in Doly's
small queendom.

They share a few glasses in his kitchen in a friendly vis-à-vis, exchanging news.

'I be doing out the cottage,' he tells her. 'Puttin' it to rights. Then it be going on the market.'

'What will you do? Where will you live?'

'Don't really know. Maybe abroad. Goin' to give me a hand?'

'All we seem to do,' Doly jokes as she helps him clean, 'is scrub for others.'

But in that place she doesn't mind. He's put his hand to his heart once more. Which could well be the last time. Doly imagines that's why he wanted her to join him.

He's most unapproachable when he's most adrift. That's when he clings back to his old accustomed ties. And for the short time he's living there he comes into his own again.

They step from the house into the sunny courtyard where the hedges have been well trimmed. A moment of gaiety before he opens the gate and sees her safely out.

He telephones a few days later. 'I've missed you.'

'Hello, Piers. Why not come over to Dramlings? The wing is all ours.'

A moment's hesitation. 'Right. I'll come.'

Tired, she guesses, from his day's labouring. Perhaps no longer up to that job.

Doly gives Piers the grand tour of the spring-cleaned cottage waiting for new tenants. She prepares a simple supper they sit down to in the wing. And wallows in doing the ordinary things that ordinary couples do. Eating without saying much, then sitting by the fire.

'Thank you, dear.'

Dear. Warm currents of desire mixed with serenity. As if nothing were any longer ordinary. Domesticities pierce his face with sadness. She can see his strength is almost gone.

'Hadn't I better drive you home?'

The resistance is momentary. His bike is loaded into the boot. They drive through lanes whose overhanging branches are denuded now. Gaudy autumn colours have been shed to blanket the earth. Leaving the trees exposed to the frosts of winter.

The dark shadows on his face have deepened, the low timbre of his voice has sunk lower. 'Next time I be stayin' longer.'

She doesn't get out of the car, merely stares straight ahead. 'Maybe.' She waits for the slamming of the door and drives away. Content just to see him. Not conditional on anything besides.

Dear Diary,
Beloved Piers. At this point in your life you may think you haven't achieved anything and have missed out on much. I can see you're overwhelmed with confusion. Yet there you are like some haunting landscape not to be put out of one's mind. That's solid, true, eternal.

Two weeks later they're together in Petersfield. Splitting up to go into different shops, meeting again in the High Street. They've never shopped together before. They drive home. Lunch at the *Flying Bull*.

Doly feels an alien nostalgia. Has age caught up with her, tied her down with chafing bonds to wish for dreams to come true?

How nice to do this once a week. So companionable. And so unlikely.

Two phone calls that same night. 'Reckon as yer should be more chary with yer telephone number.'

She looks in on Bepton on Friday. To take something to him from Midhurst. She stands drinking a beer in the kitchen. 'I'm having someone to stay for the next fortnight. Ring if you need any shopping done.'

There's no further word for the whole two weeks. She drives over to his place after her visitors have gone, leaves the car parked in the road. Shy of looking him up in his lair without being asked, shy of ringing first.

He's been clearing underbrush. She sees him sitting next to his wheelbarrow. Quite still and breathing hard. The face he turns towards Doly is guarded and infinitely sad.

'I can easily do some shopping if you'd like.'

He doesn't even turn his head to meet her eyes. 'They be delivering my stuff.'

'You've made the garden look wonderful. The cottage, too.'

Monosyllabic yes and no. A remote sadness which doesn't leave him. Giving her the impression that she's some garden fixture which needs dealing with.

She recognises the signs. He's totally alone — and wishes to be so. Or at least not intruded on. She leaves quickly, realising he's been entirely on his own the past fortnight. He's got into the way of it. She assumes he takes refuge in working to the best of his ability, as if stopping for a moment would lead to breakdown. Nothing she can say will comfort him.

It is the way of their relationship. One day the gates are open, they chat like neighbours, drift time away. The very next time the gates may be locked, making Doly feel unwanted, a trespasser.

If she could put it down to moods she could shrug it off. But he is wholly given over to some private grief enclosed inside himself. And talks about the weather. Except for one evening. When there was a laying of ghost riders outdistancing the storm.

The next phone call is a month later. Always a Wednesday. A child full of woe. 'Hello, Dorinda. I be walking into Midhurst today.'

'Piers. What a shame. I'm sorry I can't join you. But I'm in the midst of doing the house out and cooking for guests.'

She has so rarely refused, but knows it isn't that which makes for another month of silence. She drives past his place one evening and sees light behind the tall hedge, flickering flames through filtered thoughts.

She's in no way put off by his temperament, his moods. His behaviour has no bearing on their relationship. But last time they met he mentioned a strained arm, said he'd seen his doctor. And given it too little emphasis.

So, again on a Wednesday and after lunch, she takes her courage into her hands and drives to his cottage. She catches a glimpse of him working behind the hedge, the check of his shirt contrasting with the twisted twigs of hawthorn, and sounds her horn.

He walks on to the drive to meet her. 'Dorinda.'

'Are we still neighbours?'

His eyes are half closed, as though he were too weary to lift his eyelids. 'Bettern all that London crowd.'

'Well, why not give yourself a break and come and have tea at Dramlings?'

He shuffles backwards. 'Can't be stoppin' in the middle of me work.'

She waits for enlightenment.

'In case I don't feel up to startin' agin.'

He tells her nothing. 'You've done a brilliant job of the walled garden.'

At first the beginning of a smile, then his whitening face. Even the nod seems too much for him. He doesn't ask her in.

'Will you walk me to the gate?'

He shuffles over. His features are so shut in she knows he doesn't want to give anything away. He stands alone, a clear-cut stranger of whom one takes indirect and immense notice.

She nods, says goodbye and doesn't look back.

Sussex, Winter 1969/1970

He telephones on New Year's Eve a year later.

This time her answer to 'Know who this is?' is a truthful 'No'. Because his voice is a whisper, harsh, almost unrecognisable.

But it stirs the memory of another New Year's Eve. A dance he didn't come to. 'Why suddenly remember Dramlings?'

'It be jest like a book read and liked, one I be readin' over and over.'

'Nicely put. Thank you, Piers.' She hears the low rumble in his voice, the breath which doesn't come easily. This then their leave taking.

Sussex, Spring 1970

She meets his mother in Midhurst that spring. Hears of his illness, mumbles conventional phrases. But doesn't ask if there's anything she can do.

He dies in early summer. Doly plants a smoke bush, often called a wig bush she grins to herself, at the end of her garden. Where she can see it from the kitchen window.

CHAPTER 9

Sussex, Summer 1971

Years meld like comfortable leather, worn but not out. Ross is back from Austria and a visit to the States. Living in Snare's Wood only a few miles away. A married man.

Erskine, a one-year widower, is welcomed to stay with Ross and Sally. There's a strong tie between father and son in spite of the many miles between Sussex and Somerset.

'Why not bring him round?' Doly suggests. Eager to see what life has made of the man she thought she loved but actually only pitied.

'If you like.' Shrugged shoulders, head turned away.

Always that impatience now. Is it since he met Sally, or did it start before? In any case, whatever Doly says, or does, Ross gets irritated. Doly swallows her dismay. 'Do come for lunch. Sally too, of course.'

'She'll be at work. I've taken a few days off. There'll be just the two of us.'

Ever resentful of his mother, blaming the past on her. What sort of stories has Erskine been feeding him? Even so, Ross can't resist trying out the role of a son with two parents. True, he's missed out. Join the bloody club. And what, just what, did Doly leave undone about it?

Erskine is a greyer long ago, a thin rake bowed. The smile is subdued, there is no outstretched hand.

Doly takes him for a trip around Dramlings showing off improvements, the new wing. All is pronounced impressive in a happy friendly session which could have been a family constant. If Erskine had not chosen elsewhere.

He nods at the new wing, stares at the roof, widens his nostrils. 'We've booked tickets for Chichester tonight. They're staging *An Ideal Husband*. The three of us are going. Don't think they're sold out. Will you come too?'

Sally is in front with her husband, Doly is in the back seat next to Erskine. Aware of his body touching hers. The faint odour of remembered intimacies. She feels an odd gentleness, a fragile precious peace which balms the empty chasms of her life.

Afterwards they walk on the broad green outside Chichester Festival Theatre together. They watch their son and daughter-in-law ahead of them, arms twined around each other's bodies, in love. And smile at each other as they remember Tours.

Ross holds the car door open for Erskine.

'Wouldn't you rather have Sally in the front with you?' His voice, always polite, is questioning, without the reproach of preference.

Doly feels joy, contentment. That he should want to sit beside her! To enjoy again their easeful proximity brought out of the past and into the present.

'You'll be more comfortable in the front, Father. Your legs are longer than Mother's.'

They managed on the way to the theatre. But Ross, determined, ushers Erskine into the front passenger seat, settling Sally beside Doly in the back. Jealous? A strange concept for Doly. Extraordinary, but very clear.

He can't take away Erskine having sat next to her on the way to the theatre. During the silent journey back she hugs a quiet joy. Which no putrid green emotion can destroy.

'Do come in for a drink.'

She offers elderberry wine in pewter goblets, a Christmas cigar Bobby left on his last visit. Erskine smokes slowly, evidently with joy. He isn't eager to be gone but Ross insists. And makes no further arrangements for them to meet.

Next day Cynthia Greenell rings, the one-time neighbour from Riverside. She's the parent who drove her son and Ross to Seaford College every day. Now she's been left penniless by her straying husband. Life's turncoat strategy is not confined to Doly.

'Shall we drive over to Snare's Wood together? Drinks at six, Ross told me.'

Doly feels the raw, tight clamp of shock. 'Fraid…' Ridiculously high. She clears her throat. 'I'm afraid I can't make it, Cynthia. A previous invitation to Midhurst. I'll drop you off.'

The huge unexpected hurt leaves her gasping, using full strength to stop the tears. She deposits Cynthia on Ross's doorstep, eases the car out before anyone answers the ring. She hurtles blindly through the winding lanes to Iping Common, parks. 'Walk, Buffy.'

She welcomes gorse shredding her blundering hands, old bracken stalks clinging to her shoes and holding her back. The smart of heather stumps burned black by summer fires, the tear of thorny brambles bring welcome wounds. She grabs at dying nettles with bare hands. The transference of pain gives her a little comfort.

To be looked on as a rival to Erskine's affections is the weirdest thing. To be treated as one almost unbearable. It doesn't help to be aware that Ross could have been expected to be pleased the meeting went off so well. And that he clearly wasn't.

Life has already set up so many high hurdles. Why does Ross choose to be another? Because he hasn't learned to handle disappointment except at someone else's expense?

Doly sees herself at Ross's age. Swapping between young lovers, queening it at Riverside Hall. Or was she younger? It's irrelevant. She must often have hurt people she cared about a good deal less than Ross cares about her. A passing phase, she tells herself. A weapon youth uses to accent victory over age.

She tries to black out her need to be with Erskine. She subdues the longing to enjoy the total lack of hostility, the friendliness. Which Ross prevents. A share not to be shared?

The heat of despair makes Doly tear off her coat, her cardigan. She welcomes whip-lashing wind howling over a whirling van Gogh landscape. Spent heather stalks dig into her calves, draw blood. Steel raindrops cold shower her clean and dispel hot mother love turned to despair.

She whistles in the wind. Buffy charges towards her straight as an arrow, ignoring prickly heath and pot-holed paths. His tongue hangs out, a panted greeting of love. The long plod back to her car brings physical exhaustion. She leans back in the seat and naps, wakes to Buffy's licks.

She starts the motor, putters home, stretches out in front of a warm hearth. Buffy barks a love song, Pusscat purrs welcome laced with demands for food. Doly strokes the eager back, the rising tail. Is all love conditional?

First Erskine, then Lieselotte, Faith, Piers, Ross. She's left with her pets. And Dramlings.

Doly watches the moon lighting the cornfields. Then clouds obscure the moonbeams and she lights candles to brighten up her dulled spirit. It's nothing very new for Doly to be so alone. But it still hurts.

She draws an indifferent Pusscat on to her knees. And strokes her fur first backwards, then forwards. To make her sleek again.

PART 5

EEL QUEEN

1972 – 1991

CHAPTER 1

Vienna, Summer 1972

It's so totally unexpected. So very unlikely. Last night Gabby and Hans went to the Musikverein, to a concert of Hans's beloved three Bs — Bach, Beethoven, Brahms. Neither he nor the conventional Viennese favour anything later than the nineteenth century. Schoenberg was booed off the stage for daring to invent.

Gabby's taste in music is not taste at all. Her ear is attuned to military marches, the folk songs she remembers from her childhood. But she sits patiently through concerts while working out her next business move. Enforced boredom yields magnificent results.

'How d'you mean he's been taken to hospital, Greti?'

'There is no how about it, Gabriele. Perhaps you mean when. At ten o'clock this morning.'

Gabby doesn't suspect Greti of killing her brother to stop him leaving Vienna for a holiday, but she's convinced there should have been some hint of trouble last night.

'We were travelling to Schwanenbruch tomorrow!'

'You may, of course. Hans will be delayed. They're operating right away.'

Gabby's experiences of medical crises are confined to Doly and Bosch. 'What, exactly, is the matter Greti?'

'A blockage. He was in great pain. I'll be in touch.'

Hans never regained consciousness. He ignored the symptoms of prostate cancer, no doubt because they were embarrassing. Perhaps he was right. He was better off without the protracted agony of useless treatment.

Gabby paces the living room which still bears traces of last night's Sobranies. His glass is not yet washed, and there's the lingering faint smell of well-worn clothes. A living, breathing, speaking being is now forever silent. No longer there for dinner on Monday, Wednesday, Friday. No meetings after Sunday Mass. No regular companion for concerts, theatres, exhibitions. No joint holidays in Schwanenbruch.

She's grown accustomed to him. Like an old pair of shoes, he was more comfortable than anything new. Their lives have run parallel for over twenty years. Much longer than any other relationship she's ever had. She's restless, tidies the room, though she knows she can't tidy the memory away. She crumples into a chair, overwhelmed with the anguish of a loved-one gone.

He's left a vacuum in her life. It hits her with a force which knocks the breath out of her body. She was in love with Hans. Unworldly, old-fashioned, carping, infuriating Hans. Her one true love. Extraordinary. She didn't know. Not consciously, not actually.

Her heart contracts, tears cascade. Why, oh why, Hans rather than Greti?

The annual trip to Schwanenbruch is delayed until Hans Weiss is buried. Gabby studies the codicil Hans scribbled in his own hand four years ago. On the back of an envelope. *I leave half my estate to Gabriele Dohlen Bosch. Hans Theodor Weiss. May 21st, 1968.* Witnessed by the pharmacist and his wife in the shop on the corner. They are still there.

Gabby can't decide whether to demand her share or not. Hans wrote the codicil when he thought he'd lose her to another man, would do anything he could to keep her. Except get married. Or go to a lawyer to add a codicil to his will in the usual way.

She no longer actually needs his money. She has her flat, her antiques, the car. Her business is thriving, her income generous. Kamilla is grown up. But it was his wish that she should inherit half his estate. She makes several copies of the codicil and takes one to Otto Venn. And, with the help of Hans's inheritance — another inheritance she grins to herself — she can foresee the Villa Dohlen brought back into her family.

'Is this legal, Herr Doktor?'

He always ponders where others think. Longer of late. 'The witnesses are still available?'

'Yes.'

'If we can establish the identity of the handwriting I believe it is.'

'I can show it to his sister?'

The shakes are emphatic. 'I advise caution. You don't want two corpses on your hands.'

That does depend. Gabby hides her feelings by blowing into a handkerchief. A delicate lace one which helps her see but not be seen. As it did at another time with Czezina. Will the results be as treacherous as before?

She doesn't care. Hans's will is her right.

Who can she talk to apart from Venn? Still active in his nineties, but not as sharp as even he used to be. She invites Miles Havering for a pre-dinner drink. Without his girlfriend. Her constant trivial chatter not only interrupts interesting discussions, it drives Gabby to unchristian thoughts. Why are men such slaves to sex?

'I'd rather like to ask your advice, Miles. If you could come without Jennifer?'

The very slightest hesitation. Then he agrees.

Gabby explains the circumstances of the legacy. The past. The complicated inter-familial relationships.

He listens carefully. Encourages old tales retold. He's always loved Gabby's stories of the past, the recent present. Hangs on every word.

'I think you should go for it, Gabriele. In my opinion you are as much entitled as any wife would be. If you were married you'd collar the lot. Greti Weiss is lucky he didn't make it all over to you.'

'She'll go to court.'

'I'm sure she will. Never mind. You claim your rights. She'll hardly be destitute.'

'You don't think I'm being greedy? I'm very comfortably off without.'

He grins. 'Change your Beetle for a BMW. Double the size of your flat. Buy clothes, and splendid furniture. Travel first class.' He opens another bottle of wine. 'If you have trouble spending the loot, I'll be delighted to help.'

'You and Jennifer.'

He pours, smiles that downward smile. 'And Jennifer. Of course.'

If she wants another admirer to take her to social events it's clear he'd be very willing. Jennifer could be trained to think of Gabby as 'business'. Which, indeed, their relationship is all about.

'My brother never mentioned a word about this to me.' Greti's grim voice brings Mustapha the umpteenth to attention.

Gabby doesn't wish to speak ill of the dead. But she will if she has to. 'Perhaps he wasn't quite specific enough, Greti. And it was a long time ago now.'

'This crumpled old envelope? You expect to make a claim against Hans's estate with some stupid little scrap of paper like this? I won't accept it. It's utterly ridiculous.'

'I imagine you recognise the writing, Greti. What other reason could Hans have had for penning this?'

'It won't be taken seriously. You forced him into it!'

'Forced him? How do you think I managed that, exactly?'

'Moral blackmail. Exactly what you always use.'

'I should explain that I have taken advice. There was a long-standing relationship between Hans Weiss and myself. The engagements, as you know, are well documented. The original will was changed to take account of that.'

'But you didn't marry, did you?' She feeds a Mozartkugel to Mustapha. His size is legendary.

'Indisputable. And the reasons are also extremely well documented.'

'That might well count against you.'

Perhaps. She knows they're more likely to count against Hans's memory, which is a consideration. 'I think you should know that I am going to apply for my rightful share, Greti. And that I'll get it.'

She does. But the fight is as protracted, and as unpleasant, as Greti can make it. At the hearing it was Czezina, one of a small number of material witnesses, who testified that the writing on the envelope was Hans Weiss's. Reluctantly, but firmly, even under strong interrogation. No doubt he remembered Gabby's threat some twenty years before that she would have him struck off if he prevaricated.

Gabby hasn't seen him or come across him for years. Still working, still quick, but clearly in no mood to take Gabby on.

Vienna, Autumn 1972

Gabby, proud owner of half Hans Weiss's properties, is a very wealthy woman. But her capital is inaccessible. It consists of enormous town houses within the city of Vienna which are rented out to Austrian tenants. And not under her direct control. A static situation when all her instincts and inclinations tell her she must be dynamic. She's ready to trade rents for capital, and that means a direct approach.

'Greti? This is Gabriele. Could we perhaps meet...'

The phone slams down. Her letters are not answered. Greti may be being forced to pay half the receipts from the apartment houses to Gabby but she has no intentions of doing anything else. Gabby's only other possible contact with Greti Weiss is through Czezina. Will he be willing to play go-between again?

That rather depends, Gabby knows, on what pressures she can bring to bear.

She phones the lawyer at his office and makes an appointment to see him. The following afternoon.

CHAPTER 2

Vienna, Autumn 1973

'I was hardly expecting to see you again, Frau Bosch. What can possibly bring you here?'

'I'm sure you've already guessed, it's a last resort for me.'

'So what is the reason for this dubious pleasure for us both?'

'You are, of course, aware that Hans Weiss left half his estate to me. That the judgment of the court was in my favour. And you know the result: my interest in half Hans Weiss's property was upheld.'

Plumper hands through greyer hair. 'You know I did not represent Frau Weiss. I felt it would be inappropriate. And I'm shortly about to retire. You also know I was called to be a witness in the case. What can I possibly add to that?'

'I appreciated your honesty.'

'Perjury is a serious crime. The point, gnä' Frau?'

'The income from the apartments is not negligible. But I'm not interested in income. What I'm after now is capital. Frau Weiss refuses

373

to speak to me, or to answer my letters. I therefore have no choice but to try to approach her through someone else.'

'And you really think I am that person?'

'Let us say that I think you might have good reason to approach her.'

His back is against the window. As ever shadowing his expression. 'You have a business proposition, I take it.'

'I will give up all other rights if Frau Weiss agrees to one of the apartment houses being transferred into my sole ownership. To do with as I wish. That's one out of three. They're all worth much of a muchness, and it would leave her with two-thirds rather than half the estate.'

'I'm quite sure she won't contemplate such a suggestion.'

'Why not? She would be doing very well.'

'I think you already know that that's completely beside the point for her.'

'In that case, I shall have to show muscle. Two things: I will insist on half my share of the chattels which, so far, I have not asked for. The other — '

'Fascinating, Frau Bosch. Nothing whatever to do with me.'

She stands, eyes bright, back straight. ' — the other is that if you do not persuade Frau Weiss to consider my proposition I will report you to the Law Society. For suggesting to me that I break the law.'

'I haven't been involved with you for over twenty years, Frau Bosch!'

'There's no time limit on bringing a complaint.' Not a good case. But she has some basis for a complaint, which is all she needs. 'You did suggest I pretend I had obtained an annulment.'

He laughs in her face. 'That old stuff? Rubbish. That's completely unsubstantiated.'

'Perjury is still a serious crime.' The lace handkerchief is put to use again. 'But I wasn't going to rely on proof, Herr Doktor. I suppose I would have to trust to your colleagues' understanding of human nature. Would I bring such an accusation, at this stage, if there weren't some truth in the matter?' A small smile as Gabby applies the coup de grâce. 'Does it matter whether they believe you or me, Herr Doktor? You are about to retire. They will know I can get no pecuniary advantage. It's just that — well, mud sticks.'

The liquid hatred shines through the shadows. 'Moral blackmail.'

'Leverage. I really prefer to call it leverage. All you actually have to do is persuade Frau Weiss's lawyer to present my proposal to her through him.'

'I rather think you overestimate my influence, Frau Bosch. Greti Weiss hasn't spoken to me since the last fiasco about Hans's marriage plans. And, as you know very well, it was my testimony which clinched your case about the will.'

'To be specific, you agreed it was likely that Hans Weiss didn't go to their lawyer to add the codicil because he was afraid of his sister finding out.'

'And that compromises me in some way?'

'It sets a precedent for your assessment of Hans Weiss's character. It makes my contention about your plan to bypass the Church credible.' She looks directly at Czezina. 'And I don't think Frau Weiss wants all that history brought out in court.'

His hands are steepled, a silent prayer. 'I see you are using yet another hidden talent. Maybe you should take up practising law, Frau Bosch.'

'If example were the only criterion, Herr Doktor, perhaps I would!' There is no answering laugh. 'But I do think we may have the beginnings of a business deal. As you know, one should never mix business with pleasure. But I always think that a good business deal is a pleasure in itself — as long as it works for both parties, of course.'

Vienna, Autumn 1975

Gabby takes out a substantial mortgage on the apartment building Greti writes over to her. The cash allows her to make down-payments on a number of properties she thinks strategically placed to rise in value within a short time. Modern ones, in the less wealthy parts of the Inner City. She rents them out in the meantime, so that their mortgages are paid for by the foreign tenants she places in them.

Dohlen Real Estate has a new chief executive. Gabby has reverted back to her maiden name. Gabriele Dohlen hires a secretary, opens an office in the Graben, advertises in the *International Herald Tribune* and *The New York Times, The London Times, The Sydney Morning Herald.* The business grows with eagle soars, bulldog bounds and kangaroo leaps.

Three years after Hans's death Gabby is in a position to approach the Schwanenbruch Council about buying the Villa Dohlen back. She no longer bothers to drive the car — now a Mercedes she has bought herself

— up for a short visit. She books her first-class flight to Hamburg, then a chauffeured car from the airport to Schwanenbruch.

Nor does she any longer stay with Ursula. Her requirements are a little more demanding now. She rents a purpose-built apartment because she wants her retreat in Schwanenbruch to be available the whole year round.

The Council, alerted to Gabby's visit, depute Herr Fosse to begin negotiations. He invites her to the Villa Dohlen, an invitation she graciously accepts.

'We are anxious to keep a house like this for future generations of our country to enjoy,' he begins nervously, pouring a large snifter of outstanding schnapps into one of the few remaining Cornish glasses from old Dohlen's time.

'I do agree, Herr Fosse. You will appreciate that buying the house outright is not entirely what I have in mind.'

Gabby lights up her cigar, tosses back the large schnapps, settles back into her father's chair. The one Herr Fosse has, just by the way she looked at it, put at her disposal.

'My suggestion is this, Herr Fosse. We agree a price on the property. And that price takes into account that I will reconstruct the house as nearly as possible to the state it was in when we were children.'

'You mean refurbish it exactly, Frau Dohlen? Will you remember how it was?'

'Perhaps not on my own. What I have in mind is to ask my brother and sister to help me dredge it up. And perhaps we can enlist the help of some of the younger servants of that time. Between us I really think we can reproduce the original. Same colours, same decorations, same furniture. The only thing we cannot replace is my mother's portrait. I will engage a painter to imitate the style of my father's, with my mother's likeness taken from a photograph.'

'And in what way would that persuade the Council to sell the property back to you?'

'Because, Herr Fosse, the Council gets back cash. And the house, when refurbished, will be opened to the public when neither my brother nor sister, nor I, are in residence.'

Herr Fosse's bulk is hard to accommodate on the plastic chair. 'That might not be very often.'

'It will be most of the year for the time being. I might well retire to Schwanenbruch in my old age, but I do not anticipate that as starting until my eightieth birthday. Eleven years from now.'

'I still don't think…'

'And after my death I intend to leave the house to the village. In perpetuity. That will be part of the sales agreement between the Council and myself. With enough capital in trust for its future upkeep and necessary refurbishments. On one condition: the Council agrees never to change the house to anything but a show house.'

He stands, looks out of the window at the St Nicolaikirche. 'That sounds quite an attractive proposition, Frau Dohlen.'

'One more rider. I wish to stipulate that anyone in the direct Dohlen line will be allowed burial in the Dohlen Mausoleum. If they so wish.'

'I'm afraid that last condition is outside our jurisdiction. Your father arranged a private agreement with the Church authorities. You'll have to discuss that with them. The rest, I think, will be very satisfactory.' He smiles. 'All we need do is agree the price.'

Gabby smiles in her turn. That, after all, is the business she's in.

FLYING HORSESHOES

A farmer riding from Schwanenbruch to Bremerhaven came across a little man in a red coat, with shaggy hair and laughing eyes.

'Your horse only has three shoes,' he said. 'What's happened to the fourth?'

The farmer dismounted, saw the little man was right, thanked him and asked him if he knew where the nearest smithy was.

'Take your horse by the bridle and follow me!' the little chap said. And led him round a small hill where the farmer saw smoke rising from a smithy, and three little men standing by an anvil with a horseshoe at the ready.

'What luck,' the farmer cried. 'Please shoe my horse for me.'

The small smith and his lads were happy to oblige. They merely asked whether the farmer would like shoes for trotting or shoes for galloping. And suggested he have four new shoes. But the farmer turned that down, thinking the other three would last some weeks yet.

'What do I owe you?' he asked.

'A drink from your wine bottle,' they said. And by the time they'd each had a sip the bottle was empty. The farmer smiled, and went off. Not worried because he had another bottle in his saddlebag. But he hadn't gone far when he found one of his horse's feet galloped while the others walked. So he had to return to the smithy.

The smith was happy to reshoe his horse, and only asked for another drink. He emptied the second bottle, which didn't worry the farmer, for it was a cheap way to reshoe his horse, and the inn wasn't far.

What a ride! The horse's newly shod feet fairly flew over the roads, and the farmer found himself at the inn in no time.

'That's a good animal you've got there,' the innkeeper said, while the farmer put back a couple of bottles.

'He's a good horse all right. But it's not just him, it's the new horseshoes. And they only cost me a couple of bottles of wine! So, innkeeper, what do I owe you?'

'The four horseshoes.'

The farmer couldn't believe the innkeeper's demands. When he refused he was taken to see the nearest judge who agreed that, since the farmer paid two bottles of wine for the shoes, and had drunk two bottles at the inn, it was a fair exchange.

The innkeeper ripped off the new horseshoes, but the farmer thought that wasn't the end of it. So he led his horse back the way he'd come, and looked for the smithy again. He couldn't exactly remember where it was, but he heard the 'Trippiditank, trippiditank' hammering on the anvil, and that led him back to the smithy.

'So what happened to your horseshoes this time?' the little man asked.

The farmer told him his dismal story and begged to have his horse reshoed again. This time the smith offered him the choice between shoes for galloping, or shoes for flight. And the farmer chose shoes for flight. But he had no bottles of wine this time. The little men told him not to worry, but to bring them when he could.

The farmer swung himself into the saddle and, it seemed, his horse's hoofs didn't even touch the ground before he found himself back at the inn. He asked for two more bottles of wine with which to pay the smith.

The innkeeper gave him the bottles, then demanded the new horseshoes in payment. But this time the farmer wasn't going to wait for judgment. This time he set off to pay his debt to the smith. And the innkeeper rode after him, on a horse shoed with the gallop shoes. He was about to catch up with the farmer when they came to marshy land. That's when the innkeeper's horse sank into the quicksand, but the farmer's horse flew over the quagmire without touching it.

However hard he tried, the farmer couldn't find the smithy again. 'Well,' he shouted out, 'so take what is yours!' And he threw the two bottles into the air. And never heard them fall. All he heard was 'Trippiditank, trippiditank!' Which sounded like 'We give you thank, we give you thank.' And the farmer rode happily home.

CHAPTER 3

Sussex, Winter 1975/1976

'My God, Doly. How on earth did this happen?' Gemma stares at the blackened chimney and charred walls of the original cottage. The fire brigade was able to save the wing.

'A big mistake in choice of tenants.'

'You mean it wasn't an accident? They actually set fire to it?'

'No, Gemma. I mean I knew I didn't take to them, but convinced myself it was prejudice. The Taylors weren't my usual sort. I should have known as soon as I found out about the fireplace.'

Doly and Gemma are standing on Doly's lawn, contemplating the scene of devastation. The trim little cottage, with its white window frames, gay flowerbeds and enormous chimney is no longer smoking. But it is disconsolate. A gaping hole in the roof, the chimney blackened, the window-frames burned.

'What about the fireplace? Did they make it into a fire hazard?'

'Decorative damage. Remember it's Elizabethan. An enormous

thing — the way they built them then. Large enough to roast an ox or a deer. You must remember it. Little alcove seats on either side so that one can sit right inside the chimney. Absolutely marvellous.'

'What did they do? Hack it out?'

'I suppose I might have noticed that. They chose a quiet death. They painted the beautiful old bricks. Black. Shiny black.'

'You can't be serious?'

'They brushed modern gloss paint onto those porous old bricks. Impossible to save them now.'

'Tenants, and they painted your fireplace?'

'They thought it would be easier to look after. That they were doing me a favour.'

Gemma's breath comes in fits and starts. 'So how did the fire start?'

'Taylor did some electrical work in the attic. Under the angled roof space. He added illegal wiring and overloaded the circuits. Then they went off for a weekend to visit family in London. By the time I discovered it the place was in full flame.'

'You didn't notice at first?'

'The wing's quite separate — built on, not into. The fire itself started in the roof. Fortunately my phone was still working. The fire brigade got here in record time. One hell of a feat all the way from Midhurst. They did their best.'

'What are you going to do, Doly? Move?'

'I've thought about it. But no. This is my home. I love it, and I'm staying. Stone doesn't burn, and the fairly primitive construction means it can all be put back together again.'

'You were insured, I hope?'

'One of my few responsible actions. I remembered Castle Bath, the East Side People's Baths. Can you believe it's all happened again?'

'Not gangsters this time.'

'I suppose I wouldn't call the Taylors gangsters. Criminally negligent might be a better description.'

'Social psychopaths.' Gemma has tears in her eyes. 'What a hell of a thing to happen.'

Doly and Gemma are sitting by the small fireplace in Doly's wing. 'I'm sorry about your father, Gemma. I heard from Gabby that he's been poorly for some time.'

'You remember Rolf's third wife died? He never really got over it. He spent his time mourning her, was terribly lonely without her. I think that's what made him ill. The Swiss doctors chose not to tell him what he was really suffering from. So he flew to New York, thinking American doctors would be able to cure him.'

'What was wrong, exactly?'

'Oesophageal cancer. By the time he arrived in New York he could hardly swallow. Nina and Laurence took him to the Memorial Sloan-Kettering Cancer Center, reputedly the best cancer hospital in the world. The doctors there told him straight that he had cancer. And told Nina that if he didn't have an operation he'd starve to death.'

'He was staying with them?'

'Yes. He made all kinds of difficult demands. And, you know, Nina and Warren live pretty close to the edge. Both work freelance, you see. Warren never knows whether he's got assignments or not, her stringer's pay is pretty minimal, even working for *The New York Times*.'

Doly's smoking has not decreased.

Gemma coughs. 'D'you mind if I open the window, Dorinda?' Fond of her aunt, she's never called her Doly, feeling that was for other people. Gemma and Nina agree on that.

She blinks. 'Sorry, Gemma. Shall we go for a walk? It's lovely out.'

The woods, weighty with rain and summer scents, are soft underfoot.

'He wanted a new bed. Nina's guest bed wasn't good enough. He had to have fresh fish, and everything liquidised. In other words, the cancer had got to him. He was panicking. In spite of what the doctors said, and they predicted complete recovery, I think he knew he was dying. Just refused to face it.'

'Nina had to bear the whole burden? With her boys still so young? Couldn't Bandi, or your half-brother, have helped?'

'Bandi's wife simply can't abide Rolf. She wouldn't have him anywhere near. She even refused to have the poor man at Bandi's eightieth birthday party!'

'And Laurence?'

'He and Carlotta have a young baby. Tricky for them. They did take over after the operation. Worked very hard, actually. Made him eat, and exercise.'

'So how did he end up in Lausanne again?'

'The doctors insisted he was cured. And, since it's his home, he went back to his apartment. He was lonelier than ever. Crying all the time, according to the maid. The cancer came back. Riddled his whole body. Leonard and I were visiting Gabby when the news came through. We rushed over to Lausanne.

'The Swiss consultant told us he was dying, to get the family over. We were all there: Laurence and his family, Bandi and Anne, Nina and Warren, Leonard and I.

'One entertaining bit. He wasn't actually interested in any of us! He'd got to know this rather amiable middle-aged woman. He'd clearly fallen in love with her. She visited quite often. Very decent.'

Doly smiles. Gemma is too young to realise that romance doesn't die with age. 'I always liked him, you know. A decent honest man.'

'He did his best, and left us reasonably provided for. Thirty per cent each of his money and stocks. The rest went to Laurence. We've inherited a decent amount, Doly. Mary was well off.'

'I'm glad for you.'

'So if you need any help both Nina and I will be delighted to…'

Doly takes Gemma's hand. 'That's really sweet of you. Both of you. I don't need handouts any more. Maybe I'm not in Gabby's class, but I've worked out a little idea all of my own.'

'You're going to get a job?'

'I'm using the insurance money to have Dramlings restored to its former self. And then I'm going to sell it. Prices for country cottages within commuting distance of London have skyrocketed. This one is in an idyllic setting. It's worth a bomb.'

'But I thought you just said — '

'I'll live in the wing until I die. The people who buy the main cottage will have first option on the wing. Places like this are at such a premium now, I think I can get away with that sort of condition. And I'll be making quite a bit of money for myself!'

'Good. About time you were comfortable.'

'There will be enough for me to give Ross half. Then he can pay off his mortgage.'

'Don't you think you should think of yourself, Doly? You might need something — '

'He who has sufficient, has enough.'

THE LOWLY BISHOP

Over a thousand years ago, when bishops were rulers as well as shepherds of their flocks, the town of Mayence was fortunate to have a very holy man in that high office.

But Bishop Willigis did not come from aristocratic stock. Quite the contrary, he was the son of a poor wheelwright who had risen to his elevated position through good works and diligence. And, though the citizens of Mayence honoured and loved their pious ruler, they had one complaint. They found it hard to bow low before a man who, like themselves, had come from peasant stock. A man brought up in a humble cottage rather than a castle or a palace.

Bishop Willigis, hearing of this, preached from his pulpit. Condemning snobbery and too much thought about the riches of this world rather than those of the next. A sermon which did not altogether please the worthy burgers under his care.

They met in secret, made fun of the man of God, and decided to play a trick on him. One warm, dark summer night they assembled outside the bishop's palace and chalked enormous wheels on each one of his portals. Then they went chortling to their beds.

The devout bishop, up early the next morning to say the first Mass, soon noticed the scoffers' malicious work. He walked from one chalked door to the next, and stood in silent contemplation. Until, at last, a large smile creased the episcopal features. He turned to his chaplain and ordered him to send for a painter. Then he instructed the man to paint enormous white wheels on a scarlet background wherever the chalk wheels were drawn. And under each wheel the painter was to write out a slogan:

Willigis! Willigis! Just think what you have risen from.

And that was not the end of it. He ordered the town wheelwright to make him a plough wheel, and to set it above the bishop's chaste bed.

In memory of his humble origins.

The scoffers were put to silence. And the good people of Mayence began to honour and esteem their worthy bishop who, though exalted far above his birth, did not give himself airs.

Since that time the coat of arms of the Bishops of Mayence, now Mainz, has carried the distinctive white wheel on a red ground.

CHAPTER 4

Schwanenbruch, September 1976

'Well, here we go again. Twenty years later, Gabby. Seventy instead of fifty. How does it feel to be an old woman?'

Gabby's small face, trim figure and carefully chosen hairdo belie her age. She looks in her late fifties, and knows it. 'Old age depends on the way you look at life, Doly. Mine hasn't arrived yet.'

'The other thing that hasn't arrived is your buying the Villa Dohlen, Gabby.' Emil shakes with the effects of Parkinson's. Has difficulty walking. And resents the helping hands.

Gabby signals to the waiter at the *Restaurant am Pier* in Cuxhaven. Which she has booked for the celebratory dinner. 'You've put the Moët I ordered on ice?'

'Of course, gnädige Frau.'

'We're ready for you to serve it.'

'Real champagne, Gabby? Isn't that ridiculously extravagant?' Emil's face takes on a sullen look. Fixed by the paralysis.

'Sparkling wine is very good, I know. Particularly German sparkling wine. But tonight we're celebrating something special.'

'Hear, hear.' Gemma smiles at her mother. 'Gabby has done brilliantly in the last twenty years. I remember her fiftieth birthday. A budding real estate agent who hadn't come near her potential. No need to think in terms of years alone — after all, anyone who lives long enough becomes seventy. No, Gabby hauled herself out of trouble by her own doing. Quite enough cause for celebration with any amount of champagne!'

The waiter has opened three bottles and has started to pour.

'Thank you, Gemma. I appreciate your little speech. And of course it is my seventieth birthday, and I am very happy — and grateful — to be celebrating it with my family. But it is not the reason for the champagne.'

Doly's smoke rings are perfect. As ever. 'My God, Gabby. Don't tell us you're engaged again. Who is it this time?'

'No, Doly. No more Hans Weisses in the closet.' She grins around the table. 'Any more guesses? What about you, Moppel? Any ideas?'

'You've bought your umpteenth house?'

'True. But not the whole truth.'

'On another massive mortgage, sure...'

Gemma, sitting opposite Gabby, radiates across. 'You've done it, haven't you? I won't spoil your announcement, Gabby. But I always knew you could. Would! I am so proud of you.'

Gabby stands. 'Gemma is right. And partly, I have to say, her faith in me helped me get there. I signed the papers this morning. I have bought the Villa Dohlen back from the Schwanenbruch Council.'

'Are you crazy, Gabby? You've bought back that white elephant of a place?' Emil's scalp, a mottled puce with scabs of healed skin cancer, narrows already tiny eyes. His ears are mutilated stumps of flesh, the healed scabs like currants in a bun.

'You've really done it, Gabby?' Doly's eyes water. 'But what on earth are you going to do with it?'

'Before we go into all that, please rise. I would like to make a toast to Emil Julius Dohlen. Not to the man, who had his faults, or to the money he made, which he couldn't take with him. What I would like you to raise your glasses to is to his spirit. Which transformed a poor, downtrodden wheelwright's son into a millionaire when that was what amounts to a billionaire now. The grit which made him travel to the New World with a few marks in his pocket. The grasp of what that world had to offer. The spunk which helped him through early trials, the courage which helped him to see the silver lining. His spirit — and all it stands for. That was his legacy to us. It's taken me almost seventy years to recognise the true Dohlen Inheritance!' Gabby lifts her glass high, and drinks.

'The true Dohlen Inheritance!' Gemma, Nina and Kamilla chant in unison.

'It wasn't our only inheritance.' Doly stares into the dregs of her glass. 'There was another one. And we all have it.'

'You're talking about the Bender Inheritance. Something none of us who have that gene can ever quite forget. If it shows its bald patches when we're young, we cringe and hide it under a wig as quickly as we can. If it doesn't strike till later, we live with the sword of Damocles blighting our youth. Leading us astray.'

'Exactly, Gabby. Neatly put.' Doly lifts champagne to her sister.

'Thank you, Doly. However, what none of us have ever voiced is that a negative may be just as important as a positive. Maybe more important.'

Gemma's head jerks up. 'As far as Mathematics is concerned, the negative *is* just as important as the positive. And, of course, two negatives make a positive.'

'Perhaps psychology is more to the point. Transforming a negative into a positive is what gives the strength to achieve.' Gabby takes a long drink. 'I'm not getting at my mother. She had many sterling qualities. But she thought that the man who married her without worrying about her errant gene was what she had to celebrate. That's what she taught me, handed on to me.

'It took me a long time to discover how wrong she was. Two husbands and a man who wouldn't commit to marriage, to be precise. After he died, I had to stand alone. With or without hair. That's when I really knew.'

'Now Nina has found the cure it's no longer significant.'

'It's still there, Doly. Still hanging over whoever inherits it. Still demanding to be taken account of. Emma's prize was a man big enough to ignore the threat, to kick it in the teeth. And all of us here have a part of that. It isn't enough.'

'Your prize is to know you don't need handouts. That what you're saying?'

'I'm saying I don't need a prize, Gemma. All I need is to make the best of what I've got.'

'The parable of the talents.'

'When you've finished congratulating yourself, Gabby, what the hell are you going to do with that bloody white elephant?' Moppel's eyes cloud milky blue.

'That's where I need your help, Moppel. And yours, Doly. I'd like to reconstruct the house to an exact replica of how it was when our parents were alive.'

'What on earth for?'

'As a present to Schwanenbruch. And Germany. Now that Gemma and Nina are well provided for by courtesy of Rolf Ferent's third wife, and Kamilla has inherited Yolanthe's house, I'd like to spend the money I made on the Villa Dohlen.'

'But what are you going to do with it, Gabby?'

'While the three of us — Emil Julius's children — are alive, and wish to spend time in Schwanenbruch, it will be at our disposal. After our deaths I want the house to be given, in perpetuity, to the village of Schwanenbruch. With a large enough trust fund set up for its upkeep.'

'But that will cost an absolute fortune!' Moppel's head shakes, not only with Parkinson's.

'Money is relative. I have the means to do that, and I don't think I'm doing anybody down. Future generations of villagers can be proud of one of their most illustrious sons.'

'And daughters!' Gemma puts in.

'And, I hope, his issue down the generations. To show what Germany was, and what she can be again.'

THE EEL KING

Many years ago, before the new dyke was built, farmer Peck and his wife Sill lived just beyond the dyke. At high tide the couple's two pitch black horses were harnessed to their large wagon and pulled along the beach for Peck and Sill to gather all the driftwood right from under their neighbours' noses. That's how they kept warm while their neighbours shivered.

Peck was as rich as he was miserly and mean. He fed his workers the worst food in the whole village, and if anyone asked him for a bundle of straw to bed down on, Peck would slam the door in his face. There was never any question of Christmas or Easter gifts for the children, and if a beggar should chance to come to their farm Peck and Sill would set their big black dog on him.

One autumn night Peck and Sill wandered on to the beach after dusk. They saw a golden star fall into a small creek and Sill noticed an eel, as thick as Peck's arm, snaking across and making for the deep black pool which was obviously his home. He wore a golden crown on his head and had a silver bangle round his tail.

'Look what I've found, Peck!' Sill cried out. 'It's the Eel King himself.'

Peck rushed over, speared the big fish with his pitchfork, tore off his crown and silver bangle, and shoved him into a sack. Then he threw it on to the cart.

The eel cried out:

> Peck and Sill
> This is my will
> Take the silver and gold
> Which you may hold
> But woe betide if you take more

Neither Peck nor Sill allowed themselves to be deterred from their foul intentions. 'Sunday's the day after tomorrow,' Peck told his wife. 'That fat, juicy eel is just what I want for my Lord's Day breakfast. I want him fried up good and fine.'

The couple drove home and Peck slipped the fish into the eel basket kept in the water-filled ditch next to the farm. No sooner had the pair gone to bed that night than a huge storm blew up. Hail crashed against the windowpanes, the wind howled in the chimney. Yet in spite of all the noise they could hear the eel's refrain:

> **Peck and Sill**
> **This is my will**
> **Take the silver and gold**
> **Which you may hold**
> **But woe betide if you take more**

The couple again ignored the warning, even when they discovered half their barn roof missing the next day. The following night another storm blew up. Lightning, accompanied by a cacophony of thunderclaps, lit up the sky as though it were daylight. Their whole house shook, and the couple could hear the Eel King call out as before. And, though lightning struck the big oak behind their barn and split it into a thousand pieces, Peck and Sill still looked forward to their Sunday feast.

Peck could hardly wait for daybreak. No sooner had Sunday dawned then he fetched the fish from the basket, cut off his head and pulled the skin over his tail. He brought him, still wriggling, to his wife. 'Here's our Sunday feast!' he called out.

When the other people on the farm heard Peck's shout they were horrified and ran out of the house, up the road and to the village church. Except for Sill. She lost no time in cutting the fish into pieces for frying.

That's when the storm broke out again. A huge black cloud advanced over the Watt, a large black arm came out of the clouds and threw a glowing thunderbolt at Peck's house, smashing it into smithereens. Not content with that it went on to make an enormous hole in the dyke. Fire leapt out of the earth, and the floodwater streamed through the dyke.

After the floods had subsided the village people came back to Peck's farm to inspect the damage. The place where the house had stood had turned into a deep dark pool surrounded by the smell of sulphur and pitch. That's how the villagers knew the devil had taken Peck and his wife down to hell with him.

The men tried to repair the hole in the dyke before the winter frosts. Nothing seemed to work, every time they built it up it crumbled. Until a limping old woman, her stick as gnarled as her face, appeared from nowhere. She was carrying a bucket in which she had three young eels.

'These are the sons of the Eel King,' she told the astounded villagers. 'Sell Peck and Sill's land, use the gold and silver you get for it to make three golden crowns and three silver bangles. Set the crowns on their heads, and the bangles on their tails, and put the Eel King's little sons back into the pool their father came from.'

The desperate villagers followed her advice and from that moment the dyke held.

Ever since that time three young eels live in the deep black pond. And when a golden star falls from heaven their silver bangles can clearly be seen glinting through the water. This happens only rarely. But when it does, those who see the bangles are blessed with luck for the rest of their lives.

CHAPTER 5

Schwanenbruch, Summer 1981

'Surely the red salon was decorated in red, Doly! Why else would we have called it that?'

'You've got it wrong. The wallpaper was white.' Doly sits with her legs out straight. Her figure is too heavy for the crossed ankles which rucked a tight skirt high, showed off sexy legs.

Gabby closes her eyes. She travels into her childhood, sees their mother rocking in her chair overlooking the garden, her sewing basket open by her side and Vater's holed sock heel stretched over the darning mushroom. There were always fresh flowers in the room. Red poppies, roses, tulips. 'I think we're both right. The paper was a deep red flock on a cream or white background. A symbolised flower.'

'The Lieblingsblüte — the legendary flower of purest love.' The rigid mask of Parkinsonism on Moppel's face almost becomes soft. Washed-out blue marbles are sunk, unmoving, in the dips and bumps of white scar tissue, his ears amputated into small flaps. The skin cancer legacy of messing about in boats. Under a Long Island sun cruel on a naked North German head.

'You're absolutely right, Moppel. How clever of you.' Gabby's affection has grown to love with frequent kindnesses. On her part. 'It reminds me of the old story: when faced with telling her prospective husband about the errant gene, our father said: "I have enough for two". That's what the flower symbolises.'

'I guess so.' The gargoyle smile turns sister into mother. Scuffed shoes shuffle behind the agile women. Fangs of dribbling saliva alienate strangers, mumbling speech needs a translator. Bedwetting weakness, no memory, demands without compensations are shutting doors even Gabby can't prise open. It's his last summer in Schwanenbruch. The poor man doesn't even realise it.

'What happened to Mutti's boats?' Doly stalks round the room frowning at gold-framed Rhine maidens displayed on cliffs. Behind glass. Not Emma's style at all. 'She had a collection of wood-framed prints. Tall ships, beautiful clippers, skiffs and sloops. And luggers plying the Elbe.'

'All looted. Why don't we visit antique print dealers? You'll spot the right replacements, Doly. Maybe even discover the originals. We'll see the walls are dressed again.'

Doly's eyes are as marbled as Moppel's as her nostrils flare at her sister. 'The chairs were covered in red-plush velvet. Braided at the back. You were never any good at decorating.'

Gabby remembers something else, lets it pass. Her decorating skills are one of her business triumphs. 'We'll choose the right material, don't worry.'

The Villa Dohlen is, as Gabby promised, being lovingly recreated from childhood memories. With help from servants who remember domestic quarters better than the Dohlen inheritors. Except for the kitchen. Moppel remembers Rula. Her arsenal of wooden spoons. The scrubbed table, the stone sink, the enormous range. Each burnished pot and pan, the fluted jelly moulds, the bread tins baked black. The steel knives are still there, pitted with rust.

Ursula's grandson is a heating engineer cum plumber whose craft has been handed down the generations. He restores the original central heating system, the boiler, the wash-house with its tiled floor, the weaving shed.

The bathroom is still a marvel of plumbing skill combined with touches of decorating genius. The small, furled tub with mixer tap and showerhead is centred on the longest wall. The large room is tiled in plain cream surrounded by an enchanting frieze of tulips and flags, marguerites and flax fluttered by butterflies, hovered by dragonflies. The marble double basin for Emil and Emma, the indoor toilet with solid oak seat and cover, are all intact. With the original terra cotta floor laid in the Lieblingsblüte pattern.

A single tile-picture of a swan ovalled in green rushes swims majestically towards the bather.

What vision. An indoor bathroom few of the older village cottages have even now, outclassing the cubicles built into modern houses.

'One thing we haven't seen to yet, Gabby.' Doly opens the door to the steep staircase leading to the turret room. 'Vater's last hobby. His leather volumes of Roman and Greek classics. He had them moved up there. When he turfed Tante Hannah out and took the room over.'

'Brilliant, Doly. I'd entirely forgotten. There was no sign of them when Ursula and I looked at the place. There was a terrible mess of bats and birds, spiders and woodworm. Not to mention dry rot. Can you remember any of the titles?'

Past memories stir old muscles into young spurts. Doly tries to scamper, wheezes up, pulls at the roof-space cupboard door. Painted in.

Gabby and Moppel, labouring after her, hear heaves and bumps, kicks and drags. Moppel produces a penknife. Doly loosens the paintwork, they all pull.

Doly sweeps aside cobwebs and mouse droppings, crawls in. Her head reappears. 'I stacked them like building blocks to hide behind. See?'

She heaves the doors wide. Clouds of fuming mould convulse them in sneezes. Disturbing scuttling beetles and scurrying spiders. 'They're heavy as well as filthy.' She blinks away tears as she remembers the time, so long ago, when she hid here to avoid being sent back to the States. A time when Liese still cared and stopped her throwing herself off the window ledge.

'Good work, Doly. Ursula's grandson can drag them out. We'll salvage what we can, replace the rest.' Gabby tours the almost-empty room their father used to hide his loneliness. 'We need a desk and chair. Some bookcases. Anyone remember anything else?'

'Not off hand. This needs a bit of thought, Gabby.'

'No rush.' Gabby leads Moppel to the only chair available. The St Nicolaikirche bells ring noon. Filling the turret with triumphant reverberating chimes.

Schwanenbruch, Late summer 1981

'Well, Doly. You sound quite spry. Though a little heavier.'

'Gardening keeps me fit. Walking with Buffy through the woods forces me out even in the worst weather. No complaints, Liesi.'

'I wouldn't expect any. Hard to think of you as seventy! Both of us. How did it happen?'

'Beats me.' Doly basks in Liesi's smile. It reminds her of the love and friendship the two of them shared in their youth, seem to have left behind for so many years.

'I've always wanted to see the Aurora Borealis.' Liesi's voice is husky. 'Has to be this year or never. My eyes are letting me down.'

Doly's blue irises blur with tears, not age. Lieselotte's once sturdy frame is too fragile. Her iron grey hair points the angular jawbone. Deep folds from elongated nose to thin lips suggest pain.

'I've come up with an idea. One last trip, Doly. You and me. Let's take a cruise to the Arctic Circle. My treat this time.'

'Just the two of us?' A caress whispered on the breeze.

Stick arms circle Doly's plump shoulders. 'You be my eyes, Doly. Stand at the rail with me, fill in what I can't see. You've always been poetic.'

'We'll see the Northern Lights.'

'Only in winter, Doly...'

'They've been known in summer. Eskimos say they're spirits playing football with a walrus skull. Sounds like us when we were young, so I know they'll greet us.' They're also known in the Artic as flaming torches carried by departed souls guiding travellers to the afterlife. Maybe she and Liesi will be in a shipwreck, drown together, enjoy eternal friendship.

'Let's book now, Doly. Go on the next available boat.'

Doly's feet dance across the cobbles, her arm links through Lieselotte's, dragging her along. 'Remember Morocco? That awful Consul in Madrid?'

'Are you expecting us to cause that kind of havoc as septuagenarians?' Liesi's deep laugh hasn't changed.

'I think we should have a damned good try.'

'I'm off with Liesi for a month, Gabby. Then back to Sussex.'

When her lids cover her eyes, shutting out animation, Gabby's age shows in a shrunken frame and rounded shoulders. 'We've nearly finished the house, Doly. Don't you want to celebrate the grand finale?'

So many summers in Schwanenbruch in succession. And this her last. Older sister adversary has been hospitable, put everything at Doly's disposal, paid the bills without reckoning.

Now that they've recreated the rooms of her childhood, Doly's dreams are all used up. Only the eternal ghost riders and the dykeman left. Time to return to more recent roots. Where the lanes lead nowhere in particular.

'I'll be back to say goodbye after the trip. My Schwanenbruch times are over.'

Gabby's drained face. 'You aren't well?'

'The restored Villa Dohlen is your house, Gabby. This year sees it complete. I know you did it for all of us, and I'm grateful. But I've never wanted to be the spare wheel.'

'It's as much yours as mine...'

'Not true. For the first time in my life I'm all out of fantasy. Your achievement, Gabby. Solo. Congrats.'

Gabby kisses her sister's cheek. 'You have your own world, Doly. Your own achievements. This time we'll part as friends. What do you say?'

'I say amen.'

Arctic Circle, October 1981

'Just look at this Smörgåsbord, Liesi. Isn't it enough to make you want to spend all our time in the dining room?'

'Wonderful. What d'you think this is?' Lieselotte's head nods agreement, but her spoon clatters the dish, splatters oily fish.

'Your favourite Matjes herring! You can't have forgotten.' Doly piles her plate high, shrugging aside medical warnings. She's got the painkillers. Why worry about length of life when quality is what matters? 'Hold on, Liesi. You're spilling that soup all over the place.'

'Sorry. I can't get used to the movement of the boat.' Lieselotte looks at another diner's plate and misses Doly's. 'Aren't you taking rather more than you should? Remember…'

'No medical lectures, please. This is our last fling.' She slaps her plate on the table, catches her friend's arm. 'I didn't mean it literally, Liesi!'

Her friend's sudden paling, grabbing at her for support.

'You feeling seasick? There's hardly any swell.'

'I'm going to have to tell you, Doly. I'm going blind. I should have told you before we came, but I'd hoped…'

'It's all right, Liesi. You asked me to be your eyes. I'll lead you to our table, then heap your plate with goodies. I'll choose well for you, blood sister. Because I remember your passions. Vividly.'

'Hold on to my arm, Liesi. Are you cold? Should I fetch you another cardigan?'

'I'm fine. What do you see?'

Mist dipping into an inky sea. Dull grey sky without a star in sight. The Northern lights a Canadian memory. 'Such beauty, Liesi. The sky's midnight blue streaked with licking flames. Crimson and orange, with stabs of green which look like swords cutting the sky to shreds.'

Lieselotte's hand is warm in Doly's. 'I can hear the crackling of charged electrons. All round us.'

'They're turning to streamers now. Luminous, expanding arcs circling the sky in red and orange. Like the fireworks at the Schützenfest but on God's scale. Can you sense the light on your eyes, Liesi? Feel the magic?'

'Not really magic. Magnetic fields. Trapped particles impacting the upper atmosphere.'

'It's Odin riding his eight-legged horse in his race with Hrungnir.' Was Liesi always so unpoetic? She remembers her blood sister before the Nazis and the medical career took over and turned her from the sublime to the banal. 'Before he's slain by Thor with his hammer Mjølnir. They're galloping across the sky at the speed of light, the horses' iron shoes scattering brilliant showers.'

'The collisions between solar and terrestrial atoms result in the glow in the upper atmosphere called the aurora. The glow may be vivid where the lines of magnetic force converge near the magnetic poles.'

'Nothing like that at all. The aurora is the golden arc of friendship. Which will live forever in a firmament of fire and love which no earthly force can destroy.'

'Your flames are still hot, Doly. Good for you. Mine are nothing but grey ashes.'

'Glowing embers. All they need is a puff from my bellows, dear Liesi.'

'What I thought success was illusion. All that ambition kept me from my girls' childhood. You were the one who got it right, Doly. You spent your son's childhood in his company.'

Where Liesi's three daughters think the world of her, Ross resents Doly. Because he prefers his father and cannot stomach his mother's capriciousness. Which did affect him. How did that happen? 'Only the one of them.' She can't acknowledge that other, even to Liesi. Nina is kinder, more thoughtful than Ross. And has visited as often as she can. On her way to see Gabby.

'Better than my none.' Searching hands wrap around Doly. 'I wrote this note for you. To post after you'd gone back to England. The coward's way out.' She tears the letter up, throws it overboard. 'I haven't told my family yet. You're the guinea pig. I have cancer. Terminal. I'm going blind because the fastest growing tumour is in my brain. Pressing on my optic nerves.'

Doly's sobs are swallowed by the wind. Her tears are distinguished from salt spray by warmer temperature.

'I've been in treatment for a year. No one can help me. Not Joseph, not my doctor daughter, not me. Cancer still conquers medicine most of the time. There isn't a cure. This is goodbye.'

One last adventure with the woman who filled her youth with love. With whom she travelled to Morocco, to Spain, to the Lüneburg Heath. Her constant companion through life. In spirit, if not in the flesh. And now the flesh will soon be gone.

Their spirits will ride the Watt like the ghost rider. Two lone, white figures on a darkening plain.

THE HORSE'S SAVIOUR

A pious man, a freeman from a humble house, had ridden hard through autumn mists and gales to attend evening Mass in the nearest prayer house to his home. The district had no church, for it was too poor. But the man did not wish to miss the celebration for the great apostle of the Saxons, St Willehad.

As soon as the service was over, the devout man saddled his horse, prepared to brave the wind which had risen to storm force, and the waters of the River Weser which had already burst its banks.

The other churchgoers did their best to dissuade their fellow worshipper from riding home that night. But he told them not to worry, he'd foreseen the problem and had left a light burning in his window. It would guide him safely back through the dark, tempestuous night. And he set out on his way.

He had gone a good way when, quite suddenly, his guiding light went out. His horse lost his footing and stumbled into marshy soil. The rider was quick enough to jump off as soon as he noticed the danger, but he couldn't avoid his animal being dragged into the mud. He tried everything he knew to save the animal, and he called for help, but his cries were carried away on the wind.

That's when he prayed to the patron saint of horses and smiths, St Loye. He promised him a chapel on the spot he was standing on if he saved his horse for him.

Within minutes the lone man heard the sound of wagon wheels and the stomp of horses' hooves. The local miller was driving home late that night. The two men managed to drag the horse out of the mire and save him.

The reverent freeman kept his word. He built a small chapel on the very spot where his horse nearly lost his life, as a reminder and a warning for all who were fond of animals.

CHAPTER 6

Sussex, Autumn 1991

'All right, Buffy. All right, boy. We'll walk round the garden.'

Doly clips the puppy's lead to his collar. She can't manage a proper walk. No more roaming through the deep enfolding woods around her. No coming across the sudden flight of pheasant, the dart of deer. Her garden is her world. Better than nothing.

She's tired of the terrier puppy's lurching strains and thumping tail, longing for sleep as soon as the sun leaves a golden haze over the cornfields. Buffy the sixth seems livelier than earlier Jack Russells. Perhaps she's the one that's changed. How did she make eighty indulging in all those forbidden smokes and frowned-on habits? So much for keeping to the straight and narrow.

Ross arranged the birthday party. A low-key family affair. Her son, divorced and without children, invited Gemma and her family. It was too strenuous a trip for Gabby. Buffy the fifth was barely alive, and Erskine was dead. The present appears peopled with ghosts. Not just the generation previous to hers. Piers, Lieselotte, Moppel, Roger Quinnel, Ursula. And Gabby disconcertingly benign.

A tour round Ross's splendid new offices, a beautifully set out meal. Polite chit-chat while walking on egg shells.

Doly's thoughts fled to Schwanenbruch. Lieselotte's will left Doly a piece of irascible Karl Waldeck's land. The home paddock where Flitsi galloped in answer to Doly's spurs and Lieselotte's claps. The true Schimmelreiter now.

Doly's eyes mist with faraway scenes. Riding on the Watt, swinging on an old branch with a bosom friend, stalking the future. What does it profit a woman to outlive her friends?

Ross is making noises about a nursing home. She's shrugged them off. She's staying put in her little wing at Dramlings. She's compromised by wearing a panic button to summon telephonic help in an emergency. Not that she wears it. What can go wrong, here, in her home? Who'd want to steal bits and bobs of furniture little better than firewood?

Half the proceeds from selling Dramlings are safe in a building society account. It brings in enough income for modest needs. She has beauty and privacy. The new owners of Dramlings are only in residence during school holidays.

'Not so fast, Buffy boy!'

Doly keeps her frame upright and her arms strong by gardening. A younger man has taken old Fred Hawkin's place. He digs for her. Leaving Doly to kneel in beloved soil, to plant her spuds and lettuces, peas and beans.

'I saw death walking beside the old man,' she told Gemma the last time her niece visited. One last, surviving friend, younger than Doly's contemporaries who are no longer there.

'Heel, Buffy!' She pulls the lead tight. She'd love to let him go, give him his freedom. Too irresponsible. She's only had him for two weeks. He'd charge off into the woods where she can't follow him. Was she wrong to take on a puppy now?

Right or wrong, she needs him. The warm licks across her face, the strong lunge of a young body jumping up at her, the love he shows.

She bends down and hugs him. His muscles judder excitement as a bat whirls round them. He strains away. Even Buffy has no time for her. She straightens, feels the lead slide from her fingers, grabs tight through the loop to hold it. She won't be able to sleep all night if Buffy rushes off.

September balm. A harvest moon flits in and out of clouds. Bunny eyes brighten into jewels as moonbeams dance a tango of marauding theft in her vegetable patch. Buffy's terrier muscles stiffen, his nose points. Longing to guard his territory, to give chase.

'Just a walk, Buffy, dear.' She slips the lead loop further up her arm, twists it tight.

A wolfish spring as the puppy, unable to restrain himself, charges forward. 'Stay, boy!'

She isn't strong enough to hold him. She teeters reluctantly, using what strength she has to tighten the noose around her wrist.

The thump of the buck's warning, his white tail up, devastation scurried through her vegetables. Buffy leaps and bounds, dragging her unwillingly along.

The forgotten rake left lying on the path is invisible. It hits her on the forehead, stunning her. She falls on hard stepping stones, hears the crack of bone. And Buffy yapping madly, frustrated from the chase.

The pain is agony. Sitting up is worse. The puppy prancing around her, barking, wild.

'Sit, boy.'

Commands should be loud, determined, strong. Hers are murmurs of love, not direction. His grunts turn wild, loud, insistent. He tugs at the lead. Circles her.

'Calm down, Buffy dear. I can't...'

Her leg is enmeshed in the straining lead. Cold, hard fear chokes further sounds. The rescue button is on her table indoors. She's fifty yards from her back door, sixty from the phone. And helpless.

The dog's decreasing circles increase her terror. He yelps into her face showing fangs. She finds the strength to untwist the lead, slip the loop off over her hand.

The terrier circles draw the lead tighter, then he turns, charges 'round anti-clockwise and clears away. Straight through the beech hedge she planted decades ago. Howling after his prey, deaf to her cries.

The pain has become excruciating. Her voice has gone as spittle runs down frozen lips. Her fingers clutch at the cracks between the stepping stones. To try to drag herself indoors for shelter. To summon help.

She hasn't the strength. Or the will. Death at last? Here, alone, at one with the earth she's always loved? Buffy is back. Lying beside her on the path. Giving some warmth. The night is damp and cold. How long before she dies?

Night dew falls. Thicker clouds obliterate the moon now whitening. Bats swoop, owls hoot. The busy night life of the country surrounds her. She grabs at dying lavender, breaks small branches, places them under her head for a pillow. A bier of herbs.

THE YELLOW EMPEROR'S INTERNAL MEDICINE CHEST

When a human being grows old, the bones become dry and brittle like straw (osteoporosis), the flesh sags and there is much air within the thorax (emphysema) and pains within the stomach (chronic indigestion). There is an uncomfortable feeling within the heart (angina or the fluttering of a chronic arrhythmia), the nape of the neck and the top of the shoulders are contracted, the body burns with fever (urinary-tract infections), the bones are stripped and laid bare of flesh (loss of lean muscle mass), eyes bulge and sag. When the pulse of the liver (right heart failure) can be seen but the eye can no longer recognise a seam (cataracts), death will strike. The limit of a human's life can be perceived when he or she can no longer overcome his or her diseases. Then the time of death has arrived. Not to strike. To set free.

(Huang Ti Nei Ching Su Wen (The Yellow Emperor's Classic of Internal Medicine, 1,500 BC)

CHAPTER 7

Vienna, September 1991

The pain is overwhelming. Gabby gasps as she feels her vertebrae jar. Ominous signs were already apparent in Schwanenbruch. Two weeks before she left, she stumbled against the uneven cobbles in the Osterstrasse, and fell. She was furious with Schwanenbruch Council for refusing to replace old cobblestones with smooth macadam.

Osteoporosis has caused problems for years. Never ones she couldn't overcome. Willpower combined with analgesics allow her to choose her path. Dead end is better than a chauffeured highway. Today she's looking for a lay-by.

Gabby heaves her right leg over the bedside with both hands, pushes the left leg after it. She slides slowly off the bed and tries to stand. Sinks to the floor.

Weak flesh must be overcome by a strong spirit. Gemma and Marina are arriving from England this morning, Nina from New York tomorrow. One last enjoyable birthday celebration with the gang of four — Nina, Kamilla, Gemma and Marina. She's Gabby's only granddaughter. She's always wanted a son, and now that she has six grandchildren Marina is the one she's closest to. Promoted her to honorary daughter for the annual pilgrimage to Vienna. Golden September days after the Schwanenbruch summers following Gabby's seventy-first birthday. She still spends her summers there, but always celebrates her birthday in Vienna. With four honourable daughters. Feasting in Yolanthe's house, where Kamilla is sole heir.

Gabby lies in hope for several minutes. The pain increases. She can't move, can't reach the phone. She places a tentative finger on the red button 'the girls' arranged for her. Is this the emergency they droned on about? She can't even crawl. Her index finger presses down.

'Hello? Can you hear me, Frau Dohlen?'

Hear, yes. But she can't answer. What have her vocal chords to do with bone disease?

'We'll be with you in five minutes, Frau Dohlen.'

Doubts cross her mind about the wonders of modern technology. Would she be wiser to welcome stealthy death? She's nearly eighty-five, well over her biblical score. Why be greedy?

The rescue squad is already at her doorbell. They ring. And ring.

'I can't get over to let you in!' Her voice has returned full volume. Do they think she's summoned them for company?

'Your key is blocking us, Frau Dohlen. We'll have to get a locksmith.'

She leaves the key in the lock so she'll remember where it is. Nor forget to take it with her on her daily outings. Embarrassment surges adrenaline. She clutches the bedstead, levers to her knees, crawls. Grabs at furniture to help propel her. 'I'm coming.'

The doors in these old houses are so high, the locks out of her reach.

'We'll sort it out, Frau Dohlen. Just take it easy.'

She's not a child. She grabs the door knob in her left hand, hoists herself up to reach the key. Turns it.

A worthy trio of busybody middle age blusters in, concerned and voluble. Great bumbling bottoms unbalance her, lead to her bed.

It takes time to get her breath back. 'I'm so sorry to bother you. If you could find Frau Kanneva for me.' The Hausbesorgerin phones every morning to check on her needs. Shops, cleans, chats if Gabby wants it. Never rattles at her with stupid questions.

Frau Kanneva has already arrived. She ushers out the rescue services with honeyed words. She helps Gabby dress, straps her into her corset, her best clothes. Gemma and Marina are due any minute.

Gabby is longing for a nap. She sits upright in her favourite chair, ramrods her spine, swallows the pain away, slips in and out of consciousness, dozes. She signals Frau Kanneva to bring another painkiller. Hears the doorbell ring.

'Grüss Gott, Frau Kanneva.' Gemma's puzzled voice. 'Is something wrong? Is my mother ill?'

'Welcome to Vienna, gnädige Frau.'

Gabby can't make out anything more than the mumble jumble of treachery. Is even Frau Kanneva going to let her down?

Gemma and Marina throng the double door with ivory smiles. Gabby's forgotten to put in her teeth. She keeps her mouth shut, her lips wide and nods fit to bring on a headache. She succeeds in producing a response of kissing which she can do without. She stops the nodding. They sit down.

They talk. She hears the singing of the North Sea waves washing the shore. Here there's only the boring ebb and tide of small talk. She fixes her lips wide in a lie, leaves out the nod. Gemma produces a bottle of brandy. Bright girl. All Gabby needs is a drink.

'You get the glasses, Marina.'

More chatter. Less demanding, more casual. Gemma and Marina flit about. Produce coffee, pour brandy. Why don't they help her put the glass to her lips? Gemma catches on. Sends Marina on an errand and catches the drips of liquid trickling down stiff lips. But manages to pour some down. Excellent.

'Perhaps you'd like to have a rest, Gabby?'

How will she get undressed, get into bed?

'We'll help you into bed, shall we? We'll just take off your shoes.'

She blinks her gratitude at tact. Avoiding nods. Frau Kanneva can help her undress. Later.

'Make yourselves at home,' she whispers at them. 'Help yourselves to anything you like. I'll be better within the hour.'

There are no chinks of light through the curtains. She must have slept till nightfall. Have Gemma and Marina left for the apartment she puts at their disposal?

She needs all her strength to throw back the Federbett. She repeats her manoeuvre of the morning, lands in a heap by the bed.

The door opens and Gemma rushes in. 'We did ask you to call us if you want to get up, Gabby. You're quite weak, you know. The doctor came and said there was nothing to be done except rest.'

'I'm better now. I want to sit in the living room with you. Hear your news.'

Gemma and Marina twitter around, irritating her. The ringing of the phone. Gemma answers it. 'Who is it?' The staccato scratchings are so loud they travel across the room. Gemma looks at Gabby. 'It's Erika. From Schwanenbruch. Shall I tell her you'll ring her in a day or two?'

'Hand me the phone, Marina.' She'll take calls in her own house. She may be dying, but she's not yet dead. 'Erika! How nice to hear from you.'

Bubble, bubble. Toil and trouble.

'How's Tante Martha?' Ninety-three years old and doing well…

Babble, babble. Senseless gabble.

'I shall be back again quite soon,' she hears herself say. Looking down from the ceiling. 'I've already booked my ticket. Soon after my birthday. That's when I'm coming home.'

The receiver drops from hands whose muscles are too frail to hold it. Marina picks it up, Gemma adds another cushion behind her back. They sit and keep her company. And though they talk Gabby can't understand a word they say.

They call Frau Kanneva to help her undress, wash, get to bed.

She always reads in bed. Tonight is no different from any other. 'Marina. You will find my book on the bedside table.'

She takes it, opens it at the page marked with her bookmark. Places it on the Federbett in front of her.

Complete gibberish. The letters slide and blur and she can't make them out. Has Marina given her a different book? In an unknown script?

Marina takes the book out of her hands, gently turns it round, places it back again.

She's too tired to read. Why do the young think they know it all?

'If you need us, ring this bell.'

Kamilla's turned up as well. What for? They're not going out to Grinzing until her birthday. Tomorrow. And tomorrow and tomorrow. Sweeps on its rapid pace from year to year. And ends life all too soon.

She wakes to find the lights on in her room. Why? She likes to sleep with them off. She leans over to turn the bedside lamp off, feels a piercing stab of pain. Can't stop a cry.

The rush of three pairs of feet into her room. 'Something wrong?'

'I had this vivid dream,' she hears a gravel voice. Echoing from behind the curtain across the window. 'There are three ladies in my room. I would like to leave, but I can't go until the fourth one comes. Where is she? Where is the fourth lady?'

'Don't worry, Gabby. Nina's already left New York. Her plane gets in at eight this morning.'

What are they talking about? Not Nina! 'The fourth lady! Where is the fourth lady?' She sees her lying in the huge four-poster, surrounded by cream silk sheets.

'Take it!' she remembers Mutti saying. Forceful. Unmistakable.

She never wanted the locket. Not then, not now, not ever.

'Nina will be here when you wake up.' Hands push her back. Not unkindly. She hasn't the strength to fight.

'Many Happy Returns, Gabby!' Gemma's cheerful morning face glows round the breakfast table. Set with birthday cards, presents, red roses. Fresh coffee steaming welcome. And Nina has arrived.

Almost like old times. Gemma, Nina, Kamilla and Marina with Gabby in her apartment. Fresh rolls collected from the Augustinerstrasse. Just down the road. Best baker in Vienna.

The last breakfast. Her life, long, eventful, with its violent ups and downs, is coming to its close. She is content. Because she has achieved what she set out to do. Survived being orphaned, the wretched gene, two world wars. Made a myriad mistakes but — Holy Moses! — learned the lesson. The hand life deals you is a given. What counts is how you play the game.

Divorced, widowed, jilted, she finally triumphed over the ties to men. The bonus years from seventy to eighty-five were as good as any of the others. A baton to be passed on.

But not the locket!

Concerned faces all round her. 'How do you feel? Would you like Kamilla to call the party off?'

'No. You're all here with me, Kamilla has prepared a feast, my friends are invited. We will celebrate.' She feels the strain already sapping her energy. A crucial task still left to do. 'One thing before we go.'

'A nice long rest? We should leave you to it?'

Why chatter instead of listen? 'I want to give each one of you an unbirthday present. You'll have to help me.'

'Presents? On your birthday?'

'Marina, you admire Max Weiler's painting. This is his finest. Take it now.' The gap on her living room wall will not matter to her.

Goggle, goggle. Flip the toggle.

'You always wanted the inlaid table, Kamilla. It's yours.'

Wind and weather. Spoils the heather.

'And you, Nina. I'd like you to have this chandelier. To reflect your brilliant writing as it syndicates throughout the world.'

Never, never. Gone for ever.

Her father's portrait stares down at them. As if he were still alive. The old man's look has lost none of its air of determination and success.

'I want you to have his likeness, Gemma.' Silver fish eyes whose blue is almost gone gutter into life. She doesn't know why herself. The eldest child? Neither here nor there. The liveliest? Not true. The one she values most? Not really. The least obvious of the quartet. And therefore the right choice.

Gemma stares at the portrait on the wall. Enormous, weighty, ungainly. 'Thank you, Gabby. I'll take good care of it.' The soul behind the smile Gabby has never been attracted to before. 'I'll see he lives.'

'I'm not suggesting Gemma's too old, Gabby. But she's over sixty. She can hardly emulate your father at this stage. Shouldn't you be handing him on to Marina? She's Gemma's daughter, after all...'

Meddle, meddle, push the pedal.

It's not a question of qualifications. Quite the contrary. 'Now then, children. That's exhausted me. What about pouring me some coffee? Don't forget to add a decent measure of schnapps.'

'Shall I help you get ready, Gabby?' Marina is watching her as she tries to put on her jewellery, to comb her hair.

'Perhaps you could do the pearls up for me.' She knows she can't see to tidy the wig she's just had made. White, a hint or two of auburn to stop it being snowy.

The perfume spray doesn't work. Marina turns it round and presses a few bursts around her. Takes her comb and carefully arranges strands of hair around her face.

'You look beautiful.'

A bald woman cannot be beautiful. And neither can an old one. She's beyond beauty. Of body, that is. Still burnishing her soul. In hopes.

A comfortable wheelchair is waiting on the terrace at Kamilla's house. All her old friends. She can remember saying yes and no, please and thank you. And trying to stay upright in the chair.

'I think it's time to go home now.' Gemma standing by her side.

Gabby's smile is toothless because her teeth aren't in. But she can feel its radiance. 'Right, girls. I'm ready to leave. Undo the brake and wheel me home. So, which one of you is going to drive Miss Daisy?'

So tired. So tired she doesn't think she'll ever sleep enough.

They help her undress, get into bed. There's one more task left to her. Before it's too late.

She waits until they're out of the room. Until all is quiet. Then eases herself off the bed, on to the floor. It's dark now. Hard to find her way to her bureau for the keys to the safe across the hall.

They mustn't find it. She'll flush it down the toilet and no one will ever know what's happened to it.

Gabby drags herself slowly, infinitely cautious, across the well-loved room. Her beautiful apartment, her antiques, her expensive clothes, her flourishing business, her healthy bank account. They are as nothing. But there is something in the safe which is still dynamite.

She finds the key, crawls on all fours to the safe, opens it. Drags out jewellery, her will, share certificates, trust fund and other papers which no longer matter, are no longer hers.

Dust thou are to dust returnest was not spoken of the soul.

At last. A small, lone box right in the back. Where it has lain for years. Black leather opens to show the gold locket nestling in white silk. She tries to take it out. Can't find the strength to undo the catch. How will she flush it down the loo in its coffin?

The kitchen dustbin. She'll chuck the whole thing into that. No one is going to examine the coffee grounds to look for a locket which they won't realise is missing until it's too late.

Gabby hoists herself upright with difficulty, moves across the dark apartment towards the kitchen. She stumbles on something soft lying on the floor. Her slippers. She can't stop herself from falling. Feels the bones crack.

Gabby slips away peacefully. The Requiem Mass is arranged in the Karlskirche, her parish church. A large congregation of clients and friends attend. Kamilla arranges a wake in Gabby's splendid rooms.

'We need to have a funeral in Schwanenbruch,' Gemma reminds her sisters. 'We have to put her to rest in the Dohlen Mausoleum. She won't be at peace unless we do.'

'You're right. I'll see to the red tape, drive her ashes up to Schwanenbruch,' Kamilla promises family members about to leave for Schwechat airport. 'We can all gather there for a final ceremony. At a mutually convenient date.'

'There's only one date which will work.' Gemma, about to get out of Kamilla's car at Schwechat airport, turns round to Nina and Marina. 'How could I have forgotten?'

'What d'you mean?'

'Emil Dohlen died on July 4th, 1916. On Independence Day. Why don't we aim to have Gabby's ashes placed in the Mausoleum next summer? July 4th, 1992.' She lifts the locket dragging on her neck. 'After all, she wasn't just his daughter. She was the standard bearer of the Dohlen Inheritance.'

'What a brilliant idea. The day our grandfather died, and the day Nina was born.' Kamilla's eyes smile.

'Brilliant. That's exactly what she'd want.' Nina, tears still lurking, brings out a new handkerchief.

'And that locket, Gemma. She obviously meant you to have it. Don't forget to bring the precious locket up to Schwanenbruch,' Kamilla reminds her sister.

'I suppose so.' She fingers the locket reluctantly. 'I'll try to remember.'

'Wasn't there some old legend that goes with it?'

'Gabby told us the story dozens of times, Nina. When we were children.'

THE FLOWER OF

TRUEST LOVE

Hundreds of years ago, when Otto the Great succeeded his father Charlemagne as Holy Roman Emperor, Archbishop Adaldag was ruler of the marshes between Hamburg and Bremen. Great rulers need great castles, so the Archbishop built a special one near the little town of Hagen. And that's where many nobles and knights gathered for festive hunts of boar and deer, wild goose and duck.

The local farmers were expected to drive game towards the hunters while their wives – each chosen from an area long renowned for producing beautiful women – were expected to serve the hungry men.

Hiltrud was farmer Heino's wife. Blessed with shining black hair, lustrous dark eyes and blooming red cheeks, her colouring marked her out as a special flower among the flaxen-haired, blue-eyed beauties who were more numerous in these parts.

One brilliant autumn day the Archbishop and his retinue assembled in the upstairs hall, while the ordinary hunters' tables were set below them in the cellars. They ate as good meat, and drank as good wine, as any of the Archbishop's finer guests. But they drained their tankards at greater speed.

Hunter Egbert saw Hiltrud standing by the door. His loud voice sent a volley of lewd remarks at her. She turned away, ran up the stairs. But Egbert had always had a hankering for her. He ran after her. And Heino noticed, and followed him. Discreetly. Because a farmer is of the lowest rank.

When Heino saw Egbert straddling his struggling wife he rushed headlong to her defence. He grabbed Egbert's shoulders, threw him down the stairs and so back into the cellar for all to see. Wounding his body as well as his pride, prompting loud oaths spelling out Heino's fate.

'Let's get away from here,' Hiltrud whispered to Heino. 'If he catches us we're done for.'

The main door leading to the moat was locked. They ran to find an opening above the moat and jumped through onto the icy waters. Heino swam across with Hiltrud clinging to his neck. But when they reached the other side Egbert was already sitting on his horse, waiting for them. He had his hunting knife in his hand, and aimed it straight at Heino's heart. Where it found its mark.

Hiltrud dragged her beloved husband into the field beyond the moat, laid his head in her lap, and tried to stop the streaming blood. In vain. Heino breathed his last, and Hiltrud sat silent and tearless, forgetting time and place.

Next spring, at that very spot, a flower which had never been seen before grew and bloomed. Pure white petals surrounded a black calyx. And when the delicate stalk bent over, drops of dew flowed like tears. Just the way Heino's blood flowed to save his beloved.

The bloom they call the Lieblingsblüte – the flower of truest love – still thrives in that meadow, outside the little town of Hagen. But only true lovers will ever find it. And when they do they know their love with last forever.

EPILOGUE

Schwanenbruch, July 1992

Gabby's nearest and dearest crowd into the St Nicolaikirche pew which still has **FAMILIE DOHLEN** carved into its side. Gothic and ornate, but not the front pew. Because the Dohlens, though grounding villagers, were latecomers to the good and the great of Schwanenbruch.

There are no Dohlens in the village now. Emil Junior died without issue nearly five years ago, Dorinda's ashes are scattered over the fields surrounding Dramlings and Gabriele Dohlen (Ferent, Bosch, nearly Weiss) is ashes in her urn. Her portrait hangs beside her father's in the Villa Dohlen across the road.

The resonant tones of the prized Klappmeyer organ are amplified by three local trumpeters of uncertain talent but unstoppable zeal. Klapp, Klapp.

Gabby's family weren't consulted about the hymns trumpeting out today, but the old Lutheran favourites she loved so much are bludgeoned out to send her on her way:

The Church protestant. Wolderich Lappe jealous of his heritage.

Last summer Gabby, in pain most of the time, sensed her last visit. She sought out young Pastor Bintermann taking old Pastor Anderson's place. They agreed a mention of her name, during the Sunday worship before her remains are laid in their final resting place.

Negotiations for burial in the Mausoleum were a little difficult, almost beyond Gabby's strength. Her father's will states that his son Emil, and his successors, are entitled to be buried there. Which privilege has been exercised. Unfortunately without successors. There is no mention of Emil Senior's daughters, whose issue do not bear the Dohlen name.

Gabby argued successfully — a heated discussion clinched by a generous donation to the St Nicolaikirche — that blood is thicker than name. The young pastor's lips parted politely. A brilliant toothpaste smile lit up sapphire eyes without a soul. Gabby accepted the nod as agreement, shook hands on the deal and made sure the contract was pushed across for the young man to sign. With a flourish of Schwanenbruch signatures added as witnesses. Big and bold, using swan quills dipped in permanent ink.

The first beneficiary was wicked Tante Hannah, Weber née Bender, whose sister Martha begged to have her remains shipped over from the States. Not quite what Gabby had in mind, but she paid the costs.

Today Gabby's family rustle in their Sunday best, wearing expectant hats. The long sermon consists of copious Lutheran texts to illustrate the dangers of popery. Brimstone and hellfire feature in detail. The name Gabriele Dohlen is not part of a long litany of dear departed.

Most of the family sit quiet and amiable. They don't speak, or even understand, German. Gemma, Nina and Kamilla do. Their eyes shine with emotions more suitable to the battlefield than sacred ground.

The congregation, though vocal, is sparse. Sunday worship isn't much of a contender against sport and television. The young pastor stands outside, greeting his ageing parishioners, shaking hands.

Some of the devout — Erika Schonter née Bender, one or two of Gabby's school friends, children of servants in Emil Dohlen's household, the head of Schwanenbruch Council, recent friends — march meaningfully behind the three mourning hats shaking with grief. And less suitable emotions. Nina's beautiful lace handkerchief is sodden.

Gemma's German is rusty. Nina has suppressed hers.

'You cheated an old lady!' Kamilla lives in Vienna and has no trouble voicing her feelings. Loudly. Histrionically. 'Not even to offer a prayer is a disgrace! Call yourself a Christian?'

She's backed up by Plattdeutsch from the locals. 'After all she did for the St Nicolaikirche!' Swastika memories hiss like hornets around the Pastor's head. 'And for Schwanenbruch! The Bishop is going to hear about this and no mistake.'

The gift of tongues returns to Gemma. 'I understand you promised my mother a mention during today's service. To sustain her on her last voyage, to meet her God.'

'Quite impossible, gnädige Frau. Your mother was a Papist.' The voluminous sleeves of Pastor Bintermann's righteous alb flutter impressively. Like wings of the wrong colour. 'I would like to remind you that the St Nicolaikirche was the main Protestant church in Land Hadeln after the Reformation. Magister Andreas Gardin from Lüneburg delivered the first evangelical sermon here. On September 29th, 1526.'

'Four hundred and sixty-six years is beyond even Schwanenbrucher memory, Herr Pastor.' Fury enhances mental arithmetic.

'The Magister offered the body of Christ in both its forms — bread and wine.'

Does he see himself as Luther's successor? 'If we could concentrate on living memories, Pastor Bintermann. This church led the way to ecumenism. When the Catholic refugees from the East found asylum in the Villa Dohlen, services were held here for both Protestants and Catholics.

A cheer of encouragement from a depleting congregation.

Not loud enough to quell the fires of dogmatism, though the flames no longer roar. 'That finished when the British Occupation left in 1955. Our church is — '

'Your church is the House of God. The God we both worship.'

Cries of 'shame' are amplified by a sudden downpour. Heaven's tears drum out the learned preacher's words with guttural splats and tutting drips.

'Are you denying you promised to remember my mother during today's service?' Gemma, spurred into confrontation, neglects her hat. A gust of North Sea wind kites it away. It climbs as high as the twin towers behind them.

'Your mother was an old lady. I think some misunderstanding —'

'You signed a contract she herself drew up for the upkeep of the Mausoleum. Dated July 1st, 1991. Hardly an act of senility.'

A giggle of wind rounds the bell tower. Is that Gabby's laugh as she rides the hat out to sea?

Sapphire blue turns to ultramarine. 'Perhaps a compromise, meine Damen? The big bell will toll Frau Dohlen's remains to her final resting place. Tomorrow, I understand. High noon.'

Emil Julius Dohlen's elder daughter Gabriele, who made her fortune in post-war Vienna, is placed in the Dohlen Mausoleum on July 4th, 1992. Seventy-six years to the day her father died. And she was the one who took up his banner. Who will it be now?

As the cortège leaves the Villa Dohlen on its way to the churchyard, her eldest child, her daughter Gemma, lifts her bowed head, looks back. She stares at the house her grandfather built, her mother restored and the village has inherited. She raises her eyes to the arch below the eaves, sees the inscription there.

DEUTSCHE ART TREU BEWAHRT

Gemma's shoulders square. Her right arm entwines with Nina's, her left with Kamilla's, with Marina behind. Gemma marches forward with the tolling of the bell, the locket her mother clutched as she lay dying swinging for all to see. She walks to the rhythm of lines she can hear Gabby sing:

> Maikäfer flieg
> Dein Vater ist im Krieg
> Dein Mutter ist in Pommerland
> Pommerland ist abgebrannt
> Maikäfer flieg

Ladybird, soar
Your father's gone to war
Your mother waits in Berlin town
Berlin town is burning down
Ladybird, fly

Gabby's 'daughters' troop down the steep, twisting stairs to the crypt with the ashes Kamilla brought from Vienna. Gemma unclasps the locket around her neck. 'Gabby doesn't need it, she never has. She did not pass it on to anyone, and she died holding it. Let's bury it with her.'

Nina takes off the lid, Gemma places the locket on top of Gabby's remains. Kamilla replaces the lid, they seal the urn. The locket is safe with Gabby for eternity.

Meine Damen und Herren, Gemma reads out to the mourners assembled in the small chapel of the Mausoleum. *All of us here, family, friends, colleagues, know very well that my mother Gabriele — her nickname was Gabby, because she talked so much — was more than a brilliant storyteller. She was a most unusual woman who filled her eighty-five years to the very brim. Hers was a chequered life. A roller coast up, roller coast down kind of life. But her unshakeable optimism was more than justified. She was, in the end, remarkably successful. During the bonus years: after her three score years and ten.*

If asked to sum up her life I would say she always saw the glass half full rather than half empty. With the best schnapps available, of course.

Gabby was not perfect. Some would say very flawed. For me she was more than a mother — she was life's positive interpreter. She left us all the greatest inheritance anyone can leave. She showed us that even the coarsest fibres can be spun into fine yarn, and fashioned into silver nets to catch the golden apples.

CPSIA information can be obtained at www.ICGtesting.com
Printed in the USA
LVOW110908101111

254331LV00001B/192/P